THE CODE

Rose Sandy is the author of the worldwide-acclaimed Decrypter series. The technothriller action-adventures feature government cyber agent Calla Cress. Rose's books have been described as 'technology and espionage meet history in pulse racing thrillers'. The first Calla Cress book spent several weeks at #1 and continues to hold a dominate spot on Amazon's Kindle chart.

Rose grew up a global nomad, moving from continent to continent and from culture to culture. She calls herself a mélange of all the places she's lived including: Baghdad, Northern India, Berlin, Paris and the UK where she picked up four languages and enough cultures to inspire her to create for years. Rose likes to take her character's to where she has journeyed.

You can find out more about Rose and her work on her official website:
www.rosesandy.com

ROSE SANDY

The Code Beneath

www.rosesandy.com

www.rosesandy.com

ISBN-13: 978-1523939657

Cover design by Jason Sandy
Cover image © mark_hubskyi

Love is composed of a single soul inhabiting two bodies.

Aristotle

HIMACHAL PRADESH
THE HIMALAYAS, NORTHERN INDIA

TODAY

Leal Trelles opened his eyes and fixed his gaze on Jewel. Her breathing steadied as she slipped into an uneasy sleep. What had caused the short, rapid intakes of breath last night?

She lay next to him.

Still.

Sinking deeper into a fog of weariness, her slumber soundless, her petite build lay bundled in a windproof fleece under an insulated sleeping bag. The sheepskin he'd extended over her before dark slipped off her tiny frame. He spread it over her and sat upright as he unzipped his sleeping bag.

Icy conditions in the snowcapped, Dhauladhar mountain ranges could be unforgiving. He knew it well, yet he'd asked Jewel to go with him on this expedition. At ten thousand feet above sea level, and in reach of the Indo-Tibetan border, Keylong, 'the land of monasteries' lay several miles behind them on the snow-congested road. The mountains stretched for miles, dominated by valleys where the river Bhaga meandered. A range of mountain peaks towered high. Finding small patches of flat terrain in the entrancing Buddhist milieu was like locating a stream in a parched desert.

A howling wind beat on the tent. Though not as brutal as the one that had caused obstruction to their passage back to Keylong, it whistled as dawn broke over the Eastern ranges.

Leal's jaw clenched. The peaks were prone to avalanches. A year ago, snowstorms had halted all motoring activity near Rahla Falls, more than one hundred kilometers away. And now, how long would they endure without more food supplies? Trapped on an impassable footpath between Kullu Manali and Keylong, they waited for help like elephants resting on sinking sand.

Leal cleared his parched throat as cold air seeped through the gaps between the tent's opening, triggering thirst and a mild throat ache. Close to freezing on the range, maybe a little less,

Leal took in a deep breath. He rummaged through his backpack, his hand grazing the water canister.

Empty.

His hands shivered, frigid like Antarctica crystals on an ice cave. He rubbed them together for warmth and reached under his sleeping bag for his windproof gloves. A hostile wind beat against the mountain tent. Leal's nerves remained taut as a nauseous feeling gripped the pit of his stomach. A frosty chill spread through his body, sapping more of his diminishing strength. Dawn all right. He checked his satellite phone. 6:17 a.m.

Had he slept?

They'd stayed warm despite the blizzard that swept the range from the Eastern Himalayas several hours ago. The sound of pulsating blades of a helicopter, though faint, caught his ear. He nudged Jewel with a gentle hand. "Jewel, they're here."

Her eyes struggled to open and he gravitated upward rubbing them with a mittened hand. "They are here?"

Her voice had turned hoarse and Leal managed a faint smile as she blinked her eyes. "Yeah. Must be the chopper I radioed last night. They'll take us back to Manali."

Leal pushed himself from the frozen ground and pulled Jewel to her feet. He rubbed his hands along her shoulders steadily warming them. "Come."

When they'd shrugged out of the sleeping bags, they scrambled out into the blizzard cloud brought on by the helicopter's rotor blades. Icy snow pelts bit at their faces as the helicopter attempted to land. They stood immobile, chins raised in the slashing winter cloud of the chopper's rotating blades that deafened their ears. With hands shielding his eyes from the onslaught force, Leal glanced through the squall and scrutinized the advancing rescue pilot.

"Kya aap theek ho?" hollered the officer in Hindi.

Leal could barely hear his words, but understood the concerned stare in his face. Were they all right?

"Yes." Leal said. "Thank God, you're here."

The man muttered something in Hindi as Leal and Jewel approached him.

"What did you say?" Leal asked.

The man switched to English. "We've room for only one person."

Jewel shook her head. "No..." She stretched her words out in despair. "You can't be serious? We have to leave now. All of us."

"The helicopter doesn't have the capacity." The Indian officer's assertive voice bellowed in the clamor. "Only one. We'll come back."

Jewel despised the conviction in the pilot's forceful voice. His furrowing brow told her she couldn't coerce him. Leal whirled round, to face her. "Go with them. I'll come right after you."

"No. We go together. There's another winter storm coming. I can feel it," Jewel said.

"She's right," said the officer. "Manali just radioed us."

He glanced over at his co-pilot still seated in the driver's seat. The second officer lowered his window in haste. "We need to hurry if I'm to make this climb again."

Leal scanned the four-passenger-capacity helicopter before peering into Jewel's eyes, his look firm and demanding as he gripped her arms. "I'll be right behind you, Jewel. Now, go."

The pilot tore her out of Leal's grip, his forced tug throwing her off balance. She held her stomach as if pained, her feet moving reluctantly toward the chopper as the pilot guided her under the rotary blades. "I can't go without him. Leal!"

Leal edged her on with dauntless eyes. "Go."

Three other mountaineers sat clutching their seatbelts, their grips knuckle-white, as Jewel took the last seat in the confined space. The pilot slammed a seatbelt around her and hurled the door shut before taking a seat in the cockpit. Jewel's frozen glance begged Leal to consider. She glared at him through the open window unable to see his full frame in the snow tormented air as he hastened toward their mountain tent.

"Leal!"

The accelerating blades muted her cry as Leal reached back inside the tent for her backpack. Seconds later, he reopened the door and placed it at her feet.

She peered into his eyes. "Come with me, Leal."

Her hands gripped his broad shoulders, digging into them. Though his look was consoling, she knew her protests could change nothing. He shot the pilots a trusting look as their hands maneuvered the chopper's controls. He leaned toward her. "I can't. You heard the pilot. There's no room. It's not safe for you and the others."

He reached across and set a fervent kiss on her moistureless mouth and the dry throbbing of his lips made her shift closer. "They're coming back for me," he said.

The pilot clenched the twist grip between the front seats, setting the engine into mobility. Leal stepped away from the helicopter and thumped the door shut. The clang reverberated in her ears as he sped toward the blood-red tent. Jewel's eyes didn't leave him once even as the pilot twisted the cyclic controls, creating a deafening sound from the engine. What was worse, the chopper's dainty engines or the mountain's oncoming blizzard? Leal was mountain savvy, but it wasn't enough to reassure her. Within seconds, the pilot sent the chopper into a sideway ascent at full throttle. The mountain gales picked up momentum, culminating with the helicopter's hastening paddles and tail fins as it ascended skyward.

Her eyes fell back toward the mountain and to the man she'd failed. Couldn't she see it? Wasn't it obvious in his eyes? Even as the helicopter wrenched her away from Leal, his words still rang in her ears, *I'll be right behind you.* She had to believe him.

The chopper's canopy jolted and slumped-nose down a few feet in a pocket of air. Furious wind speeds catapulted it off its southbound path as Jewel held her breath and found her hands grinding the leather of the seat.

"Not to worry," the first pilot said.

"Get her back on course!" said the second.

Jewel clung to her seatbelt, seated next to a petrified elderly woman in mountaineering gear. She glanced down at the steep peaks. *Is this it?*

"Hang on!" said the pilot. "She's not steady!"

Another colossal gush tossed the chopper to its left. The pilot fought the controls and slammed the pedals. The motion controlled the tail rudder, steadying the helicopter once more as he regulated the amount of sideways thrust. Once vertical, he accelerated the chopper's speed and they rose above terror to steadier cruising over the Dhauladhars. Jewel glimpsed through her side window.

Nothing.

Wait!

Leal's vibrant-red snowsuit came into view. He tore at the wind with gloved palms and hurled himself into the tent that stood steady against nature's forces.

Was it the look in the man's eyes across from her? Or was it the way voices built around her as each took in the scene on the mountain that brought a stifled scream to her throat.

Her eyes widened as she witnessed the full magnitude of the mountain's anger. The woman next to her blasted out a loud gasp.

Jewel's lips parted. "Leal."

A whimper, not a shout. It was all she could articulate as a roaring tsunami of snow scurried down toward what had been their night's lodging. The avalanche crushed the tent, swallowing the canvas as it raced with ferocious volume.

Was it the amplifying blood rushing to her head? *No.*

A somber red flag, the tent's alert marker, zipped down with nature's scourge. The only evidence of color hurtled into the depths of the valley.

Chapter 1

FOUR YEARS AGO

The sparkle on her bodice, adorned with Swarovski and Bohemia rhinestones, intertwined with sequins and beads, caught the gaze of the spotlight. Jewel lengthened her neck like a swan in flight over an aquatic landing, every inch of her illustrating perfection. Her chin moved toward her shoulder and, with an amiable smile, she waited for her cue.

The crowds roared. The cacophony, though deafening, was applause to her ears. Jewel Carlone, the expressive eighteen-year-old, strode on the Montpellier arena platform. Her body performed with the poise that befits a rhythmic gymnast. With her chocolate mane gathered in a tight sparkling bun on top of her head, she took center stage. She waited for the first tantalizing bars of Chopin's intoxicating Nocturne in B-flat Minor.

The arena burst with frenzied masses. Twenty-four teams waited to compete for six Olympic places. Soon, the audience quieted. Jewel rehearsed each detail of her routine in her head, organizing each movement in her mind. With the anticipation of the crowds stilling, she trusted the rhythm of her drumming heart, a heart that beat for her passion, her much practiced art; art that had catapulted her to stardom.

She heard it. The buzzer sounded and the Chopin released a rhythmic freedom, and she elevated her leg with precision, soaring with her ribbon. She smiled for her audience, her makeup impeccable, and her mysterious artistry accurate. The bold choreography demanded flawless execution, and meticulous elegance and harmony.

The smooth Chopin music lifted the audience. Stirred by her movements, they edged her on, the melody floating with her. She was their champion. Enamored by brilliance, they wanted her to win. It didn't matter she had forty-one medals split between the Olympics and the World and European Championships.

She spun on her pointed toes and took another twirl, creating faultless coils with her fluid ribbon. Her body moved like ebbing water from an Athenian fountain. Her pirouettes landed with solid perfection followed by flawless turns on robust toes. Her splits strong, she danced, lost in her world, determined to enchant the judges.

She had to score above nine points, in particular in the artistry and difficulty categories. Youth was on her side. Blending the agility of a gymnast with the confidence of a ballerina, she took control of her apparatuses with skillful command and symmetry that sent the audience into her fantasy.

Halfway through the performance, perfect scores awaited her. She took a deep breath, preparing for the final step. In her dance, she became the sole occupant in the arena. She took the concluding leap, her finale. Jewel had practiced the step many times. She could not fail. Practice makes near perfect. *Doesn't it?* She could dance it with her eyes shut.

Then, it came. The jump.

For a moment all she heeded were the gasps and fear-ridden faces that gawked at her tumbling frame. Soon she sensed the faint tear of ligaments and skidded to the ground. The unthinkable became the inevitable as the snapping sensation in her right knee concluded the otherwise flawless routine.

Blustering sirens of the racing ambulance, agitated voices discoursing in French of a regional hospital in the center of Montpellier, filled her droning ears. Several moments later, emergency teams hoisted her fractured knee-joint on a pillow and strapped her into a reclined wheeler as the monstrous ambulance arrived at Montpellier CHU hospital.

Medical staff scrambled to her side and a throbbing around her right knee had caused intense swelling in her joint. Attentiveness guiding their movements, they rolled her on the bed in what resembled a private intensive care unit. In minutes, she lapsed into semi-consciousness as the anesthetic took immediate effect.

Several hours later Jewel spied through groggy eyes at a white ceiling. Noiseless like an abandoned church, the hospital room became more visible. Even then, her head couldn't take the fluorescent overhead rays. Once more, she drifted off to a nauseating sleep and roused later, stirred by quiet movements in the room.

Motion drew her eye as soft-footed, brisk steps shuffled around the door.

Then closer.

By her pillow.

Had the movement been quieter, she would've assumed it was a routine staff check. After a strained interval, she sensed someone, inches from her.

Jewel trailed her head toward the door. Was it the doctor?

"C'est vous, docteur? Is that you, Doctor?"* she said in a suppressed voice.

With no answer from her visitor, she attempted to pull herself up, but it felt as if a lead brick had been hammered into her head. The unsolicited visitor shuffled toward the table and checked her medical notes. Dark, stocky and masked, he held a small device narrowed at its outlet.

She raised her arm, but it wouldn't move. A heavy feeling sank in her stomach as she saw the man tread toward her. Only then, did she notice her right hand was cuffed to the metal bed.

Oh God! What's happening?

After short reflection, she tried to wedge it free, but the sedatives had numbed her senses.

The man moved his hand to her mouth and gagged her with pressure-sensitive tape. She lunged forward in one involuntary movement pushing her leg upward. That too was tied with a chained constraint held fast to the hospital bed. After examining the door for interruption, the intruder set several medical objects by the bed.

Jewel gasped for breath and her muscles tensed as the man moved with stealth, clanging his collection of surgical instruments. A lump crawled up her throat and she smelled the putrid leather of his gloves as a tight grip inched to her neck. He fought her free wrist in one abrupt jerk, forcing the sleeve on her cuffed hand backward.

Spasms shot through her limbs as rigid muscles failed to move and she closed her eyes. This was no doctor.

8

* * *

Jewel's eyes widened at the sight of the homicidal syringe. Its spike menaced toward her. The man grappled her right arm and pinned her left with his elbow. The excruciating squeeze that followed made her swoon and as quickly as the pain had begun, tears fighting horror ebbed from her eyes.

She tugged at her cuffed wrist. The jerk loosened her left arm from his elbow and her hand crawled to the far side of the bed, locating a metal cylinder full of surgical instruments. It took her full strength to heave its weight and jet the contents at her attacker.

The metal smashed his jaw; he propelled to the tiles and slammed a fist on the floor. Staggering forward, he surged up and spat. As if debating, he retrieved the discarded syringe before storming once more toward her.

Jewel tugged harder at her cuffed hand, ready to dodge out of reach. With eyes fixed on her masked attacker, she didn't notice the door jolt open and slam against the wall, launching a loud clang in the small room.

A second man plowed for the grunting assailant and slugged him from behind in the shoulder. He zipped round and lost balance. As he fell back he banged his head on a rolling table that overturned as it crashed into the far wall.

The concussive crash whined in her ears as more medical instruments and glass smashed around the men's feet. The goon wavered to his feet and shuffled for the exit without a backward glance.

Jewel's lips and chin trembled as she watched the second man. He was tall with dull-blond hair and had his back to her. For a few seconds he stood motionless monitoring the door then angled toward it and shut it without a sound before turning the lock.

Jewel's body launched into an uncontrollable shake. Her shoulders tightened as the robust figure, swiveled her way his jaw tight as he advanced toward her bed. Her pupils dilated as the man set his hand over her jaw. She drew in a sharp breath, her face became ashen. Yet, he didn't smother her. Instead, he eased the pressure tape off her lips, inch by inch. The motion was painless, medically calculated. His hands moved to the leather

9

straps and cuffs on her wrist and legs and unlocked them with a key he removed from his pocket. "He won't be back. Try to rest."

The dialect was crisp and confident, East Coast, maybe upstate New York.

A cold shiver ran through her and Jewel maneuvered her body with difficulty turning toward the voice. Shooting pains shot through her leg as the drugs overcast her vision and obstructed her senses. Her temples pounded, as if a thousand marching drummers had used them for rehearsal. While the anesthetic on her injured knee had worn off in her struggle, she'd ignored the increasing fire throbbing in her stiff knee. As if breaking free from a spell, she found she could move easier if she kept most of her weight on her left side. Jewel fought to get a clearer glimpse of the man's eyes and his full, lean build.

Close to six feet tall, his blue eyes framed a handsome face. His neat hair fell like frozen waves on his head, culminating into short, sand-coloured sideburns around his ears. He was dressed in a white coat, under which he wore dark denims and outdoor boots.

"Are you a doctor?" she said.

"Yes."

He strode to the nurse's station, found her prognosis and scrutinized the details. A raised eyebrow arched above his eye as he scribbled hurried notes on the medical chart. He removed the bottom sheet of paper from the clipboard and placed the notes in his pocket. Until now, he'd yet to explain his intrusion, but re-read the chart. Satisfied, he replaced it on the desk.

Curled to one side, Jewel attempted to sit up again breathing in short breaths. "Who was that man? Did you call the police?"

The man muttered in hushed tones as if she wasn't in the room. His lack of response urged her to change the subject. "How bad did I hurt my knee?"

He crossed the length of the tiny private room. "Nothing time and rest won't cure. You sustained an Anterior Cruciate Ligament tear, or better known as an ACL injury. It means you tore a ligament that joins your upper leg bone to the lower one."

"How serious is it?"

"You'll have pain around your knee and slight swelling."

His voice rang smooth to her ears, so much more self-assured than most doctors she knew. Her coordination refused to cooperate as medication forbade her to focus.

The doctor leaned over her and set a hand on her feverish forehead. She sensed his faint cologne, a mixture of ocean breeze and musk. He had no badge, and nothing else that identified him, except his words.

Jewel glanced up at him, seeing his full face for the first time in the light of dawn that broke through the shaded windows. His shimmering blue eyes pierced hers and for a moment, the arresting gaze became surprisingly welcome.

His strong facial features held a certain sensuality as he leaned forward and touched her face with a gentle stroke. A small scar under his chin drew her attention for a moment. As if wrestling with his will, he dipped his head and brushed soft lips over hers.

Jewel drew a deep breath and forbade herself to tremble as she propped into him, closing her eyes. She placed a shaky hand up against his firm chest.

He pulled away and studied her eyes. "You'll perform again."

"Who are you?"

He rose without explanation and proceeded to the door. Stirred by a last thought, he glanced at her one final time then unlocked the door. "You were beautiful out there."

Chapter 2

PRESENT DAY

Leal woke in a cold sweat. It came on with abruptness leaving his skin cool and damp. He couldn't do it. He was in one heck of a nasty bind.

Jewel Carlone was in trouble. And so was he.

He heaved himself out of bed and dragged his feet to the bathroom for a cool drink. He guzzled down a glass of chilled water, and then scrambled back into the dark hotel room of the Sacher Hotel in central Salzburg. He sank to the edge of the bed. Sleep had left him. He finished his drink and crossed to the writing desk thinking of his forgotten pajamas. He preferred sleeping in boxers anyway. Besides, the room was sweltering. Was the heat on that high? He checked the radiator. Set at 65°F, all seemed normal.

With his chest beaded with sweat, he needed a swim and considered stealing into the downstairs swimming pool. He'd toured the luxury hotel after arriving that morning from New York and had inspected the connecting indoor pool with its sweeping views of the banks of the Salzach River.

He wiped his brow. The volunteers would arrive tomorrow. His company, a giant medical corporation, Trelles Pharmaceuticals, part of Trelles Industries, had reserved thirty rooms for the volunteers in the well-chosen hotel.

Jewel Carlone was among them. After four years, that one encounter with her still troubled him. Jewel was not what he'd expected in a study patient. The last thing he needed was entanglement with his research case. If he didn't get to her, the Department of Economic Intelligence, or better known as the

DEI, would send someone else. Better he than they.

Their intentions were neither safe, nor right.

Billions of dollars were being lost to foreign and domestic competitors who targeted economic intelligence in flourishing U.S. industries and technologies. The DEI existed to safeguard the country's economic secrets, and Trelles Industries was a key corporation in the economy, dominating medical research. Seventy percent of the company was privately held by the Trelles family with Leal as president and chairman. He controlled most of the Trelleses' interests in the firm. Co-founded with his grandfather, Trelles Industries remained a semi-private biopharmaceutical company and a market leader in biotechnology. Leal and his global researchers engaged in the development and commercialization of medicinal and biotechnology products. Trelles Industries owned many pharmaceutical and diagnostic sites around the world with an annual revenue of fifty-one billion dollars.

Leal had thought of Jewel several times in the last four years hoping she'd resumed her gymnastics. How could he have been so foolish to allow his attraction to her consume him? For months, he'd put the episode in the Montpellier hospital behind him until he'd visited the New York Institute of Photography two months ago. He'd gone to discuss photography work for a new yellow fever drug advertising campaign he wanted to run in Mozambique and spotted her.

He couldn't mistake that athletic frame—trim today as it had been four years ago. A little private investigation confirmed she was a student at NYIP and had registered for a charity trip to Austria. Students at NYIP sometimes took on various projects for work experience with Trelles. A few students at NYIP had worked for Trelles Pharmaceuticals traveling with medical teams and researchers to raise awareness of disease, a project Leal had instigated to educate on global health concerns. When Leal asked his investigator about Jewel and her gymnastics career, he discovered, now at twenty-three, her art lay behind her.

Leal reached for his backpack and pulled out an electronic tablet. He wiped his brow, snapped on the desk lamp and located his research, a thorough study of infertility in rural communities. The cellphone on the desk rang, distracting him from his files, and a quick glance at the tablet told him it was 3:16 a.m. local time. He didn't need callers now and let the phone ring several times. When its shrill became unbearable he answered it and a pinched expression set on his face.

"Yeah?"

"Dr. Trelles? I hope you have everything set."

"What do you want?"

"Just making sure the DEI won't have to recruit stern measures to get the ball rolling on that sample you need *and* on the vaccine."

"My answer is the same after seven years. Research takes time."

"Just keeping watch. Okay, now explain it to us non-medical folks. Why did the tests on Mahina Carlone's DNA tests fail? She was after all the one who had Jewel Carlone, why can't her blood give us answers?"

"Mahina has two different sets of DNA present in her body, a defining characteristic of a chimera. Ever heard of that? That's when a single person has genetically distinct cells. This can result in two blood types, or even subtle variations in form."

"You're kidding me."

"I never kid about my work."

"So Mahina's blood work shows she has many signatures and therefore it's invalid for your research?"

"Exactly. Chimerism is not visible on casual inspection; however, it has been detected when proving parentage. Mahina is definitely Jewel's mother. I tested all the blood work going through the lineage of her family, however, her blood work is very different from Jewel's. That's my conclusion until I can get a sample of Jewel's DNA and blood work."

"I see. So what now?"

"You wait."

So furtive were the DEI's methods of economic monitoring in the United States that, lately, Leal questioned their effectiveness. A sharp tone came to his lips. "I first believed in your projects, but you governmental guys are now more concerned with economic espionage than providing our country with sound economic intelligence."

"We like to keep abreast of things."

"I don't buy it for a second. You can't stand medical intelligence and trade secrets leaving US soil under your radar."

"Doctor, if you knew what's at stake—"

"What a load of—"

"Easy now."

"Your eyes have been on every development in medicine since the Cold War. And with the pharmaceutical industry now worth five-hundred billion, you won't let me walk, even after I give you a vaccine. I told you I'll get it."

"Our patience is running low," said the grunted voice on the line. "Did you take the field training we require you to?"

"What training?"

"You want to pull this off? Then you need to think and behave like a field agent. We've trained you to think like a spy. So you know how to behave if any foreign noses come sniffing round your medical research."

"I took your damn training," Leal said.

"A trip to Salzburg sounds extravagant for one strand of DNA."

"Jewel Carlone is not a lab rat. She's a human being with a distinctive code in her blood that may help us find the cause for that blasted infertility outbreak, that, should I remind you, happened on your watch."

"Sounds like you're getting attached to our patient. Not what I'd expect from you."

"You started it."

"That Pennsylvania fiasco wasn't our doing. We're still investigating Ovatti Foods Corporation's involvement. Unfortunately, Dr Trelles, the culprit is still on the loose and left us with a huge mess on our hands."

"How could you have been so careless? Why commission such a risky thing?" Leal said.

"I've said this before; it was a minor attempt to increase the bee population. We're running out of time, Dr Trelles."

"Yeah, a mission that resulted in twelve women suffering from a disease we can't explain."

The voice croaked on the line. "Yes. We're now bordering five-hundred cases in one area of Pennsylvania alone and it's spreading fast. The patients have been taken to government research centers across the country and will remain there with each new case until you solve this for us. This unusual infertility outbreak is increasing in certain portions of our population and now one case has been identified in India."

"India?"

"We don't like that. We can't let governments across our

borders get wind of this and cause global panic before we know what we're dealing with."

"I know the numbers. It's your mess, not Miss Carlone's."

The man's hesitant voice droned. "Yes and you need to clean it up, by giving us some medical answers now. You need to get the code beneath her skin. The epidemic is getting out of control. The last thing we want is the media sniffing around us."

Leal heard the man clear his congested throat.

"Your research will help our little bee recession. I hope you agree that commercial bee-keeping needs to continue if US agriculture is to survive."

Leal understood the economic implications. Agriculture was a major industry in the US, now under threat, and they'd tried to salvage the problem by letting loose an ill-considered environmental scientist who'd set off a wave of events they couldn't explain. He would bet anything the government knew more than they were sharing. He rubbed his forehead, anguish ghosting to his gut. "I haven't found the right formula, so I suggest you——"

"Your drug must solve the epidemic *and* bridge the agricultural gap our country may face before our enemies get wind of it. See it as a service to your country. You're our only chance, doctor. And it bothers us that you choose to work alone."

"That's how I work."

"If you let us in on the details, it could go faster."

"And not get to the people who need it."

"Damn it! What'll it take to get us a drug for nephthysis? Isn't that what you've called the disease, after the barren Greek goddess, or was she Egyptian?"

A moment of silence engulfed them. "Time."

"We don't have time. You've already had four years. Do I need to remind you what you stand to lose?"

Why bother? He'd heard their threats many times. This time, they'd get lethal. Funding for governmental research was dwindling. They needed his vaccine *and* his company.

Badly.

The U.S. government wanted a flawless vaccine and drug against nephthysis, an inexplicable infertility outbreak causing premature ovarian aging in its patients. The DEI had failed to contain it for twenty-five years. Their first hope came when they'd scrutinized Leal's research into infertility trends while at

Johns Hopkins Medical School. He could keep them away from his projects as he'd done last time by encrypting his files.

If only they hadn't unearthed his secret, his nightmare.

The DEI agent, who'd never given him a real name and went by agent Hudson, let out a loud cough. "You've already developed three successful fertility drugs. Damn it, man! Think of the money you'll make."

Leal's breathing was louder than he intended. Money was never a motivation. Releasing a sought-after vaccine to a greedy industry and covert government agency was the last thing medicine needed, especially if it didn't reach those who required it most.

He breathed raged tones down the line. "Let me get on with it."

Leal hung up and set the phone on the desk. He continued browsing through killer T-cell formulas. It had to work. He had to boost their immunity mechanism and find the right substance to combat the build-up of T-cells at the vaccination location of the patient. An overstimulated immune response could generate lesions at the injection site on the skin and cause other side effects.

Think! What haven't you paid attention to?

He'd spent years studying infertility trends, conducting extensive studies on physical problems and hormonal glitches. Research in Kathmandu, Chilumba, Stockholm, Vancouver, Beijing and San Francisco allowed him to rule out ways of life or environmental factors on nephthysis, major fibroid tumors, the malignant type. The cancerous toxins found at the headquarters of Ovatti Foods Corporation where the disease spiraled were still a major puzzle.

Sure enough, Jewel was the link they needed. Her DNA and blood sample would give him the answers. Forty-eight months was the longest he'd spent on any vaccine. If only he could bury the incriminating evidence the DEI had on him. The one mistake he'd ever made and the mess his family couldn't have survived without. They'd threatened him with exposure, and prosecution would break Nonna, his grandmother's heart. The pressure of an incriminating lawsuit would strain her. It remained their one haggling chip against him. He needed to deliver this vaccine. Medicine was his life's mission and nothing could deter his conviction that there was a cure for everything. He knew it.

17

That's what set Leal above his peers, a stubbornness and refusal to accept failure, however long it took.

He checked the time again and glared at his screen at Gruenmeier's bill. He'd paid for all thirty volunteers to the Adel Theater, across the plaza from the hotel. This was his generous payment to Hans Gruenmeier, the theater director. The desperate businessman had agreed to let him explore his little enterprise, no questions asked. Leal preferred it that way. Trelles Industries would see that the theater would be restored. It had captured Jewel's interest as one of the thirty volunteers on this charity trip, organized to restore the seventeenth-century Adel Theater. He checked another bill from a leading snowboarding manufacturing brand. They had delivered his custom-made snowboard that morning at the hotel from a private company in Germany. He'd made his specifications known. The board had to be portable, fast edge-to-edge and make tight turns with the shorter side cut, but still respond swiftly to tear afternoon shadow snow without being too demanding.

Why had he left Jewel Carlone vulnerable in Montpellier four years ago? A woman he knew nothing about yet had her entire medical history on file, thanks to the DEI. Why was he forward? And now, he waited for her like a poaching predator ready to pounce on its victim.

He reached for a sterilized cylindrical bottle and a clean syringe. Would it be so easy to prick her skin? The thought of fracturing its smoothness tormented him. *Come on! You've taken blood samples a million times!*

Just one drop. *I'd be off the hook.*

He had to get some sleep.

He slipped the items in the inner pockets of his jacket that hung on a hook by the door and prayed morning would come having changed his mind.

* * *

September 1, four years ago, was the day Jewel had last competed professionally in rhythmic gymnastics. A dream vaporized into obscurity. She glared out the cool window of the high-speed train as it submerged under a rock-strewn tunnel on its way to Salzburg from Vienna. Though on schedule, they'd suffered a minor delay owing to fog with the flight from New York to Vienna.

Jewel's chocolate-honey locks cascaded loosely over her shoulders. An untamed fringe was pulled away from her face with a jeweled clasp under a woolen hat. Jewel wasn't a natural fan of makeup, possibly because she'd had to wear it for years as a performer. But also because she'd never bothered to know what suited her. She'd applied minimal hues to her face. A little chestnut eyeliner to accent her amber eyes and raven mascara to flatter her eyelids. The cherry lip balm Kaya her best friend had selected at Vienna's International Airport moisturized her dry lips. The combination, as advised by Kaya, sat well on her olive skin tones inherited from her Hawaiian mother and Italian father.

Kaya Wilda, a determined law student Jewel had known since the age of twelve, stretched catlike and let out a lazy yawn. "What's eating you?"

"Nothing."

Kaya sighed. "Let it go."

"Let what go?"

"You can't hide anything from me. I've known you too long."

"Only what I let you know."

"It's the anniversary, isn't it?"

"I wasn't thinking about that."

"Liar." Kaya breathed out a heavy sigh. "You achieved more than most gymnasts."

"You're my friend, so you're allowed to say that."

"You told me years ago that only the top twenty-four groups from previous years' championships took part that year."

"I don't want to think about it, Kay."

"You're gonna have to let it go and accept what happened."

"I have."

"No you haven't. How many gymnasts have ever gone that far in rhythmic gymnastics? Now let me see... none."

Kaya was right and as much as Jewel loved to perform, she loathed the attention champions got, especially Olympic champions.

"Can I tell you a secret?" Jewel said.

"Do share."

"I've been too scared to step into a gymnastics arena since. Or pick up anything related to gymnastics."

Kaya's eyes shone with sympathy. "Your team was proud of

you. I'm sure the Italians aren't complaining."

"You still hold the record, four years later," Kaya said, her eyes smiling.

The accident reversed everything. From the age of eight, Jewel had competed for Italy and gymnastics her dual citizenship allowed her to represent either the US or Italian teams. She'd spent her nineteenth birthday in recovery and physical therapy, and when her discharge papers were signed, the doctors' prognosis was anything but welcome. It remained ingrained in her brain in solid red letters.

Unlikely to compete again

It hadn't been easy to absorb the finite words that still haunted her existence. How could she tell Kaya that the anniversary reminded her of… him?

Could she return to the sport? Most gymnasts quit in their early twenties any way. But, her mind was elsewhere. Though unwelcome, the discharge prognosis was contradictory to the words of the man who'd saved her life. The firm glare she'd registered in his sincere eyes remained vivid in her mind and so did the little scar under his chin.

He'd believed that her knee, though damaged, would allow her to perform again. Who was he? Where had he come from? Wasn't it enough that she'd spent several months unable to sleep haunted by the memories of the attack in Montpellier?

Why was she attacked? What would happen next time someone tried? Who could stop them? She'd refused to step out of her apartment for months after the incident but her greatest failure was she'd failed to identify or trace the doctor. Jewel tugged at her ear stud. Where does one begin to search for a man in a global population of seven billion?

Terrifying as it was, the accident had catapulted her into her second love, photography. She'd lost her gymnastics career and now her shot at financial stability was success in photography. A career harder to break into than finding a snake charmer in New York City.

"Let's just chill and enjoy the next few days," Kaya said.

The words were drowned in a drawn-out yawn that left

Kaya's lips before she slumped into a snooze.

Jewel rested her head on the train window. She tapped the Nikon camera on her lap with a clean, manicured finger and straightened the cobalt-blue jumpsuit she wore with lush snow boots.

This was an important volunteer trip. Fellow students volunteered across the globe in search of rare projects to photograph. She couldn't afford to leave her mother for too long. The four-day trip to Austria was just long enough to give her a break from New York's charging pace, yet short enough to keep her part-time job at Charlie's Midtown Gallery of Fine Art.

As a student at the New York Institute of Photography, Jewel had first seen the call for volunteers on the Institute's website. She'd first ignored it, but later changed her mind when not selected for a coveted internship with National Geographic. The news had been difficult to digest, but her photographs could also do some good in raising awareness or saving careers. Time in Altstadt, the old Austrian city, would allow for startling camera work. The photographs would be part of her architecture and landscape portfolio, a collection beginning to gain momentum. If anything, it was a rare opportunity to be in Europe again.

When she'd volunteered and communicated her interests, the organizers informed her that her principal job was to photograph the fading, baroque theater. The Adel had opened in 1676 in the urban center of Salzburg and would be demolished if its governing board failed to raise fifty-thousand euros on time.

Jewel accepted the opportunity to document its rich history, and, judging from her Google search, it was one seventeenth-century wonder of architecture.

At the end of her trip, St. Johann, the center of Austria's Pongau district, and the governing city of Salzburg's sporting activities, would offer quiet-yet-daring ski slopes. On the last day of the trip, the volunteers would hit the slopes of St. Johann, a bonus for their time and efforts.

Jewel checked the details of her appointment on her cellphone. A quiver of awe filled her as she watched the train cross a lake embowered in woods. Fir trees screened the high-speed vehicle from the fervent rays of the September sun. She absorbed the scenic alpine backdrop dominated by lofty and bold mountains.

Two hours of the train ride were behind them and the trip

21

had drained her body, which hadn't been as agile since the accident. The train cornered a lofty slope that drew the idyllic township of Salzburg in sight, the birthplace of her favorite composer, Mozart.

Kaya's was catnapping soundlessly in the seat opposite her. The girl could sleep anywhere, something that wasn't easy for Jewel since the accident.

Several minutes later, the train pulled into Salzburg central station. Jewel reached for her belongings and stooped over Kaya. "Wake up. We're here."

Kaya rubbed her jet-lagged eyes and raked a hand through her glossy mane. "Why didn't you wake me earlier?" She searched through her purse and drew out a hairbrush. "I must look like a mouse on steroids."

Jewel chuckled at her stylish friend. "I don't think that's even possible. Come on, we have twenty minutes to check into the hotel and get to the theater."

* * *

MANHATTAN
NEW YORK CITY

Myranda Vaux eyed Dr. Konner Rickett, head of obstetrics and gynecology at the Merdon Fertility Clinic in Manhattan. His team scurried the floors of the spacious executive suite on the thirtieth floor of Randal Towers on Park Avenue.

Heights made Myranda dizzy. She breathed a prayer and hoped in heaven this last attempt would work. Just last week, a friend, and an influential business woman on all matters concerning medicine had passed on some critical information. *Forty percent of Merdon's transfers resulted in live births.*

This was the best in Manhattan.

Myranda rubbed her aching temple. *Only nine more months.*

She rose from the bed, and brought a restless hand to her chin. "I won't be pushed around like this."

A nurse shot her an edged look, only too aware that it was best to leave this particular patient with her own thoughts.

Myranda sneered at him and settled back on the pristine bed. She'd not seen her husband in weeks. He was traipsing the globe again. Nothing made him lose focus. He'd always been evasive when it came to her. Granted she'd manipulated him. Once, just before their wedding.

Myranda could still save the marriage, however much a pretense it was.

She'd launched Vaux Marketing onto the Forbes Entrepreneur list by leaching onto the Trelles Pharmaceuticals empire. Her husband had stood idly as she'd morphed a failing direct-mail business into a marketing phenomenon.

Trelles was one of the globe's most innovative biopharmaceutical companies and had been so for close to ten years. In any state west of Illinois, Myranda could be incriminated for the false representation that had put her in front of Trelles' business development teams

A feat she didn't regret.

Without her husband's knowledge, she'd used a connection, a drug investigator in Trelles, and learned of heavy losses that could have harmed their medical investors if the results of a key listeriosis study, a disease known to cause death from major food-borne germs, hadn't been marketed. Myranda had researched possible changes to internal procedures that could help. She'd bought information on experimental studies approved by the Food and Drug Administration. Her research into social marketing and a strategic, government-approved marketing strategy had been crucial in keeping Trelles trading at just over fifty dollars a share.

No one had challenged her sources. That's how Myranda liked it. As long as her legal team were well-compensated and kept their money-hungry eyes on the fine print, no one would dare challenge her lack of expertise in drug research and medical marketing principles, skills necessary to set foot in Trelles' boardrooms

Yet some business matters were not that simple, like this. Merdon was her last chance and she hung onto the last drop of ink in the prenuptial agreement she'd signed when she'd married a man she'd so admired in a rather unceremonious executive office in Trelles' Manhattan offices.

Myranda tilted her head to one side as a physician threaded his way toward the examination bed. Her nerves bit at her concentration when he began his work.

"Will the embryo transfer work?" she said.

23

"There are no guarantees," Dr. Rickett said. "But our success rates are consistently high, and we use the best techniques available."

He scanned Myranda's eyes, his lips stretching into a frown. "I need you to relax. This is a very delicate procedure. Proper embryo transfer isn't that straightforward. Our goal is to help you bring a healthy child into the world."

She narrowed her eyes and reclined on the clinic bed. "Don't patronize me."

"Of course not."

Myranda took a deep breath, conscious of Rickett's eyes on her. She stretched out on the bed and fixed her attention on his instruments, praying with a faith so intense it created a calm inside.

Dr. Rickett set a steady hand on her arm. "You ready?"

She nodded.

"There's no pain and therefore no sedation is necessary."

Myranda sloped further down on the operating table and begged her mind to draw in pleasant thoughts such as the sun-saturated Ifaty beach in Madagascar, and strawberries. Anything to avoid thoughts on the medical procedure about to begin.

She averted the doctor's neutral gaze as he began transferring embryos to the middle of her endometrial cavity. A sincere prayer left her lips in a whisper, her heart hoping in nature, her mind trusting in science that the embryo would attach to the wall of her womb. That alone would seal her part-ownership of the global medical conglomerate.

Dr. Rickett finished his work and removed his latex gloves. He tossed them into a nearby waste basket and wrote quick notes on an electronic tablet. "I don't understand why you and your husband don't pursue this the good old-fashioned way. There's absolutely nothing wrong with you both from the records I've seen."

Myranda frowned. When Merdon Clinic had asked for her husband's medical records, she'd had no choice but to fabricate them. She gathered the surgical robe tighter around her curvy frame, fury filling her tearing eyes. "Just do your job."

He ignored her comment with calculated disdain. "I'll leave you now for a few minutes."

Myranda settled on the bed and its stiffness underneath her shoulder blades edged in her back as she closed her eyes. It was never meant to be like this. She cursed, muttering punitive words that echoed in the private clinic room. The last embryo transfer had failed to attach. Her then-physician had blamed her clinical anxiety disorder.

On her way into the clinic she'd almost turned back, but she had to fulfill a clause in the non-negotiable prenuptial agreement. A last gamble at ensuring the security that would come with five years of marriage. *A live child birth by their fifth wedding anniversary.*

Myranda tossed a ginger lock away from her nettled eyes. The March date was only nine months away.

She had to give Leal Trelles a child.

* * *

Kaya's eyes scanned past Jewel and studied the fading Adel on Schottenring Platz. "Quite a building."

"Gotta look past the grime and grit," Jewel said raising her Nikon lens. "I wonder why they never kept it up."

"Well for one, funds around here typically go to winter resorts and accommodating tourist influxes," said an autocratic voice behind them.

They spun in the direction of a modishly dressed Austrian. He gave each woman a firm hand shake. "Hans Gruenmeier. I'm the theater director of the Adel."

Jewel studied his glinting close-set eyes. His graying hair was frosted above a square face that beamed a spirited smile. His accented tone used what Jewel would term BBC English.

"You must be Jewel Carlone, the photographer from New York," Hans said.

She slung her Nikon camera round to the back. "What gave me away?"

"Well, the Nikon for one, I studied the volunteer list thoroughly," he said.

Kaya drew a step near him. "It's criminal to let such a great building go to waste. Look there at the entrance, the walls haven't seen paint, probably since 1922 or there about."

"Nineteen-seventy-five, to be accurate. I'm sure you have great advice. I understand you have a great knowledge of international legal systems and your hobby is architecture."

He'd touched Kaya's core. She eased her stylish holster wallet. "You've certainly done your homework, Herr Gruenmeier."

Hans' eyes glanced up at the protruding twin domes of the theater set against the blue sky. "If we capture her rich history, I think your photos and everyone's enthusiasm in the next four days will help our cause. We urgently need friends and partners to support the foundation."

He advanced toward them with a grin of amusement. "Did you know the theater was originally a casino?"

Jewel tunneled her hand through her hair. "That would've been entertainment around here. When did it become a stage theater then?"

"When a traveling troupe asked to use it to perform Verdi's *Otello* in early 1905."

"And it's been a roaring success since?"

"We think so. Its main structure is still in pretty good shape, but the theater definitely needs a cosmetic lift. We can use help and need to reclaim its irreplaceable traditions."

Jewel only heard fragments of Hans' narrative, distracted by the theater's commanding outer structure.

Hans continued in a boisterous voice. "By the mid-fifties, the theater became a multipurpose venue, with a vast program focusing on modern dramas, updated works by old masters and of course, a theater for youngsters."

Jewel snapped close-ups of the double corner towers, each topped by a globe and shielded in scaffolding, before Hans ushered them on a tour of the west side. She raised her lens several times capturing the summit mast, the exterior ivory concrete and the Adel's unusual terracotta Moorish style.

She stared past the bustling plaza for a moment, incapable of moving as a bustling tour group assembled in front of the hotel. Setting the viewfinder on her camera against her eye, she caught sight of a statuesque man. Lean and athletic, he paced behind three winter sport enthusiasts with a snowboard behind his head and winter goggles strapped above his eyes. He put down the snowboard and bent it at an unusual angle.

Her complexion changed color.

She perched herself to one corner of the west wall and for several seconds she could not breathe.

Chapter 3

"Who's that?" said Kaya.

Jewel stared at the athlete in his snowboard pants under a snow jacket as he entered the hotel. Her black and red figure-hugging winter jumpsuit didn't feel as warm as she'd hoped when she'd put it on that morning. Wearing matching winter boots she glanced down through from the open balcony of the theater with a level view of the plaza. One by one, the volunteers from the hotel made their way into the theater.

She looked over at Kaya. "Who do you mean?"

"The guy you can't stop staring at. Here, take a look at this volunteer print out. I think that is Dr. Leal Trelles from New York. Seems like we New Yorkers all had the same idea for this long weekend."

"The theater solicited volunteers from art, photography and design schools in London, New York and San Francisco. I'm sure it's quite a diverse group," Jewel said.

"That's why you came, but what's a doctor doing in the mix?"

"Possibly the same thing a law student is." Jewel slung her camera behind her back. "I think I know him."

"Did you meet him in New York?"

"No. Montpellier. Four years ago."

The group of volunteers had now swept through the entrance below. Kaya started a march toward the lower floors, her sophisticated boots clicking on the tiles as she glanced back. "You got all of that from here. Must've good eyesight."

"Not me. My Nikon. Never lets me down."

Hans joined them on the balcony. "We are ready to begin work now."

The women followed him inside where the rest of the volunteers had begun to congregate in the main auditorium. Kaya shuffled her feet as she moved alongside Jewel. "It's Saturday. We are in this amazing place. I could be doing a whole bunch of things in the city."

"Yet you signed up to help restore the theater. We can see the sights later."

"I mean, when can we go see Mozart's birth place?"

"Another time." Jewel slung an arm through Kaya's. "I appreciate you taking the time to volunteer with me, but we've not hung out for three weeks. What better way than a four-day trip to Europe. You lawyers are always pressed for time."

"So what do we need to do exactly? I hope nothing manual."

Jewel sniggered as they descended the grand staircase. "I thought you read the brochure. Hans will assign us our respective duties," she whispered, not wanting Hans to overhear. "I'm sure it's not going to be too bad. We'll meet lots of new people. I think they will be in the auditorium right about now. Let's go."

Kaya held back a giggle as they reached the bottom step that led onto the main floor. The stalls had been removed and the grand room could easily be used for a ball room with its black-and-white marble floors that begged for a new polish. Jewel studied the four crystal chandeliers that stood above them.

"Are you okay being here?" Kaya said.

"Yes, why do you ask?"

"You've not been around a performance venue or arena for four years. I'm worried about you. It's not easy to give up something you love and are good at."

"That's all in the past."

"Is it?"

Jewel refrained from responding and followed Hans as the other twenty-eight volunteers mused quietly. Kaya had touched her core. Her way of dealing with a lost dream had been to repress it. *If I don't desire it, it can't haunt me anymore. I never have to face the pressure of performing again.*

Jewel smiled at her best friend whose English and Indian Cherokee ancestry had always made her slightly envious. She'd always admired Kaya's timeless symmetrical face and smooth copper skin. She smiled as the men in the group watched Kaya move toward the group. It reminded her of how the boyish men used to purchase rhythmic gymnastics tickets just to watch the group of gymnasts. And it was not for the artistry.

Jewel was proud of Kaya, an outspoken female equality

promoter with her shrewd sharp mind, that would sooner or later whisk the hawking men of the group into respect. All in decent fun.

No one understood her better than Kaya. As Hans counted heads and checked names, Jewel found herself muttering, almost chanting a mantra. *There is no performance scheduled. I'm safe from pressure, cameras, and performance.*

Hans began a moving speech with his loud accented voice. "Welcome to the Adel Theater of Salzburg."

The group turned to face him and the man the girls had been scrutinizing took his place at the back of the group.

"Thank you, volunteers. Thank you. With the work intended for the theater, yours is the simpler task. You won't have to worry about the stalls which are to be completely re-seated and re-raked. The orchestra pit will be enlarged and we hope, if funds allow, to have the air-conditioning installed and the backstage mechanical facilities considerably improved." He cleared his throat. "You are here to lend artistry in the form of painting, design and awareness. And with your expertise, that shouldn't be too hard."

As Hans addressed the expectant onlookers, Jewel's eyes peeked through the eye lens of her classic Nikon camera and circled the interior of the main auditorium. Her fingers toyed with the camera lens, zooming in at the chandeliers for a good shot.

She brought down the Nikon and held her position as a figure moved in her view. The tall man had fine eyebrows, a softly shaped jaw and wore a trendy snowsuit. Possibly in his mid-twenties, he neared Hans and stood a few feet from him.

Kaya watched him carefully. "Says here he's an epidemiologist by training and biomedical physicist who runs his own business in New York." She folded the flier. "All in a fine piece of snowboarder."

Jewel had searched the Internet for years for his identity and failed to find answers. She raised her chin slightly. "One who kisses girls and makes them cry."

Kaya turned toward her. "So it is him?"

"Shush…What's an epidemiologist?"

"Doctors whose work revolves around medical research. Often called *disease detectives*. They sort of study illnesses to figure out the cause."

"Is kissing considered an illness?"

Kaya and Jewel snickered and turned their full attention to Hans, who spoke on with resolve.

"I'm really excited that our plea to find the best in the arts and other professions has been successful. It will help us save the Adel."

Soon the man's stare followed the group and fell on Jewel's face. Jewel avoided eye contact at all cost and turned her attention to Hans. Kaya's protective nature over Jewel kicked in. "Cute, but from where I am looking, he knows who you are, too."

* * *

Myranda opened her eyes when she heard Dr. Rickett return.

"How are you feeling?" he said.

"Awful. Nauseous."

"That'll ease. You can get dressed now," he said.

Dr. Rickett slipped out of the treatment room once more as Myranda rose pushing her head upward. Once the doctor had left, she tugged on her silk blouse, pulled on some slacks and shoved her feet in her new red pumps before fetching her purse from the desk. She paced to the door, her head swooning.

Dr. Rickett saw her approach in the hallway and narrowed his eyes. "Rest is essential. Please limit physical activity for the rest of the day."

Rest? How can one rest? Infertility had overwhelmed her entire being since attending a routine gynecological check-up at age fifteen. No doctor, clinic, or medical specialist could tell her the cause of her problems with conceiving. Was it genes? Misfortune?

No!

She wouldn't let anything defeat her.

Not Leal Trelles. Not now.

With nine months left to bring a live child into the world she was seizing her last opportunity. Her whole livelihood hung on her greatest weakness.

Was it a weakness?

The word did not exist in Myranda's vocabulary. Hot tears waterlogged her eyes as she paced with Dr. Rickett toward the elevators.

The doctor set a hand on her shoulder and she slumped in a nearby chair. "I'll fetch something to help you with the nausea."

Myranda had hoped being married to a biomedical physician like Leal would help her problem, offer comfort, maybe even make her feel more adequate than she did.

She toyed with the gem-set wedding band on her left hand, a Cartier-Estinee solitaire framed by a crown and sealed with rare diamonds. How she'd dreamed of marrying the medical virtuoso on his way to greatness, and someone sensitive enough to put up with her anxiety disorder, inadequacies, achievements, and her forward style.

They were a team. Weren't they? If only she couldn't remember the sunny day so well, just after Labor Day weekend when she'd first laid her eyes on Leal. Myranda had fallen for the wealthy young doctor, an entrepreneur so unaware of his good looks, his formidable wealth and influence.

Vaux Marketing Inc., her upmarket consulting business had been tipped to pitch for Trelles Pharmaceuticals' new international marketing campaign and had focused on securing the account. She'd pitch and ensure a three-year international contract with the Trelles empire. Myranda would be their marketing partner for all global operations.

Soon Vaux Marketing generated successful results with a flu vaccine ad placement on Super Bowl Sunday, giving Myranda's consulting business, which she ran with her father, the staggering opportunity to collaborate with a global conglomerate. Every news outlet reported that Trelles Industries was the world's leading pharmaceutical by revenues with Leal driving much of the profits.

Shortly after, Myranda contacted Leal to discuss more promotional concepts on breakthrough robotics surgery, processes the medical company was conducting. Trelles had developed minuscule robotic hands that operated joints deep inside a patient's body, patented technology that was pushing robotic surgery to the forefront of medical science. Trelles Industries' R&D division enabled a growing number of centers across the country to use these methods. In that phonecall, and a casual follow-up meeting, Leal the unassuming doctor, an entrepreneur on the Forbes list of pharmaceutical executives, made more than a professional impression on her.

All the things she thirsted for in a man.

She followed the Forbes rankings like a celebrity social-media account. His personal worth alone was estimated at six billion dollars, six billion reasons to make the campaign a success. The price of drugs was soaring and pharmaceutical companies spent more and more on marketing than research. Trelles' share price increased each year and was trending at forty-five dollars.

Myranda had done her research.

The average drug developed by a major pharmaceutical company could cost anything from four to eleven billion dollars. That alone would pay for enough football stadiums to populate the East Coast. It was a staggering cost for inventing new drugs.

Leal had researched and marketed two drugs, one a fertility drug, and a vaccination against lung cancer that had experienced only one failure in the testing phase. The shot was designed for people with rooted disease, helping their immune systems to prevent the return of disease after surgery.

Myranda learned that Trelles spent on average ten billion dollars for every drug approved. Marketing for Trelles meant funds were in plentiful supply. This was the industry she needed to be in and Leal was the way in.

It took all of thirteen months to launch the 'Living' marketing campaign, and get engaged to him. He took the bait and she wasn't about to let go. If only that confounded pre-nuptial had not interfered with her course of action requiring she give Leal the one thing she couldn't give him.

* * *

Jewel's chin dipped when Leal's eye caught her stare.

"Attractive men scare you."

Jewel scowled at Kaya's remark and continued in whispers over Hans 'voice.

"Do you have enough light in here to photograph the damaged stage tower from below? Hans says that's the theater's selling point," Kaya said.

"Mom says you can spot lighting in any space. If you find beauty in the mundane, your picture won't let you down."

Jewel had turned to photography since leaving rhythmic gymnastics, the same profession as her mother's. She fell in love with the art at a young age, and pestered her single mom, a freelance photographer from Kauai, the oldest of the main Hawaiian Islands, for a camera when she turned thirteen. Mahina Carlone scanned the island for the right one and found a Nikon-EM with a 50mm Series-E lens in a downtown store that drained the talented photographer of her last savings. "It's yours," she'd told the budding teenager. "But promise to treat it well."

After Jewel's father, an Italian art dealer, who studied in Hawaii, left them in a one bedroom apartment in Italy's northern town of Udine, not one man had been in Mahina's life. They'd been high school sweethearts and the reason Mahina had left the U.S. for a life with him in Northern Italy. Jewel distrusted most men and related little to them.

She held back a choking swallow. Handling the responsibilities of a child alone would overwhelm her. Not to mention the numerous income issues Mahina had had to work out. Alone. How many years had Mahina's sole income gone to meet their needs? Her mother had foregone her own wants and Jewel had made do with any 'hand-me-downs' her mom's community of friends could foster.

They'd missed out on owning their own house, a dependable savings account, regrets that now gave Jewel a sense of responsibility toward her mother's wellbeing and continuous selfless acts.

Jewel knew the sacrifice it had been and the memory drew sadness to her face as she brought the camera down from her eyes. It wasn't right. Single mothers shouldn't have to sacrifice so much and still be manipulated by the men in their lives.

It was her turn to compensate for lost aspirations. Lost in decades of seeking safety and a roof over their heads.

As a child, many words around the home were speared by guilt, perhaps remorse. Her mother's every utterance about men was usually ridden with shades of hostility. Like the time when Mahina dated, just to have a father-figure around for her twelve-year-old. It had been a cringing thought to a pre-teenager, who'd never lacked a mother's love. Mahina should've known that a man meddling in their close relationship was the last thing she needed.

Dating was not a Carlone woman's strength. What could a man add to her life? Very little, as evidenced through Mahina's own experiences. But, then again, she didn't know any different and somehow wanted to experience what trusting someone stronger than her meant. What was it like to share common goals with someone who could encourage her and expand her effectiveness in everything she did? Like Kaya's husband Weston.

Hans's echoing voice reverted Jewel to the theater's fading glory. She cocked her head to Kaya's side. "Lots of photographers are abandoning traditional cameras in favor of digital ones. Not me. Not for everything. At least not yet. This camera will be fine for that tower. It's fed me since I was a child."

"How so?"

"It was my mother's. She borrowed it for years to continue working, and eventually bought it off the owner."

Kaya squeezed her friend's hand. "Your mother is a very special woman."

Hans cleared his throat. "We've very little time to work on the festival hall tower. Only two full days. Those working on painting please follow Frau Schmidt over there with the brown sweater. Those working on the ceiling please follow Dr. Leal Trelles."

Leal's eyes investigated the animated group. He'd not changed since Montpellier. His short sideburns were still groomed to precision, his athletic posture and walk confident and still purposeful. Leal's hair was perhaps a touch darker since their last meeting and was swept back like ripples. A copper-glazed fringe dropped in his face short of concealing his sensitive analyzing eyes that sheened with gentleness. Though she hated to admit it, his attractive face revealed confidence. Jewel was certain most people who came in contact with him were drawn by his unassuming masculine influence, stemming from his trendy style.

He'd saved her life from a medical fanatic with a syringe. The Montpellier police had never found either of them after an investigation went on for two years. They'd also not understood her mutterings that a doctor had saved her. With no security camera evidence and no harm to her wellbeing, the case was dropped.

Distracted by the memory of the way the doctor had kissed her in France, she tried hard to focus on what Hans was saying.

The beefy Austrian wandered over to Leal and set a sturdy hand on his broad shoulders. Leal had abandoned the ski goggles. Around his neck, he draped a soft-tassel plaid scarf.

"Dr. Trelles will take a group through those stairs on the

34

left and lead the repairs to the ceiling. Could I have a group of about five to work with him? That should take all afternoon," Hans said.

Leal paced past the parting group toward the staircase. Three sturdy men joined him along with two chatty women.

"Miss Carlone has volunteered her photography skills to document the progress," continued Hans. "Some of you may recognize Jewel Carlone. She's a world-class Olympic gymnast."

A flush crept across Jewel's cheeks in embarrassment and a tingling sensation swept up the back of her neck. What had possessed Hans to bring up her past?

Hans turned to Jewel. "Miss Carlone, you're free to follow the workers and volunteers around. We need as many photographs to solicit the funds necessary. Judging from your portfolio and the work you did for the restored church in New York City, this should be no challenge at all."

Jewel nodded.

Hans clasped his hands together. "I think everything's in order. We'll break in an hour for some refreshments. Miss Carlone, please follow me. I'll take you around some more."

"Later," Kaya said as she followed the group assigned to costume sorting. "Let's hit the manicure salon after this. I'll need it."

Murmers from the group subsided as volunteers took to their tasks in the separate corners of the theater grounds.

Jewel tailed Hans to the stage platform, stopped and pointed to a broken step at the foot of the stage. "That's unfortunate." She raised her camera to her eyes and snapped the broken oak, splintered in fragments and tunneling a hole in the bottom step.

"Feel free, Miss Carlone, to take as many pictures as you need."

"Thanks. I will."

Hans stole out the front entrance with an ear to his cellphone. Jewel's rapid breathing and visible sweating subsided as she was left alone in the serene hall. As odd as it was, she had never wanted to be the center of attention.

She stepped onto the proscenium-arched stage, taking in the full view of the grand auditorium, before advancing backstage to examine the aged velvet curtains that concealed the wings. The paneled stage floor raked upwards from front to back at a slight slant, contributing to a hypnotic illusory perspective. She found a

35

stepladder near the burgundy drapes and hoisted herself to the third step. Her arms rested on the top of the medium-sized ladder for a panoramic shot of the ballroom, and a perspective angle from the stage.

Jewel heard a noise behind her. A knot twisted in her stomach and she tried to lower her foot. She glanced down at her boot that had caught a loose rope she'd not seen on the step and kicked it away. The ladder cracked and began an inevitable tip to the right. All in the space of a few seconds, she lost her balance. Her mind calculated the irrevocable plummet to the timbered floor. With only seconds to think, she braced herself for the fall, shutting her eyes for impact. A precipitous jerk saved her and she turned as a steady arm enfolded round her waist.

Leal.

He lowered her feet to the ground. "You need to be careful on these floors. You don't want to face another injury."

Jewel regained her footing and stood upright scuffing her boot on the floor. She bit her lips and her voice spurted out in stammers. "I'm fine. Shouldn't you be instructing some group on repairs?"

"They're fine and now know what to do."

Leal loosened his grip and stepped back once his eyes had been assured she was all right. He drew his eyebrows together. "So you're the soon-to-be-famous photographer?"

Jewel steadied herself and took a long deep breath. "Impressed?"

"Very. I also remember you as the fantastic gymnast."

The overhead lights pierced her eyes and soon the need to put on her best theater performance nudged her, standing on a stage graced by those better at acting. Her voice diminished as she spoke. "You know me, Dr. Trelles?"

Leal's eyes warmed, his tone flirting with her. "How's that knee?"

"The same way you left it four years ago. I don't perform anymore."

"I'm sure it's healed." A chortle rolled from his throat. "No gymnast could perform the way you do and leave it all behind because of a small accident."

A contemptuous smile played on her lips. "Are you a fan of gymnastics?"

His glistening eyes admired hers. "Most sports, generally."

"You consider rhythmic gymnastics a sport?"

"I do."

Certain she had his attention, she started for the stage stairs. She turned for a reaction. "That improves my impression of you."

His cocky smile provoked her and his eyes remained engaged. "Anyone who can do what your body is capable of must be good at several sports."

"Don't assume you know what my body can do."

"Oh I'm sure it can bend at angles only architects can calculate."

He was from Manhattan, maybe Long Island, just by the way he tensed the words that rhymed with core and more.

"I'll bet you could outrun me on the Alps on a snowboard," Leal said.

"A challenge?"

"Maybe."

Jewel started a descent down the stairs with Leal following. "My knee is in retirement. And that goes for any sporting activity. Sorry to disappoint you, doctor."

"No, it's not."

She shot him a backward glance. "Excuse me?"

Leal edged closer, his face inches from hers. "You heard me. Your knee is not in retirement. I'll race you down on the slopes on a snowboard. The winner makes a request."

Was he serious? In the close proximity, she took in the inviting mild scent of his aftershave. Her eyes challenged him back. "Anything?"

His lips curled into a cocky smile. "Sounds like you're up for it."

"Don't get your hopes up."

"Oh, do let me, Jewel."

She scowled.

"You can do whatever you want, including compete again," he said.

Was he pep-talking? How could he be so casual after his behavior in France? Jewel eyed the exit. Which barred door would she use to escape him as he leaned closer? She fiddled with an unruly lock of hair. "I don't snowboard."

"It would take a world class gymnast only a few minutes to learn how to balance on one of my boards."

Why would she accept such a ridiculous challenge? Yet

something about Leal's boldness and spirit of adventure intrigued her. It reminded her of her own. Could her knee take it? She'd spent the good part of the last two years convincing herself she'd overestimated all of her sporting abilities, that she no longer had flexible mobility in her joints. Then why come on a winter sports volunteer trip? And why did he look at her with such observance, one minute enthralled by her desire to escape him and another eager to give her a motivational talk on sports injuries? Where had he been in four years?

He tilted his head. "Well?"

Jewel leaned away from him. "No."

His hand found her arm, firm and commanding. "What've you got to lose? A minute ago you were sure you'd win."

"No thanks."

His strong eye contact weakened hers. "If you win, I'll also show you a great view of the damaged hall. I'm sure it'll sizzle your portfolio."

It was tempting. A sturdy hand with well-proportioned fingers, bordered by a clean manicure reached for her chin. "Come on, champion."

She pulled away as Leal's words nudged at her spirit of competition. She set a hand on his scarf and tugged him forward. "Let's see how much snow you can digest."

* * *

The ring on Myranda's finger slipped up to her knuckle and made a halt. Her body had begun to rock in place, her hands sweating at the speed of a steaming water pot as she gripped her leather purse. Dr. Rickett returned with two small boxes and Myranda recognized the Alarax drugs.

He placed them in her hands as she rose. "These will help reduce anxiety."

"I don't think that's possible."

"You really should take the rest of the day off. Is your driver downstairs?"

"He better be."

Rickett grimaced, taking a step back.

She eyed him intently. "Will it work this time, doctor?"

"High-impact activities are probably not a good idea, not

until after the pregnancy test."

"Huh!" She gripped his white coat. "You're supposed to be a miracle worker."

Dr. Rickett removed her hand from his collar. "The miracle starts with you and the way you handle anxiety, your body and emotions. Sometimes wanting something so much can be our worst enemy."

"Don't patronize me." Myranda spat the words out, conscious of the blood rising to her feverish cheeks.

"It's your choice, Myranda." He managed a weak smile. "Once pregnant, you should be okay to resume all normal activities."

"If that ever happens," she hissed.

The doctor scowled. "I'll see you in forty-eight hours. We'll check on progress then."

Myranda strutted out of the clinic feeling more like a lab rat than a patient. She thought back to her wedding ceremony. After the formalities ended, it was clear Leal didn't love her. Why hadn't he once looked at her the way most women looked at him? Leal's touch and affection never made it past their wedding day. If only she'd been more careful. Too late for "if onlys"; four years too late. Then again, after all these years he'd still not mentioned the dreaded D word. *Divorce.*

* * *

The Obersthof Hotel's breakfast room bustled with hyped international volunteers. They'd completed their work on the Adel and herded to St. Johann for a well-earned day on the slopes between the Kitzbüheler Horn and the Kaisergebirge Alps. Before wandering to the slope, first they wanted to witness the race. The New Yorkers' loud voices rose above one another anticipating a good challenge. News had spread among them that an Olympian was taking on a professional snowboarder. Betting on the race was money worth making and eager moneymakers hurried to two bet-bookers from the group.

Leal washed down his freshly squeezed orange juice. He finished his cheese and a buttered wholegrain bagel. When the waiter cleared his plate, he rose, muscles relaxed as he approached Jewel and Kaya's table who sat with three male New Yorkers.

39

He glided their way. Getting Jewel alone on that quiet run, just a few hundred meters from the hotel was the surest way of getting that DNA code sample. He padded the syringe set deep within his pocket. He had to get the DEI away from his research and this sample would do it, along with its analysis. He and Jewel would cruise the black diamond runs. If that failed...

He wouldn't think about that now. Stealing with soft movement toward the women's table, he overheard the energetic conversation.

"I think you're nuts, Jewel," Kaya said. "Look, I know you've longed to get back into physical activity, but racing a snowboarder who trains everyday as a first step? Whatever possessed you?"

Jewel pulled her hair back into a pony tail, her beautiful soft face arresting Leal's attention as she spoke. "I like a good challenge."

"You ready?" said Leal steering the conversation his way.

"I must warn you, Dr. Trelles, I've won many challenges in my past."

"Call me Leal." He flashed a boyish smile her way as the table occupants leaned in. "I'll be delighted to eat the snow behind you."

Jewel rose with a gleam of light invading her eyes. "Let's go."

The jeers overpowered the breakfast room. Soon, the loud group shuffled outside to the front of the timber-fronted hotel surrounded by a handful of flower-decked wooden chalets set in the heart of the elegant village against the alpine backdrop.

They scrambled to the entrance points of one of Austria's largest connecting skiing regions, the Ski Amadé, a ski resort that stood only a few hundred yards away. The group clumped up a few feet to a small shed on a beaten path that led to a hidden chalet. With the temperature close to freezing, a series of howls turned their attention toward a side shed by the cabin. The barred door opened as two sleds of resilient Siberian huskies barged out and scampered onto the path, led by an Austrian couple in mountaineering gear.

The huskies came to a sudden halt in front of Leal. He stole round the animals toward their master and approached the fair-skinned man with shoulder-length thick white hair and gave him a strong handshake. He turned and winked at Jewel. "Your chariot. I'll race you to the après ski bars on the edge of the town. Don't worry. The huskies know the way."

Jewel glared at the pair of sleds, each driven by a team of eight, wolf-like creatures. "You're kidding. On these? I thought we were snowboarding."

The onlookers roared with excited jeers at the new turn of events. Leal ignored them, his eyes on her. "I wouldn't do that to you."

The ice-blue-eyed beasts panted with excitement, awaiting instructions as spectators took their places on either side of the race course.

Jewel's mouth dropped in protest. "I don't know how to race these dogs."

The female owner of the dogs placed a gentle hand on her shoulder. "The dogs know how to race you. I'm going to teach you *mush* language. Just memorize five easy words. *Hike*, for get moving, *gee*, to turn right, *haw* to turn left, *easy*, to slow down and *whoa* to stop."

Jewel glanced back at her, her voice shaky. "Are you sure? Is that all?"

The woman smiled. "That's it."

Leal watched the interaction. He smiled at her spontaneity and unintentional charm. She was beyond breathtaking, radiant with her glistening hair in the morning sun and bewitching with the velvety tones of her voice. Though contradictory to her words, they rang with smoothness and calm.

Kaya leaned forward. "You can add five more words to your vocabulary from now on."

The mistress of the huskies tossed her hip-length dark tresses and whispered in Jewel's ears. "I've given you the better racers."

Jewel mounted the sled. Within minutes, the two sporting sleighs stood side-by-side on-looking the valley.

Leal jumped on his sled and glimpsed over at Jewel. "You ready, champion?"

Jewel's mouth curved into a mocking smile. "Eat my snow. *Hike!*"

Like bolting race-hounds, the huskies charged down the mountain path with Jewel's dogs in the lead. The hill meandered at sharp angles. Both sleds gained speed gliding over the snowy paths and charged toward the vast frozen wilderness. They scampered past screaming onlookers.

Leaving the clamor behind them, the racers sped down a deserted path.

Jewel clung onto the reins and dared not look back at Leal's distance behind her, the spirit of competition stimulating her resolve. Frozen firs zipped past them and she glared ahead catching sight of the finish point they'd agreed on, the après ski bar near the local park house on the edge of St. Johann. Leal's huskies were a few feet behind her. Soon they took a parallel position to her speeding wolves.

"*Hike!*" she commanded the winter canines and they hastened their pace. She zipped her head round. Without warning, her dogs bore to the right and veered off course. As if by instinct, the Siberian huskies slowed down at a meandering stream and came to a halt meters from the edge of a slope.

Leal crossed the finish point to a small cheering crowd of pumped-up men. Jewel sank on the edge of her sled and pulled off her ear-muffs and ski goggles. Her hair loosened, falling wildly over her shoulders.

Leal steadied his beasts, his adrenaline soaring as he studied her. Her frown hypnotized him as he watched Jewel against the backdrop of the Alps. He didn't know what he'd expected, only that the last ten minutes set him on a new path of admiration for the olympian. His eyes didn't leave her and whether she knew it or not, she'd been fearless.

He jumped off his sled and trudged the frozen ground toward her sled. "I take it I won."

"Did you have to come so close to my huskies?" she said.

"Mm… do I detect a sore loser?"

Her cheeks flushed as she let out a little laugh. "I'm looking at a man who was almost beaten by a woman. I let you win."

"Really?"

She ran glove-free fingers through her chocolate mane and he watched her with fascination. She could be embarrassed, yet appear poised. Leal took a seat beside her, taking in her nectarous perfumed scent. He'd been this close to her once. The memory had stayed with him and tormented him for years knowing he couldn't be near her. His work was too dangerous for her, yet couldn't succeed without Jewel.

With his shoulder inches from hers, he helped her to her feet. "I won. You need to do something for me."

Jewel managed a defeated smile and shivered with uncertainty at his nearness. "Nothing requiring major physical activity I hope."

His hands stole to her flushed cheek and stayed there for several seconds as his eyes pored into her amber gaze. He felt her shiver and pulled her closer to him. "That all depends."

She slid her hand up his shoulder as naturally as if she'd known him all her life. "And what if I refuse?"

The sounds of the quiet village around him dimmed. He leaned in, grazing the tip of his nose against hers. "You can't."

She raised her chin, her body quivering, her lips almost touching his. "How do you know?"

"Because you're the kind to keep your word."

"You sure about that?"

"A wild guess."

Before she could reply, he neared his lips toward hers and pulled back as if uncertain. "May I?"

"It's not like you asked permission before."

Her eyes told him all he needed to know, and he kissed her deeply.

He'd failed and melted like ice on a sand dune in her presence. In her arms, he lost his sense of mission, purpose and duty. What had started as infatuated idolization in Montpellier was now a serious heart problem, and one that had nothing to do with a medical condition.

Leal knew much about her, everything the DEI had told him. Every file of theirs he'd read. He knew her height, blood type, weight and injection she'd had. Every time she'd been in hospital. Every time she'd volunteered at her local community center. As she kissed him back, the details of his mission became hazy. Forgotten.

With her gratifying scent engulfing him, he couldn't bring the syringe to her skin. The surest way was distraction. That's how many of his patients had avoided pain with his injections. But her response to his kiss was amplifying his own confusion. Her skin was the smoothest he'd ever touched. He sensed her shiver, mimicking his own racing heart. He'd expected to stay unattached. This was not the plan, just like it hadn't been his plan to stop that reckless agent in her hospital room.

His hand dove into his pocket and his fingers crawled toward the sterilized syringe, the design of which he'd

43

commissioned himself. He pulled himself together and his eyes opened.

Its prick would not hurt her.

* * *

Jewel rose from the sled untangling herself from Leal's arms. She'd let her guard down. How could Leal have known that detail? Her friends and family knew her as a person who kept her word. Sometimes it would almost drain her, but once she promised to do something, she followed it through. Like the time when her mother asked her to pick up a rare portrait of the Madonna from an antique shop in Rome while on a gymnastics training trip. The antique shop shut when she arrived and the shop attendant refused to let her in. She returned the next day at daybreak to buy it, almost missing her flight back to New York.

Jewel tipped her head back and watched Leal. "Okay, snow man. I'll buy you a coffee in town for defeating a girl."

He took her hand. "Intrigued."

Twenty minutes later, Jewel eyed Leal as they strolled through the center of St. Johann. She hadn't expected to like the New York doctor this much. He'd made her laugh and brought her witty side to the surface more than any other person she knew. All her rules about men and the doctor who'd left her in Montpellier had been abandoned, because Leal paid attention.

She listened as he spoke passionately about medicine and travel. She liked the tones of his low voice, and he spoke as one who thought through every word. Nothing was careless about the way he dressed, the way he wore fashionable slacks and jumpers as if they were the last things he owned. He made sure she finished her sentences before he spoke and listened with interest each time she raised a topic about gymnastics and photography, the things that meant much to her. Two hours later, they stopped outside the hotel entrance. Jewel failed to notice the time go by as he played with her hair. She turned to face him. "What's my punishment for losing?"

"So you'll do it?

"Depends?"

"Come, I'll show you."

Thirty minutes after returning to the hotel, with coats on, Leal led Jewel out of the lobby. Outside the building, he stopped by an ebony Arctic Cat snowmobile. Leal adjusted the detachable seat. "Here, put this on."

Jewel took the helmet and slid it over her head. "Where are we going?"

Leal took a seat on the snow vehicle. "You'll see. Bring your Nikon."

She hesitated for all of three seconds, unsure if this was a good idea. "I already have it."

He snapped on his helmet as Jewel settled on the seat behind him. She placed her snow goggles over her eyes and slid her arms around his robust body. A flutter charged to her stomach. Was it fear? A guard to protect herself? Yet intuitive surrender took charge. The latter being new to her. What would Kaya think now of her sabotaging thoughts about men and her stubborn resolve?

Jewel took a deep breath and Leal kicked the pedal setting the snowmobile's engine roaring. She clasped her arms around him and leaned into his strong back. He sped the vehicle off the parking plot and on the frozen road that wound toward St. Johann's alpine slopes.

Jewel rested her cheek against his jacket. He responded to her willingness and he reached back for her hand reassuring her of her decision, before churning up the engine.

They cruised above the Austrian valley that offered a myriad of well-marked strolling paths, hiking byways, mountain huts and protected nature areas above St. Johann. The higher they rode, the faster her heart thumbed against her ribcage. Anxiety rose to her throat as they curved away from the ski town, mirroring the sharp turns in the curved roads toward the hills. She raised her goggles above her eyes and caught the imposing view of the snowcapped slopes as they dusted the valley below. Twenty minutes into their ride, Leal decelerated the snowmobile and they came to a halt over the Kaiserbachtal basin.

As he switched off the engine, Jewel removed her helmet and breathed in the fresh air.

"You all right, champion?"

She nodded. "It's beautiful up here."

Leal stepped off the snowmobile and paced to a tipping cliff, hanging back meters from the edge. "I promised I'd show you a fantastic view of the stage tower."

Jewel grabbed her Nikon from her backpack. He was too close to the cliff's edge; it made her hold her breath. The seven-hundred foot drop didn't intimidate him.

Soon he turned to face her. "I like coming up here."

Though the words were positive, they were spoken with pain. Her lips stretched into an uneasy smile "Do you come here much?"

"This time, every day."

"How often do you come to Austria?"

Leal turned to face her. "Not as much as I should."

"Hold it there," she said fiddling toward him and lifted her camera as his eyes met hers. She centralized her lens having ditched the neck strap for a hand one and adjusted the focus on the compositional aspects of his handsome face. "May I?"

His lips curled at the tips and sent his eyes smiling. With his back against the view, Jewel snapped several shots.

"Don't get too comfortable with that," he said. "We're here to take shots of the stage tower, not me."

"Maybe I like the view." She lowered her camera and sent a curious gaze his way. "What brings you here to the mountains, Leal?"

"Remember our first meeting?"

It was the first time in three days he'd mentioned Montpellier. "How can I forget? What were you doing in my hospital room?"

"I wanted to see if you were all right." He kept his smile. "I'm a fan. I still remember how you performed, and your accident—"

"In case my doctors were not treating me right?"

"Exactly."

"How did you get clearance and access to the secured wing? I was in intensive care."

His eyes were sincere. "I had to see you. I hate to say it but it was easy. I said I was your doctor from New York."

"How did you know I was from New York?"

"It's not hard finding information on Olympians."

"Why did you just disappear after you—"

"Kissed you? I've thought about that for a long time."

He took a step closer to her lessening the distance to him. "How is your knee holding up? Must have healed by now."

Jewel cast her eyes toward the valley and inhaled the crisp air. "I've not done gymnastics since."

"Why?"

"I don't know."

Leal fell silent and drew his shoulders upward. "There's something about these mountains and the fresh air that makes one feel they can start again. Maybe they're speaking to you."

"What would I be looking to start?"

He turned toward her and took her hand in his, pulling her to him. His ungloved skin warmed her cheek. Leal slid his other arm around her middle and his face stopped inches from hers. "It's time you fulfill your promise."

Jewel stiffened and her neck strained up. She was close to a full head-size shorter than him. Leal lowered his face. She closed her eyes apprehending yet inviting his forwardness.

He jousted back. "I'm sorry," he said ambling toward a snow coated fir tree and stared at the valley in silence.

She followed him with her lens and snapped a few awkward shots. "Are you okay, Leal?"

"Yeah, let's get out of here."

She studied him for a few seconds. "All right. I have all the shots I need. I'm done."

"You hardly took pictures of the stage tower."

"My lens has found a more interesting subject."

Leal handed her the helmet. "I still haven't claimed my prize for winning."

What on earth did he need her to do? Why was it so important?

"You're good with that," he said pointing to her camera. "Can I put you to good use?"

"I'm not as good as you think."

"I doubt that."

"Jewel?"

She looked away from the lens eye. "Come with me to India." His eyes begged her. "Just for a week."

"India?"

"I have a small project out there much like the charity work with the Adel yet different that needs even more help. More publicity. I think your photos could help us."

47

"Us?"

"I run a medical clinic in the Himalayas, near Kullu Manali."

Jewel knew little of India. Her knowledge reached as far as Bollywood and an article she'd read once on the maharajahs of Northern India. The Met in New York had borrowed some of the treasures of the maharajahs, which left the country for the first time for an exhibition. She took in another deep breath. "Is it a research trip?"

He smiled and fastened his helmet. "Maybe. Will you come? I need to hire you for a week?"

Was it the need for more adventure, or more of Leal?

No. She didn't want him to leave her and nodded. "All right."

Leal's lips curved into a cocky smile.

She stroked the small scar on his chin. "A bad accident?"

"More like a bad medical experiment."

"Be careful, doctor."

"You're safe with me, Jewel."

"I want to believe you."

"Then do."

They straddled the snowmobile. Seconds later Jewel's eyes fell on the path behind them. Uncertain why she'd looked back, yet on the ground by a fir tree lay what looked like a discarded syringe. Jewel shrugged not grasping why that detail had caught her attention.

Chapter 4

Jewel inhaled the smells of the hillside, fresh, crisp and spicy with hints of ginger and curry. She strolled on the footpath. Above her, shiny *gompas*—Buddhist monasteries—gilded the side of the hill from her hotel in the small town. The morning sun seeped through the rhododendron tress, as brown monkeys – pests really – swung from tree to tree, looking for edibles to snatch.

Hotel Madras stood on the edge of a meadow sheltered by pines and spruce. It offered Jewel a panoptic view of the terrain and surrounding forest ideal for treks now that the monsoon season had ended. She'd learned much about India on the flight from Vienna to New Delhi. Kullu Manali, about five-hundred-and-fifty kilometers from the Indian capital, was a hill station nuzzled in the mountains of the Indian state of Himachal Pradesh. It stood next to the northern end of Kullu Valley surrounded by dense pine and deodar forests.

Leal joined her at the hotel's front terrace overlooking the valley. "Like it?"

"It's breathtaking, Leal. Charming."

"I take it that's a yes."

"It's so different from anywhere I've been," she said. "But it looks like it could be your second home."

"Sometimes it feels that way given the amount of research I do here."

They ambled down the stairs that led to the road in front of the hotel where a Land Cruiser waited. It had been converted to transport medicine and, if need be, patients.

"What do you do here?" she asked.

"Different things. On this trip, I'm working with infectious disease specialists in a town called Naggar among other things. It's about twenty kilometers from here. Come."

They traversed the car park to the white Cruiser, with *Trelles Pharmaceuticals* painted on its side. Leal pulled the door open for her and she settled on the black leather. He strolled round to the driver's seat, took the wheel, started the ignition and engaged the gear. The Cruiser reversed, curving out onto the hillside road lined with pinewood firs on either side.

"What's happening in Naggar?" Jewel said resting her hand on the ribbed leather of the passenger seat.

"There's been an unidentified disease outbreak in some of the rural regions around here, especially in Naggar. It's been going on for some months. In my field of vaccine and drug research, you get to hear about things like this. I was called in to find the cause and a cure, and work in the affected area."

"Tell me about the outbreak."

Leal's hands tightened on the wheel. "Several school children have died from an unknown disease and over sixty-five students have fallen sick. The local health centers here can't provide even basic Citamol tablets for the sick."

"What's Citamol?"

"You probably know it as acetaminophen. It's used for the relief of headaches and other minor aches and helps with flus and colds."

"That's tragic, Leal. Does this kind of work ever scare you?"

"I can't afford to be scared and do what I do. Eradicating the breakouts motivates me. It drives me. We're one entity, one body if you like. If one part of that body is sick, it affects all of us. It's important for me to know I can help."

Jewel couldn't help but agree. The anguish was visible in his eyes and noted in his voice. He meant every word. She fell silent, musing over Leal's various sides: one day, adventuring down mountains, and other days rescuing the world. His job reminded her of a blog she'd read that explored the concept that plumbers saved more lives than physicians, just by providing clean and accessible plumbing facilities. Perhaps prevention was better than cure. Clean water eradicated waterborne diseases and here was Leal, a doctor, trying not only to save lives but also to eliminate the causes of disease at the expense of his own safety.

Why would a man she barely knew want to involve her in work so important to him? Leal was not one to be driven by accolades. He wanted to see disease gone and to help people. Alongside him, she was a mere student who'd failed to get the National Geographic internship and was yet to qualify as a professional photographer; small achievements compared to his list of medical discoveries and insights by the sounds of it. Why would he choose her? Although the subject of money was never mentioned, it seemed he could afford more experienced professionals who'd already made their mark in the photo industry.

Jewel studied his face. Who did he work for? He'd mentioned his research, but not whether he was working with a university, a research company or operating on a grant. The volunteer brochure had given little of his background.

Leal's eyes glistened with compassion and sadness all at the same time. Medical brilliance shone behind his bright eyes; an accomplished doctor and researcher from what she'd observed, and also judging from the respect he'd commanded at the base clinic in New Delhi a day ago, where they'd flown to from Vienna.

Leal sped up along the deserted hill road allowing the Cruiser to trudge in fresh mud from last night's light snow fall. The Land Cruiser plunged further up a steep hill overlooking Manali valley.

Two days ago, they'd flown out of Salzburg to Vienna, before boarding a flight to New Delhi. Jewel's quick decision made in Salzburg to do field work had been spontaneous, maybe not rational, seeing she was mid-semester. But she needed the money for her tuition and Leal inspired her more than she cared to admit. Kaya had hardly contained herself when she'd said goodbye to Jewel at Vienna's International Airport. "It's about time. You deserve a break," she'd said.

The ride from the Indian capital on humid, public trains had been gruesome. Leal had wanted her to experience the diversity and charm of India. The multi-religion nation was the seventh-largest country by area and the second most populous country with over a billion people. It was the largest global democracy, Leal had said.

The train took more than half a day to reach Chandigarh in

Northern India on the Shatabdi Express. Jewel had welcomed the deserted cabin, unlike some she'd seen on the march to the private space. Leal encouraged her to take images of curious children with permission from inquisitive parents and spurred her on to chat to them. They reveled in the attention and the generosity of earned cash Leal and Jewel left behind for their permission. She'd snapped the inspecting faces of children traveling with their families, bemused by her friendliness and easy approach.

Most people she met were comfortable with English. Jewel spoke no Hindi but watched Leal's natural ease with traveling in the profundities of India, with minimal Hindi and some Arabic. He was out of place with his blue eyes and sandy waves, but it didn't matter. India was extraordinary on many fronts. Jewel had just tasted the best curries she'd ever sampled and immersed herself in the spice-filled character of Indian cuisine.

After a seven hour journey from Delhi, she positioned her camera out the window as the train slowed at Kullu Manali station. Jewel captured images of women and men going about their day in a hillside community bursting with color, honking sounds of traffic, surrounded by fir-topped hills.

What kind of place was this? A former British colony, gifted with nature's magnetism of imposing mountain ranges. The smoothing backdrop of the Himalayas was bordered by cool pine forests, the raging Beas River and scattered temples. Nothing like the fast life of New York and her mother's home in Inwood.

Jewel's growing archive of images imprinted memories that needed to be shared beyond the borders of the Himalayas. Like the little boy who sat meddling with a wooden toy, the woman with a nose ring weaving her multi-colored blanket and a colorful mountain community of pedestrians going about the day's business in a pace fractions slower than New York. That had all been a day ago.

The wind tossed Leal's ruffled fringe from his face as it broke through the open window. He leaned his arm resting on the door as the Cruiser found steady ground.

"This morning we'll work in a clinic in Naggar that we've set up near the school infirmary in the village."

"How long have you been a doctor, Leal?"

"Four years, but I've been researching medicine since Harvard."

"What drew you to medicine?"

"I can't watch human suffering, especially when drugs can be so readily available."

She leaned back in her seat musing over his conviction. He meant every word. If no one else would, he alone would exterminate disease where he could. He smiled at her silence and stared ahead. Several minutes later, Leal parked the car outside a newly built, three-building complex on an isolated side of a hill. The complex was hedged in by apple orchards surrounded by a rocky meadow.

"We're here," Leal said. "This used to be an independent house that we converted into a clinic two years ago for diabetes treatment in the area. We've since expanded it and now do operations and fit anything needed from hearing aids to glasses and much more. There's so much need here, so we can't afford to specialize. We need to recruit more general doctors and treat whatever need there is."

"You must spend a great deal of time here."

"I'm needed. After we treat the school children, I think there's much to be done."

"That's commendable, Leal," she said.

"Why?"

"Well, you could work for any pharmaceutical company for profit and here you are using the means in your hands to give free medical care."

"There are enough people making a profit from medicine. One less won't hurt. I went into medicine to see if we could reach a point where drugs could be as freely accessible as water. Our government's not happy with that."

"The government?"

"Yeah. Free medicine and research keeps them out of control. Disease can be easily turned into a biological weapon. Don't you agree?"

"I suppose, Leal. We take a lot of these things for granted. Don't we?"

They headed toward the clinic entrance. "Are you from New York, Leal?"

He reached for her hand. "My family has lived in the city a long time. It's where I was born. I do have some Italian ancestry through my father's side."

"Really? My father's Italian and my mother was born in

53

Hawaii. Her family migrated there in the forties."

"Where in Italy is your family from?"

She bit her lower lip. "My father is from Udine. I don't know much about him. He left my mother when I was two."

Leal's eyebrows pulled down in concentration. "And you've never forgiven him."

"That obvious?"

"A little."

"I wouldn't know who to forgive. He's always been a mystery."

"You grew up partly in Italy? When did you become a New Yorker?"

"When I was twelve we moved to New York. It's all I've ever known, although my mother made sure I never forgot my Italian roots. It's her way of making sure I embrace both sides of my family. That's why she insisted I compete on the Italian gymnastics team and train in Italy in my last year of high school."

Leal smiled. "I'd like to meet your family someday."

She fumbled for the right words. "It's just me and mom now."

They stopped outside the canary-yellow clinic. Leal pushed open the entrance and let her in before him. They advanced into the main reception where three doctors and two nurses attended to patients in one large room. Two walled-off rooms led off the reception area, where Jewel imagined they performed surgery. The interior walls were painted white and a single board hung on the far side of the reception carrying information about vaccinations, water safety and general disease prevention.

"Jewel?"

She turned to face him.

"I'd appreciate any photos you can take of the work here. This little project of ours is now recruiting for its next expedition for April. We need physicians in all specialties, but mostly general practitioners. Getting them to the Himalayas is the problem. I would like us to recruit a team of well-compensated doctors here. We'll use your pictures for a global campaign. Once we are done here, I want to show you something special. A project close to my heart, in the mountains near Keylong. We'll go at the end of the week."

"Another clinic?"

"We've got three. Plus, a patient who needs special

attention."

"Are they one of the people affected with the mysterious disease?"

"No. This is research. And don't worry the disease there and here won't put you in danger."

"I'm not, Leal. I want to help in any way I can."

A striking local man wearing a checked shirt and dark jeans glanced over to where they stood. He wore a stethoscope around his neck and his eyes lit up when he saw Jewel and Leal approach. He finished attending to a young mother with an infant and met them halfway across the room.

Leal gave him an amicable slap on the back. "Jewel, I want you meet Dr. Vikranta Patil. We just call him, Vik. He runs things around here and is an exceptional researcher."

Jewel shook Vik's hand. "Pleased to meet you, doctor."

"Call me, Vik," he said.

Jewel scanned the waiting patients, some looking healthier than others. "How many people does the clinic serve a day?"

Vik followed her curious gaze. "Last year, a team of six doctors and nurses, alongside a group of volunteer healthcare professionals from England, saw close to three-hundred patients a day. We have fewer people helping now. That's the most we can see in twenty-four hours. People travel for days to reach the free clinic. Leal here makes sure they receive the treatment they came for."

Jewel's eyes caught the face of a toddler bouncing on her mother's knee. "That's incredible. Are there many children?"

"Apart from the school children we are treating most are adults here, but we do treat children. That's where the greatest problems are. The locals won't bring children to us until they're severely sick," Vik said.

"Our hope is they come early so we can get in there fast and stop infections before they take over. It's a sure way to fight many preventable diseases before they become an epidemic," Leal said.

"I see."

"I realize this is quite different to the charity work you've been doing, Jewel, but your pictures will tell our story," added Leal.

"Photography sometimes communicates better than we can say in words," Vik added.

An ache crawled to her throat. The need she saw was

overwhelming. These doctors were doing more than most.

"I'll do my best," she said.

Leal watched her shy away from the compliment. "You'll do fine."

Leal and Vik paced back toward the clinic entrance as Jewel walked at a distance behind them. She needed to know everything there was about Leal and his research. To capture the pictures they required of her, she wanted to feel in tune with his mission.

Leal had ignited her passion for a cause greater than herself.

Inside the reception area, several patients waited to be served. Their eyes lit up when they saw Leal and the team of other volunteer doctors. Jewel snapped photographs where convenient. Patients were fitted with earplugs, given vaccinations, and advised on general disease prevention. By mid-afternoon, the lines extended outside to the meadows as the kitchen staff attended to hungry patients.

When the afternoon sun came in, Jewel pulled her hair into a bun. She soon fit in well with the local women who smiled at her attempts to make easy conversation. It had warmed up to close to fourteen degrees Celsius, unusually high for September. Jewel was glad she'd dressed in comfortable jeans, hiking boots below thin layers of a T-shirt and a light cashmere jersey.

At five in the afternoon, medical staff stopped for tea on the front porch overlooking the valley. Chai, as Jewel learned, was standard refreshment in India. Served in delicate, ornate cups and flavored with cardamom, Jewel savored the hot drink, which cooled her off despite the beverage's heat. The clinic's eccentric view over the Manali valley sank into her memory as she finished her cup. She glared as far as she could where the valley gave easy access to other rural towns, and more secluded villages on the mountainside.

Leal watched her talk with the women. The children took interest in her Nikon and laughed when she replayed digital images on her smartphone. He sent her a reassuring smile as he administered vaccines from a quiet corner in the main room.

Jewel took in a deep breath. For someone who'd lost the greatest passion in her life, giving time to others seemed to have filled the void.

Leal ambled over to her. "You've found your element here."

"The children are charming. They don't seem to be bothered by life's challenges and are more content than most children I

56

know in New York. I can't wait to visit the other clinics. Leal, you're doing amazing work here."

Leal's cellphone rang. He pulled the device from his pocket and shot her a reassuring wink to tell her he wouldn't be long. His face suddenly changed color, shrouded by a stern frown. In one sharp movement, he turned his back to her and walked away to a side office off the waiting room before continuing outside.

Jewel observed from a nearby window as he spoke, pacing the front yard. His free hand curled into a fist and then relaxed before his fingers tapped in rapid movements on his denims. A patient swung through the doors, allowing Jewel to catch part of a strained conversation.

"Well, she damn well better have a good reason," she heard Leal say.

The person on the other end of the line spoke for several seconds before Leal replied.

"It must be done today," he said.

With the little she'd picked up, Jewel knew he wasn't talking about a medical procedure.

* * *

Myranda rubbed her forehead with her moist palms. Her limousine parked out at the front entrance of Washington Towers. Scott the chauffeur swung round to open the door for her. "Afternoon."

Myranda made no response and slumped into the cushions of the leather seats as Scott held the door open for her. Soon he inclined the car toward Darien, Connecticut. The journey to her suburb home was slow. Her integrity, career, and everything she possessed depended on the results of her earlier test.

Short of an hour later, the car pulled up in front of an L-shaped plot that housed a conventional residence, with wings growing from either side of the main building. Myranda's work with the architects had helped construct a home deserving of Leal's stature. He'd never set foot on the property that boasted English influences and was located on a secluded spot on the island.

Myranda stepped inside the richly-decorated interiors of the house. Pepper the housekeeper walked into the living room.

57

Myranda sank into an Edelman leather couch and raised her feet, settling them on a little cushion at the foot of the expensive upholstery. Her eyes fell on a photograph on the mantle opposite of her and her father, Adan Vaux.

"Should I serve dinner now, Mrs. Vaux-Trelles?"

Myranda brushed the housekeeper away with the wave of a hand. "Don't bother me."

Myranda had taken the married name of Vaux-Trelles and few people called her Mrs. Trelles. The housekeeper left and Myranda shut her eyes, blocking out distraction. What harm could an early pregnancy test do? Her eyes opened and veered to the silver-framed image on the mantle. Growing up with a father in sales hadn't been easy.

They'd moved several times from state to state and Myranda harbored feelings of rootlessness and lack of attachment to anything or anyone. Her father had never held a steady job, dragging her from one town to another, drudging at jobs he hated. Eventually, the single dad settled in Pennsylvania and found a job as a senior sales manager at Ovatti Corporation, a small foods company.

At age thirteen, Myranda promised herself she'd do whatever it took to make a success of herself. She'd study hard, remain focused on her passion for successful brands and maybe, just maybe, she'd avoid slaving through life like her unambitious father. She'd claw past procrastinators at any cost. In high school, she'd manipulated a teacher into giving her a higher grade so she could graduate with the right credits necessary to get into college. Never mind she'd failed to complete the extra credentials required for a grade change.

Myranda succeeded on the first leg of her plan and slid her way into Northwestern University, graduating with an honors degree in international marketing.

Most people moved out of her path. Those compassionate and close enough soon reasoned her anxiety disorder often got the best of her, a state that left Myranda with few acquaintances and even fewer friends. After a series of internships with multinationals in New York, and a bad run-in with a male superior in an international cosmetics company, Myranda resolved to start her own consulting marketing firm. Her father, Adan, noted her determination and dissolved his savings account to fund her endeavors. After several false starts, a colleague informed Adan that Trelles Industries was looking to collaborate with a new marketing agency.

Myranda opened her eyes and hurled a fashion magazine at the photograph. Would a nap help? And Dr. Rickett's recommended rest? Five minutes later she rose and headed upstairs and changed into a charcoal silk nightshirt, before drifting into her adjacent home office.

Where was Leal? She'd not heard from him in two weeks. His damn, guarded personal assistant spoke of a trip to India when she'd called two days ago. Or was it Austria? The man could never sit still but, more pressing, would he follow through on the prenuptial, if she didn't get pregnant?

Myranda cringed at the thought of Leal learning of her IVF treatments. Maybe he'd change his mind. Leal longed for children more than an infant thirsting for milk.

She cursed and stepped back into her bedroom. It would be Leal's word against hers on the paternity of any child she bore.

* * *

Jewel stood under the lukewarm shower, her chocolate-colored hair weighed down with spurts of water mixed with fruity conditioner.

What had angered Leal?

She turned off the shower, seized a white towel from the nearby rack and knotted her dripping hair in soft threads before reaching for a larger towel. Jewel advanced into the living space of the moderate hotel suite. She glanced out at the darkening sky and turned on the radio, scanning the channels for the local news. The station announced heavy snowfall in the higher ranges of the mountains. Winters in Manali began in October and continued through February. The September weather, so far, contradicted the usual climate as the forecasted chill crawled into her limbs. She reached for a wide tooth comb from the dressing table, ran it through her thick mane and sank into a chair. What time was it in New York? Kaya was expecting a call sometime today. They'd been in the foothills of the Himalayas for three days and she'd yet to call Kaya, for a sanity check. Was Kaya still worried? She'd approved of Leal so far.

Jewel envied her best friend. Kaya had been married to Weston Wilda for two years, a human rights lawyer from Atlanta. Kaya's resumé so far read like that of a UN diplomat. Valedictorian of her graduation class, Ivy League education at Princeton where she met Weston in a Supreme Court advocacy class. Kaya graduated quicker than most and had married Weston in a glitzy Manhattan wedding. She would finish Law School, and then sit for the New York Bar exam after which Weston would hire her in his new legal practice specializing in family and corporate law, along with three other lawyers. Having started the second trimester of pregnancy, Kaya wanted to wait a year before immersing herself into the fast lane of family law.

Jewel drew in a short breath. Her career would never be as affluent as Kaya's. Photography didn't bring much money, not anymore, unless your photos stood out in the crowded market. But money, though scarce, wasn't her motivation.

Would she find a man like that? Was Leal the one? She leaned back and closed her eyes, her mind ringing warning bells. Leal was drawing closer to her guarded insecurities, something she'd sworn no man would do.

* * *

Myranda shot up perspiring. She glanced at the vintage clock on her bedside. It was 2:00 a.m.

Beads of sweat moisturized her night clothes. She reached for a cool glass of water from the bedside and placed a hand over her stomach. Mild pains burned through her abdomen. Drowsy with sleep, and drugged with pain, she lumbered to the bathroom for a painkiller. Only then did she see the blood stains on the ivory floor tiles.

The symptoms hadn't gone away.

Nephthysis.

* * *

Jewel found her laptop. She breathed in a lungful of air. Men brought trouble to Carlone women. Her mother Mahina was a prime example of failed relationships, having married twice and still never found love. A knock on the door interrupted her thought and she spotted a snug bathrobe hanging on the door. She reached for it and folded it around her body before answering the door to a hotel attendant holding a large gift box.

"Yes?"

"A delivery for you, *memsamb*," said the smiling man.

"Who's it from?"

"Dr. Trelles asked for this to be delivered to your room."

The ornamented clothing box drew her eyes. Tension left her face as she took the delivery into her hands. Conscious of the attendant's eyes still glued to her, she smiled. "Thank you."

When the attendant left, she eased the door shut and lifted the velvet cover of the box. Her eyes fell on a silk fabric and its dazzling colors intrigued her. It was a *salwar kameez*, a sparkling local attire she'd seen many women wear, and had spent ten minutes admiring at a local shop the day before. It was a traditional outfit worn in the northern states of India.

A note was attached to the two-piece silk dress and trouser purple garment bordered with a contrasting turquoise trim. She drew the dress out of the box. It's front flowed in plain purple chiffon with panels of print fabric and further sections of embroidery. Though a traditional wear of India, the garment flaunted a modern cut. Her attention turned to the note and she read it slowly.

Let me see the colors of the Himalayan jewel.

L.

She smiled to herself as petals of a Himalayan border jewel flower dropped to the floor from the envelope. It was refreshing to see Leal's hidden, yet sensitive side. Without hesitation, she slid it on after locating her under clothes, and then reached for a matching multipurpose scarf that accompanied the outfit and slung it over her narrow shoulders. A nurse at the clinic had told her she could wear a *bindi*, a forehead decoration believed to retain energy, strength and concentration. Sure enough, Leal had included one in the delivery. Jewel also found a clip-on nose ring and hesitated a few seconds before placing it on her left nostril.

Her hair was nearly dry. Still, she found her faithful travel dryer and styled her tresses bone straight, until they glossed and fell below her shoulder blades. Jewel surveyed the result in a floor-length mirror by the bathroom door. Had she not been Italian-American, she could almost take her place among South-East Asian ancestry. She smiled at her reflection in the mirror. "You'll do."

Jewel returned to the laptop on a small table by the bed and found a stable wireless network. Once booted, she scanned her e-mails.

A subject line caught her eye.

SUBJECT: *Job offer Photography Services—Vaux Marketing Inc.*

* * *

DEPARTMENT OF ECONOMIC INTELLIGENCE (DEI)
NEW YORK CITY BRANCH

The skinny man hurried into the director's office. "Sir, Dr. Trelles is in India. The bug we put on him is sending a GPS signal from the Himalayas, near Manali."

"Let's see that."

The assistant hurried with his laptop toward the director's desk. "Son of a…! That's where his former medical partner is, isn't it? We told him his research couldn't leave our borders. You sure it's him?"

"Yes, sir. You told me to keep an eye on this bug. You know, my first real case before I make agent."

The director squinted at the ambitious face and moved away from the desk toward the window. He placed his hands behind his back and clasped them together. "Tell agent Jones to activate Operation N.

Chapter 5

Jewel scanned her memory. She'd not heard of Vaux Marketing and hadn't applied for part-time work. Her fingers tapped on the edge of the laptop and she decided to study the details later. Soon her laptop connected onto the wireless network service and she video-dialed Kaya in New York. After a few attempts with the webcam, the signal stabilized.

Kaya's face drew into view. "Jewel, how's India?"

"Different from any place I know. How was your trip back to New York?"

"You abandoned me for a man—"

"Hey—"

"No offense taken."

"You and the baby okay?"

"Still nauseous. It's just past the first trimester, but no one warns you about the morning sickness. It should be called twenty-four hour sickness. It lasts all day."

Jewel couldn't imagine what pregnancy felt like. A mystery that failed description. Maybe it was a different experience for each person. She rested her back against the small wooden seat. "Shouldn't that be wearing off right about now?"

Her pregnant friend attempted to breathe easy, moved the laptop to a comfortable bone-colored couch and slumped down. "You'd think."

"Still working on that prenuptial case?"

"Yes, we're almost done. Just missing a sizable piece of research. I need to make a few calls."

"How's Weston?"

"Walking on ice around me," she sighed. "The most considerate man ever."

Kaya gave her a long shrewd glance. "I've never seen you glow so much as when Leal's around."

"Just here to take photos for his office, add them to my portfolio, and... I'm learning a lot."

"All to do with human biology and anatomy, I imagine."

"Maybe."

Kaya threw her head back laughing. "I like him. And don't worry. I'll do an extensive search on him just to calm your nerves. You finally have someone to take care of you."

"I don't need anyone to take care of me. I'm focusing on finishing photo school, getting a job and some stability."

"What makes you think you can't do that and still have Leal."

"Have? He's not a prize."

Kaya's eyes narrowed. "I like him for you, Jewel. He's hard-nosed and smart."

Jewel grimaced. "Almost perfect—"

"Is that cynicism in your voice?"

"Maybe. The perfect man only exists for people like you. Not for me."

"Jewel, don't. Every man has to earn his way with you. Not every man is your father." She breathed in a solemn half-whisper eager to shift the conversation from Jewel's father, a topic that left fog in the air each time they addressed it.

Kaya drew in a sharp breath. "Anyway, you're really working that outfit, are you going out tonight?"

Jewel glanced down at her *salwar kameez*. "Do you like it? Leal got it for me."

"And you want to shy away from him, why? How many people go through all that trouble? Don't be afraid to let good things happen to you."

"They don't."

Jewel's voice rang with disappointment and bitterness. Everything she'd ever wanted had disappeared from her life, gymnastics and a father she couldn't remember. And now her only hope of a meaningful life was securing a career in photography.

Leal's phone conversation that she'd overheard came to mind as Kaya scrutinized Jewel's face. "Take it a step at a time."

"Something's wrong, Kaya"

"What?"

"I mean with Leal. He got this phone call today and... Anyway, just forget it."

"Seriously, Jewel, don't be so guarded. You're not your mother. Be happy."

"How'll I know if I can trust him... you know, like you and Weston?"

"You can't know. You just take chances. To experience love, you must first give it away. Leal's a genuinely sensitive man."

"Those are your hormones speaking again."

Dignified as a royal, Kaya covered a faint cough with her hand. "And rightly so. Listen, Weston will be here any minute; he wants to cook me dinner. It'll help with my mood swings."

"I don't think anything can help with that. All right, I'll speak with you in a couple of days. Tomorrow is our last day before we fly to New York."

"I'll see you when you get back." She hesitated. "Jewel, be happy."

Jewel nodded before switching off the tablet. She peered out the window at the pitch-blackness of night. Unlike New York, the town at the bottom of the hill was quiet. She finished dressing and dabbed on a mild fine fragrance of orange blossom and water lily. She lined her eyes with dark kohl eyeliner, which accentuated her amber eyes and brushed her lips with a faint cherry lip balm. Within minutes, she was downstairs and scanned the lobby for Leal.

"Miss Carlone."

She turned her head only to lock eyes with the kind face of the hotel manager. "Yes?"

He bowed his head slightly and presented her with an envelope on a bed of a rare Himalayan bamboo orchid petals.

She glanced down at a note addressed to her.

"Dr. Trelles has sent me with a message. He wants you to meet him in the hotel cliff garden, our private outdoor restaurant. I'll show you the way."

Jewel studied the note. "What's this note then?"

"That arrived a couple of hours ago when you were out."

"Thank you."

The mild fragrance of the petals floated into her nostrils. She ripped open the envelope as the manager left.

Her eyes widened at the bold words.

MONTPELLIER WAS JUST THE BEGINNING...

* * *

SCARSDALE
NEW YORK

"Yes, it will be done on time."

The man's raw voice sent Kaya's pulse pounding. How dare the idiot think that pregnancy could stop a woman from anything? Didn't her damn case partner know she could sue him? Could it be hormones? Or desire to stand in equal waters with her male counterparts?

Austria's fresh mountain air had been welcome, something she readily admitted she lacked in New Jersey where she spent the work week. It had only set her back a couple of days on research for her supervising attorney and Professor Vayle Torres, also a former U.S. Attorney for the Northern District of New York. Kaya had been ecstatic to be selected as his research assistant. She bit her lip, anticipating the huge amount of research a prenuptial of this kind would entail. Vayle would be livid if she missed her deadline.

He'd passed the New York Bar in the eighties and practiced civil litigation with an exclusive focus on family law for the past decade. The family case Kaya had been handpicked at Princeton to participate in involved a prenuptial agreement between two well-known parties with a headlining divorce looming. Vayle was arguing for his client, a steel billionaire, against Paulina Steigers, a social climber. The agreement was anything but bashful in language and demands. In the event of a divorce, Paulina would receive an astronomical amount the appellate court had to find atrocious in relation to the rest of the estate. At least that's what needed to happen, or she'd be fired and Vayle's assistant job would move to the next candidate.

Kaya hung up the phone and placed a hand on her protruding belly. She rose from her desk and approached the window, a deep, asymmetrical light penetrating the upper level of her Scarsdale house. Vayle needed a lot more than she'd found on similar prenuptial cases in New York. She needed to research a case similar in compensation status. In essence, nothing short of a billionaire's prenuptial.

She glossed over *Society & Conscious*, a classy celebrity magazine that had arrived for her that morning. Kaya decided she needed to familiarize herself with as many similar celebrity cases as she could before presenting her research to Vayle in a few hours. Although not a fan of celebrity gossip, her career depended on the lavishness. Where better to learn from than the gossip news?

She flipped through a few pages before her eyes landed on a local story. As an aspiring family lawyer, the society pages would have much interest. The cases for divorces, split-ups and prenuptial agreements could fill volumes at her local library. Unfamiliar with the family in question and conscious of her time constraints, she scanned the article.

> *Myranda Vaux is no typical society madam. But we'll give her A for effort. Hitching up with a billionaire was never going to be an easy feat and she sits deep in wells of prenuptial disharmony waters.*
>
> *As Vaux faces a momentous decision ahead of her, we all know that prenuptial agreements tend to be a private affair, at least, their contents. But in this networked world where your secret is tomorrow's headline,* Society & Conscious *have unearthed jaw-dropping details within the Vaux-Trelles prenuptial.*

Kaya stopped reading. *Trelles?*
She took a deep breath and read on:

> *Sometimes known as "ante-nuptial" or "premarital agreements", these exclusive arrangements between parties thinking about marriage alter or confirm the legal rights and obligations that would otherwise arise under the laws governing marital bliss. For you and me, it's entertainment, for our more endowed counterparts it's a serious cash flow matter.*
>
> *And yes, that means, dear readers that it's no*

longer divorce or death that concedes an end to the relationship, but a lovely annotated signed paper, legal or not, we're not here to judge. Forgive the pun.

In the Vaux case, the marriage and the prenuptial took place in the state of New York, or so we think. New York, a state more liberal with its prenuptials than others. There was no comment from the groom's party.

Today the debate at hand is will Myranda Vaux fulfill the one requirement that was stipulated in her prenuptial. May a bride welcome a simple groom's request? No?

Is it a moral thing or duty to ask a wife to hurry and deliver the goods, an heir set against the ticking clock of five years? Surely five years is reasonable to produce an heir for any empire… such as Trelles?

Kaya bit her lip. How would anyone think to put such a thing in a prenuptial? How had the media gotten a hold of the details? This marriage was clearly a business arrangement. It was hard to digest the information and love was the last thing on any of these arrangements. Misleading statistics had disciplined a generation to doubt the altar, and hence the saving grace of a prenuptial.

The thought boosted her resolve to become a family lawyer. If she had her way, perhaps she could.

She glanced again at the article. Somewhere a shadow crawled to the page. She slammed a break on her thoughts, disrupted again by the last sentence she'd read. Her eyes caught sight of a name she'd come to know. With every part of her screaming, the magazine shot to the floor. She knew that name.

Leal Trelles.

* * *

Heaviness set in Jewel's gut as she re-read the note. The four-year nightmare awakened in her. With Kaya's encouragement still ringing fresh in her head, she held her breath. Her skin tingled with stings of needles as she re-lived the events of the intensive care unit in Montpellier. Someone knew she was here. Months of shock therapy dwindled as she re-read 'Montpellier'.

How?

When?

She had to park her thoughts and considered her options. Would Leal be able to help her? Kaya? Weston? No, she wouldn't tell anyone. Not until she could make sense of the note.

She pulled a thick wool shawl over her shoulders and stepped out on to a grand veranda that left the hotel by a line of stepping stones. It continued into the gardens full of color, an idyllic oasis above the quietening hillside. She followed the trail as had been directed by the concierge until she could no longer see the hotel. The gardens ended along a cliff side overlooking an abysmal valley, where a pale sky of nightfall had set in. Above her, the stars peered in and out of the half-overcast sky.

She inhaled the fresh air, reminding her of how much she adored the smell of pine, and cedar. Jewel glanced to one side of the clearing where a thick traditional garden canvas-tent, as those favored by Indian princesses, stood. Bathed in torch light stemming from two upright lanterns that stood on either side of the entrance, a small table was set around floor lounge mats. Persian rugs and cushions surrounded by subtle garden lighting adorned the inviting warmth of the tent. Handcrafted by skilled artisans, the arched doors opened to an inviting setting, complete with weatherproof heaters, positioned within the interior.

Jewel made her way into the tent and inspected the carved low-seating of the intimate setting, around the teak carved table. Hot chai, served in a traditional gold canister sat on a bamboo tray as aromatic incense fragrance drifted from a jasmine-scented bowl in the middle of the table. Jewel stepped outside the tent and paced a few feet. She drew in the view beyond the valley before taking a seat on one of the rock stumps and gazed at the sparkling villages below.

She breathed in the night air. Her rehearsed speech clogged

in her throat. Who'd sent that note?

A shiver ran through her as she heard the tread of approaching footsteps.

"Jewel?"

She turned to face the level voice. Leal donned a cream jacquard stone, embroidered attire, a *kurta* with a maroon art silk *dhoti*. It was a pant and top design that manifested the richness of Indian tradition, coupled with contemporary style. What she'd imagined came as a traditional relaxed wear for men in the rural parts of India, fell on the boarders of his broad build like a *maharajah*, a king claiming his army.

A thrill shivered through her senses, as she rose with a glance of appreciation. "Is this why you insisted I wear this outfit tonight?"

Leal watched her in the dazzling attire. "You needed a local souvenir, so I thought I'd join you," he said and drew close. "You're beautiful."

The words were sincere.

"Thank you."

He wrapped her shawl around her with an affectionate glint hitting his eyes. "Wasn't sure you'd want to be on a mountain again with me after losing the race in Salzburg," he said.

She jerked under his touch. "Mountains and I have a good connection."

Jewel took in his warmth against her. His hand floated to her hair and tunneled through its length. The whiff of night rhododendrons in the nearby brushes, coupled with her senses spinning with the intoxicating musk scent of his body, made her close her eyes. Leal's strong hand settled on her shoulders, loosening them. A head shorter than him, she turned her head into his chest and relaxed her muscles.

"Jewel?"

She retreated and exhaled, her hands trembling. "I—"

"Sh... you don't need to say anything. Let's just take this in and make sense of it later."

"Leal, I hardly know you and want to somehow—"

"There's so much I want to tell you."

"What do you need to tell me? "

"Once we visit my patient in Keylong at the end of the week, I have something important to tell you about me, my work and everything I care about. I need to protect you."

70

The delivered note came to her mind. "From what?"

His eyes narrowed and fell on her face as if he'd not heard her. She gazed up into his eyes as he tugged at his left ear, a habit, she'd noticed when he was concentrating.

"Do I stand a chance with you? Jewel, I want to be with you. But it has to be done right... It's the only way I can protect you."

"From what... Does this have to do with Montpellier?"

"That and more—"

"What's going on Leal?"

"I will tell you, Jewel, but tonight let's just…"

"Take our time—"

"We don't have time, Jewel. I'm trying to say I'm falling in love with you. You hardly know me, but... once we visit a patient up in the mountains, we could talk on the way down." He kissed her forehead. "Let's talk about it then."

The seriousness in his voice scared her. Was she really in danger? Was this connected to her attack in Montpellier?

"All right," she said. "I'll wait till then. Before I forget. There's something I want to give you."

She took a deep breath. "You said something once and it meant a lot. Your words kept me going these last four years. I want you to have this." She pulled out a Polaroid photograph from her shawl. "It was taken when I toured with the Italian gymnastics team. If you hold onto it, you'll hold me accountable. Who knows? Maybe I'll do gymnastics again."

Leal's face broke into a proud smile as he took the picture in his hands. "I'll hold this always, until I see you in your element again. Jewel, do you know how good you are?" He shifted closer. "You cold?"

Jewel shook her head, her lips trembling. "No."

He took her hand, kissed it and touched her trembling lips with one finger.

Jewel drew in his scent. She'd lied to herself. The truth was she'd never been more frightened in her life and it wasn't the note that scared her. She was afraid to love Leal.

* * *

"Careful how you handle those," warned Vik as he walked into the little cluttered office.

He spoke with a slight Indian twang, yet his English was of a brilliant, British upper-middle class caliber. His short, modishly cut hair was dark and glossed like a raven's coat. Thick, bushy eyebrows curved above his wide almost childlike eyes that glistened when he smiled, giving him a rather expressive face. He sported an elegantly shaved goatee that added years to him, though he wasn't a day older than thirty.

Jewel had been curious all morning about the glass cabinets in the storeroom behind the patients' waiting room. She picked up two small bottles and cradled the delicate test tubes of substances foreign to her in her hands. Vik smiled and held out his hand for the bottles, his profile expressing authority and intellect.

"What are these?" Jewel said.

"Vaccine samples."

She examined the label-less bottles. "Against what?"

"To be honest, I'm not sure. Leal brought those with him on this trip. He moonlights by trying to find new vaccines." Vik smiled as he replaced the bottles. "*And* other remedies against disease and infection. He quite enjoys it."

"Where does he do his research?"

"Everywhere I suppose. You should ask him."

"I did, but didn't get much out of him."

An inexplicable look of withdrawal crept over Vik's face. "That's Leal. Sometimes he spends hours in the mountains here thinking, contriving or even examining plants, and life in general. This gives him ideas for his formulas and then we test them out in this little office."

Jewel's eyes scanned the cluttered laboratory that made do as an office fascinated by the rows of chemicals and plant samples. A crowded bench lab held several files, research instruments and to the back of the far wall, she saw a half-open door. "What's in there?"

"It's a temperature-controlled cold room."

"Does Leal share all of his research with you, or does he work alone?"

"I've known Leal since med school. He entered Harvard at seventeen and we met in our last year there. One of those medical prodigies. Let's see, if he is twenty-seven now... I must've met him about six years ago."

"That's a long time, Vik."

A flick of mocking amusement showed on Vik's face. "By the

way, I've never seen him happier. Must be something to do with you."

A momentary look of discomfort crossed her face. "How do you mean?"

"I think you know."

Jewel blushed. "I'm just helping Leal on a few projects. We'll be back in New York in a couple of days and return to our lives."

"Leal does most of his developmental work in New York."

"You mean at the pharmaceutical company."

"Yes and no."

What did that mean?

Drops of moisture clung to Vik's forehead as he busied himself with files on the little desk. Jewel paced the room, her brows creasing with inquisitiveness and spotted more medical samples. "Have all these vaccines been tried or tested? I mean are they major breakthroughs, or extremely valuable?"

"Even if they were, Leal's the last man on earth who'd market them for profit."

"Even with his company?"

Vik stopped what he was doing. "Jewel, how much do you know about his company?"

"Nothing at all actually. The brochure in Austria said very little, something about him running research, and I haven't asked him much about it."

"Do you read *Science Magazine*, or any other scientific journal on medicine?"

"No. I subscribe to literature on photography or sports. What does his company do then? Trelles Industries?"

Vik passed a hand over his forehead. "Too much, sometimes I don't get it myself. Mostly scientific technological research and drug development. In college, Leal wanted to find answers. He's a naturally inquisitive guy as if the quest is more intriguing than the end goal. It fuels him. I wouldn't be surprised if he's actually come onto something big that's sitting in that brain of his."

"I see."

"I doubt Leal has ever wanted to run a large, successful organization."

"Large?"

Jewel reclined in a chair near the desk and heard the tread of approaching footsteps.

"Vik's painting a dark picture of me, I see."

She followed the direction of the voice. Leal stood in the little doorway. His robust shoulders filled the waist length coat he wore, over a pair of snug jeans, and a dark woolen sweater. Her eyes fell on his mountain boots, slightly wet from a possible woodland hike that morning.

Jewel unwound her legs and rose, cutting his stare as she slid over toward him. "Vik's told me all your secrets, doctor."

Leal stretched his toned arms above his head and shot Vik a weak smile. "Vik has a few of his own, but we won't get into that." He drew a step near her. "Are you ready to visit some of my patients? I'm taking more samples today?"

Jewel nodded. "Where are we going?"

Leal slid his hands in his pockets and leaned his sturdy frame against the door. "Up to a place called Tandi, not too far."

"When do we hit Keylong?"

"Soon."

Ten minutes later, they hopped into the Cruiser. Leal navigated a tight bend and eased the sturdy vehicle onto the hill road. The car shuddered to a halt on the roadside along a grocery stall where Leal purchased mangoes, lychees, flat bread, and cereal. He set the groceries on the back seat. "For my patients."

He climbed back into the driver's seat and started the engine. "I want to show you something few people know about. Something you can help me with."

Jewel fell silent, learning that it was best not to ask Leal questions, but let him ease out with his conversation. She melted into stillness as they drove for over an hour past the livid green valley bathed in a golden beam in the morning sunlight. The September sun broke between the clouds bringing in a temperate wind. The monsoons had ended not too long ago. She stripped off her cashmere sweater and the feathery wool sparked as she set it beside her.

Leal glanced at her. "Warm?"

"The climate here is quite confusing." Her voice edged as she spoke. "You know more about alpine climates than I do."

He reached for her hand. "You learn as you go. It's not so difficult. If you've got an interest in something, just go after it and slowly the answers to the questions you have fall into place. I like to see medicine that way."

Leal believed what he said. He glanced at her before returning his focus on the windy cliff ahead. An arrested expression crossed his face before he fell deathly silent. Despite his closed expression, she knew he'd drifted off, focusing.

"Something wrong?" she said.

The road ahead cornered at a sharp cliff.

Leal slammed the brakes. Her body jolted forward, only to be hauled back by the powerful force of the seatbelt that constrained her in place.

Leal gripped the wheel as the Cruiser ground the gravel. He screeched the monstrous car forward for several seconds before it came to a quaking halt inches from the cliff's rugged edge. The driver's door burst open and Leal fell out of the car onto the road. He rose unharmed and crouched beneath the Toyota. He examined the engine underneath, swerved round to the front and threw the front hood open.

Jewel slowly unfastened her seatbelt and leaned forward. Like Leal, she was unharmed. She swung the door open on the passenger side and only then did she realize that the front wheel of the Land Cruiser hung over the lethal cliff.

The blood drained from her face and her voice trailed with short breaths. "Leal."

It was a whisper at best, but enough to capture his attention.

His eyes caught hers through the windshield and a shadow of alarm passed over his face as he mouthed the words: "Don't move."

* * *

How did you get an interview with Myranda Vaux?" Kaya asked the *Society & Conscious* journalist the receptionist had pointed her to, as she entered the cramped room.

"Interview? Myranda Vaux doesn't do interviews," the journalist said.

"Really?"

"She's as evasive as they come. I had to use my own resources," came the reply from a distinctive voice.

Kaya shot an intense look at the man's granite face. She'd made her way to a bright office with rows of cubicles at the headquarters of *Society & Conscious* downtown in Manhattan. The man in front of her was the columnist for the article she'd read. A freelance journalist, she was told, who went by the pen name of Rowell Saunders. With what charm had he managed to coerce information from any modern female? For clearly he had none.

That was his source. A woman close to Myranda, he'd said on the phone. At first Saunders had refused to entertain her request for a meeting. Clearly one who guarded his sources until she'd surrendered she had information on Myranda.

"Miss?"

"Wilda." Kaya narrowed an eye. "Mrs. Wilda."

"Mrs. Wilda, why are you so interested in Myranda Vaux?"

How could Kaya persuade the stern-faced man with a plump build who, if he had any appeal, he didn't necessarily use it consciously? "I'm trying to help a friend, who may be in trouble," Kaya said.

Would it matter to him? Kaya took a deep an unsteady breath. "My friend, a former Olympic gymnast, Jewel Carlone, may be in trouble."

"Did you say Jewel Carlone? You know Miss Carlone?"

"Yes. Do you?"

"Let's just say I watch all sports including the Olympics." His face eased up. "Mrs. Wilda. I know nothing about you, but I sense you want to help a friend and I, on the other hand, want something too."

"What's that?"

"Let's just say anything to do with Myranda Vaux and Trelles Pharmaceuticals interests me." He cleared his throat. "I know one of Myranda's former housekeepers."

Kaya raised an eyebrow. What had made him change his mind? He eased into his seat in the bustling open office. "We had drinks the other night and, after a few tequilas, it all came pouring out."

Kaya took a seat on the edge of his desk. "How could the housekeeper know about the pre-nup?"

He leaned in. "That's her business, but what interested me was she'd kept a copy secured for months."

"For what?"

"Security. Myranda owes her money and dismissed her without compensation. She can't claim any criminal behavior against Myranda."

"Why not? In this country, you can sue someone for not paying you what is owed. In fact, it's called stealing."

Saunders squared his shoulders. "Poor miss maid has no green card. So, you see, she obtained another form of security."

"Do you think Myranda knows?"

He shrugged. "That's her business."

"So what did the maid want? Money?"

"Her legal fees paid for the assistance in obtaining a green card."

"What if Myranda comes after the magazine?" said Kaya.

"We've got a copy of the prenup here. It's now become our security."

Kaya wasn't sure what the legal implications were; she would investigate later. She thought for a moment, her mind torn between helping her friend and furthering her career.

Something grew coldly determined inside of her. "Could I get a copy of that prenup if I made it worth your while?"

* * *

Leal moved to the side of the van and opened his door with caution.

Jewel's face was ashen, her shoulders tight. She dared not glance at him or at the drop below, her eyes shut tight.

He lowered his voice to a whisper. "Jewel, look at me."

An involuntary tear crept from her left eye. She shook her head.

Leal slid his hand across the seat until it found hers. Moist and limp, he gripped it." "Look at me, Jewel. I'm here. Give me your other hand."

His hand reached for her forearm.

She shook her head in short jerks. "I can't."

"Jewel." Leal's voice grew firm. "Yes, you can."

Her expression remained a mask of stone.

"Lean toward me and give me your other hand."

Her shoulders tightened and her eyes blinked but Jewel remained immobile. The car jolted, losing balance and splintered a shower of rocks down the steep cliff. In one abrupt movement, Leal hauled her entire weight and heaved her back with him. The jerk threw them both onto the road. Leal had seconds to witness his Cruiser slide and plummet over the edge. He heard it roll for several seconds, crashing against the stone of the cliff, before it ground to a halt.

Then silence.

He checked her pupils. "Jewel?"

All animation had left her face. She rolled her eyes slowly and made contact with his. She took all of three seconds to realize the ordeal she'd just escaped. Her hands gripped his neck, and clawed nails stemming from intense shock, dug into his back. Her grip was sharp, yet he held her until her breathing subsided. For several moments he held her close, a mounting desire to protect her creeping into his gut. Her rapid breathing subsided and her throbbing pulse stabilized.

She pulled her body from his, her words stammering. "What happened, Leal?"

"Sh…"

She shook her head. "I couldn't do it." Jewel took a deep breath swallowing gallons of air as she spoke.

"Sh… It's okay. You're all right," Leal said. He leaned forward and held her on the roadside for several minutes longer, neither one saying anything and the rapid pacing of her heart beat against his chest.

"I can't believe, I almost…" she began.

Leal wiped a rebellious tear. "You didn't. Try not to think about it."

A sky-blue Mazda curved onto the road and decelerated to a rolling stop. "Are you okay?" a man from the driver's seat hollered.

Leal rose bringing Jewel up with him. "Yes, thank you."

"You sure? Can we help?"

Leal sensed a cramp in his thigh he hadn't noticed earlier. "We're okay… thanks. Do you have a phone?"

The man stepped out of the car and drew out a cellphone. "Here."

Leal scrutinized the deserted hillside and took the phone. "Thanks. Won't be a second." His eyebrows drew together as he dialed a number.

"What is it?" Jewel said.

Leal leaned into the phone before turning her way. "The Cruiser has been tampered with. I noticed sounds from the car's axles while the brakes were not in use."

Jewel studied his face. "Tampered with? Who?"

Leal cursed under his breath. His stomach filled with nausea, and he willed his every muscle to relax. "Someone got a hold of a good wrench and mutilated the car's engine."

Jewel's eyes clotted with horror. "Why would anyone tamper with a medical van?"

"I don't want to frighten you. It's probably nothing."

"That's not what your eyes say."

Chapter 6

Leal's jaw clenched as he observed the fear in Jewel's eyes. He headed toward the road's edge, unable to relax. The temperature under his skin rose as a state of numb dread gripped him. His mountain boots trudged the ground of the unpaved road as he waited for Vik to pick up. When his feet reached the cliff edge, he stood a few minutes glaring at the snowcapped mountains in the distance. Had his tumultuous, free spirit let him down this time?

He'd always considered himself fearless. That was before he'd known Jewel, someone he had to protect at all costs, even with that damn syringe nagging him to take a sample of her blood. If he'd delivered it by now, then maybe they wouldn't have come after him. Why would the DEI use scare tactics? Or perhaps it wasn't them? Who was it then? It didn't make sense. With him out of the way, they had nothing.

Not too long ago, he'd have gladly sat helmetless, jammed behind two or three moped passengers and woven through the impatient traffic of New Delhi, or raced at daring speeds along potholed roads on flat-boarded pickup trucks down questionable Himalayan roads. Meeting Jewel had launched his sensible nature, something that no other person had ever done.

He drew in the mountain air as the phone dialed. No pick up. "Come on, Vik."

He threaded his way back to Jewel, overcome by a sense of helplessness. "Jewel, I'm sorry."

She searched his face. "It wasn't your fault, Leal."

"I was the one who asked you to come here."

He hitched himself next to where she sat on a kilometer marker. "It happens around here. I'm sure some desperate mechanic wanted spare parts for their car."

It couldn't be further from the truth.

Jewel's head bent toward him, fitting into the hollow between his shoulder and neck. The silky weight of her hair slid over his shoulders as he tried Vik's number again and then the clinic. He dialed three times before he got through.

"Vik?"

"Leal?"

"We have car trouble."

"Where are you?"

Jewel kept her head on his shoulder as Leal cradled the phone against his left ear. "Thirty kilometers out."

"Give me half an hour," Vik said. "You sure you're okay?"

"Yeah. The car's gone though."

"What? What happened?"

"Don't ask."

Within forty minutes Vik pulled up onto the narrow road in a Jeep accompanied by a second man, a janitor from the clinic. Vik burst out of the truck, his face ashen as he pulled off his sun shades. "You guys okay?"

Vik's eyes fell on the skid marks that ran over the side of the cliff and proceeded toward the edge, his usual grin washed away. He stepped to the cliff's edge and whistled.

Vik turned to Leal. "What in God's name…?" A worried look fell on his face. "What do you want to do? Should I report it to the police?"

Leal shot up, his hand dropping out of Jewel's. "No need to involve the police."

A flicker of surprise arrested Vik's face. "But—"

Adrenaline rushed through Leal's veins as he shot up and stomped toward the edge. He stifled a curse and in one abandoned moment, rammed a foot into the kilometer marker. The weight behind his kick sent the heavy stone several hundred meters over the cliff and into what was left of his Cruiser. It rolled several times, smashed against a rock and fired up in flames mangling and charring as it catapulted to the pits of the deserted valley.

Jewel rose wide-eyed, paced to him and placed a calm hand on his shoulder. "Leal, you're scaring me."

His hand found hers and patted it. "No baby, but someone better be."

Jewel slowly walked to the car.

Vik's voice was level as he inched toward Leal watching the

smoke from the flames. "You need to settle this, Leal. You know who it is."

Leal glanced at Jewel, who'd settled in Vik's Jeep.

Vik drew into Leal's line of sight. "You think it's her? She's out for you."

"She wants me out of the way," Leal whispered.

"Does she have it in her? This can't be just about your money?" Vik said.

"She wants something no amount of money can buy."

* * *

Jewel stretched to pick up the ringing phone back in her hotel room. "Miss Carlone?"

"Yes?"

"We've never met. My name is Myranda Vaux. I'm a marketing executive from New York. I understand you're a student at the New York Institution of Photography. You live in New York, right?"

"I'm sorry, who's this?"

The call to her hotel room came only minutes shortly after they'd returned to Manali. She'd been distracted the entire route back as the tow truck pounded the rocky road, winding round traffic toward civilization and a hot meal. They'd made it to the hotel shortly before dark.

Thoughts of running home to New York haunted her. She was torn with a deep desire to understand Leal. If he'd let her. Someone intended to harm her, she understood that. But why? Now with the accident.

The receiver slipped slightly in her hand. Perspiration filled her palms. "Yes. Ms. Vaux. How did you get this number?"

"That's not important." She sensed a grin at the other end of the phone. "I've heard great things about you."

"From?"

"Didn't you get my e-mail?"

Jewel was annoyingly aware that the woman on the line had not answered her question. "Yes, but—"

"Good. Don't bother with how I found you. I've an eye for New York talent. Marketing people always know the best photographers. I've a proposal for you. I need a photographer to take some pictures of my house. I'll pay you twenty-thousand dollars."

Jewel reached and turned on the light in the darkening room. "That's a lot of money for straightforward real estate pictures," she said with slight doubt in her voice.

"There's nothing straightforward about what I commission," said the woman.

It was a demoralizing snap that Jewel chose to ignore, tempted by the chance to pay off the debt on her tuition."

"I think you're worth it," Myranda added.

Though Myranda's voice was as smooth as velvet, it was void of emotion.

"I'm not in the country right now. Could I contact you when I'm back in the States?"

"Miss Carlone, I'm on a plane right now for India. That's where you are, isn't it?"

How did the Vaux woman know all this? What sort of person can't wait for a plane to land before she calls? An influential one who doesn't take no for an answer.

Damn it! She could not think straight with the events of that afternoon still haunting her existence. This woman knew more about her itinerary than Jewel was comfortable with.

"I've some business in New Delhi," Myranda said. "I'll be at the Santi Palace Hotel. Do you think you could come down and meet me tomorrow?"

"I'm ten hours' drive away from Delhi, Miss Vaux?"

"I'm sending a chartered fight to Kullu Manali Airport. You will be met for a transfer down to Delhi and back. It will only take a few hours."

"But..."

"No buts. I won't take much of your time and you'll be back in Manali the same day. Don't miss this chance."

Jewel's mind raced. She wouldn't go to Keylong till the last day of their trip. A full forty-eight hours away. Leal had indicated he would be tied up most of the afternoon the next day. It would only be a half day. In and out of Delhi in a day.

Her voice trailed. "I'm making no commitment until I hear the full spec of the job."

"My pilot will wait for you at the south terminal tomorrow at 7 a.m. Don't be late."

"Okay, I'll give—"

She heard a click. The line went dead. Jewel set down the receiver and stared at it blankly. "Give you my cellphone number."

She drew in a sharp breath; Myranda Vaux had it already.

Chapter 7

Myranda strode into the *maharani* suite, the queen's suite of the Santi Palace Hotel.

Dirty shades. *Atrocious.*

Unreliable staff. *Unforgivable.*

It was no Waldorf Astoria. She bit her lower lip as she inspected the silk-padded queen bed, the glass-tiled bathroom visible from the main room and the Indian-style decor. A swooning fan jutted from the generous ceiling as her eyes fell on the delicate frescoes and artistic Victorian furniture. The milieu swept one back into the days and glory of the lavish Rajput clan.

She let out a sigh trying not to think of her recent miscarriage. Could she call it that? She'd not alerted Dr. Rickett. Why bother? She wanted her money back for his below-standard work.

Despite the extended efforts, the suite fell below her standards. She slumped into an upholstered sofa, and muttered to herself. Was this all Pascal, her assistant could find at the last minute. Didn't he know her requirements by now?

Pascal had been exceptional in locating Leal's whereabouts when none of the others had. He was a former private investigator's assistant who'd been unable to land a job when Myranda's employment agency rang her with his number and credentials. It had been a quick decision, but one she was glad she'd made. She needed someone with a sharp mind, deep wits and not afraid to dig for hidden information, legal or not.

It was eight months since she'd seen Leal, and a lengthy investigation by Pascal had cost her seven grand. Leal was in India... with a woman she'd never heard of. An Olympian, Pascal said, a very beautiful one. Leal could have his pick of women, but showed interest in none. Not until this long-legged, athletic brunette.

Myranda stared at a photo taken at the recent summer Olympics Pascal sent to her phone. The Carlone girl was beautiful. Attractive with assets in all the right places. Myranda was used to Leal's disappearances and usually took off for months on so-called research trips. His assistants guarded his whereabouts fiercely until, Pascal, a provocative rogue himself, dated one of them. Yet another of Pascal's discoveries.

The name Jewel Carlone came from Leal's drunken assistant after Pascal spent several hours with her. She told Pascal she'd booked a trip to Austria and then to New Delhi for Leal and Carlone. There was more to investigate on Leal, and Pascal had made good progress, but what was Leal working on?

The room would do. She was here for a day and took a deep breath before checking her cellphone. Carlone would be here any minute.

A rattling knock on her door interrupted her inspection of the rest of the room and she advanced toward it. "What're you doing here?"

"Is that any way to welcome a guest to your quarters," said the elegant man standing in the hallway.

Two adjectives formed in Myranda's mind: seedy, posh. A contradiction, but the only words she'd ever been able to use to describe the hooded-eyed man with straight hair the color of midnight sky. A lover, most of the times; adviser, whatever time was left.

Myranda stepped aside as Devon Chesser made his way into the suite. "Dressed down, Devon. Must be a social call. What are you doing here? This isn't your kind of town?"

"Even I have my off days."

His expensive English accent was melodic and full of expression, an elegance that gave Myranda the feeling she belonged in higher ranks of society, nothing like her rural upbringing. Myranda took in his tone and wished she could eradicate the lustful smirk on his face as his azure eyes peered into her, just the right shade of purplish blue, reminiscent of a sky before dusk. The casual shirt above sleek slacks fell neatly on his tall build. Not a suit he typically wore, yet the salmon tailored shirt complimented his jet-black hair, styled with caution, no hair out of place.

Devon was a scientist, smarter than most and once Leal's best friend at Johns Hopkins. He always made her think of a waiting vulture ready to pounce on unsuspecting prey. His flattering good looks complimented his tall and thin build, she hadn't been able to resist for years. They'd dated several months and Myranda had broken it off before her marriage to Leal. As her on-off boyfriend for years, he knew too much for her comfort.

Born in London and a Johns Hopkins medical graduate like Leal, Devon owned a quiet strength and though she hated to admit it, charisma. Despite the mutual attraction they had, Myranda doubted he was one ever to commit to anything they would have together. He'd proved that when he married a wealthy French girl nine months before her wedding to Leal. Devon needed status. Money he could get and Myranda was an unassuming girl from Benton, Pennsylvania, unknown to half the civilized world. Though Devon had always been attractive to her, he was never one to be called handsome. Robust, yes. Suave? Maybe. But not a man most would call good-looking.

She'd battled her way to the elite circles of New York and would never forget the best thing he'd done for her: introduced her to Leal.

He made his way toward her, towering close to a head above her. "Let me run you through how this'll work when Miss Carlone makes an appearance here," he said. "You've got to keep a straight face. Otherwise, we won't get that blood sample," Devon said.

"I don't know why you treat me like an idiot."

"You've had two shots at Trelles Industries, to make Trelles research ours and to get pregnant, I hate to admit the obvious, but you failed. We can't lose Trelles. The research and intelligence stored in secret places that you and I can't access unless we have at least fifty-one percent control of Trelles is crucial. Have you forgotten? Focus."

"Don't patronize me."

"I lost my hands on Trelles when you decided to drink too much on your wedding day and spill the beans on our little scheme. For all we know, Leal may already have developed that vaccine now that he's been with Carlone for almost a week and a half."

"Is he having an affair?" she said.

"That's the least of my concerns."

Myranda narrowed her eyes. "I—"

"Get over it. He's a billionaire, whose pockets run deep. Did you think he was yours to keep?"

"Careful, Devon."

"Or what?"

"Don't for one second think you can do this without me."

"Is that a challenge? I love it when you challenge me. Now listen, Carlone's DNA is thought to have answers we've spent years trying to find. Answers that may cure nephthysis, a rare emergence of fibroid tumors that began with an epidemic in Brenton, Pennsylvania twenty-five years ago. I hope you read my e-mails. Or did you *spam* them?"

Myranda sighed deeply. Yes, she knew of nephthysis. Sometimes it felt like that's all she knew, a disease that had gripped her body the day she was conceived. "How is this Jewel connected to this?"

"You didn't read them." He watched her, leaned against the far wall and crossed his arms. "Jewel was the only live birth from the original twelve women who were affected by the disease."

"But if Leal develops this vaccine—"

"Leal will never market it."

"He might."

"He won't. But you and I can. Leal has everything a scientist and researcher wants. I have nothing."

Myranda drew back from his bark and pursed her lips.

"I want to market it and take the DEI for all they've got," he said. "They've been on my case for years. I promised them answers regardless of whether Leal would cooperate or not. I need Leal's research or the next best thing. A dip into Jewel's bloodstream will establish me as the scientist I've always wanted to be. No more sneers from the scientific world. It's my name that'll go on the Dickson Prize, and the Gairdner Foundation International Award. Not his."

Devon wouldn't rest as long as Leal was a researcher. The two scientific minds couldn't exist on the same planet. Two opposed ideals. Best together, worst against each other. Myranda swallowed hard. "I see."

"That's why I'm here. There's too much at stake to leave it into your pretty hands."

Myranda watched him, her nostrils flaring yet admiring the

determination in his voice. He of all people knew her deepest wants, the longing and the aching. He would see her through it.

"How did you find out about this Carlone woman?" she said.

"I've always made it my business to watch Leal's every move. Including the women he socializes with."

Myranda rose and shot him a sharp glare. "Does he love her?"

"How do I know? I do know though that she's of medical interest to him. If Leal develops that vaccine for the DEI, he and Trelles will surpass any medical development in infertility research in recent decades. Remember the DEI came to both of us and somewhere along the line, Leal was more what they needed, with or without me."

Devon's jealousy was evident in his eyes. He'd always been envious of Leal's mind, intelligence and scientific influence. "Is this just about an accolade for you?" she said.

"Leal has always been a step ahead. Not this time."

"Why won't you let me handle this my way? I can deal with the Carlone girl."

"You've never taken a blood sample before. Just making sure you won't be skirmish."

"I can handle this."

"Keep your emotions out of this. This isn't about you and Leal's interest in Carlone. It's business. For you, it's survival."

Why did she have such a love-hate relationship with Devon? He'd tried her patience with every encounter. But then when he spoke, the world around him faded, the snotty grin disappeared and that was it. His suave upper-English tone had to be it. Or at least that's the best she could describe it. Myranda had never set foot on English soil, but Devon's accent had to be a London or Oxford one. What was the difference, anyway? Isn't that where all sophistication hailed from? An accent, so urbane, it dripped off his lips like honey and melted butter.

"I'll manage," she said.

Devon pulled out an envelope from his side pocket. "Now make sure you hand it to her like so."

Devon pointed the sharp corner of the envelope in her direction. "Just underneath my thumb, here, is a small prick, invisible to whoever holds it, but make sure it doesn't get you."

"Will it hurt her? Will she notice?"

"Only if you screw up."

He threw her a boyish grin. "You'll do fine. Once she has the envelope make sure you retrieve it pretending you handed her the wrong one."

"Why?"

"Because, my dear, you want it back. It'll have her DNA signature on it."

"That's it?"

Devon nodded. "Science isn't as complicated as people make it out to be."

Myranda took the envelope from his hands and laid the one with the prick on the table. She set the other on the desk next to the window and turned round to face him. "You'd better go. She'll be here any minute."

"If she's even one bit suspicious, we won't have the sample. Make sure she handles the envelope properly. Like this." He flipped the envelope indicating the manner. "It's loaded with invisible pricks on that far corner. We just need one to prick her."

"I got it. Now go."

Devon turned toward the door as Myranda paced a few feet behind him. He turned abruptly and set a hand on her back. He set eager lips on her tight mouth. "Be good. It'll be over soon."

Myranda pushed him, sending his back hard against the door. "Enough. Go."

Devon smirked before pulling the door open. "I'll see you tonight."

Once the door shut, Myranda straightened her pin skirt, feeling a heat to her cheeks. Her hands perspired as she turned and inched toward the bed taking a seat on its edge. It would be over soon. She took a mental note of Devon's instructions and only stopped when she heard the bedside phone ring. She picked up the receiver. "Yes."

It was the front desk.

"Have her come up please," Myranda said.

Jewel had been the first woman Leal had taken a deep interest since their marriage. Was it just for her DNA or was there something more? Perhaps this whole thing could work out to her advantage. And now, with only nine months to go. She could not turn back. Nothing would get between her and Trelles. Not now.

* * *

Jewel studied the elegant entrance of the Maharani Suite.
She'd been told downstairs that *"maharani"* stood for queen. The
porter's hand pounded softly on the door before he paced back to
the elevators.

Jewel stood waiting for several seconds. What kind of
woman would Myranda be? A rich New Yorker by the sound of
her accent and her command on the phone. What the heck? She
needed the money for her semester fees and studio lighting
equipment. She had her eye on a new muslin backdrop, and a new
twin-head kit. Jewel wanted to learn how light-emitting diode
kits, now known as LED kits worked—and she needed one as
soon as she got back to New York.

The door fell open and Jewel's eyes fell on a woman dressed
in a striped, chiffon tie-back zip-up dress. She was perhaps two
years older than Jewel and had the most attractive smile Jewel
had ever seen on a woman. Every inch of her was perfection, from
the ginger flaming hair set neatly on top of her head with ringlets
dancing around her ears framing a round face. Her aquiline nose,
and sparkling almond eyes reminded Jewel of a bisque porcelain
doll. Cool, ceramic good looks stared at her with youthful charm,
yet commanded authority. Jewel could've sworn that no one had
softer, milkier skin, with just the right amount of freckles to give
Myranda a girlish yet grown-up charm.

Myranda smiled and held out a hand. "Miss Carlone, please
come in."

"Thank you."

Jewel stepped into the expansive suite, examining the exotic
murals that hung on the wall. Her eyes fell on one of the Goddess
Kali, a figure she'd become accustomed to in the last few days
etched on shining black glass, dominating the expansive drawing
room. Designed in bronzes, blacks, chrome and mirrors, the suite
was deserving of the queen for whom it was built.

Myranda took a seat in the plush Ruhlmann sofas along the
far wall of the drawing room next to an alluring mirrored bar. An
exquisite private terrace with a spectacular view of New Delhi
greeted Jewel as she breathed in the spicy scents of the exquisite
space.

"Please take a seat," Myranda said.

Jewel took a seat across her and set her bag on the coffee

table in front of them.

"First time to India?" Myranda asked watching Jewel.

"Yes and it doesn't cease to impress me. How about you, Ms. Vaux?"

"Call me Myranda."

Jewel glanced around the room.

Myranda studied her without comment.

"I guess I can start by asking what is it you'd like me to do for you," Jewel said.

Myranda raised her eyebrows. "Of course, Miss Carlone. You must think it improper of me. I haven't truly introduced myself."

"Please call me Jewel."

Myranda squirmed her lips. "I like beauty and rumor on your campus has it you take great pictures."

"What rumors?"

"Don't be bashful, Jewel. I make it my business to keep an eye on upcoming talent in the arts."

Jewel leaned forward. "I'm still a student."

Myranda rose and paced to the bar to pour herself a drink. "I run a marketing business in New York and I'm into marketing interiors. I'm wondering if you could assist me. I'm a busy woman and I've recently purchased a home that requires redecorating. Before I select a decorator, I want to photograph the place." She flipped her head round. "By you."

"I'm flattered."

Myranda pursed her lips. "Hm..."

There was something perplexing about the way she phrased her sentences, short, and meticulous, almost rehearsed. Jewel leaned forward glimpsing an envelope on the coffee table with her name on it. "Ms. Vaux, I'm sure you can find a lot more experienced professionals, especially in New York, who could get this done for you. Why me?"

"The kind who gets to the point." As Myranda moved, she left a trail of perfume, a majestic aroma of sandalwood, vanilla and musk. "Actually, you're right, I have an ulterior motive."

Jewel watched the lines in Myranda's face harden. "Have you ever wanted something so bad and were unable to get it?"

Jewel shrugged. "Don't we all?"

"Well mine's got a time limit attached to it."

Was she talking to herself? Jewel set a finger on her chin...

"Excuse me?"

"Never mind." She faced Jewel. "In that envelope you'll find all the terms of the agreement. I hope you'll find my offer generous."

Jewel picked up the envelope. "May I?"

Myranda's face broke into a courteous smile. "Please."

Jewel's eyes fell on the amount in bold. "Fifty-*thousand* dollars?"

"I'm generous."

"Just for a day's photo shoot?"

"Maybe two. I've another property in mind. Come on, Jewel. We girls need to help each other out once in a while. Why should men have the best pay?"

Jewel's eyebrows squished together. "When do you want this done?"

"Well, let me see, doesn't it say?"

Myranda reached for the envelope and took it by its far edge. Her face remained unreadable, unembarrassed by what she'd proposed. She strode to the desk. "I'm willing to pay well and take care of any inconveniences. You know, missed classes, hellish hours, but it's worth it, you'll see."

Myranda placed the envelope on the desk and picked up a second one before handing it to Jewel. "I'm sorry I gave you the wrong one. Here, this is the right one."

This time Jewel opened the envelope without hesitation. "It's a check for a hundred-thousand dollars. That's insane—"

"I'm offering two jobs."

Jewel dropped the envelope on the table. "I can't accept this money for a simple photo shoot."

"Whether you accept it or not, it's being wired to your account."

"How do you have my account details?"

"Many ways. See it as an investment in your portfolio. You can later claim to have photographed one of the most exquisite properties in New York."

It wasn't right. The money was too tempting. Nothing in life was that good. That easy. Fate and chance had never been kind to Jewel. Why now? She shuffled her feet as she sat. "Ms. Vaux, I don't know how you found me, why you jumped on a plane and traveled so many miles to see me, but I really need to think about this."

Myranda continued. "It's simple. I don't take no for an answer."

Jewel narrowed her eyes as her cheeks began to heat up. Had Myranda not understood *no*? It was daylight robbery on her side. What kind of pictures were worth that, especially from an unknown photographer. "Ms. Vaux. I don't even have a studio or the right equipment for this type of job. I'm not sure I could meet your timescales."

"I'm not in a hurry."

Myranda sank into her seat and sipped a dry Martini from the bar. "I'm in no hurry, Miss Carlone. Be careful of rejecting my proposal, that is, if you want to work in New York as a photographer."

"Aren't there other photographers willing to do this incredible job? Why me?"

"You've the right training and the right approach I need. Now think carefully before you say no. There are many starving artists in New York."

Jewel's stare intensified. "I'll think about it."

Myranda twirled her jeweled necklace displaying a finely manicured hand. "Don't keep me waiting. This offer won't last for ever. I'll expect an answer by Sunday."

That was three days away and Jewel would be back in New York having completed Leal's projects.

Myranda rose and led Jewel to the front door. "That'll be all, Jewel." She shot her a smirk. "I have a feeling we'll be friends." She found a business card from a vintage purse by the door and set it in Jewel's hand. "Contact my office with this number. Now, enjoy the rest of your trip in India."

Jewel stepped out into the hallway cradling the card in her hands.

"One more thing," Myranda said leaning against the door, her facial skin stretching into a snarl. "I'd keep my distance from Leal Trelles. He knows nothing about photography."

* * *

Leal pulled Vik into the clinic office.

Vik rubbed his forehead. "I don't like what Myranda is doing to you."

"It's not a big deal."

"You can still walk out of this marriage with no consequences. It was a farce from the beginning. Myranda's blood work has never given you any insight into nephthysis and the formula for Tharnex."

"Why do you think I married her, Vik?"

"Come on, man. You and I've been friends a long time. You've always been transparent to me. It was for her blood work wasn't it."

"Yes."

"How far will you go for medicine? Is Myranda connected to Brenton's outbreak?"

He watched his friend. He could no longer keep lying to him. "I'll let you continue speculating—"

"End it now, Leal and tell Jewel the truth. She's the one you need. She'll understand. Damn it, man, you love her."

"I can't."

"If it means anything to you, tell her. She feels the same way. If I'm correct, she'll gladly surrender her blood work. Myranda and Devon may have done you wrong but you can stand above their idiosyncrasies."

"The prenup is up in nine months. I just need nine more months. If Myranda doesn't deliver, the marriage dissolves anyway. That's how we worded it and the truth is she can't get pregnant."

"If she decides to get nasty and the courts find out about your plan, they may rule in her favor. But if you divorce her now... whatever the prenup says doesn't matter."

"Jeff will handle it."

"Do it quick, Leal. You deserve so much better than you allow yourself."

When Vik left the office, Leal eased the door shut and sank into the office chair. He dialed the clandestine number Jeff Avent had had him memorize.

Jeff was an attorney who'd worked for several years within the Office of the General Counsel of the CIA before starting his own firm. An agency accessed only by referral, serving a niche clientele of people with big problems, large bank accounts and international importance. Jeff's clandestine services handled a wide range of legal issues, from both civil and criminal litigation to foreign intelligence and counterintelligence activities.

A clear cold voice came on the line. "Yes?"

"Trelles."

A slight hesitation grew on the line. "You've decided to accept my advice?"

Leal reached deep into his pocket and pulled out a surgeon's scalpel. He fumbled for the desk drawer and drew it open, pulling out a bottle of sterilizer and a cotton swab. He used the scalpel to slit the skin under his wrist with the precision of a surgeon. Underneath the epidermis, where a barely visible raised swelling lay, he drew out two paper-thin data chips, no bigger than a finger nail. He placed each inside identical, custom-made flash disks Jeff's office had wired.

"I have them here." Leal hesitated a second. "What do I do next?"

"How lost do you want them to become?"

"No one must know about this code, Jeff. It's not safe with me anymore. How can I get it to you?"

"Don't. I run a global enterprise. Where are you exactly?"

"Kullu Manali, Northern India."

Leal heard typing on the line before Jeff's voice re-emerged. "In exactly two hours, a man answering to the name of Sameer Khan will meet you at a local food joint called Abhay's Kitchen, in the bazaar on Chandigarh-Mandi-Manali road. He's a former agency worker and will know who you are. Hand him the chip in an envelope. We'll take care of the rest."

"Thank you. I've also got the information you requested all here, Jeff. This proves everything."

"I need to ask you one more time, Leal." Jeff was being careful. "Are you ready to do this? You risk losing everything."

An image of Jewel came to his mind. Leal clutched the phone tighter. "Yes."

* * *

Jewel left Santi Palace Hotel with tightness in her gut and spilled out onto the congested street. She veered onto a small enclave in the southwest part of the city that blended bustling restaurants and boutiques. Hagglers bumped elbows in Karol Bhag bazaar. It stood across a vast tapestry of ancient buildings.

She'd not graced Myranda's words with an answer. How

could she?

Jewel trotted faster than she intended and trudged up the street where she would catch a taxi to meet her flight back to Manali. The honking traffic failed to interrupt the disgust in her gut brought on by Myranda's proposal.

Cornered in a one-way street, she'd not thought of getting a taxi at the hotel. Jewel's fingers tightened into a claw as she approached a taxi stand at the end of the busy street.

She needed to think. With no taxi in sight, the wind started to toss her loose hair over her face. She had to get back to Manali. Her flight left at 3:00 p.m. She would then hire a cab up the hills to Manali. There was no reason to contact Leal and tell him where she'd gone. Would telling him be worth the hassle? He'd tried to call her an hour ago.

Jewel couldn't give into Myranda's threats. Was the high-strung executive really that powerful? Myranda was right about one thing though. Photography was a profession some considered a hobby, the kind that's hard to break into successfully in an economy where many made do without unnecessary luxuries. Expensive photos were a luxury. Her photography instructor once said that, *jobs that scare you the most are the most important ones to get under your belt.* Could this be one of them?

Jewel longed to be more of a landscape photographer, perhaps an architectural one. But what if Myranda's job was the type that paid? And what if her reputation was at stake before she even had one? Jewel wanted to do more research. To get more information.

She pulled out her cellphone. She still had time as Sunday was only a few days away. She would tackle it then.

Jewel lost her footing as she hailed a taxi. She fell forward, slid to the ground and hit her foot on a protruding brick.

Damn it!

Several onlookers observed her writhed frame. Her purse gushed open spilling its contents on the gravel. A Delhi commuter, a local woman, stopped to help her up. "*Memsaab* are you okay?"

The woman gathered the spilled contents and replaced them as Jewel rose with the woman's help. Fire shot through her foot. She checked her ankle. No major injury.

"You should be careful *memsaab*. Do you have a car?"

"A taxi please, I need to get to the airport."

"I'll call you one."

Within minutes a black Ambassador car pulled up to the curb. "Here," said the woman. "Your bag."

Jewel inventoried her belongings and glimpsed up at the woman. "Where's my cellphone?"

The woman studied her puzzled. "Maybe you didn't have it."

"No. I did and that's why I fell, I was trying to make a call."

The woman shook her head and squinted her eyes slightly. "Was it new?"

"Yes."

"This is New Delhi, *memsaab*. You won't see that phone again."

* * *

Leal glanced at the hotel's entrance as Jewel stepped out of a cab. He'd been worried the last several hours unable to reach her.

When she stepped into the lobby, he rose from his seat in the hotel where he'd settled to wait for her and put away his reading as she paced to where he sat. "I was looking for you. Where were you?"

Jewel shot him an exhausted glance. "In hell."

His eyebrows gathered. "Are you all right? I tried to call you."

Jewel staggered up to him. "My phone was stolen." She swallowed hard. "In New Delhi."

"You went to Delhi. Why?"

"I flew there to meet a client."

"A client? I thought you weren't taking clients." He tilted his head to one side as if realizing something. "Except me."

"I'm not, Leal."

"Do you want to talk about it?"

"Not really. I want to forget it happened."

He hadn't seen this closed side of her and hoped she'd not been victim to blindly believing any advice from the hordes of street dwellers who'd only be too glad to help a frightened foreigner.

Leal took her hand. "Why didn't you tell me? I could've come with you."

"You were busy, Leal. You've enough to do here."

He relaxed his face. "I'm a good listener, Jewel. What's wrong?"

She sighed and her eyes found his. "Why is it that people with money think they can buy anything? And that woman—"

"What woman?"

"Some New Yorker found me and wants to hire me to photograph her house and says if I don't I'll never work as a photographer in New York. How does she know so much about me?" Her voice rose with every syllable she uttered.

The woman, whoever she was, had upset Jewel. Did Jewel really despise people with money? Sure he'd revealed nothing about his background, hardly anything. Jewel wasn't impressed by wealth. In fact, he found that part about her very intriguing. Many times he'd wished wealth hadn't come to him at all. It had caused him more problems than he cared to count.

Leal took her to a seat in a quiet corner of the busy hotel lobby. "Then don't take the job."

"I have to Leal. I can't work for you for ever. We'll be done in a day or two. Then life continues, I go back to my course in New York and you'll continue traveling and researching."

It couldn't be further from the truth. He could stop researching and take her anywhere she wanted to if it meant he could see her every day. "You don't have to do anything anybody tells you, Jewel. I let no one walk over me. And I won't let anyone walk over you either."

It was a new ultimatum he'd adopted minutes after the car incident on the cliffs. If only so many people didn't need Tharnex.

All the wrong people.

Why Jewel? Why did she have the right gene? The right DNA.

"Leal, I have to pay for my education and there's no shame in working for it."

He searched her tired face. Why couldn't he tell her she didn't have to? He was losing his confidence around her. If his plan worked, she could photograph Greek Islands for the rest of her life if she wanted to. If it meant that they could work out a life together.

She was breathtaking when she was angry. Leal took a deep breath and watched Jewel squirm. "When does this job start?"

"I've got till Sunday to decide, but I'm guessing after I get back to New York."

"Won't that interrupt your courses at the Photo Institute?"

She smiled. "Like this isn't?"

"I like to think I'm special."

Her frown disappeared and her face softened. "Leal, I wanted to do this. To come here with you I mean. Being away from you is affecting me."

He took her in his arms despite the brief stares they were beginning to receive in the lobby and kissed her hand. "As a matter of curiosity, who's this client? I may have a word with them." He shot her a cocky smile. "I may extend my contract with you. So Miss Carlone, tell them you are already employed."

"Oh what was her name?" Jewel drew out Myranda's business card. "Ah yes, Vaux, pronounced *vo*? Myranda Vaux. Some marketing executive from Manhattan."

Chapter 8

The waiter served Jasmin tea from a canister.

"Did you use bottled water?" Myranda said.

"Yes, Ma'am."

She gestured the room service attendant away, and he left promptly. A tear grew in her left eye. What went wrong? Had Leal loved her? Cared? How did they end up like this?

When had she first seen Leal? It had to be at the Waldorf Astoria in front of researchers and members of the scientific community. Leal stood presenting the Trelles' company vision with such ease. He wasn't like anyone she knew. He'd walked into the boardroom in snug jeans and a Daft Punk T-shirt like a high-school jock. His hair was longer than she cared for, but well groomed. Leal spoke with intelligence as his medical vision unfolded, as if he was speaking not for Trelles Industries, but on behalf of the earth and global infertility research.

He inspired Myranda and she needed the Trelles account. Leal's teams had invited seven marketing agencies looking for the right partner. The agencies had been asked to pitch over two days after Leal's presentation. Not just the account. She wanted to know this man who had so much knowledge and experience for his then twenty-two years.

After the presentation, Myranda asked to see Leal. It started on a genuine note.

"Thank you for the presentation on your marketing proposal for Trelles Industries," Leal said.

Myranda smiled. "I'm moved by the passion you use when you speak about your products, but most importantly, the people you want to help."

Leal returned her smile. "I've spent a great deal of energy on our business model."

He was handsome, a clean shaven face with sparkling eyes

and a body that lived in the gym. "How did you get into medicine? You have a knack for it."

"I don't like to see human suffering. If you hang around, you'll start to believe there's a cure for everything. That's how I energize Trelles's teams and it's written in our motto."

Myranda beamed at him. "I hope we can bring the same passion to the marketing campaign."

"Sounds like you have the account already."

"I have faith in your cause."

"It's not a cause. It's a global problem."

She breathed hard. "Whether we get the account or not, I'll remain a fan. In fact, I think I would call the campaign 'Cure'."

"As simple as that?"

"You just said now in your presentation that healing begins in the human spirit. You believe it, don't you? You have me converted."

Leal studied her for a minute. "Ms. Vaux, you're smart. I'll give you the account. Tell the others they can draw up the paper work. You start on Monday."

Myranda was ecstatic.

The next several months she worked along Leal observing how he worked. She gained insight into his mind and developed a hunger for a cure of her own. Myranda followed him as he treated a woman in Lithuania with a rare malignant tumor.

"Leal, can I video as you work with the patient? We can use footage of you working on the campaign to launch the medical line."

Myranda observed and took notes. She worked nights not wanting to forget the things Leal had said. How he talked to the children, entertained them with ease. Myranda could not help but admire his gentle way with them. On a trip that July to Mozambique, Myranda asked Leal why he spent so much time in the developing world.

"It's where I think. I observe people who are immune. What makes these people different?"

"Does that give you many answers?"

"In the medieval ages, Europe was haunted with the black plague. What made the great plague disappear? Why did a third survive? Was it in their make up? What did they have that others didn't?"

He smiled. His first smile directed at her. "I've found

patterns in the human immune system by studying the bubonic plague among other epidemics."

"Are you going to tell me what you've found?"

"That'll remain my secret."

That was now years ago. She couldn't lose Leal and would keep him by giving him a child. It hurt so damn much that she wasn't able to.

She picked up the phone. "Devon?"

"Did you get it?" he said.

"Come and get your sample."

* * *

Leal's boots pounded the ground as he hurried toward the clinic. Jewel stood watching him from the porch as he strode toward her.

"I need to go into town for an hour. Will you be okay here? Vik will help you with whatever you need."

"Sure," she said. "Is it work?"

"Sort of. Can I still interest you in a trek to Keylong? As a thank you for what you're doing and to share my most interesting work with you. Just the two of us."

She nodded. "Hey, you're paying me."

Leal took her hand. "I still want to thank you. Vik will drive you back to the hotel when you're ready."

He pecked her on the cheek. "I'll see you later."

Leal stepped off the porch toward a new Cruiser Vik had bought. His stomach churned and he brought down a fast fist on the steering wheel. He was being unfair and sat a few moments in the car before turning on the ignition. Why had he taken that damn trip?

He'd fought not to go to Montpellier all those years ago. But once there and when he saw her confident ease on the platform, Jewel's effortless performance in the arena made him forget why he'd come. When the accident happened, he'd raced behind the ambulance and stolen into the intensive care unit to make sure she was all right. He couldn't just walk away. The DEI wanted that sample and if he didn't get it, they would.

What was it about her? Her smile. Yes, it was dazzling. Her

103

skin radiated with a smooth complexion. Her eyes reminded him of the sunsets in Venice and Jewel's lustrous hair fell on her shoulders like a silk shawl from the hills of Positano. He'd never felt attracted to someone so delicate and vulnerable. He'd seen many exquisite women, but not like Jewel. Meeting her had been like discovering a rare flower in the mountains. What charmed him most was she didn't know her effect on him.

Jewel was the only woman who'd ever made him question his purpose and convictions about right and wrong.

She was a ready target but he couldn't touch her. Not without betraying himself. The image of the day he'd married Myranda came to mind. He knew why he'd married her. But why had she?

He could still hear the shrill in her high-pitched voice as she'd nestled her head in Devon's chest minutes after he'd married her. Still, Myranda slipped into his life offering companionship and a sharp business wit. She'd taken over the marketing and social responsibility departments of Trelles after their marriage.

He hated the office.

She was drawn to the power it gave her.

Why had he been so quick to marry her? He needed her on medical research grounds, but he knew he'd also let himself trust her. The marriage had been a huge mistake and was costing him more than mere money. It gripped his soul like a merciless demon. His motives blinded him and sure as heck he was paying for it now.

He'd never proposed. It was a business arrangement agreed upon over a glass of smooth Pinot Grigio. He accepted a future of promises about marketing campaigns and global corporate responsibility programs, affairs Myranda could handle well. Maybe he should've cared about the details and now he hated himself for ignoring Jeff's timely warning. He had nowhere else to go but to Jeff's expertise at handling legal corporate and personal crises, swift, prudent and damn well got the job done.

He had to end the nightmare. It had been four-and-a-half long years. How had he let himself get into this mess? Being born into wealth hadn't helped Leal's upbringing. He could still remember being treated differently all his life; the chauffeured cars to Murphy-Lax Private School, the gigantic houses that were empty of love and warmth, the nannies and the privileges of every luxury money could fetch and the emptiness of love it left behind. His family had always been an easy target.

And now, the nightmare lingered as long as he was head of the pharmaceutical giant, owned by his family with him as its CEO and founder. Seventy-five percent was privately owned giving him control of its nine pharmaceutical subsidiaries and a leading medical research company Trelles Consolidated, which later merged to form Trelles Industries, all on the credentials of two cervical cancer vaccines and a drug Leal discovered at Harvard. The drug, Dilotyn, combated a rare but very serious disease that wreaked havoc on the skeletal muscles of a patient.

Leal stared ahead. He'd lost his mother on the same bed on which she had given birth to him. When his father could no longer bear losing her, the selfish moron left him at age ten. To this day, no one knew what happened to Sean Trelles the day he went off on that yacht.

Leal's father was known for his abrasive personality, his wealth, his lavish gambling habits, his expansive business empire built on exporting heavy industrial machinery, and his clashes with the Inland Revenue authorities. At the time of Sean's disappearance, he had been one of the richest and most influential men in the United States. A substantial trust fund and assets held in bonds kept the family business afloat while Leal grew into an impulsive young man who harbored a quick temper and turned snowboarding and motorcycles into dangerous sports.

As an elusive adolescent, he knew the weight of running Sean's empire would one day fall on him and took a keen interest in sports to avoid any responsibility related to the business. In high school, his chemistry teacher saw he was gifted with exceptional intelligence in research and science. Yet his lack of social skills was evident.

He had no close friends. After hours, he'd lock himself away poring over microscopes. Leal traveled on his father's company expense budget, curious about disease and human anatomy instead of being the playboy many thought he should be. He wanted to learn about rare diseases and document new ones.

Leal stepped on the gas and swerved down the Indian hillside. He drove for thirty minutes until he reached Jagar bazaar and parked the car. After a few moments, he stretched for the glove compartment, pulled out his electronic tablet and video-dialed Myranda.

The program fired up, distorted due to signal weakness, but within seconds she picked up.

"Leal, where are you?"

Myranda's image appeared on the LED screen. She peered at her camera trying to gain clues from Leal's surroundings. His voice was low and controlled. "We need to talk."

"You still haven't told me where you are."

"Doing research."

Her face softened. "Leal, when am I going to see you? I was thinking about—"

"Stop. We're getting divorced. It shouldn't be a surprise to you."

"Why now, Leal?"

"You saw this coming."

She was silent for several seconds, before her voice rose, calm and collected. "After all I've done for Trelles and you—"

"Everything you've ever done Myranda was for you."

"Leal I can still get pregnant if—"

"You trying with Devon?"

Their wedding day, if it could be called that, came to mind and the way Myranda's arms had wrapped around Devon's neck. They'd laughed unaware he was watching, celebrating their gain of twenty-five percent stake control of the company, a move Jeff had warned him against. Myranda had marked him just as he had her. Though Leal could have halted the wedding at any minute on the day, he hadn't.

"Devon's your friend and that's what he is to me." Her eyebrows gathered. "Why now, Leal? Why have you waited four years? You could've ended this marriage a long time ago? Why not when—"

"The day I let you think you'd gotten away with lying to me? Let's just say I had my reasons too, just like you've had yours. It was never a marriage."

"You can't just...Leal, I'll fight this."

"Why would you want to be married to me?"

"Because I—"

"You don't love me. You've always loved the idea of us."

A vein in Leal's forehead throbbed. "This marriage has been a cover for your family business for years and God knows what else." He lowered his voice. "I want a quiet divorce. You'll be okay. I'll leave you enough money for you and your business along with what was set out in the prenuptial."

Myranda threw her head back. Her almond-shaped eyes narrowed as she neared the camera. "You can't divorce me. Failure is not in your vocabulary."

Myranda stared at the tablet. "You're not in New York. What are you up to?"

He narrowed his eyes and breathed deep. "Any shares you have in Trelles will be liquidated. Feel free to take them somewhere else. Trelles' legal counselors have drafted the papers. I suggest you contact your legal advisers."

Myranda shook her ginger hair from her round face. Light from the window reflected in her eyes giving her porcelain skin a glow. Her face was made up with crisp and distinctive winter shades distorted as the Wi-Fi signal wavered. Her dress-suit, though tinted by the screen, was a bold red over a white blouse that contrasted her shiny hair.

She pouted her lips. "Leal, can't we talk about this?"

Desperation rang in her tone negating any attempt at persuasion.

Leal's eyes darkened. "We're done talking. After this call, we never need to speak. You'll find the settlement quite fair and free of grudges for what you've put me through."

"I won't allow you to treat me like this."

Leal's eyes wandered to the off button. "It's over. I'm sorry. I should have never married you. It's your chance to start a new life. After tomorrow, the paperwork will be finalized."

"Is there someone else, Leal?"

His index finger hovered over the off button. "Be smart, Myranda. Take the offer."

Her eyes rouged. "No, Leal. We'll have a civil conversation about this when you come home."

Hadn't she understood or had she chosen not to? "Goodbye, Myranda."

He tilted his head to one side and hit the off button. His words echoed through the car as he stared at the blank screen.

The skin on Kaya's forearm tingled as she set the phone down. Jewel hadn't picked up her phone in the last twenty-four hours and neither had Leal. Jewel didn't need this. Why hadn't Leal told her he was married?

Weston appeared at the door. "You need to rest. I don't think it's good for the baby. You've been working too hard."

Kaya nodded and peered into the eyes of the man she'd fallen for six years ago. They'd met in high school. She was a freshman and he was three years her senior. He was soon to graduate and she'd been impressed that he knew much about Native Indian culture. Weston had come from a line of lawyers who'd defended water rights in a Native Indian reservation when their land in Connecticut was under threat.

Weston practiced international corporate law and recently assisted UNESCO on revamping the World Heritage List's standard setting in Paris. His firm Wilda and Wilda Associates was a promise to Kaya, to one day run the practice together, once the baby was at least a year old. He had taken over his father's legal business and then started a new firm with hopes for Kaya to join him as soon as she passed her New York Bar exam. Over the last two years, they'd gained three partners, covering an array of legal fields including human rights, family, corporate and securities law.

"Honey, I'll be down soon," Kaya said.

"I made risotto tonight."

She smiled as she shut her laptop. "Weston, I'm scared."

"Scared?"

"Have you heard of Trelles Industries or Myranda Vaux?"

"Sure, the society woman who thinks she is a pharmaceutical goddess. She was in Forbes three months ago."

"Really?"

"We studied the Trelles portfolio for consideration over an FDA argument."

"What does the Food and Drug Administration want with Trelles?"

"The FDA constantly monitors any drug they produce. They needed a legal firm to partner with them in forensic pathology, medical ethics and also to act as a medical adviser."

"I just got hold of some disturbing information." She picked up a set of papers she'd just printed. "This."

He took the documents and his eyes scanned them briefly. "Myranda Vaux's prenuptial with Leal Trelles. How did you get this?"

"Never mind that. Leal is the man I was telling you about last night. He's Jewel's new man, the guy from Montpellier and Austria."

"What?" Weston's raspy voice echoed in her ears. "He's married. You didn't tell me it was *the* Leal Trelles."

"Yes."

"Does Jewel know?"

"I don't think so. And babe, Jewel's in love. She may not know it, but I do. And what's worse she is in India with him right now. I can't reach her."

"That's huge. The Vaux family has been involved in a couple of legal cases over the years. Some attorneys have shied away from meddling with their corporate and personal practices and others, well... let's say they take the money and look the other way."

Kaya's eyes widened. "Are you serious?"

"Oh yeah. Not proved, but they've never been good for Trelles Industries. In fact it surprises me that a family as smart as the Trelles teamed up with them."

"Jewel can't get involved with Leal. The lying snake didn't even tell her he's married. Look at the prenuptial. Have your ever seen anything like it? Myranda needs to conceive within five years of their marriage. Look at the date."

He read it. "That's nine months away."

"If she doesn't, it's an automatic end to the marriage and any stakes in Trelles. I've dug up quite a few things on her. Like the time she swayed Mayor Brinna Marshall in the incorporating of her business Vaux Marketing." Pain surfaced in Kaya's voice. "I'm really worried, Weston."

"I'm worried about you. I like Jewel a lot. You two are inseparable and I agree, let's warn and help her, but don't get mixed up with the Vaux business. From what I hear they hire the shrewdest lawyers who can convince a jury a murderer is as innocent as a new day. These aren't the sort of people I want you dealing with especially when you're pregnant."

"I have to do it for Jewel."

"Jewel's a big girl. She'll handle Leal I'm sure. She's no push over."

"It's not right. I don't like that Leal is lying to her. Somehow, I can't help but wonder if he is also a victim here."

"What do you mean?"

"Why would such a successful epidemiologist marry a conniving woman like Myranda? *And* take caution with a very specific prenuptial?"

"It's not our headache. Just get a hold of Jewel and let her make her own decision about Trelles and his intentions."

"Leal's a good guy and very smart, Weston. Yes he lied about his marriage, but there must be more here. It doesn't make sense for a billionaire to be pushed over so easily. Why is he really involved with Vaux? And why protect himself very specifically and I quote, *'Myranda Vaux is to forfeit all claim to Trelles Industries if she doesn't conceive a child after the allocated period in section 53-A.'* It just seems so premeditated and confining."

"Leave it, baby. Stop. Forget you ever saw this prenuptial. I wouldn't even mention it to Jewel. Just drop it and come down for dinner."

With that Weston turned and headed for the stairs.

Kaya turned to her laptop and searched the folder of documents she'd obtained from Saunders.

Her hand move lightly above the delete button.

She paused.

* * *

AHBAY'S KITCHEN
CHANDIGARH-MANDI, MANALI ROAD.

A piquant scent from sizzling frying pans wafted into Leal's nostrils. Ginger, curry, cumin, turmeric and coriander scents wafted through the air of the local *Dhaba* restaurant as he found his seat. His fringe fell over his eyes. Locks of sandy blond hair made the restaurant owner's children gawk at the stranger in local attire. He'd let his facial hair grow for three days, embracing the self-determination that the mountains gave him. Leal welcomed the freedom not to be tied by systems and regulations like most things in New York City.

He moved his hand to his pocket and pulled out the flash

disk, no bigger than a finger nail. Encrypted with fertility research and vaccine formulas, the pint-sized piece of technology stood between what potentially was a risky find or the key to his struggle with nephthysis. This chip, containing data worth millions of dollars, would eliminate the mental and physical burden that was threatening a growing number of women in Benton. It was spreading across the US and possibly across several nations by now. But, the drug wasn't ready. It needed to be tested and testing took time.

He couldn't risk it going to the DEI or any hands. Leal could make millions for Trelles Industries, millions he didn't need. Millions that would draw the wrong interests. Isn't that where the blasted problem had begun with his earlier discoveries?

No, not this time.

Only yesterday, he'd seen encrypted files leave the secured cloud systems of Trelles's research labs. Someone was watching his work. He needed the formulas and blood sample vaulted, and one person could get the job done with discretion. Vaulted and protected the sample and the theories had to disappear even from the one place of solace he'd always had, his family. The blood sample and replicas had rejuvenated the affected cells and organ tissues of the fibroid tumor he'd worked with the day before.

He was so close.

A boy bordering puberty set a hot *chai* at his table. He sipped his cardamom-flavored tea and waited for the man Jeff was sending. The adolescent smiled at the generous tip he was given and scuttled off to his next customer.

Would Leal recognize the agent, possibly a former spy that Jeff was sending? Jeff was connected to just about every global intelligence agency and if he needed an agent he damn well got one. Feeling much like a duck in a hunting game, Leal raised the steaming metal glass to his lips and waited. The valued data seemed to scorch his pocket as he glanced at each trucker, merchant, or hiker who stopped in for a hot curry.

Would his sister Sofia approve of this decision? He hadn't seen her in a long time. The last he'd heard she'd been touring with a theater group in Australia, or was it New South Wales?

Beneath the aloof and sometimes glacial exterior, Sofia was more sensitive than the average person. Her intuition was well developed and she could read Leal a mile away. Though extroverted, she held her privacy dear, being rather secretive and often an enigma to him. Even though he didn't see her much, Sofia was closer to him than anybody else except for Nonna, his paternal grandmother.

Leal helped himself to hot *naan*—local bread—set before him. His lips stretched into an optimistic smile as he thought of seeing Sofia's face soon. She was coming up to New York next week. Sofia knew him well and now he wanted her to know the whole truth. Though she'd disapproved of his marriage to Myranda, surely she'd forgiven him by now.

She'd never understood his decision then and would never understand his current actions. But he needed her. Damn it, she'd always been his conscience. Sofia opted not to ever meet Myranda, commemorating the first of his problems with his estranged wife. For several months she'd not said a word to him.

A dark man with wide smoke-gray eyes made his way to Leal's table, dressed in a long jacket with exposed buttons through the length of the placket and a sarong tunic tucked over the waist. Short with a wide-chested build, Leal watched the robust man shuffle heavy feet and slide into the seat across from him.

He shot Leal a stern glance. "Dr. Trelles?"

"Yes."

The man narrowed his eyes. "Once a sedative and treatment for nervous tension, the ion of this element is now a commonplace expression?"

It was a trick question and the password to his secret lab. The man's fluency in American English betrayed his otherwise seemingly local look. Leal tried not to let his pride show as he responded. "Bromine. Various bromides have been used over time to help normalize mood, mainly, potassium bromide. This led to bromine, or bromide being used to refer to any calming influence."

"You certainly know your chemicals, doctor."

That had been the clandestine watchword, a riddle he'd created for use with scientists who covertly accessed the underground labs at Trelles.

The man inclined his head. "Enjoying Manali, doctor? I see you blend in here."

Leal pulled out the state-of-the-art flash drive and placed it in an envelope. "This leaves the country tonight."

The man drew out a steel case. "That's our expertise and why you hired us."

Leal studied the man's face. "Where did Jeff find you?"

The man drew an eyebrow. "I need your thumb print to open this." He keyed in a new password. "There are only two keys, yours and the other person you specified. You now need to create a new password known only to you."

Leal slid his thumb across the laser reader of the steel box. The smooth gadget scanned his thumb print and opened. He placed the envelope in the box, not once taking his eyes off the man. Once the envelope was secured, he closed the container and entered a new password.

"Your problems have disappeared, Dr. Trelles. Congratulations."

"What happens now?"

"Avent will forward all the details you require."

"Who are you?" Leal said.

"We don't use names, locations or the same messengers twice. That's how we keep our clients happy. No need for you to know who I am."

Leal nodded, unable to speak as he examined the messenger's expressionless face. The transaction had just cost him two-and-a-half million dollars. The documents could stay concealed as long as he wished.

The man pursed his lips. "Sleep lighter, Dr. Trelles." He picked up the case and walked out of the *Dhaba*.

Leal had done the one thing he promised never to do.

Part with the data.

* * *

Leal searched the far length of the hotel's coffee bar. Jewel would be down any minute. Where has she gone yesterday? His mountain jacket, faithful to provide diligent weather protection, enveloped his lean body like a shrink-swaddled sandwich. He would tell her today. About Myranda. About the DEI.

About everything.

Leal padded the left side of his backpack where he'd placed a bundle of documents and a second flash disk addressed to Jeff. Signed last night, Trelles Industries would be safe. If only he'd managed to courier it with the rest of his data.

He'd not been ready, not until now, certain he wanted to take this step with Jewel. It shot shudders through him.

If the weather cooperated, the mountains would be a natural backdrop for his plan. Even then, a numb thought entered his bones. Was this the right thing to do? If Jewel was his, could he protect her from the DEI? He would find a way.

Leal had discarded his syringe twenty-four hours ago.

A slender figure at the top of the grand stairs interrupted his thoughts. His eyes fell on Jewel as she walked down the marble staircase. He took personal inventory of her graceful steps. She wore an olive alpine jacket that articulated her shapely shoulders worn over matching salopettes. The eye-catching outfit was sensible for high mountain adventure and he observed her fidget with the straps of the salopettes and tug at the hood of the jacket. Her lack of awareness of his stare sent his lips curling into a smile as she strolled toward him.

He rose.

"I hope this'll do."

A forgotten chocolate lock inched toward her face as she gazed with expectancy at him.

He threw her a cocky smile. "Keylong's a three-hour journey. It'll be our last stop before we head home to New York, tomorrow. Vik will drive us to a place called Gushal and we'll hike the rest of the way."

Jewel zipped her jacket and glanced at the main entrance catching the chill of the wind gusting into the lobby each time the door opened. "You picked the right day for it. The climate has turned cooler. Snow may come," she said.

"It's normal here. Just a little snow to trigger your spirit of adventure." Somewhere dimness moved in the back of his head. She was right. Roads on the Manali highway were prone to mudslides in extreme weather and in winter, most were sanctioned off by the Indian army's border roads organization. Nothing would thwart his plan. "Vik reassured me the weather will hold out. His family is from these parts and last night, he checked on the roads. They're safe and will be open until the second week of November."

Jewel relaxed her shoulders. "I'm not worried."

"From Gushal we'll hike seven miles to Keylong. It's the best way to see this part of India and I want you to meet a patient of mine up there. I'll be right back."

Leal gravitated to the front desk toward a beaming receptionist. "I'd like to check out. My bill and Ms. Carlone's will be settled with Trelles Industries in New York."

He handed the woman his corporate card and watched as she made the arrangements. No need to return after Keylong. They would take a private plane to Delhi after visiting Maya in Keylong, the puzzling link in his research.

The woman handed him his card. "Come visit us again."

"Sure will." He placed the card in his wallet and pocketed it before grabbing their backpacks. Leal slotted a medium-sized bag in his backpack that looked like a doctor's case.

He turned to Jewel. "You ready?"

Jewel nodded and they proceeded at an easy pace to the parking lot, where Vik waited with a copper Land Cruiser. The brisk air caressed his face as he led Jewel to the car.

Grateful for the fresh air and high elevations, Leal was glad altitude sickness never touched him. He opened the back seat door for her and slipped around to settle in the front with Vik. The intoxicating smell of the new Cruiser filled his nostrils as they sped off the hotel plot.

"The car is in top condition," Vik said. He glanced at Leal. "The fitted winter tires will handle the roads well."

The vehicle negotiated a tight bend that led to the Leh-Manali highway. Vik's hand tightened on the wheel. "You sure you don't want me to come." He engaged the gear. "It can get a little tricky up there in the mountain."

Leal shot a glance at Jewel. "Thanks, Vik. We'll be fine."

"I've seen Leal handle himself on a mountain," Jewel said.

"That he sure can do," Vik said.

Thirty kilometers into their journey on the meandering hill roads, they stopped on the ancient trade route of the Rohtang pass. The route provided a natural divide between the sub-humid Kullu Valley, primarily a Hindu culture south of the pass, and the northern Lahaul and Spiti valleys that leaned more toward Buddhist culture.

Despite the late tourist season, a sea of vans and jeeps carrying a horde of people jammed the wintry highway.

Vik eased his foot on the brake pedal. "I suggest we continue. You can enjoy the Rohtang pass tomorrow on our way back."

They fought traffic and deathly chaos on the crowded roads. After another gruesome couple of hours, the nestled village of Gushal appeared behind a cliff, set against the backdrop of an impenetrable screen of preset sky.

Leal jumped out of the Jeep, his legs begging for movement. He swung the door open for Jewel and grabbed her backpack. He heeded the strong moaning of the wind.

"You sure you don't want me to drive you the rest of the way," said Vik, hesitating once more before setting off.

Leal patted his back. "We'll take it from here. See you here tomorrow. I take it we should be done by lunch time."

He took Jewel's hand and led her up the meandering road expecting a slow walk toward Keylong. Although less than thirty minutes away, he glanced at his global positioning watch as they towered above valleys. They stood below a sea of white ice along a weaving road the color of coal and rust. He checked the time.

Midday.

They stopped along the edge of the cliff road overlooking a sparse valley and continued a steady hike toward the passage that led to the mountains' steep, wooded slopes. Light snow fluttered around them. They took in the views a few minutes and their lungs took in the profound air.

Ten minutes later, they caught up with a local Air Force training group, on an outdoor boot camp. Close to forty recruits trekked in uniform alongside them. Leal spoke to them casually before the two parties split a few hundred meters from the majestic gate to Keylong village.

The mountain showed its true form with its ridges and passes retaining their typical appearance of silence and solitude. A lone village girl slid past them carrying a tired white lamb. She nodded briefly before continuing at a brisk pace past them. A field of rich garden ground extended below to the valley beyond them as they caught the crooked narrow path, walled in with low rock piles.

Soon they came to a cabin on a hillside overlooking the valley. Jewel zipped round unaware Leal had stopped.

"We'll spend the night here and head out to see Maya in the morning," Leal said as snowflakes descended into a warmer layer of air and melted on his face. "Come, I want to show you this place."

Jewel admired the stone cabin huddled on the top of the hill.

She breathed in the mountain and followed Leal to the entrance. The lodge drew inspiration from the dry-packed stone houses scattered on Keylong hill. Two conifer trees, providing acorns for a chorus of mountain birds, towered above the cabin. Leal drew a set of keys from his pocket and dragged the door open. It was a one bed cabin, neat to the bone, with a desk by a small bathroom that led off from one corner of the room. The warm inviting interior was a melange of chocolate goat furs, colored linens dotted with steel and wood furniture, modern and inviting.

Jewel glanced round setting her backpack on the floor at the handmade brick laid using traditional techniques. Above them wooden roof tiles provided solid shelter from the Himalayan winds gusting from northern Asia into India.

"I hired a local businessman. He keeps the cabin clean and stocked with everything I need. The only place he can't access is the back room where I do research."

A teasing smirk grew on Jewel's lips. "Not what I expected for a cabin in the Himalayas, it may as well be in Vermont. Will you let me see your research?"

"Depends."

"Come here and I'll show you."

She smiled. "How did you get all this equipment up here? That desk there could be a medical lab in New York."

Leal set his gear down by the window, drew the shutters open to reveal a glorious view of the Keylong ranges and cracked a window to pull in a stream of fresh air. "A researcher needs his research and technology. I rent this all year from a man in Keylong and had it set up to support my work."

"It's beautiful."

He smiled. "Call it a hideout. I have two. This and one on Martha's Vineyard not too far from North Water. A quiet place I think you'd like."

She smiled. "I'm not complaining. I love it."

He studied her face wondering what was behind the beautiful smirk. "You want a hot drink?" he said moving to a corner kitchenette.

Jewel removed her overcoat and sank to the edge of the bed. "No thanks."

He moved toward her. "Jewel, I..." He approached and looked into her eyes, admiring the way the mountains reflected in them.

"Yes?"

The words failed to leave his lips. "Just glad you came."

"What's got into you?" she said interrupting the silence. "What's wrong?"

Leal closed the windows. "Nothing. Just thinking."

She set a hand on his shoulder. "Care to share?"

He took a deep breath. "I will, but first tell me this. You like New York?"

She shrugged. "After my father left us, mom thought it was a good thing for us to move there. It would give me exposure, opportunities, she said, plus we had my aunt Celia there."

"Your mother was running from something, wasn't she?"

Jewel faced him with an abrupt zip of her head. "She was." Her voice became quiet. "I don't blame her."

"And your father?"

Jewel shot him a strained look and said nothing.

"Her opinions on your dad have affected you, haven't they?" Leal said.

I hardly knew the guy." Jewel walked a few feet from him to the window and closed her eyes. Leal studied her and a break in the clouds allowed dappled sunlight to play across her face. Her arms tightened around her shoulders as she spoke. "I don't see why people get married. Why they have children."

Leal's lips pressed together in a tight grimace as Jewel continued her unintentional monologue. "A year ago, I went to Udine where I was born and to where I'd heard he lived."

"Did you find him?"

"No. It was a false lead. When I came back my mother and I fought about it."

"Why?"

She drew in a sharp breath. "I saw pain in her eyes when I told her about my trip. She was angry, possibly at him."

Leal drew her around to face him. A rebellious tear formed in the corner of her right eye. "Jewel... do you trust me?"

"I don't know. Leal, I want to but even you seem to have a part of you don't want to let me see."

"Can't you trust me without knowing it all, Jewel?"

She shook her head slowly, an anger directed at all men crossing her face. "Are you different to my dad? To the two men who hurt my mother?"

A dry ache congested in his throat. "Jewel I want to tell you everything. But I can't. It's too dangerous. For both of us."

"Then don't ask me to trust you if you can't open the dark places to me. Leal, my life's in danger. A note arrived at the hotel. I'm scared and after the incident with the car."

A tightness formed in his chest. "Jewel, we can survive all of this... together."

He wanted to tell her about the sample, and the demons that chased him and her. But he couldn't. She was vulnerable, confused about him, yet her eyes betrayed her harsh words. He lost himself in them each time he looked at her and this time was no different. He pulled her up against his chest and set his eyes into her pained gaze. "Jewel, I can't tell you because... Because I'm in love with you."

"You don't know me—"

Her words failed to find volume as he crushed her to him and touched her trembling lips with one finger. She lifted her mouth until it hovered above his. A vaguely sensuous energy passed between them and he pressed a soft kiss on her lips, aching to make her his. Leal expected resistance, perhaps a punch to his deserving face but his insistence made her shift closer. His hands moved downward and circled her waist before easing to the fastening of her salopettes. His stare was bold and assured her frankly. Something in his manner soothed her and she edged into him, wanting him as much as he wanted her. The touch of her lips sent a shock wave through his entire body.

He shrugged the heavy clothes off her shoulders and soon her fingers fumbled with his sweater. He tried to throttle the dizzying current racing through him as she let him lead her to the warm fur of the low-set bed. And when his skin met the magnet of her steering touch, he took in the scent of her hair; hypnotized by her approach.

Leal guided her hands with ease until skin met skin. Layers of resistance peeled off their bodies until no walls existed between their desperate anguish. Leal raised her hand to his lips and pressed a lingering kiss upon her fingers as she settled back against the cushions. The look in her eyes invited him into her guarded self and he took a deep breath, controlling himself with an effort.

She was so compelling and he couldn't tear his gaze from her as they took time to explore; every curve of hers molding against his muscles. Her nearness kindled feelings of fire and he moved with slow inevitability. No doctor-sense had prepared him for what her anatomy was doing to him.

"Jewel, I'm in love with you. Let me love you."

Her cheeks colored under the heat of his gaze. "I'm scared to love you."

"Don't be, Jewel."

"How can I know I'll be safe with you?"

His lips conquered hers and only lifted to give her confidence. "You can't. Let your heart tell you."

His kiss was slow, thoughtful and she kissed him back, her arms solid and strong around him. Her mouth was more persuasive than she cared to admit sending an involuntary chill through him. Jewel abandoned herself to the whirl of sensation and as he roused her passion, his own grew stronger. He felt her shudder as she drew in a sharp breath and gripped his shoulders. An exciting quiver charged through her body and he moved his thumb across her palm toward her wrist and held her hand. Raw and deep, a quick warning unexpectedly touched his core as an uncontrollable sensation shot through him in heated tremors.

For many moments they clung together. Jewel trembled against his warm, virile nearness savoring the satisfaction he left with her.

Leal had crossed a door and as he watched Jewel drift to sleep in his arms, she was now the breath he needed to survive.

An hour later, Leal opened his eyes and let them wander around the familiar room. He sat up on the bed. It was then he saw Jewel studying his face. Her locks hanging wild around her shoulders. "What is it?"

"Please trust me Jewel... for *us*."

She levered himself off the pillows. "Trust is knowing that if you jump off a cliff..." She glanced at the valley and fell silent.

He circled his arms round her bare shoulders and she took a deep breath. "The other person will catch you."

Jewel bit her lip. "Are your arms strong enough for me?" Her amber eyes peered into his. "I trust few."

That explained it. An emotional wound left by an absent and inadequate father that would be pinned on every man who dared love her. How badly had he treated Jewel's mother? How much emotional neglect had she witnessed? Why give up like that? He would tread carefully.

"Give me your hand," he said.

She obliged.

Leal reached for a package he'd left under the pillow and pulled out what looked like a flash disk. He held the black and shiny object out to her. "Let's both start now on this thing called trust. Here."

She took it in her hand. "What's this?"

He also drew out several unopened envelopes and set them on the bed between them. They were all white and blank on the outside. "Something no one knows about. These documents and this key—"

"Key?"

"Yes it looks like a phone chip but it's a key to something important. Those close to me—my family—know nothing about this." He took a deep breath. "I trust you."

He toyed with the items in his hand. "I want to change my life for the better. Mine and the lives of others."

"What do you want to change?"

"Jewel, listen, I'm close to finding the answers I need both personally and with the research I'm doing. I can't tell you everything now. What I thought would take me years is possibly only months away. I've come up with successful possibilities against infertility. This research can change many lives, but it can't get to the wrong people until——"

"What wrong people?"

"Let's talk about that when we're back in New York. But now I need you to hold onto these. There are only two keys that I've created and encrypted. You have one now and the other is safe with me."

Jewel stared down at the sealed documents and the flash disk as he smoothed his hand over hers. She examined one envelope. "Who's Jeff Avent?"

"This answers every question you've ever had about me. Hold all these things for me until we get back to New York. Then let's see what they say together."

"Why?"

"Because, I trust you."

Chapter 9

Jewel took a low seat on the warm carpeted floor across from Leal's patient in the tiny stone hut. Maya, a narrow-faced Himalayan beauty whose face was moist with anxiety took a deep breath before Leal took her blood pressure. She reminded Jewel of a benevolent angel with her straight, shoulder-length hair and round chestnut eyes. Maya lay across a straw bed, padded with sheep's wool in the shadowy space. Across the room, her husband looked on with trusting eyes as Leal's examination of Maya reassured him. He remained mute, with beady eyes firmly on Leal's every interchange with Maya.

Jewel sat a meter away observing doctor and patient. Jewel was not entirely fluent in disease analysis, but she knew the woman was not sick. Maya was a case study for him.

Leal removed the automatic blood pressure monitor from her upper arm and jotted down notes on a pad. Despite his minimal Hindi, Leal had learned the vital words a doctor needed to know and the rest of his conversation was a perplexing mixture of choppy English and even choppier Hindi.

He studied the woman's face. "This'll sting just a little."

Maya's eyes lit up. Her tone strained as she spoke. "Why can't I have children, doctor?"

The husband interjected. "Babies in village very important, doctor."

Leal reached for a clean syringe from a sterilized box and padded the woman's forearm with a soft anesthetic before drawing her blood. "I'll try," he said softly.

Red liquid filled the tiny syringe making Jewel feel like fainting just by watching.

Leal carefully placed the sample in a sterilized box before

smiling at his patient. She looked hopeful; her trust it seems was completely his and for the first time Jewel understood that most people trusted Leal when they met him. He had confidence and assurance.

Though the woman spoke little English, her fearless eyes revealed she wanted this. She wanted to be cured of barrenness, to have children so her husband would glance at her with admiration.

Leal turned to him and asked the husband in English. "How long have you been trying to have a child?"

"Nine years."

"Don't worry, Maya. I'll do what I can," Leal said.

Leal rose to his feet after giving Maya a reassuring gaze. "We'll be back and hopefully, it will be good news."

Jewel and Leal strolled out to a tiny patio around the house. Her face searched Leal's. "What's wrong with Maya, Leal? What sort of research are you doing on her?"

Leal shot her a pinched glance before answering. "She is infertile. This village's fertility rate has been dropping for years and I'm here to find out why."

"I thought infertility was only a problem in the Western world."

He squeezed her hand in his. "It's everywhere. I'm looking for patterns that can help me reverse the condition."

"Are you close?"

He looked at her earnestly before staring at the darkening sky. He zipped his snow suit. A worried look fell on his face. Jewel found herself scrutinizing the sky. Would they make it back before the snow came in? Leal took her arm and led her away from the hut with a reassuring smile. "I hope so, Jewel. Maya may help me find the answers I need. I've just tried a new drug on her so she can have children. I'm calling the drug Tharnex because I want it to be a tarnish remover, removing the stigma of barrenness."

He looked at the sky, his eyes narrowing. "We'd better go."

* * *

Leal held out a hand. "Careful, Jewel."

She glanced at the Dhauladhar mountain range, its snow-clad peaks mesmerizing her. Her backpack was heavy. They'd passed a flowing waterfall, alpine pastures and lush fruit-laden valleys on their way back to meet Vik at Gushal and they were still four miles away.

Jewel stared across the valley.

Leal followed her gaze. "That's the highest point of the trekking route. You can see the Kanga valley from here."

"How high are we?"

"Let's see. Twelve thousand feet above sea level."

She drew in a lungful of air. "Not high enough for you?"

"We'll stop when you are tired."

"I'm not. Remember, I have an athlete's stamina." She rested a few minutes on a stump, hunching for protection against the biting wind.

"How can I forget? It was fascinating watching you."

"After Montpellier, I never thought I would see you again."

He winced. "I had things to work through."

"What things?"

Leal removed her winter glove and kissed her warm palm. "I'm not trying to be secretive."

"Why didn't you try to contact me before Salzburg?"

"I was crazy not to. That's the truth, Jewel."

Leal didn't want to lose the openness she was showing. He glanced up as the wind blew snow in the distant trees and bit his lips. Come on let's move. He scuttled along the top of the slope, with Jewel tailing behind him.

"What is it?" she asked.

"I don't like the look of that wind." He took her hand. "Let's head back down a few hundred feet and see if it eases."

They trekked with steady steps. Their boots ground the snow-covered path as they inched closer to a group of Indian cedars, tall and erect with their horizontal branches. Jewel scrutinized the handsome evergreens, their dark foliage dusted with thick snow. She clutched her windproof hat as more wind bit at her face.

Leal checked his satellite phone. "The forecast calls for snowfall tonight. We should return to Keylong. We'll just have to call Vik and may have to wait before heading to Gushal. I don't like the way the wind has changed."

He took her arm as the gusts howled slashing their faces.

Her eyes glared up at him and she nestled her head on his

shoulder. They sauntered at an easy pace walking with swift steps the way they had come toward Keylong.

"I need to let Vik know we won't meet him," Leal said as he pulled out his cellphone. "We'll have to stay in the village."

Hard snow crunched under their sturdy mountain boots as they footed the tough ground. Leal walked with the silence of forest hunters. Something was plaguing his thoughts, not just the change in the weather.

Jewel pushed forward with measure toward a dry tree stump in the shelter of some woody shrubs and watched Leal try to reach Vik.

She sensed a cold flake fall on her cheek. "It's started, Leal."

Within minutes the snow hailed down, lashing their faces as the wind picked up. Leal drew a set of snow masks from his backpack and placed one over his face. He gave her the second visor. "Here, put this on."

He pulled out a compass and studied it with the skill of a seasoned explorer. "We need to descend to ten thousand feet if we can. We should be able to camp if the wind stays the same."

Jewel studied the towering views of the Kangra valley thousands of feet below them. "Leal, are you sure we can make it?"

He looked into her frightened eyes and smiled. "Yes, we can."

They started the descent. Within an hour and a half, they'd reached a lower range just below ten thousand feet above sea level.

Leal drew out his feature-rich climbing watch. He zipped round and caught the sun's last rays as they disappeared in the wake of the Himalayan range. He turned to face her as the wind tore at their skin. "We won't make it to Keylong before nightfall. We must set up camp here. It'll be dark soon."

Jewel rubbed her knees for warmth. "I thought we weren't far?"

"I took us on a different route. Sorry Jewel, I didn't know the weather would change on us."

He reached in his pocket and grabbed a set of hand warmers. "Here, break this open for your hands. And here is another for your feet."

She took the packs and opened them as instructed. Overwhelmed with nausea and faintness, she tried to shake it off as Leal set his backpack down and pulled out a light tent. He snapped it open and within minutes, it stood steady inviting them from the blistering chill of the Himalayan wind.

When he'd finished, he trudged over to where she was sitting. "I'll call for a helicopter."

Jewel looked ahead of them at the snow-covered tussock grasses. Dwarf trees, small-leafed shrubs and heaths told her they would be their shelter against more winds. Perhaps the only plants that could survive in this climate. She rubbed her frozen hands against the warmth of the packs and made her way toward the windproof tent Leal had set up. Barely able to feel her legs, she sensed the blood pounding in her temples. Even with mountaineering gloves and foot and finger heat packs, her hands against his skin were like ice. She leaped at the sight of a mountain grasshopper and held her breath wishing she possessed enough courage to stay on the mountain for nightfall. Soon darkness began an ominous descent over the horizon.

Leal made a call. "Yes. Search and rescue? We are at six-thousand-and-fifty feet. What's that you say? Okay... okay."

Jewel listened as Leal radioed with the rescue teams. He placed the phone in his seasoned backpack and he held her close. "Don't worry." He kissed her trembling lips. They were warm against his cold skin. "We'll be fine. They'll be here in the morning. The forecast looks okay for tonight. We have to spend the night here. Snow has covered the roads both to Keylong and to Gushal."

Jewel's mind refused to register his soothing words. If only they didn't contradict the fear that was growing inside her. Once inside the safe tent, Jewel edged into him fearing for their lives. Gusts punched at the flimsy-looking-yet-stable tent, whose double-layered frame was fashioned to withstand extreme climates.

Several hours later, darkness engulfed the lone tent on the deserted slope, hugged by the towering mountains. The indomitable Dhauladhar squalls howled and beat at the tent. A snow storm seemed probable. Jewel's face turned ashen and pinched. She wouldn't let fear control her even though the Himalayan climate was one of the coldest biomes in the world because of its high altitude.

She hadn't checked the climate before setting out but was sure the alpine conditions here only rivaled the arctic. Nocturnal temperatures were almost always below freezing.

She cradled her knees for warmth as Leal lit a tiny lamp and cracked open a tin of salty tuna and a bag of dried fruit.

He handed it to Jewel. "Here, eat. I'll just step outside and raise a red flag. It'll make it easier for the teams to spot us in the morning."

Jewel rose terrified. She watched as the wind punched from the outside at the two-person tent. "Don't leave me, Leal."

"I'll be a few minutes."

Food was the last thing on her mind even though her stomach contradicted her words. She settled and cradled a small, sheepskin blanket over her knees, glad Leal had thought of everything and trained for these severe cases. He was a perceptive doctor and it gave her some assurance as to their safety.

She peered through the opening as Leal fired off three flare guns and set up a red flag. A few minutes later, he reappeared through the tent opening allowing in a stinging wind for several seconds. "Done. Now, come here."

He took a seat on the floor of the tent beside her. Reflected light glimmered over his handsome face and Jewel obliged and settled into his waiting embrace. He held her against his shoulder. She followed the rhythm of his heartbeat. "I don't want to be anywhere else but with you, danger or no danger."

"I won't let anything happen to you. I've been mountain climbing more times than I can remember. This kind of thing sometimes happens," he said. "We'll be on a plane back to New York before you know it."

"Thanks, Leal." It was all she could manage to lighten the mood against the gusts punching at their tent.

She heard him chuckle as her head sank under his chin.

"I miscalculated the time it would take us to get down to Gushal. I had a very charming distraction."

Without warning the wind tore at the tent and slashed a tear in the front opening, ripping the entrance open.

"Leal!"

He rose and inspected the damage. "It's okay. It's not broken. Just tore at the zip." He repaired the rip with ease with a strong glue tube and strips of duct tape from his backpack. "It's just a small tear."

Leal was ready for anything including a medical emergency as she watched him stuff his essentials, including his doctor's bag back into the mountain pack and what looked like more mountain equipment. He returned to her side and she settled once more in his arms. Anguish crossed his features.

A shudder passed through her. Was it his nearness or the pain of waiting and praying that rescue would find them soon?

* * *

TWENTY KILOMETERS FROM KEYLONG
THE HIMALAYAS
6:02 A.M.

Leal opened his eyes and fixed his gaze on Jewel. Her breathing steadied in her uneasy sleep. What in heaven's name had caused the short, rapid intakes of breath the night before?

She lay next to him.

Still.

Sinking deeper into a fog of weariness, her slumber soundless, her petite build was bundled in a windproof fleece within an insulated sleeping bag. The sheepskin he'd extended over her before dark slipped off her tiny frame. He spread it over her and sat upright as he unzipped his sleeping bag.

Icy conditions in the snowcapped Dhauladhar mountain ranges could be unforgiving. He knew it well, yet he had asked Jewel to accompany him on this expedition.

At six thousand feet above sea level, and within reach of the Indo-Tibetan border, Keylong, "the land of monasteries" lay several miles on the snow-congested road behind them.

The mountains stretched for miles, dominated by valleys where the river Bhaga meandered. Mountain peaks towered so high, finding small patches of flat terrain in the riveting Buddhist milieu was like locating a stream in a parched desert. A howling wind reverberated outside, beating on the stable tent. Though not as forceful as the one that caused obstruction to their passage back to civilization, it whistled steadily as dawn broke over the Eastern ranges.

Leal bit his lower lip. The peaks were prone to avalanches. Just last year, vicious snowstorms had brought life to a standstill near Rahla Falls more than a hundred kilometers away. How long would they endure without more food supplies? Trapped on an

128

impassable footpath between Kullu Manali and Keylong, they waited for help like elephants resting on sinking sand.

Leal cleared his parched throat as cold air seeped through the gaps between the tent's opening, triggering thirst and a mild throat ache. It was close to freezing on the mountain.

Maybe, less.

He rummaged through his backpack, his hand grazing the water canister.

Empty.

His numbed hands shivered, as cold as Antarctican crystals on an ice cave. He rubbed them together for warmth and reached under his sleeping bag for his windproof gloves. The invasive sound of a growing hostile wind beat against the mountain tent. His nerves remained taut, a nauseous feeling gripping the pits of his stomach. Soon, a frosty chill spread through his body, sapping more of his diminishing strength. It was dawn all right. The sun came up at six. He checked his satellite phone.

6:17 a.m.

Had he slept? They'd stayed warm despite the threatening blizzard that swept the range from the Eastern Himalayas several hours ago. His ears caught the pulsating blade cuts of a faint helicopter. He glanced down at Jewel and nudged her with a gentle hand. "Jewel. They're here."

Her eyes still bleary, struggled to open. She gravitated upwards, rubbing her sleepy eyes with a mittened hand. "They are?" she said, her voice hoarse with anxiety.

Leal managed a faint smile. "Yeah. Must be the chopper I radioed last night. I still can't reach Vik. They'll take us back to Manali."

Leal pushed himself up from the frozen ground and pulled Jewel to her feet. He rubbed his hands along her shoulders. "Come."

They shrugged out of the sleeping bags and scrambled out into the blizzard cloud brought on by the helicopter's rotor blades. Icy snow pelts bit at their faces as the helicopter attempted to land.

They stood immobile, chins raised, within the forceful winter cloud of the slicing chopper's blades that deafened their ears. With hands shielding his eyes from the onslaught force, Leal glanced through the squall and scrutinized the advancing rescue pilot.

129

"*Kya aap theek ho?*" hollered the officer in Hindi.

Leal could barely hear his words, but understood the concerned look on his face. Were they all right?

"Yes!" Leal said. "Thank God, you're here."

The man muttered something in Hindi as Leal and Jewel approached him.

"What did you say?" Leal asked.

The man switched to English. "We only have room for one person."

Jewel shook her head. "No." She stretched her words out in a frenzy of despair. "You can't be serious. We all have to leave now!"

"The helicopter does not have the capacity." The Indian officer's assertive voice bellowed within the clamor. "No. Only one. We'll come back."

Jewel despised the conviction in the pilot's forceful voice. His furrowing brow told her she could not coerce him.

Leal whirled round facing her. "Go with them. I'll come right after you."

"No. We go together. There's another winter storm coming. I can feel it!"

"She's right," said the officer. "Manali just radioed us." He glanced over at his copilot still seated in the driver's seat. The second officer lowered his window in haste. "We need to hurry if I'm to make this climb again."

Leal scanned the four-passenger capacity helicopter before peering into Jewel's eyes, his glimpse firm and demanding, as he gripped her arms. "I'll be right behind you, Jewel. Now, go!"

The pilot tore her out of Leal's grip, the strong man's strength almost throwing her off balance. She shook her head in hysterics, her feet moving at a reluctant pace toward the chopper as the pilot guided her under the rotary blades. "I can't go without him. Leal!"

Leal edged her on with his dauntless eyes. "Go."

Three other terrified mountaineers sat clutching, their seatbelts, their grips knuckled-white, as Jewel took the last seat in the confined space. The pilot slammed a seatbelt around her and hurled the door shut before taking a seat in the cockpit. Jewel's frozen glance begged Leal to consider. Unable to see his full frame in the snow tormented air, he moved toward their mountain tent,

"Leal!"

The accelerating blades muted her cry as Leal reached back inside the tent for her backpack. Within seconds, he reopened the door and placed it at her feet. She peered into his eyes and her toned begged. "Come with me, Leal."

Her hands gripped his broad shoulders, digging into them. Though his look was consoling, she knew her protests could change nothing.

Leal shot the pilots a trusting glare as their hands maneuvered the chopper's controls, before leaning toward her. "I can't. You heard the pilot. There's no room. It's not safe for you and the others."

He reached across and set a fervent kiss on her dry mouth. The dry throbbing of his lips made her shift closer.

"I'll be right behind you," he said. "They're coming back for me."

The pilot clenched the twist grip between the front seats, setting the engine into mobility.

Leal stepped away from the helicopter, thumped the door shut, the clang reverberating in her ears, as he sped toward the blood-red tent.

Jewel's eyes did not leave him once, even as the pilot twisted the cyclic controls, creating a deafening sound from the engine. What was worse, the chopper's dainty engines or the mountain's oncoming blizzard? Leal was mountain savvy, but that wasn't enough to reassure her. Within seconds, the pilot sent the chopper into a sideway ascent at full throttle. The mountain gales picked up momentum, culminating with the helicopter's hastening paddles and tail fins as it ascended skyward.

Her eyes fell back toward the mountain and to the man she had failed.

Could she not see it?

Was it not obvious in his eyes?

Even as the helicopter wrenched her away from Leal, his words still rang in her ears. I'll be right behind you.

She had to believe them.

The helicopter's canopy jolted and slumped nose down a few feet in a pocket of air. Furious wind-speeds catapulted it off its southbound path as Jewel held her breath and found her hands grinding the leather of the seat.

"Not to worry!" the first pilot said.

"Get her back on course!" the second said.

Jewel clung onto her seatbelt besides a petrified elderly woman in mountaineering gear. She glanced down at the steep peaks. Is this it?

"Hang on!" said the pilot. "She's not steady!"

Another colossal gush tossed the chopper to its left.

The pilot fought the controls and slammed the foot pedals. The motion controlled the tail rudder, steadying the helicopter once more as he regulated the amount of sideways thrust. Once vertical, he enhanced the chopper's speed and they rose above terror onto steadier cruising above the Dhauladhars.

Jewel glimpsed through her side window.

Nothing.

Wait!

Leal's vibrant-red snowsuit came into view. He tore at the wind with his gloved palms and hurled himself into the tent that stood steady against nature's forces.

Was it the stare in the man's eyes across from her? Or was it the way voices built around her as each took in the scene on the mountain that brought a stifled scream to her throat.

Her eyes widened in alarm as she witnessed the full magnitude of the mountain's anger.

The woman next to her blasted out a loud gasp.

"Leal." A whimper, not a shout.

It was all she could articulate, as a roaring tsunami of snow scurried down toward what had been her night's lodging. The avalanche crushed the tent, swallowing the canvas as it raced with ferocious volume.

Was it the amplifying blood rushing to her head?

No.

A somber red flag, the tent's alert marker, bolted down with nature's scourge, the only evidence of color hurtling into the depths of the valley.

* * *

"We've to go back. Now!" Jewel screamed at the pilot.

"We can't." His words were faint over the moans of the terrified passengers and buzzing of the blades.

"We can hardly hold the chopper steady." he called back.

Jewel gawked down-frozen in her seat. Helpless. "Didn't you see what just happened?"

I can't breathe!

No!

Oh God, no!

The elderly woman next to her put her arms around Jewel's trembling body. "Have faith. He'll be okay. I have trekked these mountains for years and seen many miracles."

Was she right? Could Leal survive that beast of an avalanche?

"You must have huge faith. I'm afraid I don't have much. I hope you are right," Jewel said.

As she tried to stay calm, the woman's words did nothing to console her.

"We'll be back for him shortly. Hang on."

Silence gripped the tight cabin of the helicopter. Jewel could hear her heartbeat as it thudded in her throbbing eardrums. They sped down the mountain toward Manali. After a treacherous forty minutes, covering close to seven nautical miles at an average altitude of one-thousand-five-hundred feet, they touched down on a flat helicopter pad.

"We made it to Manali," said the pilot, his voice void of emotion.

A shiver shot through Jewel despite the warm blanket the pilots had tossed at her. Her eyes begged for information. "You're going back now aren't you?"

The winds in Manali weren't as fierce as gray dawn streaked the sky. Jewel breathed in deep as the rescue officer helped her out of the chopper and led her to the lone building at one end of the helicopter pad. "Yes, miss, we're going back for him now. From what I observed, he *knows* how to handle himself in the mountains. He'll be fine until we get to him."

Though his words were encouraging, the trepidation in his eyes was clear. The truth they all refused to admit was the chopper had barely escaped.

Three hours later, Jewel held a mug of hot vegetable *dhal*, a lentil dish of spicy soup, as she sat on the porch of the rustic mountain rescue cabin. A checked woolen blanket hung over her shoulders. She tapped her uncontrollable feet on the cedar floors sending a frantic shiver through her nerves. Her ears caught the sound of the helicopter's blades that had set off to find Leal less than an hour ago.

The woman who'd sat beside her glanced out the cabin window and joined her on the porch. Two hours later, the women accepted hot *chai* mug refills. Where was the chopper? Where was her Leal? He had changed something in her for ever. The man who'd unlocked her deepest fears and eased them. She'd not told him how she felt about him. She'd been too sacred.

Her ears caught the faint sound of propelling helicopter blades. Jewel rose. Her mug dropped with a thud, inches from her boots. She raced toward the approaching helicopter, keeping back enough to avoid its wind drift. The aircraft set its beams on the ground. As the door slid open, she scampered closer to the chopper. The pilot who'd rescued them stepped out. The second officer descended after him carrying mountain rescue gear.

She stopped running and took a deep breath. *Where's Leal?* She'd expected to see three men.

There were only two.

* * *

SEVERAL HOURS LATER

The ceiling fan above the superintendent's head swirled above them like a bird of prey. It rustled in bothersome rotating movements. Even though the temperature outside remained below freezing, Jewel needed air in her lungs.

"Miss Carlone, I need to ask you some very important questions."

Jewel's tear stained eyes, bloodshot from the pain in her temples, fired the officer a look. "What do you want to know?"

"Why were you on that mountain near Keylong?"

"Is it a crime?"

He cleared his throat. "Your cooperation will keep you out of trouble. Now let me rephrase, why take Mr. Trelles alone to a dangerous spot when forecasts had warned of bad weather?"

Jewel's hands clenched and unclenched on her thighs under the mahogany table in the secluded room at the Kullu Manali police station. She moved forward, her voice cracking with irritation. "Leal wanted to visit a patient in Keylong. We had no access to weather forecasts."

"Ah yes. Our 3G networks are perhaps not as sophisticated as those in New York. Miss Carlone, why were you with him?"

"I was working for him as a photographer."

The superintendent rubbed the back of his neck. "Did you know Dr. Trelles was married?"

Had she heard right? *Was?* Was he talking about Leal? *Married?* Had they stopped the hunt for him? Was this an announcement of his death? Her vision blurred for a second and pain gripped her chest. She shook her head. "Have you found him? Please tell me you've found him—"

"Dr. Trelles is gone. I'm sorry. He's dead," he said without emotion.

Both her hands flew to cover her mouth. A stiffening invaded her limps and her shoulders dropped as she fought back blinking tears. Squeezing her eyes shut, she rubbed her temples as the blood drained out of her face. Her breath hitched in her throat. Was Leal really gone? *No! Oh God no!*

Her body jerked as she dug her fingers into her palms. Jewel shot up in one sudden movement. "No! Go back and get him! You need to help him! Please!"

The superintendent buzzed an alarm on his desk and two cops progressed toward her. The female cop set a hand on her shoulder. Cheeks flaming Jewel took a startled step back. Leal had to be alive. He had to…he couldn't leave her.

The second cop drew near. Jewel's feet moved slowly until her back hit the wall and she slid to the cold concrete. Her knees drew to her chest and she gripped them tight as the light around her dimmed. She faded into a dark place and coldness hit her core.

Stunned silence gripped the room.

"Miss Carlone?"

She glanced up.

"Miss Carlone, please."

She tried to move and held the female cop's arm to steady herself as she moved back into her chair. The cop set a bottled water in front of her.

Several moments passed before the superintendent spoke. He turned to the other cops. "You may leave now."

Jewel took a sip of water her temples throbbing.

He cleared his throat. "We need your cooperation. As I was saying, did you know Dr. Trelles was married?"

Jewel digested his words a second time as if she'd not heard

135

him right the first. "He wasn't married."

"That's probably what he said to you, or forgot to say."

"Leal couldn't have been married. He said nothing about it the week and a half we were together. You're lying."

"Dr. Trelles' widow is here. Her name is Myranda Vaux and she's here to make a statement."

Jewel sank deeper in to the chair.

The questions swamped her mind and color drained from her face. "I don't believe you. Leal never told me he had a wife."

"Leal? I see you were familiar with one another."

"In New York, it's quite customary for people to go by the first name, officer Raj Sanjit."

His name had been staring at her, donned on him by his Chief of Police identity pin that hung on his breast pocket above a series of medals. She frowned at the way he wore his police cap, and his starched suit spoke of a man used to receiving respect from every human being he encountered.

A deep-weighted exhalation left officer Sanjit's throat. "You were alone on a mountain with a married man, and given Mr. Trelles wealth..." Sanjit cleared his throat again. "Means you went to black mail him, especially given his condition."

"What in the world are you talking about?" Jewel rose from her seat. "What condition?"

"Leal had a bad fear of heights."

Her eyebrows gathered. "That's loaded."

"Calm down, Miss Carlone. Dr. Trelles had never been on a mountain. You, on the other hand, being an experienced athlete and a skilled skier, intentionally placed Leal's life in danger."

How did this man know her affairs? He was lying and having produced no concrete evidence to support his accusations. Jewel's voice resonated with fury. "Officer Sanjit, I refuse to talk any further without a legal representative."

"Sit down, Miss Carlone, that isn't necessary. We're just trying to file the police report of Dr. Trelles' death. It's just procedure."

"Not where I'm from."

"Well, let me remind you, you are in India. As I was saying, isn't it true you went on the mountain to blackmail Dr. Trelles and coerce a hundred-thousand dollars from Trelles Industries."

"Why would I do that? What would I blackmail him with?"

"You're a beautiful woman. Anyone can see that."

A frown formed on Jewel's face.

Sanjit cleared his throat. "Services of a sexual nature in exchange for money."

"I'm not talking to you without an attorney."

"His widow has brought forward a charge that you're in serious financial trouble, money that can save your mother's ill condition and pay for her medical bills."

He tossed a set of papers on the table, her recent bank statement and a medical bill she'd paid for her mother's operation on her credit card weeks ago. Her eyes fell on a sum of money that had crawled onto her account just twenty-four hours ago. A hundred-thousand dollars from Trelles Industries. How did the inspector know details of her life? How could Leal leave her like this? Jewel's face reddened. "I refuse to talk to you without representation or Citizen's Services from the US Embassy."

"That won't be necessary. We're all friends here."

She brought down a fist to the table. "It *will* be necessary."

There was no reason to talk with the senseless officer. He was fabricating a story. What was he getting at and how did he have her financial details? Where had he fished the information about her mother's health condition?

Jewel fell into her seat as a well-presented woman entered the room followed by a discreet man. The two paced toward two empty chairs across from Sanjit's desk.

Sanjit lifted his eyes. "Ah, just in time. I was about to inform Miss Carlone that we can make all this go away quietly and that you are prepared to drop the charges if she returns the money."

Jewel's eyes widened at the sight of the woman she now recognized as Myranda, and a man Jewel assumed was her legal counsel. Wasn't this the same woman who had offered her a job? Her stomach flipped over hard. Was this Leal's wife? A perplexing energy stirred within her dangerous like a live wire. Her every muscle began to tense and her heart thudded.

Myranda's red flaming hair piled on top of her head and her frame was wrapped in an expensive snow coat.

"The penalty for involuntary manslaughter carries a heavy price," Sanjit said.

Anger thundered through Jewel. It heated her flesh and poured into her fingers. "Man slaughter!"

"While we can't yet prove it, I think you should listen to Ms. Vaux's proposal."

What was happening? Not only had she just lost the man she loved, but she was being accused of his untimely death and throwing in prostitution as well? Her quickening pulse was unbearable and her eyes blinked rapidly. She forced an intake of breath just not to faint.

The neat lawyer-type besides Myranda spoke up, watching her. "I see you've seen a copy of your bank details dated just a few hours ago. Due to the circumstances surrounding the death of Dr. Trelles, we're obliged to investigate all recent transactional dealings. We found that Leal recently employed you. A large sum of money in the amount of a hundred-thousand dollars was deposited on your account from Trelles Industries. Surely that wasn't your weekly fee for photography."

"You put it there." Her anger was directed at a quiet Myranda. "You placed that money on my account for photo services you wanted and to which I never agreed."

Myranda glanced her way, her voice ringing with patronization. "Why would I pay you for a service you have not rendered unlike the services you performed for my husband?"

Her heartbeat raced. "I can't believe this! You handed me this offer." Jewel padded her pockets for the unsigned document.

Nothing.

She'd walked out of Myranda's hotel suite without the documents and had no proof of their conversation. Her eyes pored into Myranda. "You can't get away with this. You put that money there."

"Ahem..." The attorney who'd never introduced himself cleared his throat. "As I was saying, we're prepared to come to the bottom of this and not drag Mrs. Trelles through any more grief. We're prepared to solve this issue quietly. The police here will work with us on this little criminal matter. We're willing to drop the charges."

Jewel leaned back. "Why would you do that?"

The lawyer pushed back his shoulders. "If you sign this document that attests to your witness of Dr. Trelles death, we'll simply declare all this a misunderstanding."

It didn't make sense. Two minutes ago, she was being hailed as an extortionist, a loose woman and now they wanted to make sure Leal was dead with her testimony. "Why?"

Myranda set a hand on the lawyer's shoulder. "Let me explain it to you, pretty face. I know you not only seduced my husband into going on a mountain when he was ill-skilled in mountaineering behavior. You also wanted his money."

"I didn't know there was money to be had."

"Here's the deal. He's gone. I'm in mourning. I want to bury my husband and leave this whole tragedy behind me. I need closure. If you sign this document claiming you were a witness to his death, just like all the people who were on that rescue helicopter, then, my pretty face, I'll leave you alone. Is that getting into that meaty head of yours?"

Jewel swallowed hard. She hadn't seduced Leal. He never wore a ring and he'd never mentioned his marriage. Disbelief forbade any tears and grief his death should have caused. She wouldn't stand for another charge as she watched the woman who called herself his wife. This was all wrong. Leal was dead, and they wanted her to seal his death with her signature.

Jewel cowered backward and edged into her seat. She couldn't believe the finality of her next words. "Did you find... his body?"

Myranda shoved forward. "You took Leal on a dangerous hike, knowing full well he was not capable of such activity. That avalanche killed him."

Jewel shot her a glance. "How well did you know him, Myranda?" Her lips fell dry and her race with Leal in Austria came to mind. "Obviously not well enough, otherwise, you'd have known he was remarkable when it came to winter sports."

The look in Myranda's face told Jewel she'd hit a sore nerve in a very questionable marriage. Perhaps it was best to walk away from these people, especially if Leal was now gone.

Jewel's eyes filled with fondness for the doctor she had loved and lost. She wiped an angry tear from her eye. "Leal was a brilliant doctor. He feared nothing, not even the mountain."

The room fell silent for several seconds. Myranda's lawyer maintained strong eye contact. "Nevertheless, the offer stands, sign the document and no formal charges will be made."

"I won't."

The American lawyer's tone rang with alarm. "Miss Carlone, you're in a foreign country with foreign laws. If you sign this document, you walk away free. The police record will be held at Trelles Industries and never surface. You can go home and forget you ever met the doctor. As a bonus, Trelles will not hold you responsible for the hundred-thousand dollars. See it as gratitude."

"For what?"

He had no answer. How could he? They needed her silenced. *Is this the trust that Leal was talking about?* How could Leal have lied to her about Myranda? She'd been right. Trusting Leal had come back to haunt her just as it had always haunted the Carlone women. The thought of leaving this nightmare behind was all-too enticing. If only Kaya were here. What would she do?

With her mother's medical expenses and her gymnast career over, money was hard to come by. The only dignity she had left was at the mercy of a conniving cooperation and a pissed-off wife. Leal was gone, but then again, he'd never been hers. She couldn't even afford legal help if she had to get it.

If she didn't sign the document, a whole legal battle would begin and judging from what she stood up against—an army of corporate lawyers—and she wouldn't win. They would always brand her as the woman who tried to blackmail the billionaire. If they had power to seduce civil authorities from Kauai to New York for her private information, what else could they do?

Was it the fan overhead? Or the annoying way Sanjit's voice rang in her ears? Or was it Myranda's hawking glare.

No, it was Leal's betrayal. The one thing she couldn't ingest. Somewhere buried on that mountain, Leal rested, oblivious to the fact he'd taken to his grave the smallest spark of trust that had begun to brew in her belly.

Trust, you say, Leal?

Perhaps it was the strain of the last twenty-four hours or the angst in her heart. Her trembling hands reached for the papers and with a shaky grip she put her mark on the horizontal line.

Chapter 10

The New York skyline hung dense with thickening fog. Jewel glanced out the square windows of her New York apartment grateful for a Fifteenth Street apartment in Park Slope, a neighborhood that wasn't on her shortlist when she'd moved from her mother's house.

She'd overlooked the vast stretches of greenery, the countless restaurants and bars and varied retail prospects. How she'd battled the melodrama that coincided with locating the ideal New York apartment. The typical room size was that of a prison cell. She wanted to do better and keep the price low in her means. Having received inheritance money from her maternal grandmother, she tackled the task. She'd balanced the advantages between luxury high rises with intimidating doorkeepers dressed in crisp black uniforms, buildings that imposed a five floor hike to her front door. The result had been, a quiet street in the neighborhood among families, nothing to draw attention to herself and a place to lock away feelings she'd abandoned.

Jewel stuffed her duffel bag with toiletries, needing only the basics for three days in Saint Louis. She filled her lungs with air, a deep sigh strengthening her core. Would the flight be on time, or would fog cause delays? Spring hadn't arrived even in mid-April.

Kaya sat on a swivel chair swinging softly by the window and watched Jewel pack the last of her trip items. She rose and paced to Jewel's side. "I'm so proud of you. After all the hard work and now you're an award-winning photographer off to another conference as a keynote speaker."

Jewel managed a smile and Kaya studied her as she

straightened her cotton blouse and slipped on a dark caramel blazer.

"Think I'm ready now," Jewel said.

She stepped into her dark room that led off the main living area. Few still used dark rooms. Jewel found she could still use it for restoration and nondestructive testing, like the magnetic particle inspection she'd done on old photographs of her Hawaiian family.

Jewel had insisted on a two-bedroom apartment for the added advantage of a separate room so she could work at home. Kaya followed her and gazed at her collection of captured moments, crafted settings and those more candid.

Kaya's eyes fell on a photograph taken of the Himalayan landscape, one that had never found a resting place outside the dark room. "Will we ever talk about India?"

Jewel scowled, fighting a strong determination not to delve into the subject. She switched on the optical apparatus, a modern kit that projected negatives on the back wall.

"You've just developed that image, haven't you?" Kaya said.

"I was going through stuff for the presentation, that's all," Jewel said.

"You've never been the same since you returned from India," Kaya said shrugging. "It shouldn't matter now. You're the most sought-after photographer in New York. Don't underestimate that."

Jewel turned her back and grabbed a few negative boxes from a bottom drawer before welcoming her friend's compliment. "Some would say so. It's not every day you get to go to one of the country's largest photography conferences."

"And not just as a participant, I might add. As a keynote speaker."

"It's a front. One day, they'll realize I can't take pictures. It's luck."

"It's not luck. It's damn good photograph taking. Jewel, it's not how rough the fall is that sharpens us, but how well we rise after the fall."

Jewel searched through more supplies in the dark room.

"Something in you changed in India and it wasn't because you lost Leal," Kaya said.

Jewel's face filled with horror and shot Kaya an alarmed look.

"I'm sorry. That was insensitive of me," Kaya said.

Jewel selected a stack of photographs from the drying line. "Let's not talk about it. I need a couple more developments. My flight leaves at three. That gives me an hour before I need to go. I'll develop this batch before I go."

Kaya watched as the images appeared one by one on the paper as she approached. Jewel laid the photographs out to dry on the line with care. Even in the dim light, the image of Leal's face came into focus on the wet stock paper. She couldn't forget him. However much Jewel wanted to toss the subject to one side, she'd thought of him every day after leaving India.

Kaya fingered a photograph. "This is Leal six years ago in Saint Johann." She picked it up. "Despite everything and how he kept the truth from you there was something amazing about him. But I'm sure you knew that."

Jewel pursed her lips. "He had one of those faces, a mixture of adventure and mystery, all at the same time. I didn't know it was possible of anyone. You tried to make me forget him."

"Only because I was mad at myself for not getting to you sooner, especially when they made you sign that paper. The conspiring witch now sits on his fortune like a hen waiting for eggs to hatch."

Jewel's lips twitched at the mention of Myranda. "Let's not go into it again."

"As much as I didn't like that Leal kept so much from you, I hate to see that woman get away with everything. It's not right."

Jewel took the photograph from her hands. "There's nothing we can do about it now. Listen, I've got to go."

She turned off the equipment and the lights and paced toward the living room.

Kaya followed and slumped into the couch and Jewel turned her head when she heard the doorbell. "Must be the taxi."

"It'll be okay?" Kaya said.

"Yeah. I know."

Kaya edged closer and lowered her voice. "Jewel, what really happened on that mountain? Because I don't believe the things the Indian police reported."

Jewel's eyes welled up. "I don't have time, Kaya. I have to go."

She twitched her lips, her face frowning. "I know it's difficult, but you've not let go of something that happened in

143

India. You walk around with it daily. Tell me, maybe I can help you."

The doorbell rang again.

Kaya ignored it. "It's damped your passion."

Jewel took a deep breath. "I need to go." She picked up her duffel bag.

Kaya reached for her arm. "Let me help. We've been friends since we were in the sixth grade. We've shared everything since we were twelve. Why shut me out on this?"

Jewel writhed free, strode to the windows to close the shutters and checked the rest of the apartment as Kaya watched her from the middle of the room.

Kaya followed her. "I was wrong, Jewel. It's taken a while, but I now admit it. You really loved him didn't you?"

Jewel couldn't face her.

"What happened after the men from the helicopter came back from the search?" Kaya said.

If she were to make her flight she needed to give Kaya a response. Her best friend was headstrong and could drill for an answer as skillfully as an engineer at an oil rig. She set a hand over Kaya's. "I couldn't believe he was gone. I insisted they go back and look. I wanted to go too. They wouldn't let me at first, and then... they agreed."

"What happened?"

"We found the tent, but no Leal. We surveyed the area for several hours and three other rescue teams joined us. I went to New Delhi the next day to the US Embassy to get help. They told me it wasn't my affair but the Trelles family's. I went back to Manali, paid the same rescue teams all the money in my account to go back. Vik came with me for three days. We searched until the teams gave up. I was broke so I couldn't go on. As the months have grown into years, I guess I have accepted it."

"I'm sorry, Jewel."

"The strange thing is that Leal's wife just disappeared after the papers were signed. As if she welcomed his death, without an ounce of sympathy or a tear."

"Maybe she was in shock. Or maybe she didn't love him."

Jewel mused on the words. "Maybe. It doesn't matter anymore. Leal is dead. But... I'm not sure what to do with this."

She inched to her desk and pulled a stack of envelopes sealed in a reusable zipper storage bag. "Leal gave this to me the day

144

before he died."

"What is it?"

"Some stuff Leal left with me. A flash disk I think and envelopes addressed to a man named Jeff Avent."

Kaya studied the contents. "Do you think he meant to deliver these?"

"I don't know. Question is... what do I do with them?"

* * *

NEPHTYSIS VACCINE & DRUG RESEARCH CENTER
UNDISCLOSED LOCATION

"That's 'Attempt Five-Hundred'," said a man in the white coat.

"And?"

"It failed."

The scientist behind him scurried to the mixing counter in the sealed-off drug research center and sighed deeply. "It's mutating isn't it?"

"Yes," said the first scientist, a blond woman with deep-set brown eyes like two bronze coins. Her silky, straight hair was long and was worn in a utilitarian style. Tall with a lean build, she had full lips and her skin was deeply tanned. "It's more aggressive and mutating faster than we have ever seen."

"What's the total tally now according to *Operation Nephtysis?*"

"Global, ten-thousand women and girls by our recent calculations and what's worse, is they don't know it. We do not know how this disease is spreading."

The hooded man slammed his fist into the counter. "Damn it! So now it's global and migrating at two hundred percent! This disease is killing us softly."

"Within twenty-five years, if we are lucky thirty, infertility will wipe out the global population."

* * *

Kaya took the items from Jewel's hand. "Legally they belong

145

to his widow. Or the addressee."

"I can't be involved in this. I either burn it or forget them, like I've done him."

"These look important. Why would he give it to you?"

Jewel shrugged.

The doorbell sounded again.

"Must be something he didn't want anyone to see." Kaya said. "Jewel, he trusted you."

"No, Kaya, he lied to me."

Jewel looked into the eyes of her dearest friend. "What do I do with these?"

Kaya rubbed her chin. "Do we know anything about his family?"

Jewel picked up her travel items and paced to the door. "I don't know anything. The man was a phantom from the day I met him. He just appeared and disappeared, first in Montpellier, then in..." She took a deep breath. "He was harder to read and digest than a computer product manual."

"I know it's hard, but this is something that Weston can help us with. He may know how this sort of thing works."

A streak of pain appeared on Jewel's face. "You would ask him?"

"It's up to you, Jewel. Do you want answers?"

Jewel searched Kaya's eyes for an inkling of advice. She wanted answers, but was it worth the emotional turmoil? Her heart was yet to recover.

"I'll talk to him," Kaya said.

"No, drop it."

"I'm opening these."

"No, Kaya."

"Let's put this Leal thing to bed once and for all. I want my best friend back. I hate seeing you like this."

Kaya eyed Jewel closely and her hand ripped open the six-year-old documents.

* * *

"You shouldn't have done that Kaya," Jewel said as they stepped out into the hallway. Jewel turned to lock her front door. She took a few steps toward the elevator, before turning back to her front door. She keyed it open and swung it open.

"What is it?" Kaya said.

"I forgot something. By the way, I don't want to know what's in that envelope and on the flash disk. I can't get involved again, Kaya."

Jewel disappeared into her apartment, tossing her Nikon camera gear on the floor and scampered around the entryway. "Where did I leave it?"

She paced to the living room. The fog was dying down and her eyes caught sight of a large, black framed photograph, mounted adjacent to an antique library bookcase near the kitchen door. Just two weeks ago, the photograph depicting Arches National Park in Utah had won the International Photography Awards. It had been a difficult shoot due to the timing and lighting. What was it the judges had said? That they fell in love with the way her eye had captured the arches, spires, and pinnacle of the soft red sandstone deposited a hundred-and-fifty million years ago.

For a second, she forgot her mission as her eyes blinked, resting on a shoebox hidden on top of the shelf concealed by a burnished, pothos vine plant. She moved her feet across the floor woodwork and placed one foot on the bottom shelf, reaching for the sooty shoe box. She glanced up as her hands gripped the box.

She sighed and Jewel pulled it down. The amber box tumbled off the shelf, its corner stubbing the bare toes within her slip on stilettos. "Ouch! Damn you."

"You okay in there?" Kaya said re-entering. "The cab's waiting."

"Please go down and tell him I'm on my way."

Kaya retreated.

Jewel kicked off her left shoe and gripped her throbbing toe as she sat on the edge of the sofa. The box had spilled its contents of old photographs, ticket stubs, and discarded memories from her India trip. She took a moment and looked down at the cluttered items. Her knees fell by the box. Even today, the sandalwood fragrance of the incense sticks she had placed within tingled her nostrils. She began placing the items one by one back into the shoebox. Her eyes caught sight of the ticket stub she'd not seen in nearly six years. The stub from that fateful day of her train ride from Manali to New Delhi and the day her heart unwillingly said goodbye to Leal.

An older, duo-toned photograph of a young man, barely twenty-five rested behind the ticket stub. His dark blond hair fell over his eyes in an unguarded moment, as they caught the late sunset as it disappeared over the Dhauladhar ranges. A coerced smile played on his handsome face.

It was one of the first pictures she had ever taken of Leal and had not laid eyes on it in six years. Her heart fluttered at the coincidence that in just a few hours, she was heading to the same place Leal had described as one of his favorite cities in the US, Saint Louis. A reflective historical gem, he had called it. A tear welled up in her eyes and fell on the photo. She wiped it away with her bare hands and her eye caught the corner of a New York Times news clipping Kaya had sent her when she returned from India.

Billionaire Dies in Indian Mountain Avalanche. Years of Research into Mysterious Disease, Nephthysis, Dies with Him.

Confirmed sources claim Leal Trelles had progressed beyond any researcher into nephthysis, a fertility disease that has been kept secret and continues to puzzle scientists.

In a press conference at Trelles Industries yesterday, spokespersons denied knowledge of any research the late CEO had conducted...

The government refuses to comment on any knowledge of the disease breakout, but sources say nephthysis first hit American soil twenty-five years ago and is a sleeper virus currently wiping out portions of the human population...

Jewel closed the box and rose. She fit her stiletto back on, and placed the shoe box back on the shelf. With the photograph still in hand, she scampered to the kitchen, pulled open a jammed drawer, and found a lighter. She lit the photo and watched it char to ashes on the white counter top.

"Why did I trust you?"

Chapter 11

A bead of sweat rolled down Jewel's neck as she stood under the spotlight. Preparing for an audience interested in photography was still new to her, more intimidating than putting a dance routine together and performing it before thousands of spectators. In an arena, the light camouflaged her anxiety and the cheers accelerated her adrenaline. Here, her shyness was exposed. She couldn't hide behind Chopin or clever ballet steps. Whereas she'd trained in gymnastics most of her life, she'd practiced professional photography for half the time.

The preparation had kept her up three nights in a row, having to remember exposure levels she'd used, or whether she'd balanced the right shutter speeds. As an award winner, she'd be expected to come across as an expert in outdoor photography, a topic she would be addressing in front of four hundred participants.

She would face students, professionals in her field, critics, and the media to discuss her award-winning portfolio. The audience expected her to talk not only of her prizewinning shots, but to present her entire professional career. Leal's picture, a portrait that had been awarded the International Photography Award two years ago in the 'Personality' category, was in the folder. Jewel was familiar with winning awards. She'd done so a few times in the last couple of years. Today was different. She had to talk about *him*.

She'd rarely spoken of Leal and never mentioned him to anyone. Her audience would want to know what inspired her to take his picture. She would rush past it. *I'm sure they're more interested in magical scenery shots.* After signing the documents that confirmed Leal's death, she'd felt like an amateur at life.

She'd not submitted Leal's image for the competitions. Her mother had sent in her best pictures. Jewel welcomed the encouragement and the sacrifices and it didn't matter whether it was rhythmic gymnastics, or prancing around with a Nikon strapped to her neck, Mahina believed in her.

Jewel pulled out her tablet.

"I'll connect that if you wish, Miss," the stage manager said.

"Thank you."

Jewel booted the machine and scrolled through her thirty-minute presentation.

She sighed. *You can do this.*

Jewel glimpsed at Leal's photograph and scrolled through her captions, her mind battling thoughts of the mental strength it had taken to get this point.

After India, Jewel had returned to New York and received treatment for trauma and depression. She'd stayed at her mother's house and refused help from anyone for two weeks, resurfacing from her bedroom for showers and Kaya's occasional company. When she complained of body aches and migraines, Mahina called a doctor and later paid for a psychiatrist to examine her deteriorating condition. The truth was Jewel never breathed a word to Mahina about Leal, only that she'd witnessed a traumatic accident. Three months later, Jewel resumed her courses at the New York Institute of Photography and found strength in joining the local gym. She shied away from rhythmic gymnastics, opting for a less-strenuous routine with artistic gymnastics.

Two years later, she graduated and was recruited as a freelance photographer by National Geographic, then by the *New Yorker*. Jewel took many trips abroad and around the country capturing rare and unusual pictures of anything that inspired her, possibly stemming from emotions caused by loss, and exposed after the industry began to take note of her work. The money had been slow at first, but by the end of her second year out of school, she could command five figures for projects, had a list of clients ready to pay up to sixteen thousand dollars for her fine art, and she'd also had two gallery shows, one in New York and one in Seoul. She repaid her mother's investment and insisted on putting her in a house uptown, on a rent-to-buy scheme, close to Mahina's sister.

Jewel never pursued information on Leal, his work or family after India. Though she sought closure, distance from the events was as unsatisfying as imprisoning a hunting tigress in a cage. No one from Myranda's office ever contacted her after signing the documents. Aside from the flash disk and documents she held on to, and the picture she'd developed; she'd buried Leal on an Indian mountain and deep in the dungeons of her heart.

Jewel stopped scrolling through the slides and set her presentation in show mode. She took a sip of cool water that had been provided by the conference organizers. The stage manager adjusted the platform for her talk, casting a sizzling spotlight over her face. More people than she expected began a steady flock into the auditorium as she glanced out at the rows of filling seats. Jewel rehearsed her session titled "Imaging, Light and Technology".

Her legs trembled as she took her seat on stage waiting for the cue to begin. She placed her sweaty palms over her knees and prayed she would be able to stand again without breaking into stage fright. Jewel pushed feelings of incompetence to one side and took a deep breath. Her real skills may be on a different kind of stage, but she'd mastered this too, as any other creative expertise to which she'd set her focus.

Leal believed in you.

Within minutes, the four hundred seating auditorium, with its clamor of conversation and shuffling feet had been filled to overflowing. The stage manager signaled her.

Jewel rose. "Good afternoon, ladies and gentleman," she began. "Many times, I've wondered what brought me on the path of photography, but I can say one thing. I didn't start out this way. I had my eyes set on a different kind of stage."

The audience remained numb.

She paused and watched as the last few participants took their seats. Jewel couldn't help noticing a man seated in the third row who kept an intrusive gaze on her. It would have almost been rude, if she'd not been the center of the auditorium's focus. *Darn it! Don't tell me you're a photo critic? I hate photo critics! I just took a darn picture!*

She tore her eyes off him and tapped a nervous finger on the podium. "Today, I would like to talk to you about my inspiration for photography and my portfolio of musings as diverse as they may be."

So far, so good.

For twenty minutes she took the audience through shots of a humid wadi, a desert stream taken in the United Arab Emirates. Then on a shot of perching birds at sunset in the Pantanal of Mato Grosso in Central-Western Brazil and a series of shots taken at Lake Drummond, the mighty Great Dismal Swamp in Virginia. These places had taught her about nature and life. Finally, she moved on to a few favorite portraits. Her mother's sister, a graceful middle-aged woman. Then Kaya's son, a bubbly five-year-old.

And then... *Leal.*

The last photograph she'd taken of him.

She glanced up. With her throat dry, she thirsted for water, much less for it to be over soon. Jewel searched the onlooking faces, hoping an adrenaline rush would keep her going.

"Was this someone you knew?"

A casual question from an intrigued observer in the audience.

Jewel managed a weak smile, grateful that she wasn't leading a one way discussion. "Someone I knew long ago."

"Miss Carlone, I admire your use of depth of field and the way you have captured the sunset light on your subject's face. Could you explain why you chose to use sepia as a filter on this photo?" continued the intrigued woman in the front.

"It was a timeless shot. I look to capture thoughts and emotion. I believe in the photographic principle of allowing the image to communicate something in the photographer."

"What was in your mind Miss Carlone?" asked the woman.

"While I stood on a mountain side overlooking the large basin of the Leukental valley in Austria, the contrast between the freezing temperatures and the warm expression on my friend's face struck me as one of those moments you don't ever want to let go. Photography allows us to keep those memories."

"Was your friend sad, happy, musing?" asked a keen student in the back of the auditorium. "It reminds me of the expression in the Afghan Girl photograph, intense, yet captivating."

You have no idea. I never really knew what Leal was thinking!

"You can say that," she said shifting her feet. "I like to leave it at this, a picture of a good friend lost in his thoughts, yet aware that he was being watched."

"How well did you know him?" asked the brown-haired man she'd noticed earlier in the third row.

Jewel blinked from the bright lights and squinted to gain a better look at the observer. His expression was nonchalant, almost poker-faced. "How well do you really ever know anybody?" came her attempt to avoid the topic.

"The fact that you'd want to snap this intriguing photo shows there must've been more to it."

Jewel wrung her hands as she spoke. *I won't be bullied by this rude journalist, critic, or student, whatever he is.*

"Sir, it's just a picture of my friend. If there are no more questions, I'm happy to talk through the rest of my portfolio and take more questions at the end."

"Miss Carlone?"

Damn it! What does he want now?

She forced a smile. "Yes, Mr....?"

"Trelles. All I want to know is how well you knew my brother?"

Jewel jerked her head back. It was involuntary, but all she could do to keep from falling of the stage.

* * *

"I'm sorry if I said something wrong. I really liked your presentation; you're truly a remarkable photographer."

The man spoke with an American accent, but Jewel couldn't exactly place it. She took another sip of the iced lemon water, a bug-eyed look crossing her face. She'd escaped to a high-rise, top of the Riverfront cafe on the twenty-eighth floor of the Millennium Hotel. She'd fled after the session, hoping to grab an early dinner, escape the scrutinizing glare of Leal Trelles's brother, while taking in the revolving views of downtown Saint Louis.

Jewel glanced upward at the stranger who'd appeared unannounced. "You're blocking my view."

He glanced behind him for a second. "Now that wouldn't be right for a photographer. I'm sorry." He shot his head round before smirking. "Let's see... your panoramic view of the Gateway

Arch and I think that's Busch Stadium. Are you enjoying the upscale American cuisine served here?"

Extremely handsome, he looked to be about six foot-two. Healthy skin, a tall, boyish build with broad shoulders, and a thick dark-brown haircut, swept up in a businesslike style. Athletic with visibly defined muscle tones under his elegant shirt that hugged at the waist, his good stature showed energy.

"You seem the kind to get what you want. Let me guess, you're a photo critic from New York?" Jewel said.

"No to the former and yes to the latter. Well, sort of. I'm from Venice, Italy."

"Venice?"

"You sound surprised."

She studied his face. "I am. Leal hardly lived in Venice."

"Leal lived most of his life in New York. Our grandmother is Italian, and brings the delightful blood of Roman heritage into the family."

She took another sip. "I see."

"I'm sorry for interrupting your talk. I just wanted to make sure I got to speak to you."

"Why?"

He eased into the seat opposite her uninvited.

"I don't recall asking you to join me, Mr. Trelles."

"Call me Cyrus."

"No, I'll call you, Mr. Trelles."

He shot her a cocky grin. "Of course."

A waiter came by and Cyrus ordered a beer.

"How did you find me here? I assume you have a mild interest in photography?"

"It's easy to spot a New Yorker in Saint Louis."

"Hm..."

"I followed you."

"Then you know that we New Yorkers are well versed in dealing with stalkers."

"Point taken."

Jewel couldn't explain what she thought of the man. His good looks were distracting in a way she'd not expected and he seemed polite enough, sure of his alluring presence. His hazel eyes smiled as he spoke, taking the edge off of the awkward moment. Was he really Leal's brother? Aside from the sparkle in his eyes, the resemblance was as thin as fax paper, yet their height and

155

perhaps physique was similar. Or had it been so long, she'd forgotten.

The waiter returned with a frosty Pilsner and set it on the table. He left, promising to return to take their orders.

"So who's older?"

"Excuse me?"

"Who was older? You, or Leal?"

"I was. By about a minute."

"You were twins?"

"Non-identical twins. Fraternal twins."

He smiled and Jewel held her breath. Each brother could smile with their eyes and no lip movement.

Cyrus studied her face. "You're suspicious. You don't take any nonsense from anyone."

Jewel averted his stare and should've been grateful. The mystery of Leal's family that had followed her after Leal's death had finally dissipated with the appearance of Cyrus. She tossed him an unconscious flirtatious smile. "Listen, I don't know what you want to speak to me about." She took a deep breath and allowed her sentiments to transform. "I'm glad to finally meet the only member I ever have of Leal's family. I'm not sure I can give you any information as you requested earlier about your brother."

"All I asked was how well you knew him," Cyrus said.

He was forward, but not as intrusive as most men she'd known. Perhaps she'd always been hard on any man she'd met after Leal. She edged back in her seat and sighed deeply. "Not very well. I wish I'd known him better."

Cyrus swallowed whatever emotion he'd been harboring, slid his hand across the table and stopped it before it reached hers. "I'm sure Leal wanted to know you more."

She blushed.

"Leal spoke highly of you," Cyrus continued.

"I didn't realize he spoke about me to anyone in his family. We knew each other a short time. Were you two close?" she said.

"Not as most. You know what they say about blood."

The waiter returned to take their orders and Cyrus asked for more time. "I must admit, Leal failed to tell me how exquisite you are, but I see it's hard to put you into words."

A flush crept across Jewel's cheeks. "Cyrus, I'm sorry about your loss. In fact, I haven't spoken of Leal in six years. At least until I heard that they, the conference organizers, wanted me to

156

speak about this picture. I took it shortly before he invited me to go to India." Her grief-stricken eyes met his. "As you know, that's where everything happened."

Cyrus remained silent but his quiet listening edged her on. She stared down at her hands. "Was Leal's body ever found?"

He shook his head slowly.

"Was there a funeral? How did your family grieve him? I wish I'd been there. I never said goodbye to him."

Cyrus emptied his beer and set the glass on the cotton tablecloth. He placed both hands on the table. "Miss Carlone."

"Call me Jewel."

He shot her a heartfelt smile that reminded her of Leal. "Jewel?"

She searched his eyes.

"Why did you confess attesting to Leal's death?" he asked.

Jewel moved back, her breathing intensifying. "How do you know that?"

"It was filed with the report sent to my family in Italy."

"That's none of your business. You know nothing about me. How can you come here with such...?"

Jewel squirmed. She'd detested herself the minute she'd signed those papers. It was wrong, illegally handled. She shivered from hearing talk of Leal again. She'd been branded a money-hungry criminal and worse, a loose woman who'd sleep with a billionaire for his money. She'd signed the papers to rid herself of Myranda and the embarrassment of falling for an unavailable man. Jewel longed for the carpet to wrap her out of Cyrus's sight.

Sensing her uneasiness he placed a warm hand over hers. "Hey," he said softly, "I'm on your side."

Chapter 12

Beads of perspiration formed on Jewel's forehead and she rubbed her hands feeling the moisture levels start to increase. She couldn't breathe. It was all coming back. The horrors of dealing with Myranda and her legal team. The torture of not knowing whether Leal was alive. The contents he'd given her now in Kaya's hands. The way Trelles Pharmaceuticals refused to take back the hundred thousand dollars. In the end, she'd asked Vik to give it to the clinic in Kullu Manali and ten percent to go continue treating Maya. She'd wanted not a cent of it.

Cyrus tipped his head to one side, his attractive features more pronounced. "Did I say something wrong? You look like you've seen a ghost's ghost."

Jewel took a sip of water, her head feeling light. She'd not eaten since the flight and could think better on a full stomach.

Cyrus reached for the table napkin and wiped her forehead gently. "I'm sorry."

She removed his hand from her forehead. "You don't need to keep apologizing."

"You were close to Leal, weren't you?"

Her eyes glistened at him. "It was a long time ago."

"Obviously not long enough."

"I'm fine."

"Okay. Then may we have something to eat?"

She managed a smile. "You're inviting yourself for dinner?"

"You could use the company."

Thirty minutes later, Jewel watched Cyrus ease up as his *steak au poivre* arrived. The waiter set down a large Caesar salad, and poured from a bottle of Araujo Cabernet Sauvignon into two wineglasses. Jewel took mini bites although she was famished; she couldn't keep her intrigue from Cyrus's conversation about his brother. Mostly small talk about how different they were growing up and dissimilarities in interests. Cyrus was academic and focused, having to work hard for everything he accomplished, while academia and sports came naturally to Leal. When the meal was done, Cyrus reached for her hand.

Jewel found herself accepting the gesture; she thought it was friendly without being intrusive. He stared into her eyes. "Is there something else?" Cyrus said.

"What do you mean?"

"Forty-eight hours before Leal's accident, he messaged about documents he was working on that were important to our family and business. He said he'd wanted to share them with someone close to him. Someone not in our family. Was that you?"

"I'm not sure I know what you mean."

"I know it sounds forward, but my family hasn't had closure on Leal's death and if there is something he gave you. We need it."

She cooled her voice as she spoke. "What would Leal have given me?"

Jewel thought back to the big speech on trust the day before the avalanche set in. "Don't give this to anyone. Keep it until I ask for it." Those had been his instructions. In fact, she'd forgotten about the items right until she returned home to New York. Now that Leal was dead, would she keep them? She shuddered at the thought of Myranda discovering their secret. Had Kaya already shown them to Weston?

Cyrus scrutinized Jewel's silence. "Listen, I'm not being inquisitive; I just need to know whether Leal gave you anything or said something unusual. You were the last person to see him alive."

And a few other willing witnesses...

She said nothing.

He backed off. "I'm sorry. I shouldn't have been so forward. Can I make it up to you by buying you a drink?"

"I already have one."

Jewel was used to confident men and though Cyrus's charm had seemed slightly aggressive at their first encounter in the auditorium, he maintained an amiable ambiguity that drew her interest. After all, he was Leal's brother. But would he understand? What if it were a trap?

She eased up. "How is your family now? I knew little about Leal's family. In fact, almost nothing. All I know is that he was a smart doctor and researcher who loved to work with medicine and discover new vaccines."

"Leal never told you anything about us? What about Sofia?

"Who's Sofia?"

"My sister. She and Leal were close, almost inseparable until his marriage."

An itch scratched her arm at the thought of Leal's connection to Myranda. She was yet to meet anyone who'd been content at that union in matrimony. What she couldn't figure out was, was he? Was Leal ever happy with the marriage? She tilted her head. "Where's Sofia?"

He let out a laugh. "She's in Venice visiting my grandmother. Nonna hasn't been well since she lost Leal. She suffers from anxiety disorder and in old age, it doesn't get any easier."

"I'm sorry."

"Leal's leaving us six years ago brought the family back together, as awful as that sounds."

Cyrus leaned closer. He'd been holding her hand the whole time and slowly let it go. Comforting her was natural to him and his eyes told her that he still grieved his brother.

"Jewel, we both lost something that day on the mountain. I don't believe you meant to sign those documents."

"You don't?"

"Leal loved you. Why else would Myranda want to coerce you into an agreement? She must've sensed a rivalry."

Jewel shifted in her seat. "That was six years ago. I don't know what I was going through. A few years before, I'd suffered an injury that took my career into photography. I have Leal to thank for giving me back my confidence and... belief in me."

Cyrus studied her.

"What is it?"

"Would you like to meet Sofia and Nonna? I know it would mean a lot to them. Give them closure with Leal."

Jewel didn't respond for several seconds. Meeting Cyrus had somehow brought Leal back, or at least the memories. Perhaps it would give her the resolution she needed and the chance to set the record straight. She ran a hand through her hair. "I'm not sure they would like to meet me."

"I'm certain they would."

"How do you know?"

"Thirty-some years of having them in my life. Leal changed after meeting you and Nonna talks about how he changed when he saw you perform in Montpellier."

"What about his wife? He never spoke of her." Her voice had risen within earshot of three tables.

Cyrus glanced at their audience before responding softly. "You met her. Can you blame him?"

He was right. Anyone married to Myranda would have to walk on coals. She eased back in the chair. "Doesn't make lying to me right."

"Myranda has never communicated with the family. She continues to show no respect for us."

"How do you know I would?"

"You have a gentleness and a sincerity that Nonna would feel comforted by. Seeing you may give her some needed closure with Leal's memory. She knew he thought highly of you."

"How do you know that? I thought you weren't close to Leal?"

"We were different. We didn't grow up together, but as I said, we were tied to the hip in many ways. A brother thing."

Jewel finished her water. "I don't know."

"Promise me you'll think about it. I've taken enough of your evening and you still have more presentations to give tomorrow. Please take my card."

He placed it on the table.

She read it.

CYRUS TRELLES
MANAGING DIRECTOR
MANCINI CORPORATION, VENICE, ITALY.

"What exactly do you do?"

"Come to Venice, I'll show you."

He reached for his wallet to pay.

"No need, Cyrus Trelles, this one's on me."

He smiled. "As the lady wishes."

He rose and peered into her eyes.

Cyrus paid extreme attention to detail in his appearance.

161

Business grooming apparent in all his mannerisms. Leal had been more outspoken and if she recalled correctly, had a deeper voice. Cyrus was well primed and suave.

He took her hand and kissed it. "Good night, Jewel. Please come to Venice."

"I don't—"

"Leal would've liked you to."

Damn, the guilt trip!

Could she face his family?

* * *

A crisp afternoon breeze colonized Kaya's home office as it drafted through the open terrace windows. The breeze kissed her cheek and the sun's warmth tingled her face. She gazed out the window and listened to laughing voices. Spring had arrived and Kaya knew just about every New Yorker would be sprawled out in Central Park. March hadn't been as cold as February, and April looked promising although the temperatures had been lower than usual. Scarsdale's town mansions and gated communities blended with upmarket apartments and golf courses.

Kaya didn't mind the half-hour train ride from the city's Grand Central Station as Scarsdale offered her trees and enough open space for her five-year-old son Brysen. How she missed the old days when Jewel and her would go out into the city without a burden in the world and lounge in one of the downtown Manhattan cafes.

Kaya looked over the papers on her desk, and in particular one envelope she'd hijacked from Jewel's pile and opened last night. The documents and flash disk had something that Leal was keeping from the world and perhaps something that could explain Myranda's need to get several witnesses to confirm Leal's death. But Jewel had to be convinced before Kaya could go any further into her investigation.

One problem stood in the way.

Leal's family.

The penalty for opening another person's mail lay in a small clause in the federal code. Chapter eighty-three of title eighteen of the federal code, a section called "Obstruction of Correspondence". The penalty could be high. However, her investigation had revealed the code only applied if one took a letter, package, postcard, or other item of mail from a Post Office, a mailbox, or from a postal carrier before the mail was delivered. The technicalities on how criminal the action, only a court could decide.

She couldn't afford any blunders in her career and justified it as the will to see justice served. The fisted hand that supported her cheek reached to close the pack with Leal's documents safely within. She rose and walked to the terrace window.

Brysen's voice mingled with Jewel's rich laugh and produced a smile on Kaya's face. Jewel looked content, but guarded.

She'd lost Leal, the man they'd both hoped would be Jewel's to keep. Kaya observed her son bouncing on the freshly mowed lawn, yards from Jewel, arms behind his capped head in the batting position ready to receive a pitch from Jewel's seasoned hand. Jewel could play just about any sport when she put her mind to it.

Jewel released the baseball, and little Brysen swung with the might of a ferocious cub, his bat landing accurately on the flying missile. Jewel hiked up to Brysen and ran a hand through his sandy locks. He was approaching his sixth birthday.

Did Jewel ever want children of her own? She was good with them. When Brysen was born, Jewel had come by to help and tackled anything a new mother couldn't handle alone. It was months after Leal had vanished from her life.

Jewel didn't complain once, even when she was in Weston's way. Kaya had needed a good friend around, someone who knew her emotionally and wouldn't question her irrational hormonal imbalances. Kaya's mother was in hospital battling stomach cancer and couldn't come until Brysen had reached his first birthday. Jewel lived in for two weeks helping with anything that needed doing. Grocery shopping, although Kaya's housekeeper had been more than capable. Bathing Brysen, bouncing Brysen, buying Brysen's diapers. It was as if Brysen filled a void Leal had left. The two now had an intimate bond. *Jewel, who stole the light from your eyes? Myranda or Leal?*

Jewel sprang through the open terrace door with Brysen piggy-backed to her. A bright and cheerful housekeeper, Sharie, opened the door. "Miss Carlone, I can take Brysen now, I know you and Mrs. Wilda need some time alone." She glanced at Brysen. "Would you like to frost the donuts I've made?"

The boy screeched, jumping from Jewel's back, untying her long mane in the process. Kaya watched as the boy disappeared with Sharie through the wide doors that led to the rest of the house.

"You still got it. Can pitch a baseball, like no other," Kaya said.

"Let's not forget my competitor is five."

Kaya let out a grin as Jewel slumped on the chaise lounges. "You guys have a nice place out here. I always believed you and Weston would be a fierce duo with your legal careers."

"Brysen adores you. As if you were his mother."

"I adore him too. When you asked me to be his godmother, I took it seriously."

Kaya's skin tingled each time the breeze swept into the room. She closed the terrace doors. "How was Saint Louis?"

"Interesting."

"That's an answer. Did I miss something?"

Jewel remained silent.

Kaya's burdened expression surfaced to her lips not waiting for any communication from her friend. "Weston and I read the documents and looked at the flash disk."

Jewel turned her head in Kaya's direction, her eyes not blinking, and her lips steady. "I see. How did you decrypt it?"

"We couldn't."

"What's on the documents? What do they say?"

Kaya took a deep breath. "The items were intended for legal eyes and are addressed to Leal's lawyer in Pennsylvania. For some reason, he didn't want to mail the documents or seemed to hesitate. Nevertheless, it makes sense now. After reading them, I called in a few favors and learned more."

Jewel threw her a darting gaze, shot up her hands briefly and marched to the window. "You promised me that we would leave the whole Leal matter and never raise it again. Don't you know that I have agonized day in and day out about what I signed and the consequences it created for Leal and his family. Can't we drop it?"

"No, Jewel. I love you too much to see you go on with this."

Jewel let out a resigned sigh. "Okay, what was in the files Leal left?"

Kaya took a seat at her laptop and pulled out the file she'd toyed with earlier. "Five years ago, almost six months after my son was born Myranda also had a child. She's consistently claimed that she lived up to the prenuptial agreement that Leal and her signed before their wedding."

Jewel rolled her eyes.

Kaya continued. "After his death, Trelles Industries was handed to Myranda like that without a single glance at the rest of the family. Nobody questioned it."

"It's obvious Myranda married him for his money?"

"Could it be that simple?" Kaya mused.

"How should I know?" Jewel said shrugging.

"The files raise some questionable practices."

Jewel placed her hands in her denim pockets and shifted her feet. "I should've burned those files. No one would've ever found out and we would all be happy."

"Happy? Really? You're anything but. These files can change something."

"What?"

"Give you closure."

"I don't want to get involved. I feel bad enough that we've opened them when Leal told me to just keep them."

"Why did he give them to you?"

Jewel shrugged. "God knows. Can't we just forget the whole thing? Aren't we in enough trouble already for opening files that don't belong to us?"

Kaya continued unfazed by Jewel's protests. "He had good reason. He could've used the contents himself to bring down the Vaux family months before he died and freed himself of them. But he didn't."

"Why?"

"I think you were right about Leal. He is a man of principle." She stopped herself. "Sorry... was."

Jewel turned her head toward the garden. "What do the files say?"

Kaya walked to where she stood and tilted her head. "Myranda was planning to have a baby without Leal. But..." She hesitated a few seconds. "Myranda can't have children."

"Maybe she adopted."

"Aha. That's exactly what the prenup forbids; she wasn't allowed to adopt."

Jewel's eyebrows knit. "How do you know that?"

"I have a copy of that prenup."

"What? How could you? How could you keep that from me?"

"I didn't Jewel. The day I tried to reach you in India, was the day everything happened. I received a copy of the prenup that morning and after the accident, I saw no point in following through... Until now."

"How does Myranda's having a son help us? Help the Trelles family?"

"Myranda was supposed to have Leal's child by blood. But how could she if she was infertile. The files contain her medical files that she and Leal commissioned. You see, it seems when they were married they couldn't conceive. As a medical person, Leal used his doctors to check Myranda. She wasn't aware what they were looking for. The details are all in the files in the supporting statements. Myranda planned to cheat on her prenuptial agreement."

"I still don't understand what it means."

"If Myranda couldn't conceive, she got desperate and sought other means," said Kaya

"Which means?"

"That's what we intend to find out and it could also disqualify her right to Trelles Industries. Leal died when Myranda had about nine months to go on the prenup. Although it may be tricky to prove, Myranda couldn't have had Leal's baby, at least according to these files. We've enough to go on here, but I can get some help if I make a few calls. My specialty is family law, not criminal law."

Jewel watched as Brysen went off with Sharie into the garden. "So her son is about Brysen's age, huh? I guess I'm going to have to go to Venice after all."

"What are you talking about?"

Kaya waited for an answer this time.

Jewel took several seconds before she spoke. "The presentation in Saint Louis went well, by the way, and all was going as planned until I..."

"Until?"

"Until I was thwarted by Leal's brother."

Kaya slumped into the chair. "Leal has a brother?"

"Oh yeah, and a sister and a grandmother."

"Why didn't you tell me before?"

"You didn't give me a chance. I think if we go ahead with this, we need to involve Cyrus Trelles."

166

"Would that be a hindrance, a lawsuit or a bonus?"

She walked away from the window slowly, her breathing intensifying.

"What's wrong?" Jewel asked.

"This just got complicated."

Chapter 13

Jewel's skin glistened in the late afternoon, Italian sun as she stepped onto the arrival pavement at Marco Polo International Airport. The airline captain had reported a high of nineteen degrees celsius. It was a pleasant afternoon promising not to be too warm that Jewel welcomed after being in a pressurized cabin for close to nine hours. Her dotted, cotton blouse, worn over her 1969 denim chinos breathed in the breeze coming in from the sea, as she stepped into the congested arrival disarray of the airport.

She rose on her tiptoes, peering above sun hats and mobs of travelers and glanced both ways then forward before she saw him. Cyrus had been easy to spot with his boyish smile and lean, tall physique. He wore a meticulous cotton checked shirt under a smart jacket, and was attractive, something to which Jewel hadn't expected to pay attention. Jewel grasped the handle of her lightweight suitcase, tugging its multidirectional spinner wheels as she moved toward him. Scores of travelers, tourists and pickup chauffeurs blaring above her comfortable decibel level, brushed past him as he pushed his way toward her. His eyes shone with expectation, trust, and friendliness.

She wouldn't mention the files unless prompted. She wouldn't get attached. A quick courtesy visit, then out.

"Hello, Cyrus?" Jewel said.

"It's Cyrus now, not Mr. Trelles?"

She made eye contact. "I've changed my mind about you."

He flashed her a smile that told her he approved of what he saw and seemed more at ease in this environment. He'd shaved cleanly and was relaxed on home territory.

"I came directly from the office," he said.

"You've yet to tell me what you do."

"I run an engineering company that constructs roads and highways, mostly within developing countries. For instance, I'm completing a highway contract to be constructed in Cidade Velha, on the Cape Verde islands."

"Is that a family business?"

"Yes, it is."

"So it runs in the family? The entrepreneurial spirit, I mean."

He smiled and brushed a cordial double kiss on her cheeks. "Welcome to Venice."

The Italian greeting sent her cheeks flushing and his cologne, mild and inundated with absolute masculinity, filled her nostrils with warm tuberose, precious woods and resins, sensations dutifully crafted for only women to smell. Jewel smiled. "Thank you."

"I'm glad you came."

"I was born in Udine and I'm half Italian. Believe it or not, I've never been to Venice."

Jewel let Cyrus take her suitcase and carry-on and lead her out into the sunshine. "This way. We'll travel by *vaporetto*. By boat."

She looked past Cyrus as the signs for the bus boats. "I would expect nothing else in Venice."

"This boat is private, though."

Jewel flashed him a smile, grateful she wouldn't have to deal with a crowded water boat after a long flight from New York. She reclined into the padded cushions of a vintage speedboat. Cyrus took a seat next to her in the water limousine with its spacious leather-upholstered cabin. The polished wood interiors boasted comfort, with a private captain to chauffeur them up the Laguna Veneta. They proceeded up the Brenta Canal along the waterways where the *burchielli*, boats that carried Venetian nobleman, sailed.

Soon, they cruised past the La Malcontenta, a captivating sixteenth-century Palladian villa before proceeding up the sixteenth-century trail along the banks of the Brenta. Cyrus introduced her to her surroundings. The watercourse had generated a pastoral civilization, echoes of which could still be seen in the bucolic barns of the villas, the stretches of greenery and barges docked along its banks. Jewel admired the methods Venetian nobility who, when attracted to the countryside, built their residences around the sun-dried, agrarian surroundings. The

169

homes had transformed into opulent residences. She admired the extraordinary flourishing of the villa culture and caught glimpses of courtyards, luxuriant parks, aristocratic gardens, all clothed in their immortal sophistication.

"Seems as though your family lives in one of Venice's pastoral parts."

"It's beautiful isn't it? Every time I get on a boat here, I understand why Nonna wanted to come back here." Cyrus looked toward the villas that lined the hill. "Our house was built in the sixteenth century and has been in the family since."

Jewel smiled. "So you come from nobility, Cyrus."

"Depends through which lenses you look."

"Are your offices in central Venice?"

"Yes, the offices are run from there."

They docked in the commune of Dolo where a Jaguar, S-Type Limousine awaited their arrival. The fifteen-minute ride took them up a hill before the car stopped in the grounds of a refined villa, after the plan of the Venetian medieval house. Jewel stepped out of the car gaping at the frescoes on the property. From its stylish exteriors, it had been comprehensively restructured, combining a tasteful archaic feel with modern comforts and architectural finishes. The manor house spread over more than three levels with a garden endowed with picturesque fountains, mimicking waterfalls and imitation streams that lead to a row of stables and two small rural outbuildings, possibly used as summer entertainment houses.

"I hope you'll like it here," Cyrus said.

Jewel fished out her Nikon. "May I look around the grounds," she asked, prepping her camera to explore the two hectares of well-kept garden lawns.

"Of course."

A young man met them at the entrance and offered to take her bags. Cyrus instructed him in Italian to take her belongings to the guest room. With an eye for details and expression, Jewel fluttered like an uninhibited bird through the estate lawn with Cyrus along the paved path that lined the villa. She studied the smooth, masonry cube-shape of the property before focusing her lens on the details of mythological frescoes on the west wall. She snapped a few photographs and turned toward Cyrus. "It's like a world heritage site here."

With eyes still behind the lens, she rotated toward the south part of the grounds and jolted back, startled by an object in her camera. Jewel's eyes moved away from the lens as the elegant, tall frame of an Italian woman caught her eyes whose stylish white crop was frosted with streaks of light gray as she stood several meters from them at the edge of a whistling fountain. The woman advanced toward them with a magnificent walking stick, which by the looks of it she didn't need. It was an accessory or a false security, for she moved with sophistication cultivated over many years. Defined cheekbones above thin lips gave her an aristocratic appeal. Her light-brown eyes smiled at Jewel as she approached, wearing a featherweight silk tunic, whose pink glow drifted over white linen slacks that complimented her long frame.

Cyrus stepped toward the woman and she slid her arm in his. "Nonna."

Defying age, elegance, and charm, she was one of the most glamourous woman Jewel had ever seen.

"Nonna, meet Jewel Carlone,"

Nonna advanced toward Jewel and with both hands, took her in her arms and embraced her like a long-lost daughter. "Jewel, I've wanted to meet you for a long time. You're exactly as my grandson described," said Nonna in Italian.

Her raspy voice rang with compassion. It took several seconds for Jewel to decide which grandson she meant. She presumed Nonna was referring to Cyrus. Jewel welcomed the fervent compliment. "It's an honor to meet you."

"I like her already," Nonna said to Cyrus. "I knew you would come. Seeing you here is like having him back."

"Nonna, Leal and I were hardly..."

"Shush, my dear. You're welcome here."

Nonna slid her arm into Jewel's and the trio proceeded to the front of the house. The interior of the villa displayed frescoes throughout the ground floor. She followed Nonna through to the living area, caught sight of three small lounges, a study, a second grand living room with a fireplace, and an elaborate dining room that looked out onto a porch. They attracted Jewel's eyes with glass, mirrors and ornate artwork giving the villa abundant natural light. The interior decor, using creams, gold, wine-red and deep purple took inspiration from romantic Venetian architecture, marble finishes and natural stone.

"You have a beautiful home, Nonna," Jewel said in Italian.

"And your Italian is fabulous."

Though once fluent in Italian, she had to concentrate and was relieved when Nonna switched to English. Once seated in the drawing room, Nonna reached for an espresso coffee. "Have some. I made it myself."

A villa like this was kept by at least a housekeeper, a gardener and several staff. She shook her head. "Thanks, Nonna. That's kind of you. I'll just have some water if that's okay." She placed her hand over her knees. "I'm sorry. Is it okay for me to call you Nonna? You remind me so much of my Nonna. I knew her briefly as a little girl in Udine."

"So you're Italian throughout?"

"Half. My mother is from Hawaii's Kauai Island, but my father was from Udine where I was born, not too far from here."

"Your ancestry has given you incredible genes. You are more beautiful than Leal described."

Nonna's eyes fixed on Jewel's and she loosened in her seat. "Thank you."

"You say, your father was from Udine?"

"Yes," Jewel said. "I haven't seen him since I was a little girl."

Nonna took a sip of the chilled iced tea and glanced up at Cyrus as he took a seat across from the women. Soon, he disappeared into the background as the women chatted.

"I'm happy that you came to see us," Nonna said. "In fact, if I had known where to find you, I would have invited you sooner."

Jewel shifted in her seat. "I don't know want to say." She took a deep breath. "I'm so sorry about your family's loss. Leal meant a lot to me; I learned so much from him."

Nonna smiled and cast Cyrus a glance before reaching for Jewel's hand. "I know." Her eyes glowed with fondness. "Leal made us all proud, and was the first doctor in our family. He sincerely cared about what he did."

Jewel nodded. "I saw him do it."

A sad expression fell over Nonna's hardly wrinkled face. "For years we've tried to put his memory to rest, but many obstacles prevent us."

Cyrus glanced away and strolled out to the porch as the women talked. Jewel swallowed hard watching his discomfort and the pain in Nonna's face. "I'm sorry. Did his wife prepare a farewell for him?"

"No."

Jewel held back a choked breath. "I didn't know that. I'm so sorry. Did she offer her condolences?" Jewel said half to herself remembering the not so cordial meeting with Myranda.

"No. We've never heard from her. I've never met her. Six years ago, we received letters in the mail from her attorneys telling us that Trelles Industries was to be transferred to her. According to her legal team, she was pregnant with Leal's child, which meant she could legally claim the whole estate."

Jewel sat back in her upholstered seat and glanced round the room, her voice imprisoned in her throat. Trelles's billions weren't a motivating factor here. It was not about money. This family had plenty of it. Something deeper was at stake. They were perhaps grieving a nephew or niece, great-granddaughter or son they had never met. If it truly was Leal's child.

The thought of someone having his child repulsed her and stung at her heart. However, if the contents of Leal's documents were legitimate, that child wasn't part of this family. They'd been cheated.

"Have you ever seen your great-grandchild? Leal's child I mean. I assume they are in New York?" Jewel said.

Cyrus re-entered the room. "A few years ago, her lawyer sent us a birth certificate as evidence of birth. That's as close as we've ever been to that child."

"It seemed like a transaction," added Nonna. "As if we don't have feelings. Leal was our boy and Trelles Industries was his."

Cyrus sat on the edge of his grandmother's seat and set an arm around her tiny shoulders. "Nonna doesn't care about the money or the company. It's the principle. Myranda took so much, not necessarily his money but Leal's life's work, legacy and dishonored his trust."

Jewel understood that in Italy family was important. Would they feel the same way if they knew the truth? Had she failed at her original intention of slipping in and out of this family's life? They'd worked their way into her life as easily as Leal had.

Jewel's voice choked as she spoke. "I wish I could do something."

Nonna knotted her hands over her knees. "You can."

"What?"

"Go back to New York and fight Myranda with us."

* * *

Jewel glanced from grandmother to grandson. "Why would Myranda speak to me?"

Cyrus's voice echoed with determination. "When I read about your exhibition in Saint Louis and saw Leal's picture in a photography magazine, I knew I had to meet you. For the first time in six years, I was convinced that Myranda must fear your connection to Leal and that's why she threatened you."

"What do you mean?"

"If Myranda saw you again, she'll be confronted with the truth. She'll have to dig up what she hid in a corporate grave the day Leal was pronounced dead," he said.

Jewel sank in her seat. "I can't. I couldn't."

Cyrus's tone held a note of pleading. "We need you to."

"You don't understand. I can't see her again. I—"

"You can and you can wipe your name clean," Nonna said.

Jewel bit her lip. What would they do if they knew about the hidden documents in her carry-on?

* * *

"Stop! Calypso!"

Myranda's pharaoh hound halted. He took short huffs of air and waited. Her skin flushed and her cheeks rouged with color after circling the entirety of Central Park, all the six miles of one of the three long-distance routes. Central Park in New York City offered rectitude, space for reflection and scenic distractions. Running was solace. She was uncomfortable with her fuller upper body and kept most weight on her stomach. Exercise became religion, though most men admired her figure.

"Ugh!"

Calypso barked at a white-breasted nuthatch that flew overhead, bothered by the ecological life in the park. For a hound that descended from ancient, royal Egyptian hunting dogs, he was not behaving with any trace of royalty.

Damn it! Myranda squatted like a prowling panther to catch her breath and stretched her limbs into perfect leg squats. She'd always been a strong athlete.

Myranda stared out at the terrain before her. *Will I survive next week?*

Calen's sixth birthday. Most mothers fussed over what

popular animation film theme to choose, or which of New York's leading party companies to hire. *And we have to pass a freaking DNA test!* The one Leal had slipped into the prenuptial agreement that guaranteed Calen's first installment from Trelles's family trust.

Myranda rose, glanced back at the Reservoir loop then headed to the Mall, the only straight line in the park. As she passed joggers and commuters at the early hour of 8:00 a.m., she slowed to think. *How does one beat a DNA test?* Calen had come to her like the solution to a math equation six years ago. Over the years, he'd been a security blanket. She loved the little one though his upbringing was in the capable hands of Braith, his Welsh nanny. Leal's prenuptial stated that every six years of his children's lives, they would receive a significant sum of money. What was it he had said? *"A human being develops something new in their intellect every six years."* It was his theory, one he'd not necessarily proved. It stood in the way. Calen could not receive the generous endowment of eighty-five thousand dollars every six years. If they failed, Myranda could face a law suit and jail.

It had been easy to forge Calen's birth certificate, but how could she avoid a required DNA test without exposing her lie? One she'd not expected would last. It had been a cunning five-year plan then she'd move on to dissolving her funds out of Trelles Industries. Was it greed or just a wish to get the one thing she'd yet to gain from Trelles Pharmaceuticals?

Myranda picked up her pace. Soon a tall man framed in her path, also in jogging attire. With her in-ear player at full blast, she thought nothing of it until he reached out and grasped her upper arm.

She shuddered, flipping her head to face her attacker. *En guarde*, and ready to fight her assailant, it was a face she'd hoped never to run into again. *Devon Chesser!*

She yanked her arm out of his grasp and removed her headphones, dropping her player on the ground.

"Really, Myranda? I never took you for one to avoid old acquaintances. It's been six years. I had to hound your secretary for your whereabouts."

Devon had a peculiar habit of resurfacing when unwanted. So what if he had performed a favor all those years ago. He wouldn't disappear from her life altogether, although after dealing with Trelles Industries, it was second on her list of habits to drop.

175

"What brings you to the city, Devon?"

He smirked. "A social call."

"Your calls are never social. What do you want?"

"Now, now. Is that how you welcome a dear friend after six bloody years?"

"There's nothing affectionate about our general acquaintance. What brings you to New York? Don't they have enough to keep you preoccupied within——"

"I trot between New York and London." He threw her a devilish smile. "I got bored."

"You're not supposed to contact me."

"I figured you might need some help after I left Calen's files all those years ago."

"I can't be seen with you."

"Charming as always little Myranda, but I think I'll need more respect, if I'm to assist you with your little problem."

"You have more important scientific research to do than follow me around. Have you forgotten the DEI is counting the days before they withdraw their grant proposal?"

"Precisely, my dear. That's why we need each other. More than ever now."

"I've paid my dues. I read you live on a large estate thanks to me or is it the French girl's pocket change? Leal refused to make you a partner in the firm, yet you found some way of getting to his money," she said.

"Is that how you welcome a friend?"

A vulture, more like it. Myranda started a fierce march toward the exit of the park, with Devon keeping stride alongside her. "Come, now, Myranda, you do not think I'll let you alone in this time when you need me most."

"I don't need you."

Devon stopped. "You know exactly what I mean."

Myranda paused in front of him. "You talk as if I'm a mind reader. What fee or favor have I not settled?"

"I don't need money. Never have."

"Of course not, you're an Oxford boy, why would you?"

"If money were an object, I'd have charged you Myranda for making out as if my son were yours," he said, facing her straight on.

Myranda froze. *Calen is his own son.* No wonder he got him easily. Myranda's voice quieted speaking in a delayed pitch.

"Where did you get Calen?"

"Let's just say his mother and I ended a rather distasteful relationship. She didn't wish to keep him. He came at the right time. You and I had a little predicament."

Myranda cast him a disgusted look. Every time she looked at him, she swore he could see her every thought. She cleared her throat. "If you don't want money, why are you here?"

"Calen is turning six next week. I know the rather intimate details of your little arrangement with the Trelles enterprise and I'm here to support you."

"I doubt that."

"I've come to offer you help."

"What will it cost me?"

"Nothing."

"Nothing from you is free."

"I have a DNA miracle that will help Calen pass the test."

"I don't believe you."

His answer came in smooth tones. "You forget Leal and I were roommates at Johns Hopkins."

Myranda's eyebrows knot. "With all your intelligence? Why have you never started your own medical business?"

He shot her an irritated look. "Tread lightly, or you'll walk into the abyss alone."

She'd hit a sore nerve. He was always behind Leal in any medical arena and lacked the confidence of his rival. Even with Leal dead. "No, Devon. Not this time."

"Think about it. You've no other choice if you wish to continue this charade as the grieving widow of the much-loved Leal Trelles."

"I've done my time?"

"Not yet. This will cost you just your pride. But in the game you and I play, pride is a luxury we can't afford." Devon approached, a little too close for Myranda's comfort. "I have what you need. You forget that once, Leal and I were close medical collaborators at Hopkins. Let's just say I have materials that could help."

"You're sick, Devon!"

"Not more toxic than you, my love. A woman who bribes another to bear your child, usurp a corporate throne you had no part in building, and somehow sleeps at night? How do you do it?"

Bastard! Myranda resumed her walk. The words stung her soul and every time she dealt with Devon, she paid a hefty price. First, it was cheating her father out of Trelles Industries though he deserved a seat on the board. Then, it was ensuring Devon kept a significant stake in Trelles, including voting power. Though she'd gotten what she'd set out to do when she met Leal, her ambitions had been stronger than her admiration for him. Had Leal been gullible, or did he just not see it coming?

They were meters from the exit and Myranda hurried past it and spotted her chauffeur. "I'm heading back to my office."

Devon's posture stiffened. "Just know that my offer stands."

"I'll think about it."

"You can't do this without me."

Myranda swore. He was right. She'd not worked out one way to pass Calen off as Leal's son for the DNA test. She couldn't stop now. *Well damn it!* She'd worked too hard. But could she avoid another debt to Devon?

* * *

"Leal!"

You killed him!

Jewel sprang from the moist bed. Her groggy eyes flew open. Had she perspired all night? She rubbed them until they cleared. Had it been a dream? He was so real. After six years, Leal's memory refused to leave. It had haunted her through the night as it had done the last six years. *Forgive me, Leal. I should never have left you. I should have died with you.*

She pulled the covers over her trembling body. Why was it so cold? The same dream woke her as it had for many months, teasing her senses with Leal's presence. The same mountain. The icy air breezing over the slopes. The noise of the helicopter. The terrified passenger next to her. The sight of the speeding snow covering the tent. Then, red. The last hint of Leal's existence on the mountain. Then, accusing voices, white light reflecting off the avalanche. Jewel wanted it to stop. She'd visited a sleep specialist in New York for twenty months. "Make the dream stop!" she'd cried at the New York sleep clinic therapist.

"No, Jewel, you're the one to make it stop. The minute you stop blaming yourself."

She never could erase Leal's memory, move on or meet

someone else. He'd seeped in her soul like a vaccine that would stay with her for life. Her dreams had intensified since meeting Cyrus. It had to be a brother connection although the two were so different.

The specialist told her that hanging onto any memory of Leal would hold her back. Perhaps if she released the documents to the family, she might feel better.

She slipped out of the huge bed pulling her cream nightgown over her thin nightdress and inched to the table. With eyes stained crimson, Jewel made her way to the window and took a seat on the low ledge of the arched panes overlooking the trimmed lawn. She saw movement in the grounds.

Two men trained in an Eastern martial art with which she was familiar—Kenjustu—a Japanese swordsmanship. Cyrus fought with a long pole, as did his opponent, a Japanese man and together they grappled in the ancient art. She watched them wrestle across the lawn matched in strength, jabbing and feigning as they scuttled along the grounds. Jewel checked the time on her watch. It was 6:00 a.m. local time.

A loud cry from the Japanese man brought her attention back to the combat. From the discarded shirts of the training men and the beads of sweat on their bare upper bodies, they'd been training for a while.

"This is how you deflect your opponent's bullet," Jewel heard the Japanese man say.

Jewel watched as Cyrus deflected training shots off his sword from what looked like a training pistol. His athletic movements and the way he handled his acrobatic body, reminded her of Leal. Leal had shown a similar hunger to win when he'd raced her dogs in Austria. It was a familiar boyish hunt for adventure and conquest she'd found amusing. The brothers looked different, but they were built the same, with athletic bodies that showed strength and attention to physique.

What was their childhood like? Since meeting Cyrus, she'd studied him not as Leal's brother, but as a zealous man, trying to protect his family's honor and rights. How was it that Leal was free in mannerisms, an adventurer who preferred the outdoors and Cyrus was the opposite, suave and business-focused, he'd seemed relaxed until yesterday. A pain in his eyes surfaced each time he mentioned his brother.

Jewel gripped her arm. Her presence in the family home had

to be difficult for Nonna and Cyrus.

Training ended and the two men strolled to the house. Jewel rose, advanced to the bathroom for a warm shower. Fifteen minutes later, she pulled on a pair of snug jeans, flat ballerina pumps, and a ruby halter top, that emphasized her shoulders. She pulled her hair into a tight ponytail and found her carry-on in the walk-in closet, opposite her en-suite bathroom. Leal's documents were in the inside flap of the suitcase. Its contents could alter their perception of Myranda, Leal and his family. She dropped the flash disk on the bed for a moment and fished through the case for her electronic tablet. When it booted, Jewel opened her e-mail account and scanned her inbox. Aside from the usual photoshoot requests and a reminder for a barbecue that weekend at her mother's, nothing was pressing for the moment. Her eyes fell on an unopened e-mail and narrowed in on the sender's name.

Dr. Vik Patil.

Vik.

A timely explosion from her past. She'd not been in touch with Vik since sending the money transfer to the clinic after she'd returned from India. There was no subject line. She stared at it for several seconds then drifted her eyes to the next e-mail Kaya had sent last night.

> *How's Venice? Have you told the family about the documents? What are they like?*
>
> *Listen, next week Myranda Vaux has to submit a DNA test to a special hearing committee about Calen Vaux her six-year-old son. We need to act now. The Trelles family and their legal team will be there.*
>
> *Please let me know what you decide. Either way, I'll follow your lead on this. We can drop the whole thing or give Leal's family the closure they need.*
>
> *Kaya.*

* * *

Cyrus advanced past the avenue of cypresses that led to the house. He headed through the double wooden doors of the sixteenth-century Villa Treolli. Watanabe his Kenjutsu and Kali instructor strolled beside him. Once inside, he let the warm air from the interior of the Chianti entryway brush his face. His thoughts swayed wanting to cancel his next appointment.

He needed the doctor. He'd not seen Dr. Rafaela Bartolocci his clinical psychologist for three months. What was it she'd said? "The day you went skiing in San Moritz, and saw that father fuss over his little boy, was the day the light switched on, illuminating the dark places of your struggles."

The demons in his dreams. Why did the encounter affect him? He needed the doctor's advice now. Now that Jewel was here. Now that his family needed him to stay strong. He rubbed his hand over his tensing neck muscle. *Damn it, Leal, why her?*

When he thought of Jewel, his guard fell and he could do nothing. He was struck as easily as Leal had been and slung a towel round his neck. The sound of footsteps on the marble staircase alerted him. He glanced up and narrowed his eyes.

He held his breath. That calm determination. Jewel walked down with her eyes fixed on his. Her feet touched the polished marble as she reached the bottom stair. She greeted the men with a smile and watched them make their way to her.

Cyrus wiped his face with a white towel and turned to Watanabe. He bowed. "Thank you, Watanabe-san. You sliced me at Kenjutsu today."

Watanabe returned his gesture. "You'll soon be better than I. You have such intense reflexes similar to astronauts and fighter pilots and your sword technique and speed are exceptional."

"I doubt that," Cyrus said.

"I timed you today. You went for two minutes on the simulator as training shots fired at you. That test is used in pilot fighter training." Watanabe turned to Jewel aware of her stare. "So this is Jewel-san?" He tilted his head. "I'm pleased to make your acquaintance."

Jewel raised her eyebrow and bowed in return. "You fight well, Watanabe-san," she said.

"Do you know about Japanese Kenjutsu?"

"Only a little," she smiled. "I visited Japan briefly."

Jewel shifted her feet as Watanabe left.

Cyrus watched her quietly.

Her eyes moved away from his contemplating stare. "I didn't know you liked Japanese marital arts," she said.

181

"You know about the fighting arts?" Cyrus said.

"Every sports woman should. So what's your excuse?"

"I like to stay fit."

"With exotic martial arts techniques?"

Cyrus's smile was self-confident. "Actually, yes."

"In that way, you're much like your brother. Full of surprises."

Cyrus took a step forward, narrowing the comfortable distance between them. His bare upper body was still damp, but well well built. "I need to shower and change. May I talk to you, later?"

She looked away with an inhibited smile that told him she approved of what she saw. "I'm your guest. I'm not going anywhere," she said.

He took a step to her and watched her trying to understand what it was about her that made him feel at ease and yet so protective. "Did you sleep well?"

She toyed with her hands. "Yes, thank you. Feels good to be back in Italy."

He came closer placing his foot on the first step. "You always shy around new acquaintances?"

"Only skilled, master swordsmen."

He grinned, brushing her arm as he went up the stairs.

She swung round. "Cyrus?"

He stopped at the top of the staircase and turned. "Remind me when we speak later. I have something important to tell you."

His eyes narrowed. "Is everything okay?"

"Yes. Would be good for Nonna to be there."

Cyrus watched as Jewel headed under the hallway arches to the eating area in the grand kitchen, where his family had breakfast. He stopped mid-step as he saw a figure enter the kitchen through the open door leading to the patio.

Sofia, his older sister by two years shot him a beaming smile but soon turned her attention toward the kitchen. Growing up, many had called her a typical southern Italian girl; olive skin, soft brow-ridges, straight nose and low cheekbones. Luxurious chestnut hair bounced off her shoulders and she wore little makeup over her almond-shaped eyes. She dressed well with animated charisma oozing from her style, comfortable loose clothing skewed toward classic tailoring rather than the adventurous high-street trends. Tall and with an angular build,

Sofia was used to large families, loved to chat and eat, mostly Italian seafood dishes. Marinated San Remo shrimps with caviar and scallions were a favorite and she could whip up a delightful macaroni with clams and artichokes.

Sofia had always taken her big sister role seriously, protecting Cyrus and defending him when needed. As teenagers they fought like hungry bears and though he saw her as little now, she remained his confidant. Cyrus stood looking down the railing, purposing to witness her first meeting with Jewel.

Sofia marched up to their visitor. "Hi. You're Jewel, right?"

Her English was fluent, slightly accented. Most attributed it to spending much of her upbringing in Venice. Jewel watched the swan-like woman inch toward her. Dressed in white slacks and a tight, branded T-shirt, Sofia stopped to pay attention.

Jewel took a step back, "Yes."

"I'm Sofia."

Jewel received a double kiss on her cheeks, which sent her smiling. "I thought you might be."

Cyrus watched the interaction with a curious eye as he leaned over the rail, towel over his shoulder. "Sofia, be nice. Jewel's here for a few days."

Sofia winked at her brother, cast a warm smile at Jewel and took her hand. "*Leal's* Jewel."

Jewel freed herself from Sofia's hold. "I wish I could say that Cyrus had told me all about you, but he hasn't mentioned the best part. You're charming."

"Brothers." She glanced up at Cyrus, who continued lurking down with a smirk. "I'm really pleased to meet you."

Sofia slung an arm through Jewel's arm and offered her a seat in front of a traditional Italian *colazione*, a display of fresh rolls, biscotti, butter and jam, and served her a piping cafe latte.

"You have the same warmth as Nonna," Jewel said.

Sofia giggled. "I'll take that as a compliment. Nonna's a pillar of strength around here."

They chatted at the dining room settling into a warm conversation about travel and the climate.

Cyrus continued his march to his bedroom on the third level of the villa. Nonna must've told Sofia he was in town. Was she going to play with his conscience again?

Dr. Rafaela had called Sofia a lost child who threw her problems off her shoulders to disguise their existence.

When Cyrus stepped into his room, he checked the time. Dr. Bartolocci would be here soon. He had requested an early start.

Will Jewel surrender? Will she want to help us? Help Leal? Help me? They only had a few days and as the head of the Trelles family, he needed to confront Myranda Vaux. A war Cyrus had wanted to fight the minute he'd heard what had happened in India.

He'd contacted Dr. Vik the week before, asking him to send Jewel a gentle tug. *"Via e-mail, may be best if you haven't been in touch since you last saw her."*

By Cyrus's measure and from Jeff Avent's description, Vik was a man of integrity, character and he'd known and worked with Leal. His brother had confided in him. Vik helped Leal in his research, providing the much-needed seeding ground for the infertility research in India, projects Myranda's team had closed after the accident. Leal had researched uninterrupted from the money-hungry world. And together, they set up the remote clinic in the Himalayas on Trelles's behalf, a clinic now abandoned and patients displaced. Leal's social justice efforts had been wasted.

Cyrus headed to the shower. He couldn't help wondering whether Jewel had loved Leal as they knew Leal had her. She must have. He could tell from the way she squirmed and twitched her lips each time she spoke of him. Leal's last communication had mentioned a woman he'd met who'd changed the course of his life. Though he'd meant medically, they could tell from the cryptic way Leal presented details.

And maybe there was more. And why not? Leal had everything he didn't, dangerously good looks, a chivalric attitude, that blasted cocky smile. He was analytical and though not always obvious, business-minded. Cyrus had often heard of women in his New York circles bribing doormen and restaurant owners to meet him. His brother had been a stunning athlete who indulged in dangerous mountain sports. He'd certainly been the one attracting the opposite sex. Leal had paid women little attention, including the woman he'd married, until he met Jewel. He'd been looking for one, his Gibraltar Campion—a rare flower found in the high cliffs of Gibraltar rediscovered after a lone climber found it in inaccessible cliffs and sprang the species back to life. Jewel was *his* Gibraltar Campion and Leal had been the lone climber.

Then, why Myranda?

Cyrus stripped to shower. Several minutes later, he changed

into a pair of navy jeans, a polo shirt, and leather travel shoes. *Could six years have changed Jewel?* Leal trusted her, so Cyrus had to trust her too. He had to be careful, though, as it was torture controlling his attraction to her. He was in danger of stepping into the delicate territory of Jewel's allure.

Chapter 14

Myranda waited for her cappuccino as a noisy appliance whistled steaming foam. Mrs. Thomas the housekeeper had made the first one to her liking, velvety, with equal parts espresso and milk, topped with shaved chocolate, but no sugar. The sound of the seductive opera by Handel—*Guilio Ceasare*—played in the in-wall speakers. She sighed as the hot liquid warmed her hands when Mrs. Thomas handed her the cup. The town apartment, bought after the news of Leal's death, had been renovated with details fit for royalty. A centerline view of Central Park could be seen from the nineteenth floor apartment from every room. Myranda rose to open a window letting in a slight morning breeze as the sun settled over the city in the mid-morning hour.

"It's a day for winners," said a man's voice behind her.

Myranda zipped her head toward the entrance on the bottom floor from the mezzanine. Devon strolled through smirking, let in by Mrs. Thomas. He made his way up the seventy-foot long gallery, clacking his heels on the magnificent floor of snow-white Thassos marble and scanned the room before settling into the palatial space bordered by a library and a formal dining room.

A skylight hovered above the half-stone, half-timber wall. He'd changed into proper office attire, a slim fit business suit, made from high-quality new wool.

She turned in his direction. "Okay, Devon, let me see what you've got."

"So you've decided accept my offer," he smirked. "Naturally, I'll want a tiny favor in return."

"Why am I not surprised?" she said.

He pulled out three documents from his inner coat pocket. "It's all you'll need in the mediation." He tossed the papers on the coffee table. "How much do you know about DNA testing?"

"As much as any other person."

"It's quite simple. DNA carries our genetic code and here is

Calen's."

Myranda watched as he fingered the documents. "How can I be sure it's genuine?"

"It's genuine all right and will pass in the mediation. You still don't trust me, poppet? Ninety-nine point nine percent of DNA from two people is identical. Only zero point one percent of the DNA code sequences that vary from person to person make us unique. Funny, huh?"

"Go on."

"Identical twins are the only people with identical genetic markers. You do know Leal was a twin. An identical one."

"That's not possible. I would know."

"It is. His twin brother died in infancy. I read that little detail in his family documents."

Her eyes broadened. "You serious?"

"I see that's news to you. It is to most people. Leal never disclosed much about his private life."

"But a twin...?"

"The more closely related two people are, the more likely they are to have similar genetic markers. When you, my dear, acquired Trelles Industries, and I got my forty percent voting power on all board decisions, it put me in a rather unique situation. One that allowed me access to a handful of Trelles's files. Naturally, one needs to know what they're looking for."

"You didn't dare—"

"It wasn't an easy find, even for my experienced eyes. A lock of hair was among the twins' infant items, conveniently labeled as 'twins' first haircut' by an over-sentimental mother I believe."

"How does that help me? Calen?"

"The DNA signature I've used is his twin's and will pass as Calen's."

"How did you get to *these* files?"

"I stole your access to the family archive in a Zurich private bank. It hadn't been opened in some twenty years I believe."

"You've no shame, Devon."

"Sadly, no."

"I still don't get how this helps me."

"All cells in the body contain the same DNA, samples can be taken from anywhere, you know, skin, hair follicles, blood and the like."

"What will this cost me?"

"I want more votes in Trelles, and I don't want *even* you stopping me from manufacturing what I want when the time comes."

"How much?"

"Fifty-one percent."

"You've got guts."

Devon was a biomedical scientist by training like Leal. He knew what he was talking about. Myranda rose and marched toward the arched fireplace. She wanted this, but couldn't give Trelles to him. Trelles had to remain hers. Sure, Devon could do it, but what was he hiding? Would he one day return to claim Calen? She didn't know where Devon had gotten a baby. Their contract had been never to reveal the details.

Calen was hers. He wasn't her natural son, but she'd seen him as hers since Devon had signed the documents and brought him. Since then, her life would be intertwined with Devon's. She'd known Devon since they met at a marketing conference in Philadelphia, starting a sordid affair that had always bothered her and his stylish wife. Life would be unimaginable without Calen, the result of an unfortunate affair with God knows whom.

"What if I refuse?" Myranda said.

"That's a privilege you don't have."

He's right. She paced toward the hall and picked up a baseball cap Calen had discarded on the floor on the way out to school that morning. Despite her instincts in business, Myranda had insisted that Calen's papers be legal in every way and her lawyers had checked every minute detail. Devon wasn't senseless to produce questionable evidence, and this was too important to end in court one day. With just a few days to go, discomfort crept into her gut.

* * *

Cyrus roamed out onto the villa terrace. The nectarous scent of the blossoming roses, ranunculus, freesia and hypericum berries in the manicured grounds caught his nostrils. The garden didn't give him solace. He took in the enticing scent of fresh-cut grass and crossed to the lawn, passing the swimming pool. It had been refilled for the warm months that past weekend after a torrid winter of storms and much rain.

The sun was up now. Its heat beat against his sleep-deprived eyes. Leal had tortured his dreams last night, clear he'd not put his twin to rest. Leal had unfinished business Cyrus needed to attend to. He strolled toward the outdoor house, and further to the terrace that overlooked the hills.

Dr. Bartolocci stopped reading. Seated under the ascending vines of the natural canopy on a hardwood reclining chair, the sound of his strides stirred her. Her eyes lit as the morning sun hit them. She rose and placed the local newspaper down on the garden coffee table. Her silver streaked hair was brushed back and her smile took years off her age. Cyrus guessed she was in her fifties. She had been more like a mother to him in the last several years, a psychologist he'd hired to help him after Leal's accident in India.

"*Bongiorno.* Cyrus, how are you?" She spoke in Italian with a Milan accent where he first met her, in the leading family clinic she ran.

Cyrus reclined into a designer wicker sofa opposite Dr. Rafaela. "I'm well."

She eyed him, her profound eyes smiling. "The look on your face tells me you have met Leal's Jewel. How is that going?"

He shrugged, then paused before surrendering a deep sigh. "She's incredible."

"Not getting too attached, are we? That could get sticky. Is she going to help the family?"

Cyrus poured himself a cup of espresso from her canister and into the extra cup. He swallowed the hot contents in one swig before setting it down again. He scanned the vineyard in front of them. "My guess is she'll help, for Leal."

Dr. Rafaela leaned back and exhaled. "I hope so. The sooner you deal with the past, the more quickly it'll be for you to resume your life and move ahead. You remember what I told you."

Cyrus cast her a glance and leaned back. "I don't think I'll ever be able to shake the past. Leal's past. Will that not ruin my progress? This whole business with the Vaux woman and now, Jewel is more complicated than I expected."

"How so?"

"I don't know, but it is."

"I see." Dr. Rafaela relaxed her stare. "Cyrus, I care about you. I want you to shake this. These last six years have thrown you into a deep spiral and you can be free when you tell Jewel the truth."

"I can't."

"You remember what I told you last time."

It had been three months, but how could he forget the truth in her words.

Cyrus frowned.

"Listen," Dr. Rafaela said, "you can do this." He turned his attention to her consolation. Even in the bright sunlight and calm weather, he wanted to step off a cliff with no rope for support. Would the truth he hung onto be strong enough to hold him above his failings?

She tilted her head, watching him with interest. "You need to hear this because it's important." She maintained a focused gaze. "You're your own person. Leal is gone. Think about you now. For years, you've been tormented by the intense sensitivity you felt ten years ago when you went to Andermatt in Switzerland, on that skiing trip. When you observed a father fuss over his little son, the way no father ever fussed over you."

Cyrus rose, striding toward the edge of the stone terrace and gripped the supporting canopy pole. "It was nothing?"

"That man was hefty. He was big, with no softness manner. Yet you wondered why a sizable, powerful man would take a moment to fuss with a fragile, bawling child."

Cyrus turned to look at her.

"It was beautiful wasn't it?" she said.

"I spent my entire childhood in a cold family. Nobody said anything warm, except Nonna and when my father disappeared—"

"You had to be the man."

"Sofia disapproves of me."

"Sofia wants her brother to come home. It wasn't easy for her, never having a mother or father to raise her. Ironically, she's taken the affection she lacked as a child and uses it toward others. That's why she kept running away. But she had you. She's always had you."

He sighed again. "What am I doing wrong?"

"She wants the real you."

He sensed the temperature rise in his cheeks as the sun warmed. They'd been out on the porch close to forty minutes. His muscles tensed every time he spoke of Sofia and the past. He'd never forgiven himself for abandoning her when she needed him most. She'd run off and married the idiot from Rome, twenty years her senior. She'd just celebrated her twentieth birthday, and he'd just turned eighteen. Cyrus bailed her out from the greedy grip of the Real Estate merchant. It had cost the family much money. Money was the only stability he'd known. He reviled it. It had betrayed him frequently, with the opposite sex and family.

He saw something different in Jewel. She brought a steadiness to his being when she was in the room, a quiet-yet-attractive confidence. Had she done this to Leal? Was it his twin syndrome? *I now know why Leal fell for you.*

So had he. It was not physical although her amber eyes were the rarest he'd ever seen. Her determined spirit gave him strength. It never deterred from its aim. What would Jewel think if she knew the truth? He turned and leaned against the pole, facing the sky. "Dr. Rafaela. What do I need to do? How can I break free?"

"You changed on that ski slope ten years ago, as if you'd fallen in love the first time. In love with the preeminent side of human nature. Your spirit saw something beautiful. The way the human spirit can break speared by gentleness and vulnerability and the way the father's little boy brought out a gentler side to him. Let your human spirit break free from control. Don't carry everyone's burdens. Live, Cyrus, live... Leal would have wanted you to."

Dr. Rafaela was right. She paced up to him and set a gentle hand on his shoulder. Her tenderness almost broke his stubborn will. She tilted her head. "Seeing Jewel has done the same thing to you, hasn't it, Cyrus?"

* * *

Cyrus entered the kitchen as Nonna nibbled at a buttered bread roll in silence. Sofia and Jewel conversed at the table. Jewel was now a family member and each person around the table had both Italian and American heritage.

"So you were in *Breakfast at Tiffany's* at the Cort Theater. It opened in New York to rave reviews," Jewel said.

"It comes with its rewards," Sofia said.

"Tell me about your Tony Award nomination. Have you always known you wanted to be in theater?"

191

"Yes and no." She glanced at Cyrus. "I wanted to study medicine. When Leal entered that field, I figured one doctor in the family was enough. I reverted to theater as a passion and now my work takes me to many places around the world, touring."

They had connected.

Cyrus poured himself a glass of tomato juice and took a sip of its acrid taste. He set his glass down. "Jewel has done some performing herself. She's a wonderful gymnast and dancer."

Jewel shot him a puzzled glare. "How do you know?"

"Leal."

Sofia tilted her head. "That's right, he said you were a rhythmic gymnast. It's one of those sports you don't really know much about unless you watch the Olympics or the regional tournaments. I'm impressed."

Cyrus smiled at Jewel. With the morning light against her olive skin, she looked more ravishing than he had ever seen.

Jewel looked away from him.

Had she noticed? Had she felt it too? As much as he tried he could not tear his eyes from her. Had Leal looked at her this way? The hustle and ruffling in the kitchen disappeared until the only sounds that remained were that of his heighten breathing brought on by the lure of his admiring stare. He moved his eyes from her and walked to the kitchen sink to set down his empty glass before taking a seat opposite Sofia.

"I have something to tell you," Jewel said taking a deep breath. Her tone low and muffled. "When I met Cyrus in Saint Louis, I didn't want to remember... remember anything about Leal."

All eyes turned to face her.

Jewel shifted in her seat. "I was probably the last to see Leal alive. I'll never forget when the helicopter pilots came back without him—"

Cyrus visualized her ordeal, her unimaginable pain. Nonna placed a hand over Jewel's.

"Leal left me something. I didn't know what it was until recently. I filed it."

Sofia leaned forward. "What was it?"

"An envelope with several documents and an encrypted flash disk. He said I should hold onto it and that he wanted to share everything in it with me. I put it away in my backpack when we hiked to Keylong and forgot about it until a year after he was gone. Myranda's legal team embargoed my communicating with anyone related to Leal, or they'd make my life hell."

Anger crossed Cyrus's face. "They had no right."

Jewel shrugged. "If I hadn't met you, Cyrus, this would have stayed hidden."

Nonna looked into Jewel's eyes. "Why did you let Myranda treat you like that?"

Jewel coughed and took a sip of cold water. "I've asked myself that question for years. It was my fault."

"That's not true, Jewel," Cyrus said.

"Yes it is." She sighed. "He was married."

The room fell silent for several seconds as Jewel placed her palms on the table. "I was confused, cornered. Choose any of the above. I was alone and wanted everything to go away. All I cared about was Leal and the work he was doing."

Sofia shifted her feet and looked over at Cyrus who glanced out the window.

"Anyway," continued Jewel, "I placed the files and the flash disk in a box and didn't open it till last week." She looked from one Trelles to another. "Forgive me, I did not mean to keep anything from you. It was before I met you."

"Don't torture yourself, Jewel. You're family here," Nonna said.

Jewel glanced at Cyrus. "When you asked me in Saint Louis if I had anything Leal had left me, I remembered the documents in the envelope. It had been six years."

The room's focus was on Cyrus. Jewel pulled out the envelope from her pocket. "I believe what is in here will help with the case next week in New York. Myranda has to prove that her son is actually Leal's and information contained here proves otherwise. If you want to carry it further, you may find that she's not entitled to Trelles Industries."

Cyrus took the flash disk and slowly read the contents of the documents as Jewel set a hand over his. "I'm sorry for holding them all these years, but Leal asked me to. There's a reason he didn't mail these files to your family lawyer. Can't you see that?"

"We need to act now," Cyrus said.

"What will it change? Do you want to get involved with Myranda?"

Sofia eyed Cyrus's response but said nothing.

"Can't you see that if you go ahead with this, it may not be what Leal wanted and it may dig up old wounds?" Jewel said.

Cyrus's palms moistened. Jewel could be right. He placed the files on the table. "Myranda Vaux took Leal's work, his money, and is depleting Trelles Industries. It's our chance to make things right."

Nonna twitched in her seat. "Jewel, all we want to know is the truth."

Cyrus moved to the table. He turned to the women. He hated to argue with Jewel, but he had to finish this. Even with Jewel's painful reliving of her nightmare. "Jewel, Myranda took more than Leal's company."

"Shouldn't Myranda Vaux be exposed if she has committed a crime?" Cyrus said. His eyes bathed with anguish.

"I don't know if I agree. Leal left it alone. It's your choice and little of my business. Just let me know what I can do to help. But I think you should leave the past in the past. You don't need the money, never have," Jewel said.

Jewel stepped out of the kitchen, nearly tripping over her feet. *I can't get involved again.*

She progressed out of the kitchen failing to notice Nonna who'd discarded her walking stick and leaned it against the dining table. Nonna followed Jewel as she wandered through the hallway, under the spiral staircase and found the library that opened onto a cobbled stone patio overlooking the lawns. Warmth from the open windows, touched her bare shoulders. She sighed grateful to be in a warm climate and rubbed a hand over her chest as if to say it still ached from her loss in the Himalayas. She scampered past shelves containing volumes of books from floor to ceiling and a slanting ladder that aided those who needed a glimpse at the higher stacks of hardcovers.

The view of the distant rolling hills and the graceful vineyards alone took her mind off her thoughts about Leal.

Myranda will come back fighting. Had Myranda left him there intentionally?

She shuddered at the idea and a thought had entered her mind the minute she'd learned about the prenuptial agreement. Jewel ran a hand over some volumes, admiring the vast collections on classical music, architecture, and theater. Several family photographs graced the elegant dark wood shelves with their vintage silver frames. As she walked from shelf to shelf, her eyes fell on a carved red-cedar box. It looked Indian and reminded

Jewel of the artwork she'd seen in Northern India.

She picked it up.

"Go ahead, look inside." Nonna's soft-spoken voice startled her. Jewel turned around unaware she'd been followed into the room.

"Go on," Nonna said, her glistening eyes smiling.

Jewel lifted the brass catch. The handmade decorative cover had leather panels. Her eyes studied the two-toned photograph on the inside, a young boy. By the look of the eyes, and an unassuming smile, Jewel guessed it had to be one of the brothers. "Is this Cyrus or Leal?"

"Who do you think it is, Jewel?"

She looked at the photograph. "I think it's Cyrus."

Nonna didn't respond. Instead, she advanced to a nearby chair. "Please take a seat."

Jewel obliged.

"Sometimes a connection comes at unexpected times in our lives. Sometimes importune times, but we don't choose those who change the way we'll ever look at life again. My husband was the same way."

"I'm not sure I know what you mean."

"Meeting you in Montpellier changed his life. Leal lived with purpose after he met you. You did something to him that saw him start one of the greatest pharmaceuticals in the United States. Trelles can be a global pioneer in the history of medicine."

Jewel cast her eyes down. "Leal believed in free medicine for those who needed it most."

"That's right and if no organization would do it, he would," Nonna added.

Leal had spent hours in the clinic lab in Manali.

"Forgive him for marrying Myranda."

"Nonna it was ten years ago when we first met and to be honest, I didn't know whom I'd met, until Austria."

"His marriage to Myranda was always a mistake. We all knew."

"Why didn't he tell me?"

"Bambino, Myranda never loved Leal. My grandson wanted to tell you, possibly every day you were with him. You must've sensed it."

She was right. Leal had behaved strangely in India, especially after the accident on the roadside.

"He wanted to tell you. Maybe that's why he gave you the documents. He could trust you."

That word again. Trust.

"But why? I made such a fool of myself."

"Leal was a man of principle."

"What happened, Nonna? I mean between Myranda and Leal?"

"She cheated on him with her ex Devon Chesser. Leal overheard a conversation between her and Chesser, who had been his good friend from college, hours before they were to leave for their honeymoon. The two conspired to get her to marry Leal so they could control Trelles Pharmaceuticals. Leal heard them and I think she never knew. Leal married a very questionable woman and to this day we fail to know why."

"Doesn't sound like Leal. It's too simple. Leal could smell a rat a mile away."

"When we founded Trelles, the business depended on several things. Such as the level of control Leal and his grandfather would have, given the business's vulnerability to lawsuits and financing needs."

"I'm not sure I follow."

"Leal and his grandfather set up Trelles, which also included gaining licenses and permits. The company had never been public, but privately owned by the Trelles family. Trelles belonged to our family. My husband, Leal's grandfather was head, and he turned ownership over to Leal. This happened about seven years ago. Sofia and I opted out, choosing to be directors with less than thirty percent of the shares in the company between the two of us. What we didn't expect was his marriage to Myranda not too long after he took over."

"If he didn't love her why did he marry her?"

"We don't know. But what our lawyers discovered was that she had Trelles' ownership on her mind, and its intellectual property, access to science and research."

"What did that mean to her, she's no scientist?"

"Whether or not she coerced Leal into marriage, she knew what his death certificate was worth."

Jewel sighed. "Everything, right? That's why they so needed one produced with signatures from all the witnesses on the helicopter."

"The death certificate ensured Myranda could run Trelles

Industries."

"Is she qualified, capable?" asked Jewel.

"No, but Devon Chesser is."

* * *

A new level of admiration for Leal crept into Jewel's being. "How does a person do such a thing?"

"What?"

"Marry for other than love?"

"He didn't love her. Myranda wanted the money and perhaps he needed something from her," Nonna said. "Or she loved being tied to an influential doctor in medical and technological circles."

"Maybe." Jewel rubbed her eyebrows. "There's something I've been wandering for a while now." She stood and paced the room. "Why did Leal insist on a very specific prenup?"

"We're all to blame for that. I think Leal was not in favor but owing to his standing and worth in Trelles Industries, his lawyers advised him to get one drawn up."

"But, Nonna, it still makes little sense. Why would he ask for an heir in the agreement? Does the Trelles family need heirs?"

Nonna's face fell at the mention of Leal's awkward stipulation.

"I'm sorry, did I say something wrong?" Jewel said.

Nonna attempted a faint smile. "Leal was always fond of children. The legal team asked him to think of one thing he could put in a prenuptial agreement that would prove to him that Myranda loved him. My grandson recalled a conversation with Myranda in which she said that she wanted a family, that this was more important to her than anything. It was a spur-of-the-moment thing. I think that was all it was. But thank God, he did. This may be the only way to protect Trelles Industries."

"I'm sorry Nonna. I know little about big businesses. Is getting Trelles Industries back the most important thing to the family? Leal was casual about business. He was more passionate about helping the sick and finding new and effective ways to help and cure people."

"You're right, Jewel. That's why we need Trelles Industries back. Myranda controls a fifty-one percent stake in Trelles and there's intellectual property that belongs to our family. We can't access it without her consent. The only way we can get what we need is to have full control of the company again. And to do this, we must win at the mediation in New York."

"I see..."

"I used to run Mancini Corporation from New York with my husband," Nonna said. "We moved to America after the war and started a new life. Mancini was the answer. Our family in Italy was not doing well. We would have done anything to help family and communities at home."

"Was it difficult leaving Italy?"

"When Mancini took off in New York, we opened a branch here. After my husband died, the business went to our son Sean. But he wasn't as business savvy, or entrepreneurial as my grandson."

Jewel watched the older woman, as her stunning eyes glistened with fond memories of her family, a family bond that Jewel had never had. Jewel knew little about her extended family. Her mother never spoke of her American side and life before they moved to Udine where Jewel lived until her twelfth birthday. After that, they moved to New York. She had no relationships with father figures or brotherly types and often told herself she didn't understand men. Jewel avoided any entanglements with them, all until Leal came into her life.

Her hands moistened still holding the photograph. Then her hand moved over its edges. "What were the boys like growing up, Nonna?"

Nonna rose and paced to the mahogany desk by the window where she found several photographs in a drawer. "I would like to say it was a happy upbringing, but they lost their mother at a young age. Their father, my son Sean, could not handle losing her and he passed away. My husband and I raised the boys and Sofia."

"I'm sorry."

Nonna smiled brightening the mood in the room. "Cyrus has worked hard the last six years to secure the Trelles business for his brother's sake to no avail."

"Tell me about your late husband."

Nonna smiled fondly. "Bernado started Trelles with Leal in our garage. He was a pharmacist by training when we fled Italy with a passion for discovering new medicines. I guess that's where Leal got it from. They would spend ages looking at different sequences and cures, studying medicine and epidemics in history.

Anyway, what started as a hobby and home project grew into Trelles Industries. They discovered several vaccines."

She opened a little drawer. "Come see this."

Jewel made her way to the desk and examined the contents in the drawer. It contained two rows of early samples of sealed vaccines in elegant tubes.

"This is how Trelles Industries began," Nonna said.

Jewel's eyes fell on the see-through crystal falcons. They glistened in her eyes. A sense of pride for the gifted family filled her. They were hard workers who never thought of themselves first and, somehow, they'd endured against several odds. *I have to help them.*

Nonna moved to a picture of a handsome, silver-haired man. "This is my husband, Bernardo Treolli. He changed our name to Trelles when we moved to New York."

Bernardo bore a slight resemblance to Leal with his brown eyes, wavy hair and form fitting clothes.

"Leal graduated from Johns Hopkins Medical School," continued Nonna. "My husband was keen on making sure he accessed the best medical training. He devoted hours to research and studying human immune systems. He had no desire or passion to run a business that's where Cyrus steps in."

"Did the boys ever work together?"

"Cyrus was a silent partner in Trelles and monitored company affairs from Venice and had the right of attorney in Leal's absence."

"He never got involved in the business side. With Leal gone, Myranda's lawyers overrode his fifteen percent stake with a vote from Myranda."

Jewel's eyebrows knit realizing she'd heard little of Cyrus's upbringing. "When did Cyrus leave New York? He told me he and Leal never grew up together."

"It was because of me," Nonna said. "I moved to Venice, close to my family when Trelles Industries was listed and a third of its business went IPO on the New York Stock Exchange." Nonna took heavy breaths as she spoke. "Cyrus looked after our family affairs here and has run Mancini from Venice for a long time."

"Why did you leave New York?"

"I couldn't bear to be there after Bernado died."

Jewel gave Nonna an affectionate hug, cradling her small frame in her arms. "I like it here, Nonna."

The women turned as Cyrus paced into the library. He ran a hand through his impeccable hair. "Jeff Avent, our New York Lawyer has just called. We have seventy-two hours to file a motion against Myranda Vaux. Mediation will take place next week in New York."

"Is that enough time?" Nonna said.

Cyrus shot them a pained stare. "I've sent Jeff copies of the documents you brought Jewel."

His handsome eyes narrowed as he approached Jewel. "The real question Jeff asked is will you, Jewel, stand up to Myranda?"

* * *

TRELLES INDUSTRIES HEADQUARTERS
NEW YORK, CITY

Myranda observed Terence Bradick, her chief attorney, as he took a seat in the well-lit conference room. A Mediterranean-looking man with an angular face and a narrow nose, his hair was groomed back with an unruly curl dangling over his high forehead. Two nonchalant individuals stepped into the room after him dressed in high-priced business suits, a man of a plump build and a fair-skinned woman in her late twenties with short blond hair and a modest old fashioned haircut.

Terence placed his briefcase on the table and clicked it open. The two aides took a seat in the plush conference room on the thirty-third floor of the Midtown Manhattan office building. The 57-West office spaces that Myranda had helped secure for the pharmaceutical company, occupied several floors of an Art Deco building. Situated two blocks from Central Park and a block from Avenue of the Americas, a short distance from her town penthouse.

Myranda watched Terence in silence. He was used to her demands, yet wasn't easily dissuaded. Perhaps he was as corrupt in his business dealings as she was, or knew where the best profit for the day would come from. Terence had worked with Myranda for seven years, handling all her legal matters, personal and corporate. He ensured the legality of her commercial transactions, advising her on her rights and duties as the chief executive officer of Trelles Industries & Pharmaceuticals.

Terence possessed a profound knowledge of statutory law and regulations passed by government agencies and helped Trelles Industries achieve Myranda's goals within the confines of the law. They'd met at a marketing conference in Barcelona on new digital technology within the medical field. Striking a conversation about New York led to a long and fruitful professional relationship.

Terence coached her after she acquired her MBA in Marketing at the Ross School of Business, to getting her first pitch with her father's company. He admired her wit and knew when to confront her. It was the reason they got along. Terence ignored her shouting fits, her pushover nonsense and brash comments. She couldn't afford to lose him and he'd stayed with her despite knowledge of her unconventional methods. He was no fool and could see right through her business jargon. Terence asked her never to reveal her secrets to him, but asked for the facts in every matter. If he didn't know what she would not surrender, he wasn't liable. Terence worked with facts, and facts only. As long as they added up, he ignored his clients' motives, especially Myranda's.

Terence nodded in her direction. "We have the papers drawn up."

She slid into a white swivel chair. "Did you receive the materials from Mr. Chesser?"

Terence cocked his head, searching her eyes. A disapproving look, but Myranda didn't budge. He continued about his business, pulling out one document after another with the female attorney lining them in front of Myranda to sign. "Devon Chesser has produced this evidence." He slid out a document and placed it on the table. "That there's the DNA chart of your son and the sheet underneath shows Leal's DNA chart."

Myranda studied the documents trying to understand them.

Terence straightened his tie. "They've been authenticated and will pass in court. We have submitted them in the juvenile court and obtained a court order from the child support enforcement agency. The DNA results establish yours and Leal Trelles parent-child relationship."

She pursed her lips and handed the papers back to him. "Good. Then there'll be no problem when we meet with Leal's legal team."

"Leal's family will be present at the hearing."

That I didn't know.

Myranda shifted in her seat. She'd never met a single member of the Trelles family. Terence altered his head slightly so he could watch her response. "The documents were produced after a GENESA DNA test."

"What's that?"

"The most extensive and reliable DNA test, I've found. It specializes in Y-chromosome testing, only available for males, as it checks the Y-chromosome markers to determine which paternal haplogroup, or "clan" Calen belongs to."

"Is that so?"

"I must warn you, though, that you must go through this DNA review every six years of Calen's life. If there's any reason for not proceeding, as your legal counsel, I advise you to tell me now before we present this."

She tilted her head. "What would I have to tell you? I was married to Leal for five years and we conceived a son before he died."

"I understand Mrs. Vaux, but should any ducks be out of order, you'll be liable."

So what if she'd had to walk around the office for nine months pretending to be pregnant. It had been worth it. Even if she'd had to disguise a protruding front in public, taking fake trips to the Baby Gap store, prancing around in a pair of over-sized bound underwear and a tank top folded with duct tape, an accessory from the fourth month of the supposed pregnancy.

"Terence, I'm perfectly content to proceed, unless you would like me to get someone else."

He bit his lower lip and cast Myranda an unsocial look above his reading glasses, gawking more like a professor of anthropology than a legal counselor. "I'm sure you know the law. All right, then let's go through the details. I'll present this evidence against the prenuptial agreement and say you've fulfilled your side of the bargain and that there's no reason for Trelles Inc. to go to another set of hands."

"What will Leal's family produce? What counter argument can they bring?"

"Unless there's evidence that Calen is not Leal's, none." Terence watched her as she shifted in her seat. "Is there?"

* * *

Jewel welcomed Jeff's quiet stare. He had been Leal's attorney and Leal had trusted him. She stepped out to the pool in the morning sunshine. "Jeff, could I speak to you before the rest of the family join us?"

Jeff had arrived from New York that morning. And he swung in his chair still studying her. "Of course. So you're Jewel Carlone. What can I do for you?"

"Leal trusted you. I know that now. I haven't told his family something critical, my real reason for coming to meet them."

"I see."

"I want to know what happened in India. Why no proper rescue took place when Trelles could've done it themselves."

Jeff shifted in the garden chair and inclined his head but said nothing.

Jewel continued. "Why was he presumed dead so easily? Is the Vaux family hiding something that might give me closure on this?"

"Jewel, it's difficult for us too." His eyes softened. "The only evidence we have against Myranda is related to the prenuptial agreement. If she didn't live up to the stipulation, then she doesn't legally own Trelles Industries. My advice is you help the family. It will mean a great deal. You were the last one to see Leal alive. That gives them comfort. They've suffered."

A chill ran through her although there was no breeze on the April afternoon. She sank into a chair and stared at Villa Treolli's glistening swimming pool. A gardener attended to the gleaming waters fishing for unruly leaves and debris that had floated in after last night's storm. Her attention shifted to Jeff once more as he straightened the ruffles in his sensible suit. He was sincere. Kaya had mentioned on the phone, two nights ago, that the Trelles family had known Jeff for many years. He'd also helped establish the company with Leal and Bernardo, was civil and made complete assessments of facts. But what if the facts weren't plain?

Jewel flinched as she sipped the sour grapefruit juice she'd made earlier. Bright lights reflected off the pool and shone in her eyes. "I don't agree. Something wasn't right after Leal's death, especially the day at the police station in Manali."

"When the Trelles family regains the company, they can launch an investigation if necessary."

"That could take months."

"We've no alternative. Myranda, as Leal's widow, was the only one the police in Manali would deal with at the time of his death. We have nothing to start with."

Jewel's voice was firm. "We can start with Myranda."

Jeff stared at her with dark pensive eyes, his face displaying a workaholic streak. "If there's evidence somewhere in Trelles Industries, we can get to it after this first step in New York."

"Myranda's hiding something."

"That's why we need Trelles back, Jewel, let's take it a step at a time."

"Why hasn't the Trelles family tried to fight Myranda in the last six years? Why now?"

"They didn't have you on their side and they didn't have the documents you had. Plus they had to wait till Myranda's boy turned five to even begin an investigation."

Jewel mused on what Jeff had said. Perhaps she could gain closure this way.

But somehow it wasn't enough.

Quiet footsteps on the pool's safety flooring startled Jewel. Kaya made her way to them wearing a turquoise drape dress and sank into a seat next to Jewel. "Getting acquainted? We have a lot to review," she said.

Kaya had flown in that morning after Jewel had told her everything.

"Already acquainted," Jewel said.

"I contacted Jeff after you left for Saint Louis."

"Since then, we've covered much ground on the plane here," Jeff said. "It was a risk both of you took in opening Leal's documents and taking his encrypted flash disk. I'm glad you did. The disk contained a hidden code with a bank address and vault access that contained further documents." He fingered a set of papers in front of him. "For six years, I never knew how to comfort Leal's family, even with my own suspicions."

"So no hard feelings," Kaya said.

His face rearranged itself into a grin. "The contents were addressed to me anyhow. I give you my permission in advance for having done so." Jeff jotted down notes on his laptop open in front of him. He sipped his espresso. "And thank you, Kaya, for joining my legal team on this. I can use a good family lawyer close to Jewel."

Kaya's face relaxed into a smile. "It's an honor to work with a seasoned attorney."

Cyrus and Sofia made their way from the main house and joined the trio by the water. Jewel leaned back into her seat as Kaya flipped open her laptop. "Shall we begin?"

Jeff spoke first. "The first thing Kaya and I discussed on our way here is bringing you across as credible and why you should be in that mediation room, Jewel."

"It's a mediation? I thought it was a hearing," Jewel said.

"No. It's a mediation," Jeff said. "An alternative dispute resolution to court. This way, we can resolve the issues with concrete effects and save time. Both parties have agreed to it."

"Myranda's team will want to know why I'm there."

"You're a close friend of the family and everyone here will vouch for that. You worked with Leal as his employee when he died," said Cyrus keeping his face impassive. "The mediator, in our case is Judge Tia Constanta."

Kaya set a hand on Jewel's. "She'll act as a neutral third party. She's there to facilitate the discussion next week and make sure all necessary preparation and documentation are complete." Her face betrayed a hint of persuasion. "Myranda has consented to mediation. It's less publicity for her that way. Your evidence may be required, Jewel."

Cyrus watched Jewel and she caught his encouraging eye before she shot up. "Myranda will go mental with me in the mediation room. She doesn't like me much. Don't you see? Her legal team—"

Jeff interjected. "Judge Tia will direct everyone to the facts and away from personal attacks."

Cyrus set a hand on her shoulder encouraging her to sit. "We'll all be there with you. And remember, this is a big *if.* You may not have to say anything."

Jewel took a deep breath and plopped into her seat. "I don't think I should be there."

"We've prepared a statement using Leal's documents. Leal had a complete medical file on Myranda in that vault."

"What's our statement?" Jewel said.

"It's a summary and includes DNA evidence regarding Myranda's son, Leal's rescue, and death certificate. We'll bring this to the mediation. Remember we're dealing with a paternity issue here," Jeff said.

"We're threatening to begin a paternity proceeding in a family court. This means we want to file and challenge a verified petition that establishes Leal's paternity over Myranda's child, Calen Trelles. Myranda doesn't know that during the writing of the prenuptial agreement, Leal had a full medical file on her," Cyrus said.

"Myranda may then opt to consent to an order of paternity," Kaya added. "She's already said there's no consent and is prepared to present blood or DNA tests."

"What if Leal is the father?"

The question all hadn't voiced left Jewel's lips and Cyrus's smile vanished. "The evidence in these documents proves he wasn't."

"Myranda suspects Leal and I—"

"The truth is you didn't know that Leal was married. We'll not touch on your relationship with him. Leal hired you to photograph his work. We have evidence from the workers at the clinic and many e-mails between you two," Cyrus said.

Jeff knotted his fingers. "Just so we're all clear and before we meet Myranda's legal team, can you tell us what happened that week in India?"

Jewel twitched and leaned from Cyrus. "I followed Leal around the clinic in Manali. I photographed patients and critical cases he wanted to focus on. There were many in need. Some had no access to medicine, others had deeper problems like no medical care during birth or access to clean water. Some remote villages we visited didn't have basic access to vaccines and medicine for preventable diseases. Leal saw this as an opportunity for Trelles Industries."

Kaya's face became an image of intense sincerity as she spoke. "Jewel, Leal trusted you. He gave you these files. Should they try to discredit you, it must come across that Leal wanted you to work with him in confidence."

"Won't the fact that the documents were unopened and addressed to Jeff jeopardize our case? Won't the judge dismiss it?" Jewel said. The questions echoed through silence, not addressed to any of them.

Jeff spoke first. "You didn't open the files. The legal team did."

"Won't they want to know why I waited this long?"

"We'll claim that when Myranda made you sign those papers

at the police station, her one stipulation was to stay away from the Vauxs and the Trelleses. You were frightened. That's the truth and will be credible enough for the judge."

Sofia cast Cyrus a disturbed look. Soon, Jewel's gaze settled on him. Did Sofia understand her dilemma? Did she have one ally on this team? One that wanted the truth out of Myranda?

"This shows you as a confidant and an employee who had every right to have those files," Cyrus said.

Jewel scanned the little group around her. Nothing in their faces gave her confidence. And a burning feeling in her gut told her they'd just unleashed a war that would doubtless leave severe casualties.

Chapter 15

TRELLES INDUSTRIES
NEW YORK CITY

Jewel fidgeted with the collar of her lavender, cotton wrap shirt. Her eyes shied away from Judge Constanta, who'd strolled into the room commanding its attention. She seemed a thoughtful woman whose hooded, black eyes were like two spheres of black marble. Constanta was younger than Jewel had imagined. Her tall and curvy build fit well in a paneled jacket over a knee-length, pencil skirt. She'd mixed traditional office colors with floral feminine hues. It gave her the right combination for a professional look. Her dark skin was as radiant as a summer's afternoon. Jewel studied the pair of reading glasses Constanta used to hold her ebony hair from her square face.

Cyrus hadn't left her side much after boarding the plane from Venice and was behaving more like a confidant. He wanted to make the process comfortable for her and she was grateful for his efforts. He took a seat next to her and handed her a glass of chilled water. The reset lights in the functional conference room beamed down on the oval table set for ten participants.

She took a sip of water.

"You okay?" Cyrus said.

"Yes. You?"

He nodded. "The others are on their way."

"I shouldn't be here."

"You'll be fine. I'm right here and it's my fight."

Was she ready to see Myranda again? A condescending professional some men would call attractive, and skin that lived in a spa. "Cyrus." He turned to her. "I hope your family gets the closure we all need today."

He grazed shoulders with her and his hand found hers under the table where it had drifted. He held it for several seconds and turned his lips to her ear. "You're not alone this time."

The skin on skin contact sent a delightful shiver through her. Cyrus meant what he said. She saw it in his eyes. He wouldn't leave her alone. His gesture was unexpected, yet she found her heart sprinting with hysteria. More than usual. She would get through the taxing ordeal and the new level of magnetism to Cyrus creeping into all their conversations. A cocktail of inexplicable emotions rocked her mind. She battled the new sensation and barely noticed when Myranda's legal team of three stepped into the room.

Cyrus released her hand and patted it. She swallowed hard. Then her eyes fell on Myranda, who strolled in like a gazelle with her thick, long ginger-colored hair worn in a style that reminded Jewel of a flowing cape. Her skin was perfection, her wardrobe immaculate and wore a stunning sleeveless emerald, jersey dress with a wrap front, gathered at the waist and ending on her knees.

She wore a bland expression on her face and Jewel kept a straight face as Myranda and her legal team took a seat across from her.

"We may begin," said Judge Constanta as she took her seat and nodded to the legal teams.

"Good morning, all. My name is Terence Bradick," began an eloquent attorney, his voice resonating with self-confidence. He was the same man Jewel had seen at the Manali police station. "We know why we're here. The Trelles family represented by Jeff Avent has brought forth a paternity complaint regarding the late Leal Trelles, my client's late husband."

He took a pause. "Now, under the state law of New York, if the mother and father are married when the child is born, the law says the father is the legal father. In cases where a couple isn't married, the biological father isn't considered the legal father until paternity is legally established. But this isn't the case here. At the time of Dr. Trelles's death, my client was married to him. The law gives specific rights to the child and certain legal rights and responsibilities to the father. In our case, Calen Vaux-Trelles was born close to nine months after Leal's accident. This alone would acknowledge Leal as the legal father."

Jewel kept her eyes down avoiding eye contact with Myranda altogether.

Terence coughed to clear his throat. "A prenuptial agreement was signed before the marriage." He drew out a copy and placed it in front of him. "Now, the prenuptial stipulates a paternity check before allocating the sum of eighty-five thousand dollars from the Trelles family trust fund to mother and child. The Trelles family has challenged paternity and we're here to prove otherwise." He glanced round the room, his eyes hawking at the participants as if to certify that his words were followed with care.

Jewel held her breath and caught Kaya's eyes two seats from her. Kaya winked back in silence.

Jewel hadn't known these full details of the agreement and Terence remained expressionless as he spoke. "The prenuptial states that, at age six, after a live child birth, a review would be conducted of the assets of Trelles Industries. The fund would reward the mother with increased shares and dividends, and a sum of $80,000 as mentioned earlier. Should a contest be filed, as we find ourselves, then a required mediation or hearing must follow."

"That's correct. And a vital contest it is," Jeff Avent said.

"I think we can handle this quick and fast with no further pain to both parties," said Terence.

Jeff nodded. "Agreed." He distributed several papers to the participants. "On September 29, seven years ago, a document was filed detailing the medical history and an unfortunate medical condition which prevents Myranda Vaux from having any offspring by natural means. This document was commissioned by Leal Trelles with Ms. Vaux's consent."

"That's a lie!" Myranda said. "I never agreed to an examination."

"You did," Jeff continued. "Is this your signature?"

She cast a glance at the documents. "Leal never said the examination was to explore all my medical history, just our marital compatibility."

The room fell silent echoing with her last phrase.

Jewel trembled.

Cyrus's knee knocked hers slightly reassuring her.

Jeff leaned forward, clasping his palms together. "May I continue?"

Judge Constantia nodded.

"The medical examiner was her late husband Leal Trelles himself. The document was redrafted and signed again by both parties at a private New York clinic three months before Dr.

Trelles' death. Dr. and Mrs. Trelles conducted a routine check of their health statuses and as a result, it was established that Myranda Vaux couldn't have a child through natural means due to a condition outlined here." He placed copies of medical papers in front of each participant.

Jewel studied them. *Fibroid tumors? That's the disease Leal was investigating in India.*

The sound of shuffling papers filled the room. Myranda's face stared down at the documents in question, her eyes glaring. Her body still. She crossed her arms above the table.

Jewel's hand reached for Cyrus's knee. She held her breath wanting to escape. To leave the room and the madness that didn't concern her. Her throat began to dry and although they'd been in the room for less than an hour, it seemed like hours. The mediation reminded her of the day at the Indian police station.

Her breathing increased.

Cyrus set a calm hand over hers, subduing her emotions for several seconds.

"Given the evidence we present here, action is simple. Myranda Vaux's takeover of the Trelles Industries is nullified and invalid on the grounds of a prenuptial agreement, she herself signed," Jeff said.

The judge removed her reading glasses and bit the end of the rims. "I see."

Jeff pointed to a paragraph on the third page of the document. "Ms. Vaux may have a child, but according to this medical report, that boy is not Dr. Trelles's son."

* * *

Terence's lips pressed tight. Jewel watched him and a new confidence engulfed her. She was a step closer to finding the truth. The agony of not knowing what had happened to Leal after his accident had kept her up most nights. That part of her life had to close.

Myranda's defense fell silent. Terence cleared his throat. His face tightened and the burning enthusiasm with which he'd begun the morning's proceedings disappeared, replaced by pinched eyebrows over concentrating eyes.

Terence curled forward and studied Jeff's documents. "You

211

say that Mrs. Vaux-Trelles was incapable of having a son at the time this document was developed? Circumstances changed. She carried a baby to term." He found a sheet of paper in his folder. "Here are the birth records, the birth plan administered and certified by the Mount Sinai Medical Center in New York."

Judge Constanta held out a hand and Terence placed the documents in her firm grip. She said nothing as she studied them. Her eyes narrowed and focused on the fine print.

Those hospital documents must be forged. Which of the two pieces of evidence was accurate? Leal's papers or the hospital documents. No hospital lies. And if the facts were correct, could Myranda have had Leal killed? What about the tampered car in India? But she had been at the scene. Myranda wasn't that capable. It was a natural accident. *Maybe...*

Jewel's gaze flirted around the room, not settling on one person or object for any length of time. She was faint and a streak of agitation crept into her body. Two seats down, her eyes caught Kaya. Her friend clutched the silent cellphone she never left the house without and shot Cyrus a glance.

His eyes glared at Myranda's face.

Jeff's eyebrows drew together, studying his opponents. Kaya had emphasized that Myranda's child had been born at home. *Where did this medical record come from?*

Terence progressed, his voice confident. "A son was born on October 2, six years ago to Mrs. Vaux. These tests administered show that his DNA matches that of the father. The samples used come from records that Leal Trelles filed himself with Trelles Industries. They were commissioned by him. Then no doubt this child is his."

Cyrus ran a hand across the papers in front of him, scrutinizing the fine print. "A hospital birth record doesn't prove she had that boy."

All eyes fell on Cyrus. He watched Myranda. "Why don't we hear it from Myranda?" He tilted his head. "You were never pregnant?"

The first bold statement Jewel heard from Cyrus.

Terence's calm voice broke the tension. "You can't intimidate my client. Mrs. Vaux has a signed statement of her view of the matter and is not required to answer your questions. She's the legal mother."

Anger welled up in Cyrus's tense face. His eyes averted to

Jeff. "Legal she may be. Natural is another matter. Natural is what we are here to prove."

Myranda rose, her eyes fuming at Cyrus. She slammed her manicured hands on the conference table, her action sending a coffee cup rattling. If the glance in her avant-garde eyes was anything to go by, her professional behavior was under gunfire.

"That boy is not yours. Leal proved you couldn't carry a child to term. Read the material for yourself," Cyrus said.

Myranda crossed her arms. "Don't come here threatening me with papers written with such sentimental hogwash from a man who knows nothing about me. Who are you, anyway?"

"My brother was a scientist and a doctor of the highest caliber. That's why you married him."

"You're Leal's brother? I didn't know he had a brother," Terence said. "I object to this sort of questioning."

Cyrus continued undeterred. "At the end of Leal's life, his research focused on rare cases of infertility. And believe me, if his report declared she was infertile, next to law, it's truth." His eyes glared with passion and loathing.

Judge Constanta's commanding voice came short of an erupting verbal battle and she narrowed her eyes. "That's enough now. Let's take a recess. I'm proposing suspension for three hours. I want to review this evidence with each party individually, if necessary."

She rose and left the room. A minute later, one by one Myranda and her legal team strode out of the room leaving Cyrus, Jeff, and Kaya in conference.

Jeff began. "Things are looking good. There's no way she can contest Leal's papers."

"Her DNA documents were fabricated," added Kaya.

"Or bought," Jewel said.

Jewel's confidence surprised her and from the avid peers she received from Kaya. She'd spoken aloud.

Cyrus rose. "That boy's not hers."

Even with his confident statement, something bothered him. He looked each person in the eye. "We've dealt with Myranda before. Though questionable, her legal team has always followed the law to the last ink drop." He turned to Jeff. "What have we missed, Jeff? It's improbable that the Sinai Medical Center fabricated that document."

"Are we fighting a losing battle?" Kaya asked.

Cyrus strolled to the floor-length windows that bordered the hallway and glanced out. "I'm not saying that. Terence is a smart attorney and wouldn't use fictitious documents," he said.

Jewel followed his gaze. "Then where did they come from?"

His eyes didn't leave the window once. Jewel followed his gaze and spotted Terence conferring with Judge Constanta.

She barely heard Cyrus's voice.

"That's what I intend to find out."

* * *

Myranda's breathing was above normal. She glared at Terence from where she stood a meter from him and Constanta. She strained her ear in their direction. Her future, her being, depended on today's outcome. She leaned against the far wall of the large hallway and flexed her fingers.

"Judge Constanta, I'm sure you can see this is preposterous. The evidence is clear and this'll hold in any New York State court."

Constanta's eyes caught the words that fell off Terence's arguments and she started a march to the elevators, her eyes fixed to the floor. Terence followed close by. "Can't you see that there are loopholes in this hearing? I mean, the family has had six years."

Constanta reached the elevator and pressed the call button, but didn't respond.

Myranda needed answers and strode toward them. When she approached, Terence set a hand on her arm.

Constanta peered at Myranda. "Mrs. Vaux, I'll have you know that I've been practicing family law for twenty years. Believe me, a court hearing is much worse than mediation, I hope we won't end there if we don't reach a decision. Court makes difficult situations worse."

"Why would I have anything to hide?"

Constanta approached. "Any concerns that need to be raised, I suggest you speak to your attorney here and present them fairly and conclusively in the next session."

"Naturally."

The judge stepped back into the open elevator and called her floor. "Mrs. Vaux, I don't play infantile games and I'm uncompromising."

Myranda stood motionless in front of the steel doors before sliding past Terence toward the end of the hall.

Where's Devon? She fumbled through her leather bag for her phone and headed for her office. Once inside, she closed the door and dialed Devon's number. "Sort this out, Devon! I don't know how he knows, but I don't like that brother's look. I don't understand this family."

"What brother? Calm down, Myranda. I'm in my car downstairs. Constanta is leaving the building. I'll take care of this."

* * *

Cyrus watched Constanta appear through the Trelles lobby. Soon Myranda made her way to the entrance. As she passed the revolving door, she received respectful nods from the door attendant.

Cyrus inched behind.

"Shall I get your car, Mrs. Constanta," asked the door attendant.

"No, thank you, I'll walk. I've some thinking to do."

Cyrus followed close by in his car, turned left into 8th Avenue's bustling business district, then into west 29th as Constanta tramped up the stairs of a Romanesque church building. Its large towers and spires proudly displaying a Gothic trim. Cyrus slouched against the door as he drove.

His car rolled to a halt. His hand tightened on the wheel as he parked the Volkswagen behind a Peugeot across the street. He swung the door open and pulled himself out before heading toward the church's entrance.

Inside Constanta slid into a seat in the front pews. Cyrus persevered, skulking past the font and found the side aisle. He inched from aisle to aisle until he found a discarded altar-boy chair left behind the pole nearest the front row. He slouched into a scratchy seat in the main sanctuary, his head pressed against the concrete, meters from Constanta. Ahead meditation candles in even rows, indicative of prayers offered by as many souls as seats in the cathedral burned without an ounce of warmth from their heat reaching him.

He peered from behind the pillar. Constanta had her eyes closed as several tourists advanced down the aisles. Several meters away, a minister answered questions they had on the church. Cyrus turned his head toward the entrance to see a face he hadn't seen in years.

* * *

Cyrus breathed in a half whisper. *Devon!*

Devon glided down the aisle, a confident step in his march. Several moments later, Devon stole a seat next to Constanta. "I hope I'm not disturbing your meditation, Judge."

"You?"

Cyrus took another look from behind the pillar as Constanta shifted in her seat. "What do you want, someone could see you. What're you doing here?"

"Making sure my investment is protected. How is the mediation proceeding?"

"Get out of here."

"Not so fast. New evidence has surfaced. It could jeopardize our desired outcome."

"I need to think."

"You'd better stick to our arrangement. You owe me for the life of that dear boy in Luther Medical Center."

"Leave my son out of this."

"Your son can get the medical attention and medication he needs," Devon said, clearing his throat. "Should I remind you that drug makers avoid producing orphan drugs? They do so in favor of potential blockbusters. This means your son, as a sufferer of Duchenne Muscular Dystrophy, wouldn't have access to the Corticosteroids drugs Trelles Industries is manufacturing under my supervision."

Cyrus caught the sound of controlled sobs leave her throat. Devon's bite was sharper than he remembered.

"Thanks to me, Mrs. Constanta, your son will not only live, he'll thrive. Your position as a reputable judge came in quite handy for Trelles Industries' little dilemma," Devon said.

Cyrus's mind rang bells of caution. Devon's hushed tones were as treacherous as a hyena guarding eggs.

"I need not remind you that if untreated, mutation in your

son could reach muscle degeneration and eventual death."

Cyrus leaned his head back against the cool pillar for a moment. *Criminal!*

Not only were those drugs produced by Leal's team, they were drugs Leal wanted Trelles to manufacture and supply free to sufferers. The boy suffered from a rare disease. Muscular dystrophies were a cluster of inherited disorders typified by progressive muscle wasting.

A pounding invaded Cyrus's temples. He clenched his jaw. *Damn it!*

"Let's not toy with your son's medical condition," he heard Devon say. "If you play fair today, I'll make sure our recent improvements in medicine extend the life of your son."

Constanta rose. "Leave me alone." Her voice echoed off the stone walls. "Believe me, Chesser, after today, if I ever see your face again, you'll not only end up in my courtroom, I'll—"

"Shush... Let's not make threats in the sanctuary."

Cyrus's heart began a sprint of wrath. *Sanctuary! You've awakened the claws of the mother eagle in her!*

"I have little time before the end arguments are heard," she said.

Devon leaned forward. "Then, maybe I can help you with further vital information."

Cyrus peeked again, straining his ear, invisible behind a dim shadow as Constanta raised one eyebrow.

"What information?"

Chapter 16

Cyrus stepped into the men's restrooms. Situated in one of New York's finest cuisine spots, the urban French restaurant across the street from Trelles' headquarters bustled with eager diners. He'd hurried back, leaving the Volkswagen outside the church. Had he known the distance she was walking, he needn't have bothered taking the car. Cyrus heard Devon's voice in his head and the sobs of the judge. Devon had been helping Myranda. How could he have missed that? Devon conspired with Myranda from the minute she married Leal and they'd laughed at Leal's oblivion and generosity.

Damn it! Leal, how can we win this mediation? We need to win. Myranda had planned her takeover for months, but was she the only one lying? He hated himself. Dr. Rafaela's words echoed in his head, *Deception may haunt you one day.* He needed to be a step ahead.

Cyrus threw cold water in his face. It trickled down his white shirt, and he reached for soft paper towels to mop the dampness from his chest. Five minutes later, he plodded out of the bathroom and made his way to the dining area of the restaurant. The session was to reconvene in forty minutes. He thought for several seconds. The documents Jewel had signed couldn't have been without coercion. A thought gnawed in his mind. Jewel differed from other women he knew and Leal's attraction to her now made sense. Jewel had gone through enough, taking blame and a burden she wasn't meant to shoulder.

He exited to the main eating area. Sofia had flown in that morning with them and she waited at a corner table set for two, sipping a glass of lemon water. She drained it as Cyrus approached.

"Have you ordered for me?"

She nodded. "I thought you'd like the smoked Brooklyn

Ricotta with Agnolotti and just some water."

His stomach wasn't ready to down a heavy meal. He searched her face. "So you know?"

"Jeff filled me in," she said. "What are you going to do?"

"The only thing I can. Fight this with the truth. We've waited a long time."

Her eyes lit. "Really? What if we lose?"

His voice strained as her eyes met his. "Sofia, we can't let Myranda get away with this."

"Is that the only reason?" She placed a hand over his. "I've not always agreed with your choices, Cyrus, but you're my brother and I love you. I believe in you. Please do what's right. As painful as it is, it'll make all the difference."

Cyrus lowered his glass. "Will it?"

Sofia swallowed hard. "After that, all things should return to normal. Please tell me they will."

He hated to see the pain in her eyes, but the strain in her voice was harder to bear. He needed to hear her laugh. Her distinctive laugh, a boisterous guffawing, that had always brought calm to him, signaling that life could be laughed at and any problems could dissolve. Sofia was the strong one, the keeper of his secrets and had a profound sense of companionship he'd always counted on. Her sincerity went deeper than the ice queen she sometimes was when circumstances didn't go her way. Sofia could give sound advice. He needed it, but would it hurt? Would old wounds resurface?

He emptied his water in one gulp and looked into her eyes glistening back at him like large sapphires. "Myranda will give up Trelles Industries, one way or another. The company has to do what Leal and our grandfather meant for it. I'm more convinced of this after today."

"I know." She gave up all pretense of eating her served hors d'oeuvres and reached for her wineglass. "How did Myranda get Leal's DNA chart. We had those sealed long ago."

"She's had help from an old acquaintance. Myranda is capable of anything."

The main meal arrived; a hearty display of Agnolotti ravioli served with jingle bell peppers, Meyer Lemon, pearl onions, fava beans, and roasted pine nuts.

Sofia took a bite of her ravioli. "Do you think Myranda knew her infertility problem would become known?"

"Probably not. But she was willing to take that chance, which tells me there's more than money at stake here."

Sofia pulled her plate toward her. "If she were barren, why did she sign the prenup? What a chance to take."

"Whatever happens though, she's lied to the courts, to Leal, to us. The prenuptial agreement was clear. In the event of Leal's death, to acquire Trelles fully, any heirs had to be Leal's." She chewed slowly. "Why would she fake it? Didn't she know she'd be found out?"

"She wants something more valuable than money."

"Like what?"

"Release from old favors. Myranda has made many enemies in her career."

"Yes, but who?"

Cyrus narrowed his eyes. "She took a risk, much like we have."

Sofia watched him silently. "What else is bothering you?"

He looked into her searching face. "Nothing."

"You're thinking about Jewel, and what she would do if she knew."

He glared up at her.

Sofia wiped her lips with a napkin. "Why don't you tell her the truth? Sometimes, we women want it out straight. We value honesty and vulnerability. Mystery only works for a while."

Cyrus pushed his plate away from him and took a deep breath. "I can't, Sofia. It's too complicated, too much of a risk."

"Give her the benefit of the doubt. I like her. She's probably your best ally in this. Just tell her."

"I can't Sofia, not after what she's been through." He took a large mouthful and set his fork down. "We'd better get back. They'll be waiting."

Sofia grasped his hand. Her eyes resonated with strength and determination. "The way to win this battle, the mediation, your pain, may be to give Jewel what Leal wanted to give her."

* * *

Kaya picked up the phone to Weston.

"How's the mediation going?" he asked.

"Things are looking good so far. The Vaux team didn't know

220

about our wild card. The judge had to call a recess."

"That's positive."

"Yeah. Myranda didn't know that we had those files on her. That threw her legal team."

His voice wavered. "I'd wait to open the champagne. Myranda has single-handedly clawed her way up the Trelles ladder leaving injuries behind."

"We have her where she needs to be."

"Be careful. I'll see you when you get home."

"Okay," she said, and hung up. Kaya turned as Jewel walked toward her and took a seat on a nearby bench. "Hey."

Kaya sank beside Jewel. They'd taken a casual stroll during recess seeking air and ended up in the urban oasis of Rockefeller Center's Channel Gardens. Jewel hadn't looked well after the meeting and Kaya had suggested the escape from the conference room and a stroll to the botanical outdoor promenade. Jewel's face had been a mystery all morning. Even though Kaya understood Jewel, icy indifference in her smile meant she was up to something.

Kaya nudged Jewel's shoulder. "How are you holding up?" She'd seen that look before, six years ago. "Jeff thinks this'll all be over soon. Things are looking good. Jewel, isn't that what you want?"

Jewel shrugged. Her stare was the same the day she'd stepped off the plane from New Delhi. When Jewel had returned from Montpellier with her aspiration of becoming the most decorated rhythmic dancer dashed in a single choreographic error, she'd had the same look.

"Come on, Jewel. We've talked about this. You can finally move on. Now those clinics and medical centers that Leal wanted to finish in India can happen. Then, who knows, maybe you and Cyrus—"

Jewel raised an eyebrow. Her attraction to Cyrus had been obvious to Kaya the minute she'd left for Venice. It was how she talked about him, and *to* him.

"Yes, I've been observant. What is it with the Trelles brothers and you?"

Aware of Kaya's eyes on her, she scratched her forehead. "What would I do without you? You remind me of the person I want to be and am grateful for that." Jewel linked an arm around Kaya's. "I know you've gone out of your way to sort this out. I

221

appreciate what you're doing."

"Let's go on vacation somewhere after this is all over. Perhaps, take a trip like the old days. You know, show up at the airport and get on any plane with available seats. Now let's see... or would you rather go with a certain cultured Venetian?"

Jewel chuckled. "I remember those days. Isn't that how we ended up in Salzburg and met Leal? Did we plan that trip?"

Her face broke into a pleasant giggle, and Kaya understood why she was bewitching to men when she smiled.

"And for your information, Cyrus is a nice guy who..." Jewel began.

"Who can't stop looking at you? Come on, Jewel, you've noticed it too."

Jeff strolled up to the women, sipping a cup of coffee in a Styrofoam cup. "We have ten minutes, should we head back?"

"All right Jeff. We'll be right there," Kaya said.

Jewel took Kaya's arm. "Before we go in, I want to tell you something. I'm still concerned. So far, no one has mentioned what happened to Leal on the mountain. I understand this mediation addresses the company and the prenup. But don't you think it strange that no one has raised the document I signed and why Myranda had to get so many witnesses to certify Leal's death?"

Kaya pursed her lips. "It's not important now."

"To me, it is. Whatever happens in there today, I'll still go after the truth."

Kaya's eyes studied Jewel. A victory in the conference room wasn't the answer Jewel was seeking. Hers was a deeper quest. Jewel rose from the bench, the sun hitting her eye and she slid on her sunglasses. "Will you help me?"

Kaya rose instinctively, a flicker of surprise overpassing her face. "I'm after the truth like the next lawyer, but what will you do with the truth? Jewel, wake up and look around you. It won't bring Leal back."

"I didn't mean that."

"Cyrus is your man. You have your second chance right in front of you. Take it and forget the mountain. It's been six years. Cyrus cannot take his eyes off you for a second. Shouldn't you call it a day about Leal? Take a good look at him. Be happy, Jewel, because I think the man has some serious eyes for you."

Why couldn't Jewel see what was plain to all the Trelleses and those around her? Her heart belonged to one brother or another. This was her redemption. Digging up old wounds would stop her progression and any chance of happiness.

"Jewel, please. We'll win. I promise," Kaya said.

A pang of misery was evident on Jewel's face as she spoke. "I've struggled for a long time. The only way I can move is if I close Leal's door."

"You've struggled with this since leaving Venice. I know what the problem is. Cyrus makes you feel the same way that Leal did and you feel guilty." Kaya pursed her lips. "You'll never give up will you?"

"You lose your heart once, Kaya. Look at you and Weston. I don't think many of us get a second chance."

"Come on Jewel, you seriously don't believe that?"

"I do. That's why finding what happened to Leal is my only hope."

"You can't mean that. It's been six years!" She leaned forward, her hands on her hips. "Jewel, you may never find out. Have you thought about that?"

* * *

Jewel slid into the seat next to Cyrus as Constanta flipped through several papers.

"I've had considerable time to deliberate the evidence and the arguments you've presented here today. Before we complete the mediation I've some things I'd like to say."

Judge Constanta's words filled the room. The mediation process had allowed each side the opportunity to be heard, present their grievances, and benefit from dispute resolution without the expense and delay of a trial.

Something was growing coldly determined inside of Constanta. "Seeing we left the last session further from resolution than we intended, I hope I can offer some helpful insights."

Constanta leaned back in her chair. "As I sat reflecting on this, I suddenly remembered that I'm not a fan of prenuptial agreements. They complicate lives, cause pain, but in a case like this, I'm happy to see that one was drafted as things look more straightforward."

Kaya, who'd taken a seat next to Jewel, grasped her hand under the table, firm and reassuring. Jeff held his fountain pen over his notepad. Cyrus had been quiet since re-entering and Jewel was thankful for his presence beside her. Why did he watch Constanta with such caution? More than before, scrutinizing every word she said and movement she made.

For the first time since the meeting had begun, Myranda glanced up at Jewel and the women's eyes met, as Constanta proceeded with her speech.

She ran a finger over her documents. "So that you understand, the decision reached here today will be recorded, reviewed and ordered by a different judge. Our aim is to reach an agreement. If you want to reach a decision without trial, I'll offer some suggestions. Before we proceed to duration, here are some thoughts."

The room quieted.

Constanta's words were spoken with guard. None challenged her deliberations. Jewel observed her speak with reluctance. "I've seen a wide number of reasons couples use post- and prenuptial agreements. And they aren't all because they think their spouses will get more than their fair share of assets in the event of a divorce. My role here today isn't to decide the outcome, but to facilitate your reaching your solution."

The judge's shoulders loosened. "A change or significant difference in the financial status of one party may also prompt a couple to enter such a contract. I see this marriage began well, one cannot deny. Mrs. Vaux was required to have a baby within the first five years of marriage, as stated here, in order for her to be entitled to a considerable amount of money. Let me see, $750,000 for every year they were married. Fifty-thousand dollars were allocated for general support, a house, a new luxury vehicle at the end of every lease cycle were included. There was also an allocation for fifteen thousand dollars per month for personal expenditures and two thousand a month for beauty care. A million dollars per year for each child born and a contribution to her business ventures of a hundred thousand dollars."

Myranda bit her lip but kept her eyes low.

"Now in the event of death, she's to regain Trelles Industries, provided that she'd adhered to the first prerequisite," Constanta said.

The numbers astounded Jewel. She hadn't known Trelles Industries' real worth. In fact, she didn't care. She'd never discussed money with Leal. His office had called to settle her fee in India and Jewel had only been exposed to the wealthy side of the Trelleses when she met Cyrus. Did Myranda want Leal dead to access his money? Was it that simple? Why?

"Ladies and gentleman," continued Constanta, "with the evidence the Trelles family have provided, Mrs. Vaux-Trelles did no such thing. She didn't produce an heir for Dr. Trelles."

Constanta glanced over at Myranda. "Mrs. Vaux-Trelles, I'll have the courts do a further investigation regarding Calen Vaux-Trelles. That's a serious *and* incoherent matter. It'll be handled separately."

Kaya squeezed Jewel's hand. Jewel's eyes remained fixed on the judge and she set a hand over her chest. Her heart had been pounding faster than normal since entering the room. For Cyrus's sake. He stood to lose more. It was his brother's memory they were talking about.

"Now," continued Constanta. "Where does this leave us? How can you settle matters? As I sat at a neighborhood church over on West 29th Street, I looked up and saw an image of the Virgin Mary holding the infant Jesus."

For a few seconds, the room edged into her trailing words. Constanta took long pauses, and Jewel wished she would get on with whatever her legal mind was construing.

"I then began thinking there was only one virgin conception, at least to my knowledge. History tells us there was only one miracle birth. It's one way to see things. Every other birth is a voluntary act between two consenting adults and in less fortunate cases, a result of misdemeanor. However, to use every day jargon, it takes two to tango."

"The documents presented by Mr. Avent reveal that Myranda Vaux repeatedly went in for other treatment, such as artificial insemination and IVF." Constanta looked over at Myranda. "Everything discussed here remains confidential naturally. This got me thinking, why would Mr. and Mrs. Trelles, newly married and in love... why would Mrs. Vaux-Trelles seek fertility treatment without the knowledge or consent of her husband?"

Jewel pursed her lips and shot Kaya a look.

"This is clearly before Mrs. Vaux-Trelles took a mandatory test, commissioned by the late Leal Trelles, one month into their marriage. The test as we have learned certified her barrenness yet the results weren't disclosed to Mrs. Trelles. This only tells me

225

that Mrs. Vaux-Trelles, without her late husband's knowledge, chose to use medical help from the first day of their marriage. Why?" Constanta said.

The question hung for several seconds. Jewel hung onto every word uttered. Where was Constanta swaying them? She took a deep breath, her ear straining to grasp every word the judge said.

"I'll let you know why, and this will be my final statement on this matter that should be considered before your conclusions." Constanta scanned the quiet room. "Mr. Bradick and his legal team have presented a new argument to be taken with the utmost seriousness." She fumbled for a paper in front of her. "Dr. Leal Trelles and Myranda Vaux were never intimate. This is according to a recorded testimony taken of Leal Trelles on July 2, six years ago."

The room fell silent and a lump crawled into Jewel's throat.

"And if they were never intimate," continued Constanta, "how could Myranda have ever had hope to conceive Leal's child? I'll have you know that this argument will stand in court."

Kaya gasped, unable to hide her shock. Jewel found her eyes turning toward Cyrus, his eyes narrowing.

Constanta clasped her hands together. "There's one outcome from this mediation. Think carefully. In light of the new evidence, the Vaux-Trelles legal team will proceed this case to trial on grounds of an unfulfilled prenuptial agreement. As a mediator, I stay out of the decision, but I warn the Trelles family that this will stand in any court of law." She placed her palms flat on the table. "Dr. Leal Trelles enforced a prenuptial agreement he himself never purposed to keep."

* * *

Cyrus scuttled down the stairs. and stopped to breathe, his hands clenching at his sides. It was an unconscious attempt at self-control and he cursed the world for shouldering him with hefty weights, his father for leaving him to take on the family's responsibilities, and failure for looking him in the face again. He'd failed Leal.

Dr. Rafaela and Sofia had been right. For six years, he'd waited for answers. Had Myranda really succeeded? There was no

226

time. He'd not stayed to listen to Jeff and Kaya's conclusions. He had to get there.

To Leal's secrets.

Myranda would get another restraining order against his family and Jewel. He'd not waited to see how she took the news, caught in his own frustration. How could Jewel stand up to Myranda now? As he stepped out of the fire exit into the main reception area of the building, he turned at the sound of stilettos on the marble. Dr. Rafaela's advice was to always breathe in after an attack, and that's what he'd done. Seven times.

He fought the urge to turn back into the building's escape passageway. He would head out into Manhattan to think about his next move. Myranda advanced to the exit with a celebratory contemplation in her eyes.

Cyrus followed, anger crossing his face. "Myranda!"

She flipped her head back, casting him a quick glance. "Well, if it isn't the other brother. You couldn't hold onto the money any better than Leal could." Myranda's face broke into an infuriating smirk as she approached Cyrus. "Really, Mr. Trelles, our business is concluded. Didn't you hear? Not only do I retain everything your brother owes me and everything I walked into that room with, but the best part is that you and that woman, Carlone, are ordered to stay one hundred yards away from me and my company. Now that's what I call a sweet restraining order."

Cyrus shifted closer and grasped her forearm undeterred.

Myranda retreated.

"Your company? Touch one more cent of my family's business and this may not end as cordially as you would expect."

She raised her hand to strike him. "How dare you?"

Cyrus caught her wrist mid-air and stared straight into angered eyes, his voice controlled. "You may think on paper all is as settled as the Declaration of Independence. My Roman blood wants to wring your neck, but my New York side will see you in court. This isn't over."

"You overestimate your capabilities. You can't touch my son or me. Get your hands off before I enforce that restraining order. Remember, Cyrus, you're the one who agreed to mediation."

Cyrus saw little use in arguing. "Your team fabricated that DNA report, not to mention the evidence of giving birth. It's all fakes, isn't it?"

Myranda pursed her lips.

"Own up now, Myranda. This may be your last chance and that of Calen's," he said.

Cyrus released her hand as Myranda's stare intensified and she stomped to the door the chauffeur pulled open. Before settling in, she turned around to face Cyrus. "Threaten me again and I'll take more than your company. I'll make the Trelles name dissolve from Trelles Industries altogether."

Chapter 17

The five-and-a-half-hour drive in front of Jewel would be brutal. It was close to 3:00p.m. She'd head southwest on Broadway toward Chambers Street and hope traffic would allow her to get to the I-95 N interstate route. Jewel had slipped out after the mediation and hurried off before anyone discouraged her pursuit.

With a restraining order enforced toward not only Myranda but also Leal's property, she needed to act fast. The information Leal had given her on the evening of their first date in India was all she had to go on. "On Martha's Vineyard, I've a small bungalow near North Water. She's a retreat, a little place no one knows about, not even my family," he'd said. "I keep it off the books. The only place I'm myself."

Leal's safe house was where she would find his true self. Was it still there? It had to be. It had to have answers. And why did Leal keep it off Trelles's books? She needed to see it.

The underground parking lot was quiet when she found her Jeep Compass and started the engine. In minutes, she was out in the late afternoon New York traffic. Her cellphone on the passenger seat was off. Kaya would try her phone. She couldn't afford distractions now and Kaya would persuade her to stop her investigation. She tapped her fingers on the steering wheel and stopped at a red light, spotting Robert F. Kennedy Bridge. If she swerved into the left lane, the route would lead her back to her apartment.

When the lights turned green, she set her foot on the gas pedal and the car continued right on I-95 N, following signs for New London and Providence, the route to Leal's bungalow.

* * *

The car drifted to a halt after Jewel nosed into a parking spot on a beach road stretch on the east coast of Martha's Vineyard, the tip of Massachusetts. She rolled down her window, inviting the rattling sounds of cyclists and the drones of the mild late evening traffic. The smell of seafood roasting from the beach restaurant in front of her wafted in the air and circulated through her car. She hadn't eaten the whole trip and had stopped at a gas station to pick up two bottles of still water.

She switched off the engine. Jewel had caught the vineyard tour. Her global positioning system had battled to find the right location leading her past the clay cliffs of Aquinnah, vivid elegant cottages of Oak Bluffs, and the New England architecture of Edgartown, the first colonial settlement on the island.

She gazed out the window at the waves crashing on the rocky shore. Her GPS had stopped responding about five miles back. Was she any closer to Leal's Edgartown bungalow? Her memory was shaky but could this be the road?

She checked her watch. It was close to 8:00 p.m. She'd walked through unfamiliar roads and a quaint town. The sun bathed the horizon, its violet streaks signaling it would drop behind the Dukes Country skyline. In the distance, she spotted a stately sea captain's house and two lighthouses that lent the island much of its imaginative magnetism. Jewel had never been to Martha's Vineyard, a resort island, and a summer colony that had come from the whaling industry, taking the vineyard to prominence in the early eighteen hundreds.

Three cyclists rode in from the oceanside path proceeding in her direction. She waved her arm out the window and they stopped a few feet away. Jewel leaned forward and spoke to the helmeted teenager. "Is this the right road to North Water?"

The biker raised an eyebrow before nodding and pointing in front of her. "Yup. If that road still exists, continue up this path and once you reach the sea captains' homes, you'll be on the right track."

"Thanks."

Jewel would hike the rest of the way. The car worked the city life well, but the last thing she needed was to draw attention. She found her denim jacket, pulled it on before changing her shoes for the hiking boots she left in the car. She swung the door

230

open and pulled herself from the car, turning her attention to the road that turned in to a dusty sidewalk.

Several minutes later, she stood alone on a secluded ocean path, minutes from a recently renovated waterfront home. Jewel spotted a sign.

HIMALAYAN JEWEL
FOR SALE BY VINEYARD ROYAL
ESTATES ON BEHALF OF TRELLES
INDUSTRIES.

It took her three seconds to realize what she'd read. She pushed open the white picket gate leading to the bungalow nestled on a lush, green lawn among swaying trees, a comfortable respite in the picturesque setting.

Leal had mentioned this retreat more than once. First at the clinic as they'd shared an Indian meal and later as they hiked in the Himalayan ranges. He had often called this place *where winter meets summer and spring takes over*. His Himalayan Jewel.

She reached the property and paced to the rear side that led to the beach, her feet crunching in the sand. Few people loitered round and a quiet boat sailed in the distance.

Why did Leal invest in a premier location on the shoreline of a seven-hundred-and-fifty-acre salt-water pond to one side? Jewel was certain nobody came here or used it. She tried the back door on the deck that led to the beach. When she couldn't get it open, she glanced over her shoulder noticing a small rowboat docked on the private pier. Three Georgian bar windows stood to the left. She checked them all hoping for a small crack to wedge open.

Nothing.

I have to break in.

Her heart sprang into a race. Breaking into a house the law had told her never to approach was one of the boldest things she'd attempted in her life. Glad her phone was off or someone could call and startle her, bringing her to her senses, she surged round to the front porch and tried the doorknob. It, too, was locked. The shades of the front window were drawn and she scurried down the stairs to the driveway and scouted the area for a rock, a pebble, anything to get closer to her answers.

No. Breaking and entering undetected I can handle, vandalism is another thing. She burst up the stairs and veered round to the rear of the bungalow. A French door led to a kitchen.

She tried it.

It pushed open. Had it been a maintenance person? Real estate viewers? She didn't care and rattled the door handle. The floor-length French door opened effortlessly and she dragged the door wider, then waited. Her pulse pounded in her ears in the silence as beach waves crushed on the rocks and they found their way to land. A wind that had built in the last several minutes flapped at the overgrown grass pads that scattered near the porch. Jewel took a deep breath and set her foot inside the kitchen, closing the door behind her with care. The contemporary space was tidy and inviting with its custom-fitted cherry cabinets, stainless-steel appliances and granite counter top.

She crossed the length of the kitchen and stepped into a spacious hallway off which several rooms led. Jewel studied the new bamboo flooring in the hall, new windows in the living room and carpeting in the main rooms. An impressive fieldstone fireplace warmed the heart of the room fit for an upscale home as each room of the bungalow fronted a water view. A lump rose in her throat, having learned more about Leal in the last few minutes than when he was alive. She slumped to the floor, her elbows resting on her knees as a picture of Leal's face drew form in her mind. *Damn it, I miss you!*

Jewel stayed on the ground for several minutes before continuing her investigation. She paused a few minutes at the bottom of an oak-cut, staircase with custom-made central pillar posts and spindles that led to the upper floors. She continued to where Leal's bedroom would be.

At the top of the stairs, three bedrooms led off the long hall. She tried each door before settling for the middle room. Jewel stepped into the tranquil master bedroom suite that encompassed a small seating area, distant ocean views, and an interior hallway to the master bathroom and closet. The room played off a white backdrop with early moonlight peering in from closed drapes that threw soft illumination in every corner. Consistent minimal hues of creams, browns, and caramels adorned the room revealing that Leal had been a minimalist.

Her feet moved against the carpet and she filed through the closet taking in the masculine scent of pressed shirts, a row of designer jeans and smart and casual pants. Beneath the clothes a row of outdoor shoes lined the floor, items that had been untouched in six years. *Why is it still here?*

It was impossible to bring him back, yet his scent drifted off his clothes. She took in the indulgent smell of wood, spice, and bergamot, scents she adored and had memorized. She rubbed the heel of her palm against her chest and closed her eyes. *I'm so sorry, Leal. I should've died with you.*

The fragrances lingered, floating to the back of her nostrils. Jewel slid to the carpeted floor, her back against the open closet as she fingered a light-blue pinstripe shirt. She drew in the musky scents that drew out fresh and undeterred memories of Leal. Her head dropped in her hands.

She sat on the floor of his walk-in closet holding his shirt. How long? She didn't know, nor how many hot tears collided with her denim jacket. Her attention turned to the bed and a set of bone-inlay, bedside tables. They were home to silver-plated picture frames of vacations with Sofia and Nonna. Several moments later, she spotted a collection of rare coins mounted on the wall above an undersized work desk and a Jose Ramirez classical guitar, whose dusty fret board showed use. She rose and slid her fingers over the taut strings of the instrument before setting her eyes back on the photographs.

Moving with the stealth of a famished lizard, she made her way to the bedside table and pulled the top-drawer open. "Come on, Jewel. It's not as if you're stealing," she whispered to herself.

Several letters, ticket stubs, and photographs piled on top of each other, many dating from his high school days. She picked up the first photograph and spotted Leal, probably at fourteen, Sofia around sixteen and Nonna beaming on a cruise ship. There were no pictures of Cyrus. For a moment she thought of her feelings for the brothers, both equally strong. One new and unfamiliar, one old and broken. She filed through more items before removing her hand altogether, satisfied there was nothing more here she needed to investigate. As she rose from her knees, her eyes fell on a photograph hidden under a pile of old letters.

Her hands rose to her mouth. *No!*

With a trembling hand, she reached for the picture. The same smile, the same day, the same outfit, and the only copy of a photograph taken of her and the Italian gymnastics team. It was the photograph she'd given Leal the day he died.

*** *

A thud from the front door told Jewel she was no longer alone and soon she heard rapid footsteps on the oak staircase.

Muffled voices.

Two.

A hasty man by the sound of his footsteps and a commanding woman spoke as they made their way to the top floor.

Panic rose to Jewel's cheeks. She fiddled with the drawer handle, and shut it before glancing out the window. A Bugatti Veyron had pulled up in the driveway.

Damn! She scanned the room, scrambled to the walk-in closet and cowered under the left handrail and shut the door.

She waited on the carpeted floor, took a deep breath and slid under the hanging clothes as voices neared her. Jewel's shaky hand drew hanging shirts and pants covering her frame beneath them. She dragged her feet under her and could hold the awkward position for only a few minutes. She chewed at her fingernails. Without intention, her elbows pressed into her sides and she took another deep breath. Jewel shut her eyes and her hands began to sweat. Three seconds later, the voices barged into the main bedroom. With her heartbeat pounding in her veins, she wedged further behind several hanging shirts and recoiled.

In one sudden moment, she peered through the hanging clothes and weakness broke out into her knees.

"Why are we here?" The man's voice was urgent.

With Jewel's back to the wall, she strained her ear, a bold effort that gave her minimal earshot improvement to the adjacent room.

"Leal thought by keeping this place off the books it could not reach my attention. I had my lawyer request its sale when the mediation ended."

"How did you know about it?"

"I followed Leal here a month before he went to India?"

"How did you get the keys?"

"I had the locks changed. We won't be disturbed here."

"Congratulations, little one, on your success. You can drink to many more years with Trelles Industries. I doubt they'll be back to haunt you now."

Myranda did not reply.

234

Jewel heard heavy footsteps by the closed door and a man leaned into the door, inches from her nose.

She grimaced as the British-accented man continued. "This means dear Myranda, you owe me."

"I'm not your dear."

"Come on. Leal is gone and Cyrus can no longer haunt you. Let's just finish the sale on this place and leave. It gives me the creeps."

"I doubt anything gives you the creeps."

"How about a little drink in Edgartown to celebrate?"

"We're not here to celebrate."

Myranda shuffled through drawers. "If anyone ever finds the report on Leal's death, and I mean the correct one, that we forced the police in Manali to write, everything will be over. We've got to make sure nothing here points any fingers at us."

Jewel's eyes widened. Her heart raced into a chase.

"Where's that file, Myranda? I can have it destroyed for you."

"Don't push your luck, Devon."

The man who answered to the name Devon raised his voice. "You owe me big time. Even the little trick used today. That was genius."

"You bastard. I gave you that information in confidence."

"Yes, but look how it got your victory."

"It only worked because the judge was afraid of something. I'm not sure yet what." Myranda's voice was strained. "That was risky, Devon. Constanta won't let you off easy."

"Forget Constanta. She's afraid to lose the drugs Trelles is dishing out to her son."

Jewel wasn't sure what was worse, eavesdropping on incriminating confessions or being discovered trespassing.

"What of it?" Devon said. "I pointed her gaze to the picture of the virgin birth and merely commented that there has only ever been one on this planet."

"I don't believe you."

"I may have mentioned something along the lines of 'if Myranda were to conceive it would be a miracle birth because she was never touched by Leal'."

Jewel's head pushed against the closet wall, a cramp developing in her neck. She did her best to ignore it. If Leal had refused to touch Myranda, why didn't he divorce her? He never

235

planned on being in a marriage with her. *Is that what he was trying to tell me in India?* Why did Myranda want him dead on paper? With Leal dead, it was her word against any accusers.

Jewel covered her mouth.

"Get out, Devon. I can do this alone," Myranda said.

"Only when you give me the Manali police file, the last connection we'll ever have to Leal. Don't you think it's time you surrendered it?"

"I don't care about the file. Take it."

Jewel heard Myranda shuffle in drawers. Her shifting silhouette was visible along the cracks of the sectioned closet door as she paced the carpeted floor. She ambled around the room and made a phone call.

Jewel didn't catch the name.

Myranda's voice was louder now. "You mean it's in a box? What's the number? Okay, Terence." She hung up and turned her attention to Devon. "Terence will make sure you get the file tomorrow," Myranda said.

"I want it sooner."

"My jet will fly us back to New York tonight. You can have it then, if it's the only way to get you out of my hair."

Myranda's feet shuffled by the closet door. Jewel could smell her strong fragrance, a modern perfume, fruity with warm, woody depths.

Jewel edged back and held her knees to her chest, cupping an involuntary hand over her mouth. The silhouette grew until the moonlight let it bounce off the back wall, along the bathroom entrance and the floor-to-ceiling shelving. Myranda stopped by the closet door as hangers of clothes veiled most of Jewel's vision.

The doorknob turned.

Jewel clasped her knees tighter.

"So this was Leal's little hideout?" Devon asked pushing his weight off the closet door.

"Yes. This is the first time I've been here."

"And it wasn't on the books?" he said.

"Not the ones I had access to. I own it now. I wanted to see all the properties that had been banned by Leal's estate. Leal was highly secretive and until the decision today, I had no access to him, the real him."

"I doubt there's anything of interest here. It's some place he came to think, I guess."

236

"Or brought his lovers. I didn't know about it until I saw it on the records of the full Trelles asset report after the mediation."

"Jealous are we?" Devon's voice rang with mockery. "Give me a break, that's beneath you. The whole time I knew Leal, he didn't have time to date. Too engrossed in his research."

"Still, I had to see it for myself. It could be here," Myranda said.

"What're you looking for?"

"Nothing." Myranda's voice was soft, distracted. "I'll have the movers box everything and burn it."

"A little harsh, isn't it?"

"I don't wanna be reminded of this past any longer."

"Oh well, you have to get rid of his memory."

Myranda pushed the closet door open slightly.

Jewel's hands trembled, a hysterical whimper mounting to her lips.

The door thumped against her boot.

She closed her eyes.

* * *

Jewel held her breath.

"Come on. Let's go. Leave this to the movers," Devon said. "What's this?"

The door settled at Jewel's boot, refusing to open. A bead of sweat escaped down to her neck.

Myranda moved from the closet. "Just some collectibles. I doubt Leal would leave anything of caliber here."

"If you tell me what you are looking for, I may be able to help you."

"It doesn't matter. Let's go. I've informed the movers and Pascal to bring me anything of interest they find," Myranda said.

The voices trailed out of the room, reverberating from the stairs until they disappeared altogether. She could breathe now and stretched her legs. Several minutes later, she heard the engine of the Bugatti start and grind the pebbles in the driveway. She glanced down at the picture in her hands. It only meant one thing and she intended to prove her theory.

Cyrus observed as two figures departed the bungalow. He'd flown out on a charted plane and spotted Devon and Myranda at Martha's Vineyard Airport. Myranda had always wanted access to Trelles' private files and now nothing would stop her. Her shrill laughter echoed in his ears as she strolled arm in arm with Devon to the departure gate. His flight landed minutes after theirs and he'd followed the Bugatti out toward Edgartown in a BMW rental, at a safe distance.

Cyrus needed to get there quickly and had waited close to half an hour after Myranda and Devon had gone inside the bungalow, and until the Bugatti disappeared behind the curve.

His muscles tightened as he pushed open the car door and headed to the house. The rays of the full moon beamed off the residence's elegant entrance. Perched behind Katama bay, the farmer's porch on the house and the second-story deck had always been ideal for Leal to recluse from demands and shelter his secrets.

As he advanced up the pebbled path, he spotted the FOR SALE sign. Anger swelled in his being and he wedged the hammered board from the soil.

Cyrus checked his watch.

10:00 p.m.

Myranda was selling the house. He approached the front porch and stood for several minutes looking at a third set of footprints in the sand. He brushed the thought away and fished for the door key from his pockets. The door wouldn't open. He rammed a boot into the lock and the door swung open. Once inside the house, he found the alarm intercom in a storeroom by the front door. He pressed a button that secured the alarms. If anyone returned, he'd be alerted.

How did they know about his place? The purchase papers had been sealed in a vault in Zurich. Cyrus took a deep breath, then scanned the entryway before proceeding toward the living room. He scrutinized the entertainment center, and in particular, the right cabinet.

Leal had wanted the flexibility of a safe that could fit anywhere in the home, yet was clearly out of sight. The firm he'd used designed the unit that surrounded the safe, a classic

Biedermeier piece and modern parchment cabinet that matched the rest of the living room furniture. Leal had chosen the living room, the least obvious place for a safe and the ideal gentleman's hideaway.

Cyrus opened the cabinet with a remote control he'd brought and the door slid to one side revealing a compartment whose rare, patented technology was secured with high-gloss, chrome-plated aluminum. The polished pillar of steel was under four-feet tall and less than a foot deep.

He scanned his thumbprint over the security system and switched on the overhead reset lights. The safe was customized with two sets of cabinets, watch winders and seven drawers of varying sizes. Cyrus slid open the first drawer and drew out the medium-weight snow pants worn on the Dhauladhar Himalayan slope. His hand found a campus attached to a crimson mountaineering windbreaker.

The items were exactly where he had put them.

Chapter 18

"Myranda and some man called Devon know more about Leal's death than we think." Jewel reached in her pocket and pulled out a photograph. "I found this."

Kaya took the photograph from Jewel's trembling hand. "What's this?"

A few feet away, little Brysen scrutinized aquatic life in the main hall of New York's Aquarium. The fourteen-acre facility, packed to the gills, drew oceanic enthusiasts with its biodiversity from the world's oceans.

"I gave Leal this photograph. The team photographer took the Italian team photo and Leal had it when we're climbing to Keylong."

Kaya pressed her lips together wondering where Jewel had escaped after the mediation. "I've been worried sick for the good part of the last twenty-four hours. You disappeared after the mediation without a word. Where did you go?"

Jewel scanned Kaya startled face. "Martha's Vineyard. I spent the night in a small hotel in Edgartown, before getting up at dawn to drive back to New York."

"Are you crazy?"

"When I got to your house this morning, Sharie told me you and Brysen had left for the Aquarium." Jewel raised her head. "You need to believe me."

Kaya shrugged. "Anyone can have several copies of a single picture. You're the photographer. You know that."

"It's a classic Polaroid. Can't be reproduced. That's its beauty. A Polaroid has the assurance of authenticity digital pictures can never attain. We only took that one picture. Look, I signed the date and time on the back."

Kaya reexamined the artifact. Jewel's eyes were sincere as she spoke. "I gave it to Leal and we had a whole conversation about me going back into gymnastics. I'm not crazy. There's only one picture."

Kaya reached for Brysen's hand before he took off to see the Pacific walrus exhibit in the next hall. "Then what're you suggesting? Where did you get this anyway?"

"Leal's house in Martha's Vineyard."

"What were you doing there?"

Jewel's eyes shied from her sensible friend. "I broke into his house. The window had been left open and I got this a few minutes before Myranda walked in with a man she kept calling Devon."

"Devon Chesser?"

"Is that his full name?"

Kaya handed Brysen an oats bar and sat him on the bench as he watched gliding rays and clown fish swim in the large sea tank in front of him.

Kaya kept her voice low. "You could've been caught. What got into you? The mediation outcome is final." Her voice was strained. "You can't go near anything belonging to Trelles Industries or Leal any longer."

Kaya took a seat next to her son as Jewel joined her, tunneling a hand through her tousled mane. "This photograph was with Leal during the avalanche. How did it get to his house?"

"I know you want answers. But there are none. You heard Judge Constanta, a prenuptial was made. Neither party fulfilled it. In New York, deceit about a prenuptial is enough to void the agreement. The mediation determined that Leal was deceitful when they wrote the prenup. He had Myranda sign against a prenuptial clause that he never intended to do his part to keep."

"I trust Leal. Something must've happened. She did something that turned him off."

"It's out of our hands."

"I don't agree."

"Regardless, Jewel. Myranda will keep Trelles Industries and we can't do anything about it now. If you trespass onto their property, you could be arrested." She slid a hand on her friend's shoulder. "I know it's difficult, but you must leave it."

Jewel refused to back aside. "Devon and Myranda have information on what happened to Leal in India. I heard them say so. There's a file, the real file recorded by Manali police on his death. Leal's family received a fabricated lie."

"What are you saying?"

"Myranda paid the Indian authorities to look the other way."

Kaya tilted her head to one side. "It's possible."

"I was in the room and they didn't know it. There's a file and Myranda intends to hand it over to this Devon. The truth."

Kaya held Brysen's hand as he rose. "In a minute, little one." She returned her attention to Jewel. "Okay, let's say they fabricated the account they used to serve their interests. What good will it do now? It won't bring Leal back."

Jewel had stopped listening. "If I get that file, I'll be satisfied. Perhaps the torment and sleepless nights would end. The dreams would go away." She clasped her hands together and lengthened her aching neck. "I need that file before it's never found again."

"Jewel. Listen to yourself. You can't simply walk into Devon's place and ask for the file."

"What else do you propose? We don't have time, that file will be gone by tomorrow. This picture has changed everything. At first, I thought that finding it meant Leal... Then I thought, surely if he were... Wouldn't he?" Jewel leaned her head back for a moment. "For a second, I even believed—"

"Jewel. You're not making sense."

"It's okay, Kaya. He's gone."

"What are you going to do?"

Jewel's eyes were as focused as a poacher on a hunt. "I'm going to steal that file."

* * *

A hefty swing-door beneath the drawers disappeared inside the safe when Cyrus opened it. It was large enough to fit a set of shoe boxes. He pulled out the insulated over boots, snow-shoes, water-resistant pants, a waterproof jacket, extreme-cold down parka and a pair of glacier glasses.

In the drawer above, he rummaged beneath a stack of papers, before his eyes fell on the envelope he'd given to Jeff's man in the bazaar. It had arrived and Jeff Avent had placed it here for him, in the safe that locked away shadows of the truth shared with Jeff, Sofia, Nonna and Dr. Rafaela.

He hunted under more stacks of papers until his fingers grazed three detailed, medical history files: his, Myranda's, and Jewel's. He rummaged some more and his eyes caught the ticket stub from the train he'd taken from Manali to New Delhi, the day after Jewel had left India.

Next to the papers, a printed traditional men's scarf dyed in rayon fabric, beamed its patterned print at him. He'd worn it to the bazaar, hiding his identity when Jewel boarded the train to Delhi twenty-four hours after the avalanche; the day he resigned he would never see her again. He brought the scarf to his nostrils, taking in the scents of the bazaar. Jewel had raced across the platform to get to the crowded car. She'd fought tears, her eyes bloodshot as she hustled past strangers, her face ashen and her shoulders tight.

Jewel had arrived at the station in jeans and an olive *salwar kameez* top. She'd chosen to veil her head with an embroidered white scarf. White was the only shade widows wore in India. Was she the only one mourning him that day? Disengaging herself from the preferences and luxuries of life? Perhaps scorning the habitual participation in society by those around her.

How could he have left her there? His heart still pained from the abandonment. Eyes concealed behind the ruby scarf, he watched as she dragged her minimal luggage, as if it combined the burdens of a politician's agenda scheming to solve the world's problems. Her feet shuffled, tumbling on the concrete platform of Pathankot station, the only railroad out from Manali.

She grieved, burned by lies and betrayal. She must've known by then that he'd not been truthful about his marriage, and for a second, he'd ached to run to her, unveil his identity, tell her he was alive, tell her it had all been a setup gone wrong. That he never meant to hurt her feelings or lie to her. That he'd so wanted to protect her from his enemies, and hers.

But no. His determination to stop Myranda and finish his research held him back. It was the only way he could redeem himself and yearned that, should he ever see Jewel again, she'd understand his dilemma. That he'd done it because he loved her. Feelings that surprised him when he'd first seen her in Montpellier.

As she neared her train car, he watched. Tears broke from her eyes, streaming down her olive cheeks. Amber eyes welled with every second. Those who passed her cast concerned glances her way. She cowered under her veil and fixed her eyes on her tired feet. They questioned what would cause such sadness in such a beautiful face.

Jewel slung her camera across her shoulders and stepped onto the train. An older man helped her with her ultra-functional suitcase, loading it onto the Maharajah Express train. As the doors shut and the train accelerated along the tracks away from him, he became Cyrus.

* * *

Stawnmonk, the thoroughbred was ahead. Myranda observed her father's excitement as the horse took the lead against his peers at Belmont Park in Elmont. Belmont Stakes wasn't as pleasant this year. The mediation had strained her nerves and even with her favorite horse ahead, a horse she'd followed for the last couple of years, the victory was not gratifying. Neither was the victory two days ago at the mediation.

She shot her father a long look. Adan was what was known among racing circles as a "Superfecta". He usually wagered, picking the first four horses in exact order to win. To Myranda's surprise, Adan won at least once a year, a passionate pastime that kept him entertained.

An able jockey sponsored by the Trelles foundation was manning Stawnmonk. She had also wagered it would take her mind off things. She hadn't seen her father in two weeks and needed his advice.

The latter astonished her. Most of the time, she made decisions alone. This gave those around her the impression she was as resilient as a gladiator's shield. But the person she needed to convince was herself.

Myranda couldn't lie to herself any longer.

She was terrified.

Sun broke among cloudy skies, setting a flood of sunshine on her face. Belmont Stakes was behind the Kentucky Derby when it came to attendance and even with the sizzling heat, the place bustled with activity.

Adan wore an ice gray suit that fit without a glitch and a simple, well-cut, white shirt worn with new tan shoes that matched. He roared, his voice cheering on his investment. "A brilliant performance! Stawnmonk is on a roll," Adan said, triumphing as his favorite horse crossed the finish line.

"I'm glad you find this all amusing."

Myranda had agreed to spend some alone time with her father. They sat in the clubhouse with its spacious viewing area along the window overlooking the grandstand to one side and the backyard to the other. Myranda's gaze fell to a set of office files she had brought with her. Adan's concerned face turned to formless thought.

He would see right through her façade.

"When are you going to tell me what's bothering you?" he said.

Her eyes shot up. "What?"

"Don't you see? You've won. Seven years of hard work. Now you can enjoy all. The money, the company..."

"It means nothing."

Myranda set the papers she'd read to one side. Her elegant hat, suggesting timeless, womanly elegance, had been picked for a hot day. It matched her floral organza dress that created a structured hourglass silhouette over her taut stomach and narrow hips. She'd selected pink drop, diamond earrings to cheer her up, and a matching pair of leather peep-toe sandals. As she leaned in toward Adan, her voice broke into a whisper. "Papa. I can't stop now, not when I'm so close."

"So close to what?"

"Close to the reason I married Leal."

Adan's mouth slackened. "I knew you didn't love him. He knew it too. But why I wonder?"

Myranda grasped his hand. "Papa. You'd think I should be celebrating. But money isn't the answer."

He let out a shrill laugh to signify she was joking. "Really? That's why you spend so lavishly." His mouth curled into a frown. "You didn't grow up in favorable circumstances but what more could you want now?"

She flipped her red tresses. "More."

"What could Leal's billions not buy you?"

She ignored his condescending tone. "I may control Trelles Industries' future, but the only reason I've been willing to go this far is for something far greater than money."

"What?"

A tear formed at the edge of her right eye. "Papa. I want to be cured."

Adan allowed a hard swallow to trail down his throat.

245

"Cured? From what? Are you not well?"

Myranda glared at the racetrack. "Years ago, when Leal and I first met, I was inspired by him. Most people think it was because he was so rich. And he was. Very few twenty-four-year-olds had achieved half his success. What was particularly attractive was he cared little for money and things."

"I'll give him that," said Adan, raising his glass of iced Remi Martin cognac.

"Oh, no. That was too simple an achievement according to him," Myranda said. "Preserving a whole village from Malaria was far more an achievement."

Adan set his glass down. "I remember the aspirations he had."

"Those were true aspirations. That's what first attracted me to him. His brilliant mind. His research."

"I know, my darling. But what aren't you telling me?"

"You mean why I signed that prenuptial, when I knew I couldn't have children."

"But darling, you didn't know."

"Didn't I?"

A quiver of bewilderment played on Adan's face. "Didn't you find that out after you married him?"

Her face broke into a frown. "I knew."

"You knew?"

"A few weeks before we got married, I knew the prenuptial was coming up, and though I was aware I was challenged reproductively, possibly barren, I agreed to sign it, with the risk I could never fulfill it unless—"

"Unless?"

"Unless Leal helped me."

"How could you have been certain you couldn't fulfill it?"

Myranda's eyes fell to the table, focusing on her full champagne glass. "Because, I couldn't get pregnant with Devon's baby."

* * *

Leal became a brother he barely understood; took on the identity of a twin sibling lost at age six. He traded all he knew for a lie, a fabrication that would throw him into the dungeons of

246

personality disorder. A personality that introduced experiences and behaviors far from societal norms and expectations.

He was one step on the journey. The deed was done.

Dr. Rafaela's words rang in his ears. *"As an identical twin, you took on your brother's behavior, a rare syndrome where twin pairs influence each other's conduct. Even though Cyrus died young, the few years you had spent together and the various genes you share have allowed you to switch between the two personalities."*

Nonna had first observed the behavior when he was eight, when he created an imaginary friend in Cyrus, who'd lingered with them even though Cyrus had been dead two years. Dr. Rafaela's words were clear. "It's a peer influence that stayed behind even after Cyrus died."

As he grew, Leal could impersonate his brother, and mimic him, adding variations to whatever age he would have been. Leal soon directed energies into developing the personality of Cyrus. Dr. Rafaela told him he needed to let Cyrus go. The grief of losing a brother that had lasted decades needed to end, and meeting Jewel had been the start of that recovery.

A tingle ran through his arm, as the discomfort of the surgeon's scalpel came to mind. He gripped his shoulder and massaged it. The moment he'd walked into the underground clinic in New Delhi had sealed his destiny, by becoming Cyrus.

Minor reconstructive surgery had hurt less than leaving Jewel. In New Delhi, three surgeons from Los Angeles worked on his forehead and his nose, implementing minor non-permanent reconstructions. The doctors used infrared radio-frequency technology to warm the skin beneath his dermis, creating muscle and skin tightening and uplifting skin in the required regions around the nose chin and forehead.

"What about my eyes?" he asked the surgeon.

"You've got two choices. Either we use a new method a Seattle scientist has devised that allows us to use lasers to change your blue eyes to brown. This works by destroying the blue pigment in the iris. The procedure is quick and painless. It should take only a minute to pull off and three weeks to settle. Or you use contact lenses every day."

As much as he hated anything near his eyes, he chose the latter and with the final touches to his identity, Leal would be buried beneath a new exterior, baptizing Cyrus Trelles to the world. The sensible brother, the business-minded one, the brother they would claim was kidnapped by ransom hunters, taken to Italy at age six and raised under a different name, until the family used an investigator to find him. They would claim that later, a DNA test had revealed Cyrus's true identity.

The paperwork was more complicated to fabricate, and government officials harder to bribe but they managed to get it done. A team as fierce as Jeff Avent's could get it done.

"It's not like you've not been using this identity," Jeff said. We need to kill your real one. The DEI won't be able to prosecute you for breaking the law if you are dead."

"What if I refuse?"

"Do you want to go to jail, Leal? Or do you want to finish your research on this drug without the DEI breathing down your neck?"

He couldn't go to jail. His research had to be finished and he had to protect Jewel. Leal could finish his research, use funds he'd put away, without the DEI and the government's knowledge.

The only one who stood to lose was his Jewel. And her life was in danger if he didn't show results. The DEI would send morally void idiots like Devon to hound her, and who knows, even kill her for her bloodwork.

"What will happen to Jewel?"

"We'll protect her, and as Cyrus, you can check on her from afar."

"What about Trelles Industries?"

"We have to act as if you're dead and follow the law to the tee. That way no one will suspect."

"When the time is right... we'll find a legal way to claim back your company."

Leal reclined at the table as doctors began the painful procedure. As a medical man himself, he knew what to expect. Warned of the complicated operation, he stayed awake.

"We're using a process called facial reanimation," he heard the Californian doctor say. "The facial reanimation surgery involves moving tendons and muscles from one part of your body, to your face."

The scalpels began their work. He felt nothing. Saw nothing with his gauzed eyes.

They began with his jaw area. *Will Jewel know me when the time comes?* That's all that mattered. *If I go ahead with this, I leave her behind.*

I can't leave her!

"Stop!"

His aggravated voice surprised him, leaving his throat in an excruciating roar. The numbness in his jaw allowed little sound to escape his lips. Leal removed the gauze himself and scrambled off the operation table. He fell to the cold floor, inches from the secured door.

"But..." began the doctor jerking back.

"I can't do this to her." His numb chin barely allowed him to speak.

"Who?"

"Jewel."

"Ah... the gymnast. Yes I read her file."

"She'll live and Jeff's team will keep a protective eye on her."

"It's not right."

"Listen, Trelles. Taking on Cyrus's identity will help you continue and finish the research in isolation from the hungry hands of those who should be kept away from the fertility drug you're developing."

"No!"

"You're almost there. You can't stop now."

Leal shook his head in violent streaks. "No!"

"Carlone will be fine." The doctor shook his head in disbelief. "Love is an eccentric disease, doctor. But you can do nothing now."

"Tell her the truth."

"What will that do?"

"Keeping information from those you love can damage a heart. The secrets are killing you. Its echoes are screaming in your head longing to tell her the truth."

The chill from the cement seeped into his tightening muscles and he gripped his arms for warmth. Was it the shiver from the floor? Or was it the reality of what he was about to do? Jeff and the doctor were right. Myranda would be under control. Devon would be silenced and unable to access his research. Trelles Industries left vulnerable, only for a while.

Extinction of humanity was at risk. Nephthysis was a weapon greater than any nuclear threat as far as he was concerned. Even if it meant personal cost to him. He held the one secret that had baffled fertility science for years, the one thing

Myranda desperately sought and Devon longed to market out of self-indulgence.

He'd already planned Tharnex, the vaccine they wanted without using one drop of Jewel's blood. But he needed time to test it. He kept part of the codes on the key he'd given Jewel and the other codes were in Martha's Vineyard. He'd struck a deal with another multi-billionaire in Venice. Together as philanthropists they'd created secret labs in Friuli, Italy to get the drug and others to parts of the world that needed them; Liberia, Manali, Armenia and many more without governmental eyes, greed and regulation. The deal was good for six years or it would be void and his work would be in vain. In that time he could have all his research tested. There wasn't much time and the DEI need not know.

Jewel would be left alone and he'd hire two agents from Jeff's agency to watch her twenty-four hours a day, from a distance, however long it took to test Tharnex. The documents incriminating Myranda and Devon would be safe with her and once he was done testing he'd find her. He could only pray she'd forgive him and wait for him. It wasn't risk proof. The avalanche and his disappearance could ruin everything.

A warm wetness spilled near his thigh. He peered down, unaware of the wound the doctor's scalpel had caused on his underarm.

"Come, let me patch that up before you lose any more blood."

Leal obliged, advanced toward the medical bed and sat on its hard edge. "Enough now, you've changed enough. No more."

"But your eyes."

"I'll wear contacts when I have to."

"But—"

"I said, enough!"

The doctor took a deep sigh. "I guess it'll do, once we dye your hair we'll be able to pass you off. You'll have a slight resemblance to Leal to categorize you as a fraternal twin, or brother. No one will ever believe you were once identical twins."

"That better be all."

"Looks like it is."

The surgery wounds lasted two months and when he healed, Leal awakened to a new identity.

Cyrus Trelles.

Kaya watched Jewel and internalized her next thought tugging at the belt holding her dress with a side-drape detailed in Mykonos blue. "Jewel, listen to yourself."

"I need to know what happened to Leal and the investigation after his death. And I'll do this with or without your help."

The din of crowds in the New York Aquarium halls silenced in her ears. Kaya could do nothing to convince her best friend otherwise. "In that case, I can't let you go without something." She grabbed Brysen's hand. "Come on. Let's go. I have something to show you."

Thirty minutes later, the two cars pulled up in Kaya's Scarsdale driveway. Jewel followed Kaya and Brysen into the house. Once the boy was settled in front of paints and brushes in the kitchen, Kaya led her friend to her upstairs office her palms sweating. Jewel couldn't be serious. Kaya had hoped never to share this with Jewel. But the time had come. They were going to get the file and Kaya knew how.

The late afternoon sun burned into the home office Kaya had been using since Brysen was born. A mix of surfaces, modern furniture, and decor aided by bright and dazzling colored lighting peered in from every corner of the room through the half wall-length windows.

The workstation area was black with built-in fixtures. Furnishings lined each white wall. A black-and-white themed modular desk and matching chair system had been integrated. The desk could be redeployed to accommodate computer requirements for business meetings of up to four people, which happened when she had to work with clients.

Kaya marched to the office desk, pulled the top-drawer open and paused, shutting her eyes. If Jewel wouldn't stop, maybe she could help. The oath required for admission to practice law that Kaya had taken came to mind. The flaws in most legal proceedings and situations in which many find themselves had inspired the need in her to improve the law any way she could, be it in her sphere of influence. The last weeks had challenged the oath's meaning in her life. For the first time, she understood how one might bend the law for good. In the last hour, Kaya had resigned to her instincts. She could now disregard her own conviction to help Jewel and the Trelles.

Pursuit of ideals had to wait until Jewel had settled. Kaya foraged through a drawer under her work desk and pulled out a paper-wrapped item. "Something I got before I left for Venice."

"What is it?" Jewel said.

"A security entry card to Trelles Industries."

Weston peered through the cracked door.

Kaya swallowed a lump as he strode into the room.

"I didn't know you were home, Kaya." He glanced over at Jewel with a concerned look. "I heard about the mediation. You going to be okay?"

His eyes fell on Jewel's hands. "What's that?"

"Something I've been keeping in case we need it," Kaya said.

Jewel examined the card. "It gives me access to all security control systems in Trelles Industries. Where did you get this, Kaya?"

Weston rescued the card from Jewel's grasp. "Not only is this against the law, but you'd endanger your life and career." He turned to Kaya. "Where *did* you get this?"

Kaya shied away to the window. "I borrowed it from spies. I didn't steal it, someone who did gave it to me."

"What?"

Weston's look was anything but cordial. He understood Kaya better than any other person and his response had said it all, not what he was expecting from her.

Tightness formed in her chest.

"When?" Weston said.

Jewel watched her friend with interest, and crossed eyes with a new side of Kaya.

"The day of the mediation. When the judge gave us that mini break."

"I was with you during the break," Jewel said.

"Just before we met up." She gripped her wrist. "Years ago, I made an acquaintance at *Society & Conscious* magazine, who goes by the pen name of Rowell Saunders. You know the kind that looks for corporate dirt and flashes it across page one."

Weston's eyes narrowed. "Was it for work?"

"For my research on prenuptials." She glared into the eyes of the man she loved, hoping she would not disappoint him with her next words. "He was looking for dirt on Myranda Vaux and had posed as a society columnist."

"Posed?" Weston said, his eye contact strong.

"Yes. He's a private investigator for a governmental organization—the Department of Economic Intelligence—an economic monitoring agency launched about ten years ago."

Weston's mouth slackened. "I've heard of them. But don't they monitor economic trends and predictions around the globe. What would they want with Myranda?"

"You would think. They've been spying on her for years and learned much, but can't bring her in without real evidence. The real question was; what did they want with Trelles Industries, or specifically, Leal?"

Jewel slumped slightly. Kaya could see she was speechless and slid into her desk chair. "That's their front image. They're actually a counterintelligence unit under the FBI."

Jewel stared into space. "The FBI?"

"Guys, the Cold War is not over." Kaya said. "It's simply moved into a new battlefield, one the FBI calls the global marketplace. The DEI assumes that every year, billions of US dollars are lost to foreign and domestic competitors who deliberately target economic intelligence in flourishing US industries and technologies."

Weston's eyebrows knit. "Why Trelles? So they do research."

"Trelles is on their list given its dealings with the developing world, especially where new vaccines are concerned."

"Is Trelles Industries in some sort of trouble?" Jewel asked.

"Quite the contrary. Trelles possesses research intelligence into medicine, vaccines, and prevention—intelligence worth billions—that, should it fall into foreign hands, it may be detrimental to our own economy," Kaya said. "According to the DEI, our enemies might use medical intelligence as an economic weapon."

"What sort of intelligence?" Jewel asked.

"Rare vaccines, cures and drugs. New advancements in scientific and medical technology. The list goes on. Many governments are hungry for medical intelligence, out of shelved technologies and will exploit open source information or company trade secrets at any cost. Call it economic espionage."

"What is it that Trelles needs to protect?"

"I don't know. But it seems Leal did, and they believe Myranda may too. With Leal out in India, they heightened their investigation around him. I imagine it's because he was doing his

253

research off home soil and they may have thought a foreign government had recruited him. Foreign economic competitors unlawfully seek economic intelligence commonly operating in three ways."

Weston interjected. "Where did you learn this?"

"That doesn't matter now. It's true. One way is to target and recruit insiders. Sometimes they look for people with the same national background working for US companies and research institutions."

"That's ridiculous," Jewel said.

"Is it? You remember Vik Patil."

"Yes, he was in India and a good friend of Leal's."

"Well, he's very much on the DEI's radar due to his close dealings with Leal and his education background at Hopkins and Harvard."

"So you met this Saunders and believed him?" Jewel's cheeks were reddening with every syllable. "He could've just been a liar."

Weston sighed. "Sadly, we lawyers will work with many individuals to find the truth. I trust your character instincts but did you check him out?"

"I went to the DEI headquarters and believe me; it took more security checks to enter their facilities than trying to get into a Swiss bank vault. When I agreed to help, they told me some things I wasn't allowed to know, so they blindfolded me to this location," Kaya said.

"You serious?" Weston was ready to throw his fist into a punching bag. "Why didn't you tell me?"

"I wanted to help Jewel. I thought they might know something?"

"What did they want from you? Surely, they wouldn't have given you all that information for nothing."

"Since the week Leal died I've been in contact with Saunders, whose real name is agent Amos Hudson. I'd gone to see him at the magazine. He was the first to tell me about the prenuptial agreement. When he discovered my connection to Jewel and that I was a lawyer, we got talking. He asked if he could enlist my service."

"To do what? And why your connection to me?" Jewel said.

"He knew about you and Leal. I guess they had spied on anyone connected to Leal. They'd followed Myranda a long time for mishandling, but have nothing to incriminate her. They

254

needed to know if intelligence was flowing out of Trelles to their enemies. Trelles Industries is steadily becoming the world's premier innovative biopharmaceutical company and has been since Leal and his grandfather started it."

"That's what Nonna was trying to tell me," Jewel added.

Kaya booted her computer. "They've got a few investigators planted in Trelles Industries. Hudson met a housekeeper that used to work for Myranda. She informed him she had a bone to pick with her."

"The woman doesn't know when to stop making enemies," Jewel said, almost as a half whisper.

"The housekeeper assumed she was paid to pour dirt on Myranda whose dealings with her had ended rather acrimoniously. She got many files for him, including the location where Myranda hides her most valuable items, a safe in her bedroom that requires the highest level of security scans to get into."

"The file must be there if it hasn't been destroyed."

"You can't get into the safe. The DEI tried using the maid. It's a state-of-the-art safe that requires communication of radio signals from triggered sensors to the control panel. Perhaps controlled by a cellphone. But you have to get into the phone first."

"I can get it."

"How? Saunders has needed more information from Trelles and Myranda for years. His one ask was would I be willing to get it? It would be a government service he said and this document the DEI signed certifies that I'm protected."

"Let me see that," Weston said, his legal eyes poring all over the FBI document.

Kaya left for a few minutes and returned with a closed shoe box. "There's one more thing. Here's something else they gave me, just in case."

Jewel's eyes fell on a small electronic tablet with the office blueprints of Trelles Industries in New York.

"This may help if you go, Jewel," Kaya said.

"Jewel," Weston said, his voice steady. "If you go with this and are caught, it'll be a crime. You don't have DEI's cover as Kaya?"

"It depends on how you look at it," said Kaya. "This is a government investigation, she may help them."

Weston took a seat and thought for several seconds. "I doubt they'll bail you out of anything if you are caught. Even on this agreement with Kaya, it says so. Should she be caught she is alone."

Jewel fingered the tablet. "I take it the DEI doesn't want its clandestine dealings to be public knowledge."

"You sure you want to take that chance, Jewel?" Weston said. "For Leal? Was he really worth it?"

A sinking feeling dropped in Kaya's stomach. "That's not your call, Weston." She faced Jewel. "There's one more thing."

Kaya rose and found a document in a bottom shelf. "Myranda has a licensed gun according to the DEI and may not hesitate to use it."

"A gun?" Weston said.

"Myranda grew up in one heck of a town. A town that breeds some of the best snipers around. Maybe she needs protection," Kaya said.

Weston threw up his hands in disbelief at the women. "From what?"

Jewel took the items from Kaya and placed them in her bag. "I intend to find out and I've a devious feeling that file of hers has the answers."

* * *

A choke rose to Leal's throat as he peered down at the ruby scarf. He was used to switching accents and mannerisms depending on whom he was around, aided by a few medical tricks that grounded his transformation. The lies needed to end.

Leal secured another set of files from the safe labeled "Attempt One" and "Attempt Seven". God forbid anyone should to get their hands on "Attempt Seven". The medical discovery had come to him in India so he wouldn't endanger Jewel's life and release her from the DEI. He shut the safe and the main doors of the vault.

The answers had started with a mutual college partnership with Devon Chesser. As his roommate and genetic research partner for years, they'd been best friends and medical partners on important experiments, securing a Lasker Award and grants from the American Society of Reproductive Medicine, nowhere near enough for the research they needed to conduct.

Then the DEI started to take note. The award acknowledged creation of an innovative, short-term research project focused on fertility preservation. After Johns Hopkins, Leal's focus turned to vaccine research. With his grandfather's backing and cash flow from the Mancini Corporation, the result had been the launch of Trelles Pharmaceuticals, later renamed Trelles Industries.

In just a few years, Trelles Industries, which started as a niche supplier of specialty pharmaceuticals had secured private funding packages of more than twenty million dollars, half from Mancini Corporation and the rest from existing investors. The world watched as Trelles made more profits than most pharmaceuticals, choosing to collaborate with developing governments in the supply and trade of vaccines for preventable diseases. That's how it had to be. Make the best affordable for those who needed it most, a vision he'd inaugurated at Trelles Industries that kept the company ahead of its competitors. Not long after, the DEI hounded him to share his research, gave him an ultimatum and threatened his life, family and company.

The DEI feared his research would flow out of their intelligence circles. Leal's personal focus shifted to research on the infectious, environmental and occupational causes of infertility. With the DEI set to solve the Benton mystery, he was their new best contact. Breakthrough had come with Attempt Seven. It peered at him from his hands. Leal needed to get the digital files on the data chip and hard copies out of the house where the man who'd met him at the Dhaba in India had brought them.

He grabbed the items and, moving toward the kitchen, progressed to the cabinets beneath the sink, found a trash bag, and stuffed the clothing elements inside. After a few moments, he trudged back to the living room, collected the items and placed them in a steel briefcase he'd carried in.

One more thing.

He raced upstairs, fumbled through his bedside drawer before emptying the contents in the briefcase. He then quickened back downstairs. He locked the house and strode to the back porch where he found a trash can in which he dumped the bag with the clothing into the garbage and reached in his pocket for a small bottle of biodiesel. He emptied the contents over the bag and lit it with matches from his pocket.

The items fired up in smoke. No one would think much of it. People burned trash in their yards almost every weekend. Garbage he'd been hanging on to for far too long.

Dr. Rafaela was right. To be free, he had to let go of one brother.

He'd made his choice.

Cyrus.

Chapter 19

Vik advanced to the arrival terminal at New York La Guardia Airport as Leal watched from behind a hooded jacket. It had taken a phonecall to Vik's mother to persuade him to make the twelve-hour trip on a first-class Jet Airways ticket to New York. She'd been told to tell Vik someone from Trelles Industries would pick him up. He would listen to her. The elderly woman's gentle eyes had never left Leal's memory. He'd taken note the day he'd uncovered NZT2, a treatment he'd prescribed for her inexplicable febrile illness. His treatment had mattered to her and if that had been the only reward he ever got from medicine, it would be enough.

Vik's tall frame stood with perfect posture. His face and bushy eyebrows were not to be mistaken amid the thongs of passengers arriving. He carried an aluminum briefcase under his arm and scanned the airport looking for his pickup.

Leal made a slow approach to him. He'd chosen La Guardia owing to its closeness to Midtown and Upper Manhattan. Would Vik's acute, observational skills and sharp, analytical mind make the connection? Leal looked different. But he was still Leal and Vik had been his closest friend after his first year as a Harvard undergraduate. Surely, Vik would recognize his voice.

Leal had spent much of the past evening discarding habits created for Cyrus. He had excellent manual dexterity and skill. These he'd used for mimicry, even adopting the accent of wherever he was. Could he completely discard those tricks now?

Vik filed past several travelers before stopping a few feet from Leal, looking both ways in search of his name on a plaque.

"Vik?"

Vik zipped his head toward the voice. He scrunched his eyebrows and tilted his head to the side. "Yes?"

Leal shot Vik a welcome nod.

"Are you from Trelles Industries?" Vik said.

Leal approached Vik, whose furrowed brows implied that though usually trusting and a sociable extrovert, today Vik was cautious.

"You're Vik Patil?"

"That's right?"

"This way. Your mother, Mrs. Sheena Patil told me you'd be arriving now."

Vik's eyes softened. "I'm sorry I've been on a long flight and wasn't sure whom I was to expect."

Leal shook his hand. "I understand."

"I received an e-mail that someone from Trelles, would pick me up. Who are you if you don't mind me asking?"

"A friend of your mother's."

He moved toward Vik. "Come this way. I'll take you to your hotel. I need to speak to you about Leal Trelles."

"Leal? What about him?"

"His research."

Vik shot him a mistrustful glance and pulled out a printed document. He handed it to Leal. "Are you Cyrus? Leal's brother?"

Leal shriveled at Vik's expression but refrained from answering.

"You must forgive me," Vik said. "We've never met. Leal told me about the name, but I've never met the person. It's the only photograph I found on the Internet."

Leal stepped back slightly as he fingered the image. It was taken as an executive press photo for a media interview for Mancini Corporation about three years back. Vik would think it was Cyrus. That's what the caption on the paper read. He handed the paper back to Vik and pointed toward the parking lot. "Welcome to New York. This way," Leal said.

Vik tugged at his coat's collar and matched his steps with Leal's long strides.

Leal rubbed the back of his neck. He closed his eyes and took a calming breath when they reached the elevators that led to the parking lot. He reached out a hand toward Vik. "Let me help you with your bag."

Vik held onto his luggage studying the stranger, an inquisitive glare in his dark eyes. He let Leal take his overnight bag, but he kept his briefcase.

"Was the flight okay?" asked Leal.

Vik could not stop gaping at him.

"What do you want to see me about? Surely, we could've discussed Leal's research on the phone. Why fly me all the way here?"

They walked passed rows of cars in the parking lot at a brisk pace. "I've a business proposal based on some information Leal may have left with you."

"Your brother's entire projects in India were shut down. Anything we were working on and any funding was stopped by Trelles Industries when he died." He tilted his head. "Something about you is very familiar. I can't put my finger on it."

"Let's speak in the car."

The morning rush hour from the airport was modest for Monday. New York's highways permitted easy access to the heart of Manhattan. He swerved into Fulton Street. After years in New York, although not a great idea to drive into the city, Leal had become used to the specifics. No turn on red and other precise rules designed to limit congestion at busy intersections, plus the endless streams of pedestrians and jaywalkers.

He parked at the corner of Ann, William and Fulton streets in the northern portion of the financial district. Conversation until then had focused on travel, traffic, and New York. Nothing that accommodated an entry into the topic Leal wanted to discuss.

Leal switched the engine off but remained seated.

Vik watched him with an inquiring frown. "Why haven't you contacted me until now? I'd almost destroyed the files I was asked to bring. When we were shut down, I filed them because I believed your brother had done some great research on fertility. Things that if completed would revolutionize medicine and possibly humanity."

Leal kept his eyes fixated ahead as several tourists crossed the intersection. "Vik. It's me."

Vik scrutinized his face, his bushy eyebrows in a furrowed knit. "What did you say?"

"It's me. I'm Leal."

Vik's eyes narrowed in skeptical thought. "Is this some kind of a joke?"

A chill entered Leal's bones as he turned to face his friend. "I don't have time to get into this now, Vik." He was conscious of the eyes focused on him. When he spoke again his tone was heavy. "I didn't die in India. I had to appear dead."

Vik was silent for several seconds.

Leal would have given his entire wealth to know what Vik was thinking. Vik's medical mind was calculating the actuality of what he'd just heard.

After about thirty seconds of stretched silence, Vik raised his chin. "Why?"

"I've always trusted you, Vik, and you've kept many of my affairs confidential. This is another I'm asking you to keep," Leal said.

"This could be a scam to steal Leal's research. She's always pestered me for it threatening with lawyers, calling it Trelles's intellectual property. But no, I've held onto it. Leal would not once have surrendered it. From what I hear that wife of his was capable of anything including incriminating that the woman Leal loved." Vik's gaze became intense. "How do I know it's you?"

"You just have to trust me. Think about it, Vik. I've no reason to lie."

Vik's hands trembled in his lap. "I guess you wouldn't. But then where is Cyrus?"

"There's no Cyrus. He was my twin brother who died young of a severe form of methylmalonic academia when we were six. The fatal disease caused his liver and kidneys to fail by early adolescence. Till this day there's never been an explanation why he had it and I didn't. That's why I threw myself into medicine."

"Then who's this guy in the picture?"

"It's me. Look at me. I know I don't look like Leal, perhaps a faint resemblance. But it's me. For reasons I don't have time to get into now, we revived Cyrus's identity."

"Why? It doesn't make sense."

Leal shrugged. "It's a long story. I promise, I'll tell you everything, but we don't have time now."

Vik's face still revealed indecision. "What sort of jokes are you Trelleses playing?" His voice rose to a near shrill. "Why fake your own death?"

Leal's chest tightened. "Vik—"

"What about Jewel, does she know?"

Leal shook his head.

"What happened to her?" asked Vik. "If anyone, you should've told her. She went through so much for you, trying to get rescue teams up to Keylong, spending all her money trying to work with the authorities until she was broke. After that, we lost touch, about a year after." He thought for a minute. "I liked her a lot. You don't deserve her."

Leal's heart dropped into his gut. "She's the most important reason I had to appear dead, Vik. I needed to protect her from Myranda, Trelles and the government's economic espionage agency."

Vik exhaled with a small measure of relief. "I sent her an e-mail the other day. Maybe it was overdue. I wanted to see how she was. Where is she? How is she?"

"As beautiful as ever, maybe more. She's trying to solve a mystery I started six years ago. I can't let her go through anymore and when it's all over, I must crawl back and only hope she'll forgive me. That's why I need your help."

"How can I be certain you are Leal, for one you speak and behave like him, but look nothing like him?"

"Vik, I had minor facial surgery on my jaw, chin, and forehead. Facial reanimation, to be exact. But I stopped them halfway, when I realized what I was doing. I'm healed now and look." He removed a contact lens. "I have been wearing these."

Vik stared at the lens in his hand. "Wow."

"Disguising your face can be deceptively simple if all you want to do is hide it from the public or create a new character. I had to hide from those who were out to get me and my research. Only my attorney, my doctor, Nonna and Sofia know the truth."

Vik's jaw dropped slightly; unaware he'd gaped at Leal for several minutes. He looked at him with a skeptical eye. "It can't be done? Can it?"

"The government can do anything they want."

Vik drew back sighing. "Yes, now I see. There are similarities. The hair is different; the bone structure is the same. How did you get away with it? You fooled me and I've known you since we were in college."

"Do you believe it's me?"

"Hm... let's see. Why did the sixteen-year-old boy, whose disease we studied at Harvard not age? What was our first theory?"

Leal grinned. "We found that his hair and nails were the only parts that grew on his body. We studied his DNA in search of a genetic mutation that might unlock the fountain of youth that kept him young."

"Did we find it?"

"Not yet, brother."

They burst into laughter. Vik reached for his shoulder pulling him into a hug. "It's good to see you mate. This is some crazy stuff. How—"

"As I said, I'll give you the details later. I need you to come in with me, and I'll fill in all the rest. We need to get in that bank over there. It's time we unlocked a special vault."

The men stepped into Pilman Bank, a closely guarded establishment, only known to those privileged. It resembled a private archive library from street view. They were greeted at the entrance by a bank delegate. Leal flashed a security card and passed a thumbprint scan, before the man led them down three floors through a hidden elevator.

Once on the vault floor, they stopped outside a multilayered steel door. Leal watched as three more security staff maneuvered a team of robots to shift pallets that moved the first lock. Leal then nodded to the security guard giving him the approval for Vik to escort him into a tightly secured area. The subsequent chambers could only be accessed by an elaborate system including voice-recognition and three-foot keys, before they reached a three-key safe-deposit box. Once inside, Leal closed the door.

"We'll be outside, Mr. Trelles," the taller guard said before leaving the two men to settle in the acclimatized room.

"Thanks," Leal said.

He opened the security deposit box and pulled out a second steel box. He scanned his palm print and the box snapped open. Inside he pulled out an envelope. "Here it is."

"What's this?" Vik said.

Leal's face tightened. "Biophysical characterization of the antigen in fibroid tumors."

"You mean you found the substances we tried so hard to get? These babies can create antibodies and combine specifically with those in the cancerous cells of the patient."

"Yes, Vik, I got it. I tested many stabilizers and interactions with these little babies." He pointed to a formula.

"Adjuvants?"

"Exactly. These will form part of the vaccine to enhance the ability to create protection against infertility."

"How did you do it?"

"I used an immunogen, a combination of chemicals to induce a more marked immune response."

"With this formula? Did it work?"

"Heck yeah."

"Using the DNA strand data we were missing? Did you use Jewel's?"

* * *

Adan studied his daughter. "Devon Chesser? You and he?"

"Don't get graphic, daddy. It's hard enough to admit that to you."

A grimace fell on Adan's face. "But Devon, wasn't he Leal's best friend in college?"

Myranda ignored the question. "Do you remember when I was a little girl, maybe three or four? We used to live in Benton, Pennsylvania."

Benton had been her home until she was twelve. Though less than a thousand residents lived there, tugged away in Columbia County, it held several memories. A rural beauty, home to progressing farmlands, state game terrains, dense forests, recreational parks and astonishing nature preserves.

Myranda barely remembered her mother who'd died shortly after her fifth birthday. They'd lived in a hundred-year-old single family home that her father expanded with meticulous artisanship when he worked as an environmental scientist for a beekeeper company, Solomon Bees. The company played a critical role for Ovatti. Bees were important insects as every third mouthful of nutrition was reliant on bees as pollinators of the plants Ovatti supplied. As the biggest employer in Benton, Ovatti produced apples, cherries, peaches and grapes. When Myranda was about nine years old, Adan received a monstrous bonus for his invention of a sanitary method to bring fruits from the field to the grocery stores with minimal defects.

Her father would waltz in from work with a skip in his walk. They were happy and Adan never made her feel as though she had no mother. Over the years he'd told Myranda about his esteemed job, not only saving Ovatti millions, but also bringing in enormous revenues for the beekeeper company.

Then life took a cold turn when her mother had been gone only a year. Adan suffered a tractor accident while on the Ovatti grounds, breaking three ribs and enduring a leg and elbow

265

fracture. He spent weeks recovering, requiring Myranda's only known relative, Aunt Prudence, to look after her for months. Adan returned to his job ten months later only to find his position had been given to a colleague and he assigned to work with organic honey recipes instead. Life in Benton was never the same as Adan tried to change his job several times.

Myranda released his hand. "Papa, we used to live near Ovatti Foods. They were the talk of the town when they moved to Benton and you were happy when Solomon Bees contracted for them."

Adan's eyes darkened evoking a memory he didn't want to remember. "We lived by Ovatti Corporation."

"Mother used to work there. Remember?"

"How can I forget your mother?"

"Do you recall when she came home one October with complaints about 'heavy legs' and the nurses urged her and two others to seek specialist attention in Bloomsburg?"

Adan's eyes shot up at her. "Where did you—"

"The nurses heard of a fourth case, too, and they feared workers were getting sick, that a serious disease was spreading through the Ovatti plants. Interestingly, it was only women."

"I remember that. But how do you know? You weren't born? Those incidents broke out while your mother was pregnant with you."

"One thing about money is you can pay for information. I hired a private investigator who found one woman affected at Ovatti, who also knew my mother well."

Adan's face displayed thoughtless shock before he heaved a sigh. "Yes. Your mother was at Ovatti." His fist rammed the pristine table. "And they discarded me like unwanted swine!"

"Tell me about her."

"Why do you bring this up?"

She searched his eyes, witnessing a tortured melange of pain and resignation. She spoke in a soft, raspy tone, wishing to evoke no more difficult memories. "The investigator said mom got worse and worse until she was admitted in a clinic for two weeks."

"That's right and they never discovered what it was these workers had. It hit the news big time. It was awful. That's why I urged your mother to move away. She was pregnant with you. You were born premature, and had to stay in the hospital for

266

weeks. After you were born, I asked your mother to let us move. She refused."

"Mom couldn't have any more children after that, right?"

"That's right." It was painful for him to surrender to the truth and he shifted in his seat. "But frankly, I don't think we wanted anyone else." He smiled. "We had you."

"The thing is, papa, she was still sick even after she recovered according to her doctor. Whatever the disease was, it had made her infertile. In fact, according to this investigator, and here are the papers to prove it, many women at that plant became barren because of something that happened in one of Ovatti's laboratories. According to him, this still isn't solved."

A bead of sweat escaped Adan's forehead and he rose from his seat not wishing to face her. The races had stopped as the horses and jockeys were changed. Adan fingered his scorecard. "Darling girl, I loved your mother, but she got so obsessive. I didn't want you to be affected."

He slid back into his seat. "It was never proved that the virus affected her."

Why was he talking so fast? Keeping his distance? Myranda rose and set a hand on his immaculate suit. "Papa, I know it did." She wasn't about to give up. She had to know. "I know it did, because it affected me. That's why I needed to marry Leal."

Adan's shoulders drew inward. "Why?"

"When we first got the Trelles account, Devon told me that Trelles was on the government's watch list for Tharnex, a vaccine the company was developing and Leal was developing this very vaccine. Devon said only he knew how to stop the spread of the disease."

"That can't be."

"Devon couldn't match Leal's genius in medicine even if he had a gun to his back. He's always envied Leal. Anyway, Leal was tasked with finding a cure for the illness that broke out in Benton. The disease that killed mom and now is affecting me." She took a deep breath. "It killed mom because she wanted more children. And now I can't have any either."

Adan set a hand on her shoulder. "Myranda. Your mom never died."

* * *

Leal avoided the question about Jewel, a distaste forming in his mouth. "This formula is what has kept me alive. The DEI would have eliminated me by now if they thought I couldn't get it. The economy is desperate for it and the rest of the world would like to get their hands on it. It's the complete rational formulation that can reverse infertility induced fibroid tumors."

"When did you develop it?" asked Vik.

"About two years ago."

"How did you manage with everything going on around you?"

"Remember when I researched the same solid tumors in Benton? The disease had hit the town in the late eighties. And though fibroid tumors had been around for a while, this one seemed to spiral after women consumed a certain mineral water. I located all twelve women who suffered from that mysterious barrenness. All twelve of them."

"Yes, I remember. About seven years ago. I helped conduct the calls we had for women to come forward to take part in a medical experiment. But I didn't know that's what it was. You offered a heck of a lot of money to each participant. Heck, Leal, this is big! Do you know what this means?"

Leal nodded. "Yes. A possible end to infertility. I was interested in one candidate. The only one able to bare children after that disease hit."

"We used her DNA and genetic code file to find clues. However, to no avail. I have the notes here in my briefcase."

"I stayed up all night trying to put the pieces together then it hit me. I found the answer."

"What. So did it work?"

"Yes. I developed Tharnex and that's why we were in Keylong and Manali. Several women from the village there had natural barrenness problems. Your mother had first alerted me to the problem there."

"Yes, she did. Didn't she want you to go test it on them? And did you?"

"Yes, after my assumed death. I wanted to go one step further and with the women's consent I administered it."

"And it worked?"

Leal shuffled through the box and pulled a series of

268

photographs. "Here are two women from the mountains. Before and after. I had the clinic send me pictures monthly. Both women conceived within a year. Here are photos of their children."

Vik's eyes widened. "This means the cure can work on women of all kinds of barrenness not just those affected in that village or ones with fibroid tumors."

"That's yet to be proved. This is what I have been up to these last six years, when I wasn't Leal. I had to get this done and stay at bay until it was complete. Don't you see? For Jewel's sake. The DEI had to believe I had her DNA. That's why I took her to India." He drew in a sharp breath. "I didn't think she'd change my life."

Vik's eyes were sympathetic. "What's in the actual formula? I remember you used many of them."

"The day the van went down the hill. I'd just discovered the one thing we hadn't seen all along. Something that animals around us display all the time. I remember asking why we didn't see so much barrenness in animals. The answer wasn't in chemicals."

"I see. You're keeping the specifics to yourself."

"I have been until now."

"Are you gonna tell me?"

"Tharnex works by traveling to the brain, where it partly blocks estrogen receptors. This then gets the brain to send a signal to the ovaries to produce more estrogen, which causes ovulation. It's a natural combination and results in fewer twin births when about ten percent of women treated with most fertility drugs give birth to twins." Leal reached for two plastic bottles. "Here are are some of the first samples I had made in Venice."

"This is brilliant, Leal."

"I had to find a safe and effective medical treatment to help infertility patients with nephthysis."

"I hear you. You may have found the solution to one of the most common conditions causing infertility." Vik took the bottles from Leal's hand. "You always could find an answer. What are you going to do now?"

"Destroy it. And I want you to do it for me."

* * *

Myranda's eyes widened.

269

"Your mother is alive, somewhere," Adan said. "She left me. Simple as that. Don't go down this route. You're stronger than any woman I know. You live life for yourself and pursue happiness at any cost."

"I get it from you."

"You've more money than you could ever spend, brains to match and a beautiful son, Calen. Isn't that enough?"

"Nothing is ever enough."

"Stop this trivial nonsense. Raise your son and be happy."

She brushed his hand away with a strong jerk.

Adan was taken aback by her strong response. His eyes were a shade darker and his usual sociable self was challenged. He leaned forward. "Leave this and move on. You can always adopt your next child. Birth is overrated. Ask any woman."

"Where is she, papa?"

"It doesn't matter anymore."

Hot tears streamed down her face. "I want that vaccine, that research, or whatever it is. It belongs to me. Leal owes me!"

"What does he owe you?"

"I was his wife. I'm the one who needs this most. Nobody but me!"

"Why?"

"I don't need the money. I just want to have a freaking baby!"

* * *

Jewel checked her phone. She had an incoming e-mail, but didn't have time for it. She had to get to Trelles Industries by 8:00 p.m. The security guards changed right about then. The e-mail would have to wait.

The smartphone kept beeping. It would only delay her. She slid her finger across the touch screen and opened her e-mail application.

> *Hey, it's Vik Patil.*
> *I'm in NY. I'm not sure if you still live here.*
> *If you do, it would be great to meet up with you."*

270

Could it be? Vik Patil? Jewel had always liked him. She read the e-mail to the end:

> *I'm in town on business and will be staying at the Central Park International Hotel. My number is at the bottom of this e-mail. E-mail or text me if you'd like to catch up for old times' sake.*

Jewel slid her fingers over the screen typing a quick reply.

> *Hi Vik,*
>
> *I'm on my way to Manhattan; perhaps we can meet briefly at your hotel, seeing it's on my way.*
> *I won't have much time as I have a prior engagement this evening. I can be there for 6 p.m.*

Twenty minutes later, Jewel proceeded into the lobby of Central Park International Hotel. The breeze from the air-conditioning was cool on her bare shoulders. She'd chosen a sensible outfit for the evening engagement, a sleeveless, V-neck top that sat at her waist in dark cherry and a dark-brown skirt that ended at her knees, exaggerating the curves of her calves. She would need to act as if she belonged in Trelles and passing off as an assistant was how the DEI had imagined Kaya's espionage role at Trelles.

Jewel scanned the hotel lobby, her eyes falling on the luxury marble finishes of the floors and the stunning, floor-to-ceiling windows. She ambled toward the reception desk and asked for Dr. Vik.

"A rare Himalayan Jewel."

Jewel flipped her head to discover the owner of the refined accented voice. "Dr. Vik?"

He took her hand and kissed it before pointing toward a more casual restaurant, one among five in the luxury five-star establishment. Nestled between windows overlooking Central Park and the restaurant's exhibition kitchen, the inviting gourmet aromas churned her famished stomach. She glanced over at Vik in his gray suit, worn with a white shirt. His hair had frosted gray over the last six years. Otherwise, he hadn't aged and his eyes still smiled with empathy.

Vik guided her to a reserved table, and she took a seat as a waiter helped her into the chair. Once they'd skimmed through the menu, the waiter marched off with their order of slowly cooked salmon with sliced French pickles and sauce hollandaise for Jewel, and a heavier steak order for Vik. Jewel's speeding up nerves, all in preparation for her feat later, wouldn't let her stomach take more than the light entrée. Her eyes wandered to Vik's smiling face. "I can't believe you're here. It's so good to see you."

"I was worried about you after—"

"After Leal died?"

Her eyes fell onto her napkin. She twirled it in her fingers for several seconds before placing it on her lap.

Vik encouraged her with a gentle tug on the shoulder. "Jewel, you're looking exquisite as ever. I take it you are going out this evening?"

How could she tell him she was about to break into Trelles? She batted her eyes slightly in embarrassment, a mild attempt at avoiding the question. "Are you in town on business, conducting research, or just visiting?"

"Research never ends, my dear." His face broke into a cordial sneer. "A bit of both."

"I see. How is everyone back at home? Are you still in Manali at the clinic?"

"No. I moved to New Delhi, and run a medical research lab now."

"That's great. What sort of research are you doing?"

"Vaccines. Our country still needs them."

They enjoyed a communal laugh before Vik's eyed her closely. "Enough about me. How have you been?"

"It wasn't easy after Leal died. I never really got over the fact that I fell for a married man and his wife never made me forget it."

"Is she still hounding you?"

"A week ago, I agreed to help Cyrus, Leal's brother, with a mediation. I guess they thought I could help being the last to see him alive." She fixed her gaze on him. "It wasn't easy."

"Leal would have been proud of you. You did the right thing in helping his family I'm sure."

"I miss him. But he's gone and that's it."

Vik stared at his hands for a few seconds not sure how to console her. "I missed him too, you know."

"*Missed?*"

"I meant *miss.*"

"I still miss him. Meeting his brother, Cyrus, allows me to think I've gained back part of him. It's strange, but as different as the twin brothers are, to me they sometimes seem identical. So similar in some ways yet different in others."

"How do you mean?"

"Take Cyrus, for instance, he talks of convictions about right and wrong that remind me of Leal. Both their internal standards of correctness, for example, can be puritanically demanding and act decidedly on what seems correct. Like Cyrus wanting to see his family through this mediation. He didn't do it for the money; he owed it to his family, especially Nonna and his sister Sofia. In that way, he's very much like Leal."

Vik swallowed hard. "You met Sofia and Nonna?"

"I did. In fact, Cyrus came looking for me to help with the mediation."

"How did it go?"

Jewel sighed. "Not well at all. Worst of all, I've let Myranda get to me a second time."

"A second time?"

"Her legal team made me sign a document that helped her seal Leal's death. A death certificate if you like, a police report in Manali claiming Leal was dead because I witnessed it." She choked on her sentence. "I—"

He placed a hand over hers. "I know. I mean, I understand. Don't dig it up now."

"It was legally questionable, Vik. It still is."

Vik twitched as the meal arrived. They ate in silence for several minutes as an easy Blues tune crooned out of the restaurant's speakers. Grateful she could use the chewing time to align her thoughts; Jewel murdered her gnawing fears for her evening's break-in later. She pushed her half-eaten plate away from her. "Something is not accurate about it. Leal died, then it was brushed under the carpet so quickly. I don't think that's right."

Vik looked up from his meal and wiped his mouth. "Jewel, He—"

"No, I mean it's a mystery, the way his widow handled it."

"He never loved her, Jewel."

Jewel wished she could've heard the words from Leal's lips, instead of concluding the truth from everyone's evidence. She twitched her lips. "So I've been told. But there are so many holes in the story."

"What are you thinking?"

"To be honest, I'm not sure. I found something yesterday in Leal's beach house in Martha's Vineyard. The one he used to tell us about in Manali. I found a picture I gave him before the accident."

Vik's concentration on her words intensified as she continued speaking. "Maybe it was a copy?"

"It wasn't. Then I overheard something."

"What?"

"Myranda and her accomplice wanted a file destroyed."

Vik moved forward and spoke in low tones. "A file?"

"Yes. The police file of Leal's accident on the mountain."

"Where's this file?"

She hesitated for all of two seconds. "I will find it. Only then can I put this thing to bed. I think the file is with a man Myranda Vaux trusts. Devon Chesser."

Vik scraped a hand through his hair. "Chesser?"

"You know him?"

Vik failed to respond.

She shrank from the cold of his watchful eyes. "He was a college mate of Leal's and is a medical corporate guy, who many say is really running Trelles Industries and owns a..." Sensing herself ramble, she jerked her head. "Do you know him?"

"Yes and no. We were together at medical school. Leal and I met him at Harvard. Leal's and Devon's research was similar."

"They were friends?"

"Research partners. Although I don't think they stayed friends for long after that." He set his fork down. "Sounds shady if he's connected to Myranda. I can't let you do whatever you're planning." His face turned serious. "Don't do it, Jewel."

She placed a hand on his arm. "Thanks, Vik, for your concern. I think I'll be okay." She looked at her watch. "This reminds me, I really need to go." She found her card and set it on the table.

Vik raised a hand to stop her. "No, Jewel, allow me."

She shook her head with a smile. "Can this be my treat? Seeing you again reminds me of the person I always wanted to be."

The waiter processed her card and handed it back. She placed it in her purse and rose. "Good to see you. How long are you in New York?"

"A week."

She gave him a peck on the cheek. "Don't leave without saying goodbye."

As she pulled away, he held her arm. "Jewel, be careful."

Vik's gaze followed Jewel as she left the half-empty restaurant. He reached for his phone. "Leal?"

"Yes?"

He fished down in his inside suit pocket. "I've thought about your suggestion as promised. I'll do it."

Leal's voice was assured. "Thanks, Vik."

"Jewel may be in danger. I should've told her everything."

"No, Vik. I promise to do it tonight."

"Well you'd better hurry. She might walk into something bigger than she bargained for."

* * *

Vik stepped past the two marble lions that guarded the entrance of the landmark *beaux arts* building. Myranda caught sight of him and raised her head. She'd never met him in person but had read all his Trelles employee files. Something stood out in the section titled. *Have you ever been convicted of a criminal offense?*

That's where she would focus. She greeted Vik with a little more than a smirk and they disappeared within the shadows of an adjacent room in the New York Public Library. Myranda had always admired it as the greatest *beaux arts* building in America, and one of the greatest civic ventures in the city. She had used her connections with a bald admirer of hers, an influential library director, to secure a quiet room for two hours. Vik wouldn't have dared step into Trelles Industries.

He seemed smaller than she'd imagined. She'd expected him to be as tall as Leal, perhaps like Devon, and his credentials as a researcher rivaled theirs. He'd also been easy to find, but harder to convince to attend this meeting. Myranda analyzed his smart gray suit and gave it a silent seal of approval. Why had she doubted his appearance at the library?

He has a past and anyone with a past is desperate.

She'd sent him an e-mail almost every six months since she'd left India. At first, it was to preside over Leal's research in India and thereafter, she had sent him all the corporate news via e-mail. But, with this last e-mail communication, bribery had worked its wonders as he finally acknowledged her existence.

The small meeting room on the ground floor was stuffy and overlooked Fifth Avenue. Myranda slid into a seat at the reading table. "Dr. Vik. Please, sit."

"I prefer to stand."

"Is this how we'll begin our business relationship?"

Vik reluctantly took a seat as Myranda leaned in, her eyes scanning his face. "Do you have what I asked you for?"

"Yes." He reached in his briefcase and pulled out a brown envelope. He tossed the document on the table in front of her.

"Is that it?"

Vik nodded.

She took hold of the contents and opened the envelope. "The answer to my little problem?"

"That all depends on you."

Heat licked Myranda's skin and her limbs vibrated. "What do you mean?"

"It'll all depends on your body and how well you react to the contents of the formula."

Myranda scanned the paper, not understanding the scribbling. "You had better not screw me over."

Vik's bottom lip trembled. "Why would I do that?"

"I don't know. Just remember that the details of your little sin are in my possession. I'm sure you wouldn't like that to get out. You should be happy. You can have a full lab with the latest equipment and access to technology you've only dreamed of. And achieve more than you could in that little New Delhi lab." She leaned in further. Her perfume of roses and lavender filled the little personal space between them.

Vik grimaced watching her carefully.

She shrugged. "Even better than Leal could get you in India. Yes, I found out about the clinic and your research there. Leal was up to something, which I'm sure you may know. I don't want the details, Vik. That's for Devon. But if, as you say, you've got Leal's research, it may turn out well for you."

"Leal's work was miles above Devon's."

"Just give me the results I need and I'll let you off the hook. I may even tame Devon's rage against both of you."

Vik rubbed his sweaty hands on his thighs.

Myranda knew he wouldn't dare deceive her. The risk was high. She grabbed the envelope and placed it in her purse. "When can we begin?"

"Tomorrow. I'll need about forty-eight hours."

"Will it work?"

"There were never any guarantees. What's your list of ingredient specifications?"

He tossed a paper her way. Myranda gripped the document and glanced at it before rising and shoving it in her purse. "Dr. Patel, you're an expensive man. You're making me spend more than on any other man."

"Just the price you have to pay if you don't want to gamble with your life and pursuit of happiness."

Myranda's face broke into a snarl. She flung a company card, strung onto a neck cord on the table and started a march toward the door, her back to him. "You begin tonight. That card will get you into all the allowed areas of Trelles."

Vik took the identity card, his hands shaking as he pocketed the item. "I'm sure."

"Screw with me and your file goes public. And the first person to see it will be your mother."

Chapter 20

Jewel's strut was purposeful as she stepped into the lobby of Trelles Industries. Her hair whipped up in an exquisite up-do and her attitude resonated with elegance and determination. Jewel had never met Devon but from the description Kaya had dished her, she would know him right away. *"Think of a super confident, arrogant Londoner and you can't go wrong. He may look you over. From the DEI files he is quite beguiling to women, so watch out".*

That was the only clue she could follow. She wasn't planning to make his acquaintance; the dress up was in case she did. All she needed was five minutes in his private office at Trelles Industries. In then out, posing as one of his secretaries from the other end of the country, California to be exact. According to Saunders' investigation, Devon rarely paid attention to his revolving door of executive assistants. He wouldn't know all of them.

She entered the elevators as a three-quarter moon gazed above Manhattan through the glass façade of the building.

8:21 p.m.

She called the button for the sixty-fifth floor, and held her breath as the elevator doors shut. She thought back to the instructions Kaya had given her. "According to Saunders, Chesser's office is at the end of the hall on the sixty-fifth floor. The executive and research section is at the end of the hall. You'll recognize it as the only door with a red handle."

Jewel exited the elevator, stepping out onto the sixty-fifth floor. She maneuvered through the silent halls, occasionally glimpsing late-night researchers and other workers, her noisy stilettos clicking. Jewel reached the end of the empty hallway on the sixty-fifth floor. When she came to the security entrance of what she believed was the right door, she took three paces back and glanced behind her.

Jewel peered down at her feet at a red welcome mat. It had silenced her noisy heels, cushioning her unsteady stilettos. She glimpsed once more at the quiet halls before sliding the key over the door reader.

A red light beeped back at her.

As Devon's secretary, she would be expected to enter his office and since he had seven, no one security guard would know them all.

She stared at the closed door, before a second attempt at getting it open.

Nothing.

She tried again.

No response.

"Can I help you with that, Miss? Sometimes these doors jam. It's been happening in the last day or two."

The thunderous voice from an overweight figure startled her, sending her beating heart into her throat. A night security guard stepped toward her.

Jewel swallowed hard.

The jovial man, waddling as he neared her, took her card from her hand, hardly glancing at it and scanned it for her.

The door clicked open. Jewel stared at all two hundred pounds of him, heavy on his short legs. Unusual, radiant hazel eyes gleamed at her from a gentleman who wore braided black hair.

He pushed the door open. "There you go, ma'am. You must be one of Mr. Chesser's people. How's it going? I heard you guys are a fierce army around him," he said in a New York, accent, his 'aw' sounds prolonged and dropping his final consonants.

Jewel managed a faint smile. "Thank you, I can take it from here I'm sure."

The guard handed the card back to her. "Mr. Chesser left several hours ago, but I know his assistants work overtime. That's what I hear. I'm new. This is my first week."

Jewel relaxed her limbs; stood straight shouldered and cleared her throat. "Hope you like it. Listen I need to get some work done for the board meeting tomorrow."

"Sure. Go right ahead." He turned with a bounce of his heavyset frame and continued his inspection of the halls.

Jewel sighed.

Even with her best efforts at a disguise, her overdone face couldn't resemble any secretary of Chesser's. The security guard was new to his job. That was good. But how long would her good fortune last?

She quietly entered the dark room, and pulled a flashlight from her purse. The large executive room had one wall with windows looking down at Manhattan night streets. Light from the scintillating skyscrapers seeped into the room giving her enough vision to access the space's dimensions.

She scanned the wall cabinets along the right side of the office, careful not to brush her hands along several files. Chesser's was an executive suite with magnificent dark wood flooring. A throw rug at the foot of the executive desk in the green and ivory shades of the Trelles company logo, suggested warmth and character, although from what she had heard it was not a resonance of his chilling personality.

A glass cabinet to one side of the room boasted accolades, mostly medical awards by the look of it. She spotted a photograph with Leal and her first real glimpse at Chesser on their Harvard graduation day; his was an ear-to-ear grin while Leal's silent stare into the camera suggested poise and calm resolve.

Jewel's feet moved along the throw rug, bordered by a set of dark-brown leather couches all a touch too high-priced for her taste. She stared at a rare Jackson Pollack painting above the desk before moving to the left side of the room.

She advanced to the coffee table in the middle of the meeting area, spotting several documents on the glass top. After filing through them, she couldn't locate the document.

"Where did you put it?"

After several minutes, Jewel shrugged. Shudders of revolt crept down her spine, not wanting to imagine what lengths she would have to go to complete her last break-in into Chesser's office. It was close to thirty-six hours since overhearing Myranda and Devon's conversation and she had no guarantee the file still existed.

She sank to a chair in defeat and looked at her watch.

9:30 p.m.

Where had the time gone? Jewel surveyed the room once more and decided she would need to move to her second plan. She inched to the door and squinted. With her eyes focused on the base of the door, a shadow moved into the room. She heard the murmurs of a familiar voice. She was no longer alone.

* * *

The driver stopped the limousine a block away from Brooklyn Bridge and Director Hudson glanced from his reading in the backseat.

"Why are we stopping?"

The driver didn't hear him, stepped out and left the car.

"Hey!"

Three seconds later a hooded individual pulled the driver's door open and started the car.

Hudson reached for his gun. "Who the heck are you?"

"Only a shadow from your past, Director."

Leal's face drew into form in the rearview mirror.

Hudson's eyes dilated, his breathing sped up taking control of his speech. "You're—"

"Dead? So I keep hearing."

The car continued down Brooklyn Bridge.

"Put your gun away and listen up if you want an end to nephthysis. The last I checked, we were nearing twelve thousand confirmed cases."

Hudson obliged.

* * *

"You don't know when to quit," Devon said.

Jewel bit her lower lip and staggered a few steps away as Myranda appeared behind him.

"I take it you don't know the meaning of distance, even if it's an order from a magistrate judge," Devon said.

Was it the way Devon glared at her with shameless conquest? Or was it the way Myranda's gleam pierced through her? Jewel inched a step back, the gun barrel pointed straight at her. The overweight security guard who'd joined them in the last second looked more fearful for her safety than she did.

Any minute, her knees threatened to give way. This would be her first criminal offense. Would they let her off easy?

Myranda whipped the gun from the security guard's hand, and aimed it at Jewel's temple. The cool steel soaked into her skin digging a circular mark as Myranda's piercing eyes bore into her like a goat about to ram a looming aggressor. She dug the weapon deeper.

Myranda turned her head at an angle in Devon's direction.

"What's the penalty for trespassing in New York?"

Devon stepped forward, his grin wider than the curve of an Arabian sword. "Let's see, up to seven years imprisonment and fines up to five thousand dollars, or double the felon's monetary gain, which in this case would be a hefty sum seeing the value of what can be had in this building."

Jewel staggered a few paces back, her hands falling limp at her sides. Devon began a looming, circled pace around her. "Plus any additional court costs and fees. Let me see, how much can we milk from your meager earnings."

"You don't have enough money to stop me," Jewel said.

He sniggered, his beast-like frame circling around her. "Or even better." His eyes bulged. "I should fetch my syringe and get a better sample of her blood than Myranda achieved in India."

Devon reached for his pockets.

The security guard beefed in front of him. "Hey! I think the cops should handle this."

"I don't have time," Myranda said, digging the gun even deeper into her skin. "I could just pull the trigger. We'll call it self-defense over a trespasser. Now how about it? What's worse? Rotting in a cell or a quick end to your misery. I know you seduced Leal. He never loved you and only wanted to sample your blood. So you see he used you."

Jewel's eyes narrowed. She pored into Myranda's fuming glare, before shifting it to the security guard who wasn't sure who had what authority.

Myranda's eyes flashed and her mouth twisted into an ugly sneer. "Call the police. This time, I'll make sure even a tornado cannot rip you from where they'll lock you up."

Jewel shot her chin up. "What makes you think it's me they'll lock up? Maybe I'll let you off. Let's not pretend, Myranda. Even Leal knew your frailties and scams. The truth has failed to stay silent. It's only a matter of time."

"Get her out of here!"

Devon narrowed an eye. "Wait. What does she know?"

Jewel shot them a triumphant stare. "Everything."

"Don't listen to her. She's bluffing. She's just buying time."

Twenty minutes later, Jewel sat cuffed to the security guard in the lobby as three armed police officers strode into the reception.

"You are under arrest, Miss Carlone."

She had to know. "What are the charges?"

"Theft of government property."

Had she heard right? "What government property?"

"The late Dr. Trelles manufactured a vaccine, called Tharnex that is of the utmost importance to the US government and it is our belief you stole that intelligence before he died. Trelles Industries has pressed charges for breaking, entering, and theft as well."

"What vaccine—"

"Ma'am. I suggest you get a lawyer."

There was only one person she could call.

* * *

Jewel shifted on the cold metal seat in the jail cell, her head weighing down on her hands. Her disheveled hair fell loosely on her shoulders. The disinfectant stench of the cell had given her uncontrollable nausea all night. Had it started when she was first taken to the precinct's local station for initial processing? She barely recalled the police officer's interview asking her for pedigree information, her name, address, date of birth and Social Security number.

After surrendering the information, a female officer had taken her and explained she'd be processed for arraignment. *That's an appearance before a judge,* the cop had explained.

She stared at the voucher she'd been handed for the confiscation of her apartment and car keys, her purse and wallet with three hundred dollars in cash. The other items would be held for safekeeping while in custody. Numbness ran in her fingers, sore from rigorous biometric fingerprinting. A vacant stare loomed on her face; not in shame and self-pity, but from exhaustion. How could anyone sleep in such a place? She had no idea what time it was, nor how long she'd been in the cold cell.

Will he come?

"Jewel Carlone?"

She raised her head at the braying voice through the iron bars. "The charges have been dropped. You're free to go."

Jewel raised her head from her hands as light from the hallway across the cell silhouetted him. "Cyrus?"

The officer dragged open the cell door, its iron grills slid to one side in one loud clanking slide, as he stepped into the room. Jewel rose instinctively. She hadn't seen him since the mediation and had ignored any attempt extended to contact her.

She hitched herself against him as he set his lips on her hair. Her head fit perfectly in the hollow between his neck and shoulder.

"Cyrus..."

He pulled back. "You all right? I would've come sooner, but the paperwork was lengthy."

His concerned eyes pleaded with her as if to say, *why didn't you let me in?*

Then again, why hadn't she? Jewel drew him once more into a relieved hug. She pulled away and looked into his brown eyes. "What did the officer mean the charges have been dropped? I doubt Myranda would—"

"Don't worry about that now. You're free and there's no record. I owe you that much. Let's get you out of here."

He stroked her damp cheeks. "Jewel, I'm sorry this happened to you."

"It wasn't your fault. I was the one who—"

"I'm more to blame than you know."

They left the cell with the officer tailing behind until they reached the door to the exit.

"Sign here," the officer said.

He signed her release papers, retrieved her belongings and waited until they were outside before he spoke again. "Let's get you some food. I only wish I had gotten to you sooner. I need to take you away from all of this."

"Where are we going?"

She checked her watch. "It's past midnight." A protective glare she'd not known in any man was visible in his eyes, his face full of strength. "Somewhere where you can be safe and get some rest."

He directed her to a BMW4 Series Coupé. Jewel set her palm over his hand as he shifted into first gear of the luxury car equipped with sport seats. "Thank you, Cyrus."

He reached forward and pushed her hair gently back from her face. "I... you're welcome."

They drove for two hours out to Long Island and Jewel slept

most of the way. Her eyes opened when the car halted.

"Where are we?"

"North Haven."

She scanned the dramatic bay-front enclave of Southampton, a portion of Long Island whose charm she'd admired for a long time. Kaya could trace her ancestry to this place, originally inhabited by Manhasset Indians for hundreds of years.

He shut off the engine and leaned in. "Let's get you fed."

Her face relaxed into a smile. "I like your car. Seems more like something Leal would dare me to race him in."

A conflict of emotions followed in quick succession over his face, merging into a smile. "Yeah. It's definitely his style. I'm glad you like it."

She shot him a grateful look and sighed deeply. She'd grown familiar with his attractive face and his masculine charm and peered into his brown eyes for several seconds before turning away. "I don't know why, but you're the only person I wanted to call."

"Glad you did."

Her heart leaped in her rib cage and she caught herself smiling. Hunger was the last thing on her mind. Had Cyrus always had this effect on her? She'd not felt this way since Leal had left. Just by looking at Cyrus, it was clear she was falling for her man's brother as the last days had intensified the magnetism between them.

"I'm sorry for bringing you into this. The crazy world of the Trelleses," he said.

"I would've become involved one way or another."

"Because of Leal?" His eyes were hopeful. "Why?"

"Cyrus, I was in love with your brother. I never saw it coming and felt like I let him down when I signed that form."

"He loved you, I'm sure. Just too afraid to follow through."

"Leal let me see so much and helped me when I felt I couldn't go on. Sure, he seemed abrupt and bossy sometimes, but I think it was a front for his shyness."

He opened his door and strode round to open hers and she stepped onto the gravel driveway that led to a rare waterfront property. "What's this place?"

"Home. I bought it yesterday."

"You moving to New York now?"

He glanced at her. "Maybe."

"I guess it's true what they say about brothers. You seem to both like your isolation and being by the water."

He took Jewel's cold hand as she stepped out of the car and rubbed them for warmth. "Come."

They strode the hundred yards to the front door of what seemed like a new residence. As he unlocked the door and switched on the hallway lights, she stepped in behind him and closed the door. Jewel proceeded into the vast space. Though he'd just bought the house, it was decorated to the highest standards. The meticulous charms of the interior included high ceilings, abundant natural light, terraces on every side of the house and clear views of Noyak Bay. The main living space boasted elaborate fireplaces and moldings reminiscent of Victorian palaces. They advanced into a pleasant south-facing sitting room, combining moss-green club chairs, striped window shades, and white-oak boards, decor that ensured seamless continuity between rooms.

She slid off her shoes, and tousled her hair. "Mind if I shower?"

He turned his head toward her and smiled. "Up the stairs, first door on the right. You hungry?"

"You cook?"

"I'm half Italian, remember."

Jewel gravitated toward him. He stood immobile, not sure where to look. Without warning, she placed a gentle hand on his cheek, rubbing his rough two-day facial hair. She glanced into his eyes. Intense astonishment touched his face as she drew into him, her lips inches from his. She knew he could never dare—too much of a gentleman—or was he?

Chapter 21

Leal felt Jewel's lips touch his as she let her emotions instruct her. Her lips met the corner of his and she kept her gaze on him. Only when she felt his muscles relax, did she close her eyes and he centered his lips on hers. A union of two misplaced souls became one. Leal fought a long-forgotten urge for the woman who'd stolen everything in him. The six years had heightened her rare beauty. With chocolate locks long and dark, her exquisite eyes were determined and her athletic body seemed physically stronger. She was as disturbing to him in every way as his lips continued pressing against hers like a whisper and he responded to her as if his life were wrapped in that one moment.

His arms enfolded her waist as his pulse began pounding, a drama of longing astounding him. Almost as soon it had begun, she pulled away. Leal held on tight not wanting her to escape. He had waited six years to be with the woman he'd let go. What would it be like watching her sitting next to him every day, enjoying the same things, laughing with her, joking and being his best friend? He'd had six years to wonder. Against Jeff's best advice he'd checked on her almost every month, spying on the secret agents he'd paid three-million dollars to protect her against sample seekers, following her on trips to the gym, her fine art photo exhibitions and her trips home to Mahina.

She stepped back. "I'm sorry. I don't know whether that should've happened. I'll go up and take that shower now."

"Jewel, wait..."

"Consider it a thank you." She smiled before starting up the stairs.

Leal watched after her until she reached the top of the staircase. With her hands leaning into the railing, she glanced back down at him. "Cyrus, you've been really good to me."

His face looked different, but damn it, he was the same man as he'd been at the Montpellier arena, when he had watched an eighteen-year-old on a global stage.

Jewel could be mysterious in her silences, courageous, especially how she'd handled the enigmas of India. He ached to discover more of what was going round in her mind and smash the pane of falsehoods between them. He loved her, damn it! To her, he was Cyrus, not Leal. She loved Leal. Couldn't she love him? Though he'd married Myranda, Leal only had to explain his reasons.

He heard the shower start and advanced toward the first step of the staircase, glancing up. Jewel had left the door partly open and he could speak to her through the crack. That way, he couldn't see her response, heaven forbid it be a contentious one.

He continued up the stairs, a shaky hand on the banister with emotions imprisoned for six years foaming to the surface. He wanted to eradicate confusion and smear the truth between them.

He had to tell her.

If the right words were to fail him in his narrative about his identity, perhaps he could unleash the trapped truth about his feelings. Would she understand? The battle in his mind beaded sweat drops on his brow as he dropped his leather jacket to the floor and advanced up the stairs along the top of the railing. The door stood slightly ajar as he approached and heard the shower stop.

Several moments later, Leal's hand moved to the steel doorknob and he stopped mid-stride as the door pushed open. Jewel's demurring gaze met his. Towel-dried hair, wild and enticing, loosened down her back and a large bath towel hung barely restrained around her toned frame. He knew he shouldn't look especially how any step forward would discard the towel completely to the floor. That's not why he'd come. Yes it would be more than phenomenal, but neither was prepared. The moment was off target, the sentimental details erroneous. He had willed for weeks to avoid this step. Only when...

Even as he itched to run, she wasn't bothered by his unnerved stare as determination directed all her movements. She advanced measuredly toward him in an intriguing body sweep and his eyes drank her up, impelled by his own ache. Aromatic hands wrapped around his neck, moisturized with intoxicating blends of botanicals and sent an involuntary shudder through him. Had she expected him? He was about to spill the truth, but as parting lips raised to meet his, Leal's resolve ended almost as soon as it had begun.

He pulled back. "I can't, Jewel. I don't think I'm able to hold myself back around you."

"Why do you want to hold yourself back, Cyrus?"

"I want to do this right." The more he looked at her, the harder it became to resist the impulse. "I think I've been in love with you, since we met."

She drew in a deep breath. "Then, Cyrus, love me. Love me like Leal never did."

He pulled her into his arms having wanted Jewel for a long time. Why had he been such a bastard? But he had wanted to wait and the only way he wanted to handle Jewel's skin was with commitment.

Leal's lips explored her wet skin, his arms tight around her. He had waited a long time and his body ached for her touch. She moaned in his embrace and a feverish tingle sparked through his muscles. He drew Jewel close to him and carried her in his arms. He made his way into the master bedroom where his unopened boxes had been laid. Her body cradled against his as he sensed his way through the barren room for the bed and set her against the mattress.

Jewel glanced up at him and settled in the warmth of the satin duvet. Soon he'd joined her and was struck as he'd always been by her from her slender legs to her oval face. Her scent washed over him as he brushed her skin with moist kisses, his core heating with hunger.

At the base of her throat a pulse beat. He'd not held her like this in six years and the warmth from her lips told him she was his. However much a lie it was, tonight this is where he'd belonged. He needed to be with Jewel.

Her body squirmed beneath him and arched to meet him. He couldn't stop now as her body understood his rhythm. She became his and soon a mutual shudder ran along their wearied limbs.

Darkness filled the room as Leal held Jewel for what seemed like several moments. Soon he heard her soft breathing as she drifted into a deep sleep, her body limping in his tranquil embrace.

* * *

The fluorescent light overhead hurt Myranda's eyes as she stepped into Trelles's private laboratory that was bathed in white light in the interactive research environment. Access to these specialized facilities and equipment was revolutionary even by industry standards. The state-of-the-art lab housed medical freezers, robotics, aluminum cooling sleeves for R-tubes, ECG devices to detect abnormal heart rhythms and several more instruments and gadgets she couldn't name, yet had spent thousands of dollars investing in, all of which had been set up by Leal.

"I trust you've found the facilities suitable for testing a full range of anatomical and clinical tests. Any results yet?"

Vik shot from his seat and squinted an eye.

"You're a jumpy one."

Three other scientists continued an experiment, testing batches of vaccines. With Leal's research gone, the scientists had had to start from scratch. Creating a vaccine usually involved experts from around the world and she had hired these specialists. She hated the slow procedures of vaccines and drug research usually requiring ten to fifteen years before the vaccine can be made available to the general public. If only she knew where Leal's research had gone. Even with access to all things Trelles, including all properties, secret labs and testing warehouses, no one had ever been able to locate Leal's research into nephthysis.

The researchers in the room had started afresh spending months in lab study at her expense trying to identify an antigen to prevent nephthysis. Once the test vaccines were cleared by the U.S. Food and Drug Administration, Trelles would need to endure three more phases of thorough clinical trials conducted on human volunteers for efficacy, and determine appropriate dosage while monitoring for side effects. This would be another several years.

Well damn it she didn't have several years! She needed a nephthysis drug now. Myranda glanced toward one section of the laboratory and caught sight of the three male scientists she'd recruited from various fertility disciplines with a common goal of investigating modern infertility challenges.

"I need you three to gather around. With medical minds around me, our new consultant will not fabricate lies." She breathed easy. "Let me remind you everything discussed here today is covered by the non-disclosure agreement."

The scientists proceeded to Vik's station and Myranda took a deep breath. "What can you tell me so far?"

Vik scratched his head. "You need to be patient. Unexplained infertility affects about thirty percent of the global population and is the most frequent infertility diagnosis given to women."

"Don't give me statistics. Give me results."

"Then may I call for your patience," Vik said.

Vik resumed pouring a set of chemicals into three test tubes. The substance reacted with the obscure elements and Myranda watched as they fizzled. She couldn't get her head round the details. She needed this man to deliver today. With enough dirt on him to pile a landfill, she hated to admit that he was her last hope. All her life, she'd had to make things work for herself, never depending on others. When it came to her body, she was helpless.

"I'm not sure what your previous doctors have told you, but the approach I'd like to take with you is to rule out four conditions: endometriosis, immunological infertility, tubal disease and, my suspicion, premature ovarian aging."

The words hit Myranda like a death sentence and sent her spirit shivering. She searched Vik's face. "Speak plain English."

"In my research, I've found evidence for one or more of these conditions in a surmounting majority of cases. Now, endometriosis is a very common gynecological condition. The cause is still debated, and the condition affects the cells that compose the internal lining of the uterine cavity."

"What does that mean?"

"The cells grow outside the uterus. Most commonly on fallopian tubes, ovaries and the pelvic tissue linings. Should I continue?"

Her mind worked frantically. "Please."

"Tubal infertility denotes the presence of abnormal fallopian tubes. You know, where the egg needs to be released from. This can't be overlooked either."

Frightened to the point of collapse, Myranda had never once had the possibilities of her disease spelled out so bluntly.

"Have you had this diagnosed or checked?"

"How can I know?" Myranda spoke fighting back tears of anger. How could her life and dreams be in the hands of this man?

Vik continued. "Third, I've looked for abnormal immune function. This is a sure possibility. Your blood work seems normal and that's why my last assessment of your case is you may well have premature ovarian aging."

"Is that what the women in Benton were diagnosed with?

291

Don't lie to me. Dr. Chesser was in the initial team on this."

"Like I was saying, you'll find that Dr. Chesser and Dr. Trelles's research ten years ago ruled in favor of these four conditions," Vik said.

She swiveled her head at the other scientists but kept Vik in view. "Why this particular diagnosis?"

Vik searched the faces of the other researchers around him. She followed his gaze. From their faces, it was obvious they agreed with Vik as an expert in the field of infertility research.

"Mrs. Vaux," began the shortest man. "Women are born with about three-hundred-thousand follicles and that number decreases by approximately one-half every ten years."

Vik interjected. "Female fertility reduces moderately until around age thirty-seven. Then infertility quickens in parallel from then on with the loss of more follicles."

The stocky scientist, with gray eyes like two pools of mercury, joined the conversation. "Women with this fourth condition face an intense weakening in their fertility potential and possibly enter early menopause."

One of the scientists coughed begging to get a word in.

"What Dr. Vik is suggesting is that your ovarian aging curve, for reasons which are still unclear, has been reached at a much younger age."

Vik interposed with caution. "Fortunately for you, Ms. Vaux, this formula reverses your condition and while you're still less than thirty-eight, reversal of your condition is possible."

"Is it safe?"

The stocky scientist cut in. "The State Department of Health and Substance Abuse Testing divisions have certified the ingredients. I'm sure it's agreeable."

Myranda watched Vik carefully. "Let me remind you what's at stake if it's not agreeable. One mistake and I'll make good on my end of our deal, your incriminating file will be released to the authorities disqualifying you from ever practicing medicine again, not to mention possible jail time."

Had she said that aloud? This was her life, her choice.

"May I have my papers now?" Vik said.

She pulled out a document marked confidential with the Indian police stamp. "I'm sure you're familiar with this seal."

Vik's eyes narrowed and his hands shook.

Her knuckles whitened as she gripped the document. "So I

can be sure you'll do this right, I'm holding onto this."

She tugged her lime green-cropped spring sweater and started a strut out of the room. Vik thought for a moment, scratching his head.

"You three come with me," Myranda said, turning to the puzzled researchers.

The three men started after her. She zipped round to face Vik. "How long will it take before it's effective?"

Vik raised his head. "If I'd not been dragged here involuntarily, I might have disclosed that the formula has never been tested on humans. You'd be the first."

* * *

Leal was deep in formless thought as Jewel came down the stairs. Her wet hair was wrapped in a towel in the morning sunlight that flooded the room. She had found his new bathrobe and it engulfed her small frame as she strolled into the bright kitchen.

Would she it had rather been the Leal she knew? He tried to jam a brake on his line of thought. *Damn it! I'm Leal and I didn't even have the spine to tell her as I made love to her.*

He continued stirring the last of the eggs. There wasn't much in the fridge, but he found the needed ingredients for a superb eggs florentine; butter, egg yolk for the hollandaise sauce, two English muffins, large handfuls of baby spinach and four free-range eggs for the rest. He deposited the egg yolks into a round bowl set over a pan of simmering water as Jewel made her way toward him. He added the water, lemon juice, salt and freshly ground black pepper to the egg yolks, then placed the butter in the mixture.

The sizzle from the pan filled the large kitchen that had first attracted him to the property. The kitchen floors were ornamented with river stones in spiral and infinity-knot designs. Architectural details from the Middle East and India were evident in the cabinetry make and the copper pots and kettles that hung above the counter. His interior designer had captured the heart of India, the place he knew he had captured Jewel's heart. The windows were open and a slight breeze flew in from the south deck overlooking the bay.

293

Once he'd completed the sauce, he placed the buttered muffins on a cookie sheet.

"I thought we could eat on the patio. I hope you like eggs florentine. I'm afraid the only other choice is canned kidney beans. I'd hoped my housekeeper had bought more groceries."

She threw him an alluring smile and touched his lips. "After last night, I could eat anything."

The way she said *night* sent Leal's eyes smiling. He switched off the burner. "Would you rather it had been...?"

"Leal?" She gently drew to him. "I'm falling in love with you, Cyrus."

"I've been in love with you since we met."

"I've gained something I lost long ago," she said. "Leal opened my heart to trust, so it could belong to you," she said.

He angled toward her and drew her into his arms, finding it impossible to formulate his words. Jewel ran a playful finger along his chin, before settling into a seat on the kitchen island and picked up a fresh muffin. She buttered it some more, and took an enormous bite.

He smiled as he watched her take more bites. Leal eased the steamed spinach on top of the muffins, topped with the poached eggs and tipped the hollandaise sauce over the top. He found silverware in a nearby drawer. The radio he'd set to some chill-out tunes serenaded in the background, as he took a seat opposite her. "I guess we're eating inside."

They ate in silence for a few minutes.

"I forgot to thank you," Jewel said.

"For what?"

"For getting me out of jail."

He smiled and nodded his head. "You already have." He took a deep breath. "Jewel, I've something to tell you."

Though he had more courage now than when he'd stopped at the top of the stairs several hours ago, he hoped the words would ease out. His cellphone rang. For a few seconds he stared at it, debating whether to answer it. The moment had gone, lost in the shrilling beeping of the classic ringtone of his smartphone.

He pressed the call button and set the phone against his ear, his eyes still on her face. "Yes."

It was Vik.

Leal rose from the island table, walking to the door that led to the patio. He looked over at Jewel for a brief second as she finished her plate and reached for the glass of freshly-squeezed orange juice. He walked till he was out of earshot.

"I've done as you requested," Vik said on the line.

"Is it gone?"

"Yes."

"Thanks, Vik. I appreciate it."

He strode back into the kitchen and set his phone on the table. "Sorry about that. A business call."

Reflected light glimmered over her face as she reached for a grape. She chewed slowly. "Cyrus? Will you go back to Venice? To Nonna?"

"I'm hoping you can help me with that decision."

She smiled without comment, the first shy look he'd ever seen her display crossing her face. "I—"

"I have to close all the loose ends on our family and Trelles Industries here. But after that, I plan too. Would you come with me if I did?"

Would she agree? They could stay here for all he cared. The DEI could leave him alone once and for all. He would say he'd tried to develop Tharnex that he'd used Jewel and her DNA and that nothing from her genes could help explain the disease and why it was only her mother who had conceived. He would keep the other little information from them, the notes he'd taken in Montpellier. How long had he stayed in there as she slept, until he'd fought the intruder off her? He thanked his luck that he'd gotten there on time. In time to switch her records and shield them from the DEI. She wouldn't be a lab rat for a money-hungry medical industry. Patriotism or no, her records belonged to her and her doctor alone and he hoped he could be the latter.

Jewel pushed her plate away and took another sip of the cold orange juice. "I've been wondering how to say this to you. I learned something about Leal and frankly I don't know what to think."

"What did you learn?" he said.

"The day of the mediation. I went to Leal's house in Martha's Vineyard. He'd told me about it when we were in India."

"What did you do there?"

"Looked for clues and perhaps a reason to let him go and release myself to you." She glanced into his expectant eyes. "Anyway, I found two things that are puzzling me."

"What did you find?"

"A picture I gave him in India. As a photographer I know firsthand that you can have more than one copy of a picture, but not an original Polaroid."

Leal swallowed hard and tugged at his left ear. She stared at him as if something had sparked a memory and continued. "Now how's that possible? As I was trying to make sense of it, guess who walked into the house?"

"Who?"

"Myranda and a man called Devon Chesser. I only had moments to think before jumping into a closet."

Leal's eyes narrowed.

"Then a strange thing happened," she said. "I then overheard Myranda and Devon talk about the police file on Leal's death and accident." She glanced up at him her eyes searching for truth. "I believe they bribed the Himachal Pradesh police and together manufactured a new police report they've been using for many purposes since. That's why I went to Devon's office. I thought I could find it. I think they found Leal's body and buried the details in their corporate vaults."

Leal set a hand over hers. "Why didn't you tell me, Jewel? We're in this together." He watched her. "What did you want to do with the file?"

"Clear my name." She rose. "I don't know." Her hair fell out of the wrapped towel, spilling over her shoulders.

"You really loved Leal, didn't you?"

She hesitated as if whatever she would say next would betray each of the brothers. She glanced up at him. "I'm sorry. I should stop talking about him so much. Cyrus, this morning I felt like we could—"

He rose walking toward her before brushing a lock from her amber eyes. "Jewel I want to be with you. Do you trust me?"

She hesitated a moment. "Yes."

"I'm not letting you go."

"I'm not sure you'll get what you expect."

"I'm in love with you."

"Are you?"

"Surely, you know."

"I—"

"It's okay. I realize you haven't moved on from Leal. I don't blame you." He let out a short tension-breaking laugh. "Leal was better looking than me."

"Cyrus, I just want to give us the chance we deserve, with no distractions. Does that make sense?"

He moved closer gathering her in his arms. "I hope I can help you close those issues."

Jewel glared up at him, her face a good head shorter than his. "I had no doubt about your feelings after last night." She pulled away and walked to the sink.

An echoing phone ring from the counter top broke the silence. It came from the fold of her purse. She strode reluctantly to retrieve it. "Hello?"

Her face went ashen. "I'll be there as soon as possible."

She turned to face Leal. "Can you drive me to the hospital? It's my mother."

Chapter 22

Jewel could feel the silence between them stretch in the car as they drove to Lower Manhattan Hospital.

"I'm sorry about your mother."

"She hasn't been feeling well for several years."

"You are close to her aren't you?"

"Closer than most. She's always been my number one fan. From gymnastics to photography. When I started going on shoots abroad, she stopped traveling with me."

"I called the hospital. The car collision with the delivery truck has left Mahina with a concussion."

Jewel failed to shake the guilty feeling. Her obsession with her quest had cost her mother her health. "If I'd stayed closer to home or, lived with her, this wouldn't have happened."

"It's not your fault, Jewel. The other driver has been taken into the emergency unit as well."

The room was bathed in white light when they approached her mother's bed. A female doctor sat in an adjacent seat taking Mahina's blood pressure on a quiet apparatus as she lay sleeping.

"I'm Jewel Carlone, her daughter. Can you tell me anything about her condition, doctor?"

"She went into cardiac arrest after the accident. She's now stable."

Leal set a hand on Jewel's shoulder. "I'll leave you with her and be outside the door if you need me."

Jewel thanked him and he left, closing the door behind him. "Mama?"

Mahina had her eyes closed and a bandage to her head. She moaned softly.

"She needs to rest, but you can stay here with her," the doctor said.

"Is she going to be okay?"

"We'll have to see."

"What happened?"

"ER reported she was getting into her car and went onto the road. Out of nowhere a van rammed into her just downtown?"

"Who did this, doctor?"

"We won't know until the other driver is out of a coma, but I can find out for you?"

"Thank you."

Mahina's eyes opened and Jewel edged to her side. "Oh, Mama, I should've been there for you. I promise that I will from now on."

"She went into cardiac arrest, at the scene of the accident, but the emergency teams reached her just in time to stabilize her," the doctor said.

Mahina started moving her head in response.

"Mama, I'm sorry this happened to you. If I had been there..."

The doctor rose. "I'll leave you two. Now no excitement, she really needs to rest and is on heavy painkillers. I'll be back in ten minutes."

Mahina turned. "Jewel, what happened?"

"Sh... Mama, you were in a very bad accident. Try not to talk. You need to save all your energy."

Mahina's head leaned toward her daughter. She coughed. "Jewel, I'm glad you came."

"Mama, rest. I'll stay here as long as it takes."

"I feel fine." Mahina searched her daughter's eyes raising a hand to Jewel's cheek. "Now's as good a time to tell you as any."

Jewel took her hand and squeezed it lightly. "Mama, please just rest."

"Jewel, I'll feel better if I tell you."

"Tell me what?"

Mahina drew her eyes open and raised her head. "I want you to know the real reason we moved to New York from Udine."

What did that have to do with anything? The concussion must have played with her mother's senses. "I know, you and daddy split up and he moved on. You'd always wanted to be in New York to further your photography career and inspired mine."

"No, darling. You father didn't move on. I did. It drove him crazy."

"We don't have to discuss this now."

"Yes we do. Because, finally it can wipe the sadness and anguish from your face. I can't bare it anymore, Jewel. I can't bear to see you unhappy. You run from everything good in your life, gymnastics, love, or the pursuit of it and it's my fault. I was a rotten example for you."

Mahina had never seemed so determined.

Jewel bit her lip. "Mama..." She leaned in toward her mother. "I haven't tried to find papa, in fact I've let the whole thing drop."

"I left your father because I couldn't stand to live with him and after what my ex-husband did to me."

"Ex-husband?"

"I didn't realize you were married before."

"I was and my actions robbed you of a father and screwed up your relationships with men. All because I couldn't forgive the man, who once loved me more than anything."

Jewel tried to ignore her comment. Mama had always been a role model. In truth, she brought guilt into every conversation they had about the past.

Jewel smiled, her eyes narrowing.

"Don't follow my example. Don't hate your father," Mahina said.

"I don't."

"Yes, you do. You do in the way you react to men."

Jewel bit her lip.

"Kaya told me. It's love or hate with you and that's just a shadow of my influence," Mahina said.

"It's not true."

"Stop chasing the impossible. Sometimes we have to live with the probable."

"I'm happy."

There was a note of imperceptible pleading on Mahina's face. "Are you?"

"Ideal doesn't exist. Mama, I'm not chasing a dream."

"Yes you are. For years, I've watched you, even when you didn't know. I saw how losing Leal affected you. I wish I had met him. Don't prevent happiness because of a lost love. These years will never come back. I never loved again after your father. Look where it has gotten me. Alone and dependent on my daughter for company."

"That's not true. I love being with you."

300

"Jewel, you are twenty-eight and still my baby in many ways, take chances now. That's what I wish I could do if I had my time over again."

Jewel's expression burned with sentiment. She rose, paced the room and walked to the window in silence, thinking about her mother's words. A picture of Leal and then Cyrus came to her mind. She knew she loved them both. Was that possible? How could they be so similar, yet so different?

Doesn't she owe it to Leal to love him even after death? Why couldn't she let go? Would she fail Leal if she stopped going after that file? She wasn't free, not even to love Cyrus until that file was found. A pounding singed through her temples as she stared at her mother.

"There's another thing," began Mahina. "I want you to find your sister."

The revelation stung like a centurion's dagger. Had she heard correctly or was she still in a trance of emotions. "Mama, I wondered if you'd been married before even if we'd never spoken about it, but you never told me that I had a sister."

Jewel moved back toward the bed.

Tears rolled down, Mahina's face. "I let her down just like I let you down."

"What do you mean? Why are you telling this to me now?"

"Because you need to know and there's never a good time." Mahina's look was penetrating and petrified at the same time. "Your big sister had to grow up without me because I was selfish, had an affair, and ran off with a man who I thought would give me everything. In one way he did, he gave me you. But then as if heaven was punishing me, took him away."

"Why didn't you tell me before? Who is she and where is she?"

"I don't know where she is. It all started with an accident in Benton. Did you know I used to live in Pennsylvania before New York?"

Jewel shook her head.

"Benton is a small town. When Ovatti Foods arrived years ago, we all thought we could make a good living working there. I worked for Ovatti Foods as a contract photographer."

Jewel resumed her seat by the bed as she drew in her mother's narrative.

"There was a company called Solomon Bees, a bee harvester

301

that employed many local people. My ex-husband worked for Solomon Bees."

Jewel had questions about him, but decided to listen, not wanting to aggravate Mama's weak condition.

"Then I got very sick one day. Extremely sick, people thought I was going to die." She let out a short laugh. "Later, a doctor explained that I wasn't going to die but had been contaminated by something I had ingested at Ovatti, radiation possibly, and would never have children again."

"I see."

"I was pregnant with your sister at the time. Well that almost killed me. For a couple of years, after that, I was unbearable to live with. My ex and I would fight a lot and your sister was such a tiny thing when she was born. I must've lost it one day and when your father, Piero Carlone, whom I'd known since high school called me one day, I left to be with him in Italy. You were born a year later."

"What happened to your first husband and the child?"

"He took her from me and wouldn't let me see her, even when I asked him many times."

"Is he, she... still alive?"

"I don't know. All I know was when I had you, it was like I'd been given a second chance. That I could have life with in me again. It was not until you were twelve, when we returned to the US that I thought of finding her. I never did. Adan may have changed his name and hers, I guess, to protect her from me. I really don't know much about them."

Mahina's words started to resonate with Jewel. Where had she heard similar information? She stood and stared at her mother for several moments. "Do you remember the diagnosis of your disease?"

"No. Please forgive me."

Mahina's blood pressure rose on the machine. She had to let her rest. A bitter taste stole to her tongue and Jewel managed a weak smile. "I forgive you and I'll find them."

Mama's voice was low and drifting. "I know you will."

Soon Mahina fell into a deep sleep as Jewel watched her. How long? It was impossible to tell. The details of Mama's history inundated her mind, torturing her conscience. Her hands stole to her throat. She couldn't breathe. The glimpse into Mama's past had answered many open questions and raised a daunting one. Mama's life had led her to Benton. She'd contracted a disease in that little town. The media had branded it "cursed," "unsolved," "poisoned." Ovatti Foods suffered a huge lawsuit. People had lost their jobs. Women were made barren.

Hadn't she read it in a paper years ago? Or perhaps seen a documentary on unsolved mysteries.

Barren women...

Mysterious disease...

Vaccines. No cure...

Sister?

Myranda's prenuptial.

India?

Leal must have known. Uncertainty crept into her mind and with her pulse pounding faster than she could keep up with, her vision lost focus as her head hit the floor.

* * *

Leal paced the hospital floors and almost collided into a man pushing a wheelchair. He debated whether to call Dr. Rafaela for an emergency session. With Jewel's mother fighting for her life, the last thing she needed was his confessions. His lies.

He stopped for several seconds, turned toward the far wall and rammed a fist into it. Undeterred by thundering pain, he ambled over to the waiting room and found a coffee machine, slotted some dollars into it and gulped down the warm bitterness of an espresso and tossed the Styrofoam cup into a nearby trash can. He bought a second cup. His phone rang, its shrill startling him. He set the coffee cup on the side table. "Yeah?"

"Leal?" He stiffened, agitation increasing with the heavy breathing on the line.

"Who's this?"

"It's Vik."

"Vik, what's going on?"

Several blocks across town, Vik stood in the Trelles laboratory tapping his trembling fingers on the steel desk. "I need your help. I've turned myself in to the police and they'll be here to pick me up any minute."

"What are you talking about?"

"I need you to come and vouch for me. I've created a vaccine

303

dose for Myranda using your formula and I'm afraid she might take it and it'll kill her."

* * *

Leal placed the phone in his pocket and entered Mahina's room. Her breathing was soft and steady.

"Jewel?"

No answer.

His eyes shifted toward the floor. Jewel lay face down on the cold tiles, her hair a mop around her head. He dashed to her side, lifted her head and cushioned it in his lap. He checked her vital signs, taking note of her level of consciousness. He checked her pulse, placing the tips of his index and middle fingers on her wrist with just enough pressure to feel her heartbeat through the artery. He observed her chest and stomach to see if there was movement that indicated breathing as a frantic nurse ran to his side. "Nurse I need, some help. I need a stretcher."

Leal laid Jewel flat on her back. He elevated her legs to restore blood flow to her brain. Her face was ashen, her eyes closed. He loosened her belt and jacket allowing her to breathe easier. Jewel moved her head slowly from one side to another.

Leal gathered her in his arms and placed her on a lie-flat stretcher that two male nurses had managed to secure.

"There's a free room just down the hall," the nurse said.

Leal followed the nurse, grateful for the rapid response to his request. The medical aids hoisted Jewel on the bed, her head still moving very slowly.

"What happened, doctor?" asked the nurse.

Leal shot the nurse a quick glance. "How did you know I was a doctor?"

"You certainly responded like one."

The tense lines in Leal's face relaxed and he checked the name on his badge. "Nathan, can you please get me some water. Let's place her on her side so she's supported by one leg and one arm."

Nathan obliged.

"Thanks."

"Is she okay?"

"Yes she is. Her mother was just taken into ER down the

304

hall."

Leal opened Jewel's airway by tilting her head back and lifting her chin.

"Could she be pregnant?" Nathan asked.

Leal shot him a startled glance. "I don't think so. She was just fine in her mother's room, something must have happened. Maybe some news or shock at seeing her mother in a weak state."

"I see."

"Please monitor her breathing for a second. Her pulse is normal and she should come round shortly. It's only a temporary malfunction of her nervous system."

Leal looked round the room and found a thin clipboard on the table. He quickly grabbed it and started fanning Jewel. She rolled her head slightly from one side to the other and moved her leg down gently. She rotated her head and faced Leal. "Cy..."

"Sh.., try not to speak."

"What happened?" Jewel said.

Nathan placed a hand on her forehead. "You fainted just now. How do you feel?"

"I don't know."

* * *

Jewel sat up slowly and for a moment thought she'd seen Leal.

"Do you think we could have some more water?" he said.

The nurse debated whether to budge for a few seconds before leaving the room. Jewel sat and scrutinized Cyrus as he stroked his chin. The gesture reminded her of something that had happened ten years ago. The man who'd rescued her in Montpellier had behaved the same way. He'd attended to her with the same tenderness, the same calm and look of expertise. She blinked, imagining she may still not have all her senses restored. Cyrus was beginning to remind her more and more of Leal. Maybe she'd forgotten how he'd really looked up close.

She took a deep breath. "Did I faint?"

"Yes. Was everything okay in your mother's room? What happened?"

"Cyrus, do you believe in boomerangs?"

"Huh?"

305

"That what we throw away comes back in some sort of way. Good things sowing good and bad sowing bad."

"What do you mean?"

How could she rest? Myranda was her older sister and yet they had been rivals from the day Jewel was born. Myranda may not know, yet all Jewel could think about was Myranda's unfinished business with her. Jewel had taken her mother, kisses that should have been hers, heard stories that should've been read to her.

Myranda had been bitter for years until destiny had brought them together as adversaries. A sibling rivalry that existed beyond geographies, comprehension and distance. Sibling rivalry was one of humanity's oldest problems and Jewel could only imagine, a competition for threatened resources, love and territory. The Trelles family had been their battlefield, and Leal's affections their trophy. Could Myranda have unknowingly been deprived of a mother's love and blamed Jewel inadvertently. Or had Jewel been deprived of a father's regard that she'd been trapped between the affections of the men who'd offered a substitute? They'd both been incomplete beings, searching for wholeness in whatever form of manner.

"Cyrus, I think I understand Myranda a little better," Jewel said.

"How?"

"Myranda's mother was infertile at some point but later she had a child."

"How do you know?"

"Because, Cyrus, I'm the child she had."

"How did—"

"Cyrus. This means that your brother's vaccine Tharnex may have worked. My mother must've been one of his patients."

Chapter 23

Hudson's voice was hoarse. "There you are."

Kaya observed the agitation in his face. He was as restless as the day he blindfolded her, with her consent, and taken her to the DEI headquarters. Where was it? Certainly within an-hour-and-half drive from lower Manhattan. She'd only seen the interiors of the building and couldn't describe any of it. The dock on the river was visible from Hudson River Park, one of the places that smeared New York City with maritime charm and landmarked Manhattan from Clinton to Battery Park.

A masked dog walker crossed her path, alerting Kaya that New York also had its shadier secrets, like this DEI establishment for one. As much as she could hide flaws in herself, she also tried to use her shortcomings as inspiration to change circumstances around her.

Hudson wasn't helping. Not only had he ignored Jewel's bravery in tackling Trelles single-handedly but she had a feeling his suggestion for this clandestine meeting was not going to be reasonable.

"Agent Hudson, I've not heard from Jewel. I'm sure if anything had happened, you would have."

"She got into the Trelles building, was arrested and bailed out by an unidentified source. That was the last intelligence I got from headquarters."

"I know she'll call me."

"Do you trust her?"

"More than you."

A lengthy silence told Kaya agent Hudson, whose image as Rowell Saunders, was hard to ward off, had not cared for her response.

"Mrs. Wilda, find that friend of yours before I do. There's something she needs to know. The DEI is running out of patience with the Trelleses. The deadline is approaching."

"What are you talking about? What is running out?"

"You may think you know everything about the Trelleses, but as an attorney, I would have imagined your observations skills would be above average."

Kaya narrowed her eyes. "You better make this meeting worth my time. I'm the one helping you. I despise secrecy especially when it's our government shielding us from the truth."

He drew in a sharp breath. "You should look a little closer at Cyrus Trelles."

"Why? Quit wasting my time."

"Mrs. Wilda. If Jewel doesn't make contact within the hour, her boyfriend is going to be looking for another good lawyer. Do you want the job?"

"Hudson. Your threats are even beyond you. This is a free country and—"

"Cyrus Trelles is really Leal Trelles."

Kaya lips remained open mid-sentence. "Excuse me?"

"Cyrus Trelles is a government alias we gave Leal Trelles, or should I say allowed him to keep. There's never been a Cyrus Trelles, at least not one that lived more than six years."

"What the heck has gotten into you?"

"Go ask him if you think he's out for Jewel's interest. What I am about to tell you is classified and falls under the nondisclosure agreement you signed with the DEI. Leal Trelles is alive and we let him fake his death. We had our reasons, but we're still investigating his. We believe they're connected to the two sisters Jewel and Myranda."

"Sisters?"

A weight of knots formed in her gut. It was more information than she could take. Her mind calculated the phrases, but something was still amiss. She smacked her lips for moisture as the river breeze wafted her way. "I'm not sure what to do with that." She slid into a bench overlooking the Hudson. "You're lying. Leal? Cyrus?"

"Same brother. Same man."

"No, it can't be. What sort of jokes do you government types play with people's lives? It doesn't make sense anyway. How can anyone survive an avalanche? Jewel saw it. Others saw it."

"He pulled it off with no help from us. He's quite a fit guy. We needed him to deliver a vaccine for us. He didn't need money so we couldn't bribe him with a grant. However, when we discovered criminal behavior in his family files, we had an edge on him."

"What criminal behavior?"

"Identity theft. Of his younger brother. He did it to hide company assets for his family."

"I don't believe you."

"He agreed to work with us until he delivered the vaccine, then he wouldn't face prosecution."

Though most of it didn't make sense, some of what Hudson was saying seemed probable. Leal had been extremely secretive. Kaya lifted her chin. "Who else knows?"

"Apart from his family, just you?"

"Does Jewel know?"

He extinguished his cigarette. "I don't think so. Leal was instructed to keep silent."

"How could I have missed it? Yes they're the same height, weight, but why wouldn't they be?"

"They were twins."

"But his eyes, hair, mannerisms—"

"Facial animation, my dear. The government has been using it for secret agents for years. Listen ma'am. Those who have access to the technology can create whomever we want, whenever we want, even imaginary agents. We've been at it for years. Leal was brought on as a special medical agent to complete a task. Now your task is to find Jewel and get any intel she has before we do. I imagine she had help breaking into Trelles."

Kaya rose in one abrupt movement. "I'm not interested in your insinuations."

"I'm on a deadline. I need to answer to higher authorities within forty-eight hours. You should never upset a desperate agent."

Kaya couldn't imagine what Jewel would do if she knew. It would break her more than the pain of Leal's death that she'd endured. Her eyes narrowed as she spoke. "I won't do it. I won't be the one to tell Jewel just to coerce Leal to give you whatever you want."

"Mrs. Wilda. You've no choice in the matter. We make it a point to know everything about the people we deal with. If Jewel and Leal don't come up with the drug within forty-eight hours, your license to practice law will be revoked. Don't test us."

Kaya lips trembled. "You can't do that. A bribe."

"No bribes necessary. You broke the law when you opened the contents of documents that were never addressed to you. Should I remind you of which files I'm talking about?"

* * *

Vik's voice rang in Leal's ears. Why hadn't Vik told him what he was up to? Why hadn't he destroyed the file? Jewel's breathing and vital signs were now steady. She sat up and scanned round the room. Her eyes focused on his face but she remained silent. Her hand slid to her forehead. "What happened?"

"Try to rest, Jewel."

She sat up slowly. "How?"

"Try not to think about it."

She drew in a sharp breath. "Mama... where is she?"

"She's okay"

"I need to go."

Leal took her hand. "Where?"

"There's something I need to do."

"I'll come with you."

Leal rubbed his hands through his hair and they made their way back to her mother's room. Jewel had rambled about Myranda in her fainted daze. She knew the truth now and it would be easier to tell her the rest. Moisture smeared his hands when they reached the recovery room where Mahina had been transferred. Leal hesitated a few feet from the door. Jewel's news made him weak. What if Mahina recognized him? Could she see through his disguise? He placed his back against the far wall as a hurrying nurse scurried past him and into the room. He followed her with a grim look on his face fearing the worst as he stepped further into the room behind her.

"I'm sorry, but family members only."

A groggy moan sounded out from the bed. "He's family."

Leal shot Mahina a surprised look and caught Jewel's bewilderment in turn. He paced toward the bed slowly and placed a soft hand on the nurse's shoulder as he passed her. "It's OK nurse, I'm a doctor."

"What?"

Jewel's shock was to be expected.

"But you are an engineer," she said.

"I passed all the exams," Leal answered.

Jewel's baffled look shifted to her mother. Leal knew she would question him later.

"Must run in the family," Jewel said.

"Mrs. Carlone, you are recovering well," said Leal.

"Mr. Trelles I take it? Can I call you Cyrus, because I feel I know you after hearing nothing but good from my daughter after her Venice trip?"

"Of course, you can."

When had he first seen Mrs. Carlone? It must've been the day she was brought into the downtown DEI center to be examined. Because of her, he'd been able to investigate nephthysis in-depth and first found out about Jewel. Insights from Mahina's medical files had accomplished much of what now was Attempt Seven of Tharnex. A vaccine now unleashed to God knows what. He needed to contain the damage now. He glanced down at the frail frame on the bed. Though years were written on her face, her skin still glowed. Mrs. Carlone had a composed way of growing old, with flowing flocks of thick hair, high cheek bones and excellent facial symmetry, her skin illuminating with exceptional Hawaiian genes. Leal now understood where Jewel's brave eyes, strong spirit, brown hair and the sparkle in her eyes came from.

"Are you okay, Cyrus?" Jewel said.

He turned to face her looking intensely into her eyes. "Yes. Listen I hate to leave you, but I need to head off now. Something's come up. I'll come back later."

"What is it? Please, don't go. I need to talk to you. I need your help on something," Jewel said.

He looked at her and then back at her mother. "Me too."

He wouldn't lie this time. Deception and white lies had cost him much. Isn't that what Dr. Rafaela had said. *'Once you start lying, you can continue to rationally compartmentalize the truth. When you keep a secret, you logically attempt to push it out of your mind so that you don't expose all at exactly the wrong time, which only makes you think about the lie even more.'*

"I will, Jewel. Right now, you mother needs you, but I need to go to see the police authorities," he said.

"Why? Is it to do with me?"

He cupped her cheek stroking it lightly. "No, sweetheart."

"But what do you mean the police? Is everything okay?"

"I'm not sure, Jewel." He took her hand in his. "A friend of

311

mine is in trouble and needs my help."

"Who is it, Leal?" The look in her eyes warned him not to lie.

"Someone who worked with Leal years ago. I need to go vouch for him."

"This seems to be a habit for you. Bailing others out. Who is it? What did they do?"

"His name is Dr. Vik Patil."

Jewel's eyes enlarged gazing at Leal with intensity. "I know him. I just saw him yesterday, but very briefly. Is he okay?"

"I don't know."

"He was a good friend of Leal's."

"I know. They did some amazing medical projects in India."

He squeezed her hand gently. "I need to go. I'll be back." Leal turned to face Jewel's mom. "I'm sorry to leave you like this, Mrs. Carlone, but I need to go."

She smiled at him and said, "Go help your friend. Hope I'll see you soon."

Leal started toward the door.

"Wait!" Jewel grabbed her jacket. "I'm coming with you."

She kissed her mother on the forehead. "I'll be back soon, Mama. I have to help Vik. I don't think he knows many people in the city."

Jewel's courage never stopped to stir him. Leal smiled. "Are you sure?"

"Yes."

* * *

The BMW stopped at a red traffic light. Leal glanced over at Jewel hoping for a look into her thoughts. She kept her hands fisted together in her lap and every few minutes, she would rub them together. Was she cold? It was almost late afternoon, but the air conditioner was on. The silence was torturing Leal, as he reduced the strength of the air conditioner. "You cold?"

"No, just worried for Vik. Why would anyone arrest him? What has he done?"

"We'll find out soon."

"And why was I arrested for the theft of a vaccine I know nothing about? And how did you..."

"Let's not talk about it now."

They drove for thirty minutes, leaving downtown for calmer streets. Jewel slept for most of the drive. They nosed into a parking space up at the corner of a connective corridor joining a secluded road with two warehouses and a tall stone building. The isolated properties were joined by a large empty parking lot in what could only have been an industrial district adjacent to Gowanus Canal and behind Ninth Street Bridge. From the outside, the building resembled a vintage factory.

"We're here," Leal said.

Jewel stepped out of the BMW and looked up the height of the brick and masonry structure next to the two warehouses. The five-story glass tower disappeared behind the fog beginning to form in the sky. "What's this place?" she said. "This isn't a police station."

"It's the Department of Economic Intelligence."

Jewel shut the door calmly. "What're we doing here?"

Leal locked the BMW, exhaustion shadowing his face and took her hand. "Let's go see."

"Cyrus. I'm not going a step further until I know what's going on."

He leaned forward. "Jewel it's time some of Trelles' secrets came out. Please trust me. I won't let anything happen to you anymore."

Anymore? And there was that word again *trust.* They paced the short steps to the entrance of the stone building as burdened strides forbade Jewel from keeping up with Leal. Inside three security guards approached them. Jewel rubbed the back of her neck. Her anguish must've been obvious to them as one of the security guards scrutinized her discomfort. Leal pulled his shoulders back straight. "It's okay."

"Mr. Trelles?"

Leal nodded.

"This way," said the first man. He observed Jewel quizzically. Sensing his concern, Leal took a protective step in front of her. "She's with me."

The man held out a hand and led them to a security desk. "Your things stay here."

They passed through a security x-ray. As Leal stepped through, it beeped.

Leal padded his shoulder. "Must be the data stick."

The uniformed officer gave him a knowing look and asked him to proceed.

Jewel raised an eyebrow and proceeded after him. They took the elevator to the second floor. Jewel breathed a little easier, a tightening forming in her gut. The well-lit offices showcased an upscale, modern working milieu within a tasteful lobby. Comfortable seating adorned the otherwise bare space. Original modern artwork stared Jewel in the face and the individually graded, color spectrum on the floor suggested the office was no conventional public building. Large-scale wall graphics on the walls gave directions to various functional rooms, coded with confusing abbreviations.

"Cyrus? What did you mean by data stick? I thought we were going to see Vik."

"He's here."

* * *

Leal moved away from Jewel. He had more explaining ahead of him. Once on the twenty second floor, he reached for his cellphone and scrolled through to an incoming text message. "It's this way."

They found the well-lit room a few doors down. Minimalist at best, three chairs lined against the windowless, gray-scale room and a large square table covered most of the floor. The negotiation was not going to be easy. Vik sat, elbows on the table, his head bowed in contemplation. He peered up when Leal and Jewel stepped into the room. Within seconds agent Hudson joined them. Vik glanced from face to face, his expression a shroud of anxiety, before placing his hands on his lap.

Hudson cleared his throat and turned to Leal. "Good thing I got your message or things would've turned sour."

Leal remained calm, his eyes on Vik as agent Hudson took a seat. Vik studied Leal. His eyes had lit up, flowing with relief at the sight of him.

* * *

They took a seat across Vik. Jewel's conversation with Kaya had dropped several hints about the DEI, but the organization was still a mystery. The few people she'd seen on her way up gave

314

away little clues as to what really went on. Who ran this place? Is this where they'd brought Kaya blindfolded? But most pressing, what was Cyrus, Leal's and Vik's connection to this place?

Hudson dropped a file on the desk and shoved it in front of Leal. "You may want to look at this before we proceed."

Cyrus opened the file and glanced at the notes as Jewel stretched her eyes slightly, attempting to spy on the print as he scrutinized the information. He closed the brown envelope. "What are the implications, Hudson?"

"They've already been explained to him."

Vik held a straight face.

"I'd like to speak to Vik privately before we begin," Cyrus said.

"I can't let you do that," Hudson said.

"Come on Hudson, you owe me one and you know it. This man's not a criminal. I must speak to him alone."

"Five minutes tops, Trelles."

Hudson stepped out of the room.

Vik took a deep breath. "I can explain."

"Just tell me why you did it."

"You saw the file just now. It details the time when I made a mistake."

"I'm not talking about that. I mean why didn't you destroy the elements I gave you?"

"I started to..." he looked over at Jewel. "I did. I left the building when we spoke. However, Myranda got to that information in there somehow and cornered me. She threatened to release it if I didn't create a drug for her."

"Vik, you and I know that the tests done were harmful. The side effects were still uncontrollable. Myranda is desperate like the woman who took that first dose. She stole it. Why would you repeat such a mistake?"

"But you said you had it..."

"The formula works, but it's yet to be approved."

"I wanted to vindicate myself. I got careless I guess. When I had the file in my hands, I suspected that the formula may have improved, or that I could build on Leal's work. My research brain and inquisitiveness just got the better of me. I almost had it. I just wanted to really be sure it wouldn't work before I destroyed it. I swear."

"I wanted that file destroyed."

"I'm sorry."

"Vik, I forgive you. I probably would've done the same thing in your shoes."

That Jewel didn't expect. The thought softened her face and earlier judgments of the man she'd began to love.

"What has the DEI told you? They caught me as I was finishing up, before Myranda came back with her deadline. They've given me a deal, a way out."

"What was the deal?" Jewel said.

Vik looked at both of them one right after the other. "You're not going to like it."

"What is it?"

"They will expose my file if I don't return to Myranda and tell her I gave her the wrong vaccine. They want me back in Trelles and for me to claim I messed up accidentally. They don't want Myranda to have Leal's vaccine."

"Why would you work with Myranda, Vik?" asked Jewel.

"I just wanted to try it in Myranda's lab. You see I hoped to create one real one and one phony one and give her the fake one." He slammed a fist on the table. "Gosh I don't know! I saw the state-of-the-art lab, but was given every ingredient I needed. I—"

"How did Myranda know you had the formula in the first place? Is that what I was arrested for? Leal's vaccine?" Jewel said.

Vik's eyes studied them both. "I stole it."

"From where?" Jewel said.

Chapter 24

Leal ran a hand through his hair. "Vik did not steal the file," he said. "Leal gave it to him."

Vik remained silent. "You still haven't told her?"

"Told me what?" Jewel said.

"Anyway," Vik said. "Now, the DEI wants me to return to Myranda and pretend to give her a new vaccine, the counterfeit one. That way they incriminate her for reproducing Leal's vaccine without government approval. They believe she has it. She's also wanted on a few other incidents but can't bring her in without evidence."

Jewel crossed her arms. "Is that why my charges were dropped? What does the DEI want Myranda for?"

"I'm really not sure. I overheard Hudson mention her father in connection to something, but I guess that they have some suspicions into her economic dealings with Trelles and are looking for a way to get into Trelles Industries," Vik said.

"What happens if you don't help them?" Jewel said.

Vik dropped his eyes. "They'll expose my mistakes and prosecute me here and in India."

"What mistakes?"

Leal peered over at Jewel. "Six years ago in India, Leal and Vik worked on a fertility vaccine. Tests of the vaccine showed only minor problems. Some women had a slight fever; others had redness or irritation of their skin at the site where the vaccine was given. Anyway, Leal was unhappy with the side effects. In any case, they decided to destroy the file and start again with different approaches. Unfortunately, one desperate patient stole the vaccine test samples. She overdosed and then... died."

"That wasn't your fault," pleaded Jewel.

"That's not how the police saw it," said Vik. "I've had many sleepless nights agonizing over the patient. She didn't deserve to do so, but her agony led her. Her family shamed and disowned her because she couldn't bear children."

The door flung open and Hudson marched in. "Time's up. What will it be Vik?"

* * *

Jewel analyzed Vik's face as he glanced across at Cyrus, his eyes begging for an indication as to what he should do.

"I'll do it," Jewel said.

A flash of astonishment grazed the men's faces.

"I'll catch Myranda red handed for you," continued Jewel. "No need to let Vik do it. I can go there and make up some lie about acquiring the real drug and say that Vik confessed to me that it wasn't the right one."

"I can't let you do that," Cyrus said.

"Look," she rose pacing the cement floor. "Myranda won't suspect me. In fact, she'll hate me for it. She'll believe me because of my relationship to Leal before he died. What you want is evidence of bribery, withholding information, false manufacturing. You name it. I'm sure I can get that for you."

Hudson watched her carefully. "You would do that?"

"Agent Hudson. I'm sure I could also find out whom she's sold it to if at all. Myranda has a bone to pick with me because of Leal. I could use that, somehow. I can finally figure out if she'd a hand in Leal's death or a least covering it up for her own purposes in order to acquire Trelles Industries."

Hudson rubbed his chin. "I'm intrigued. What do you boys think?"

"Myranda is dangerous, Jewel, and as you know Devon Chesser is not a walk in the park either," Vik said.

"Listen," Jewel cleared her throat. "I'm offering you both a way to get Myranda, and the vaccine. I'll explain that Vik realized he'd missed something. Vik can make up some medical gibberish and then I'll propose that I had caught up with him and he was too afraid for his life to tell her but that Vik admitted it to me. She'll believe me because she knows I know Vik. It'll work, trust me."

Hudson dodged backward and leaned against the door. "Myranda will terrorize him and you."

"Isn't that what you want?"

318

Hudson sidled over to Jewel. "I appreciate your help, Ms. Carlone, but if Myranda sees you, she'll call the cops. You're not supposed to get within a hundred feet of her."

"Jewel, I can't let you do it. No," Cyrus said.

* * *

Leal stopped outside an eleven bedroom estate.

"Some place," Vik said. "Yours?"

"Bought it seven years ago."

"So Myranda uses it now."

"Not for long. I'll sell it after all this is over."

"Bad memories?"

"Something like that."

He'd driven Vik the twenty miles to the townhouse. A *beaux arts* residence designed in 1905. Stylistically, it was more Parisian than most French houses he knew. Myranda had wanted a house that made a statement to the world attesting to her achievement. Frankly, it was *his* achievement.

"Doesn't seem much your style, though who am I to question the tastes of an epidemiologist worth thirteen-billion dollars," Vik said.

"I know. Myranda always wanted to hit the upper class neighborhoods. She ascended the ladder faster than a squirrel on Valium."

The front of the nine-thousand square feet space with eighteen rooms drew attention to the entrance with its sweeping double staircase facing a green lawn.

"When was the last time you were here, Leal?"

"About six years ago when I paid to extend the back to fit a man-made pond and two built-in gazebos."

"She really milked you."

"Only for a while."

Had he been foolish enough to imagine he could one day retire, do his research, and settle here? Leal first admired the house for its private location, generous kitchen, a butler's pantry, a considerable master suite, a formal dining room, oak fireplaces, and the library was a researcher's dream. Here, he'd imagined, he would teach his children about science and the mysteries of nature.

He turned over to Vik. In the dim 6:00 p.m. evening light, beads of sweat formed on Vik's brows like a faucet gone wild. Leal leaned toward him in the passenger seat. "You ready to do this?"

Vik nodded. "I have too. Listen, Leal, I'm really sorry, but the thought of that knowledge getting to my family... I've never betrayed you with anything and I——"

"I've done worse things in my life, Vik. Many that I need to correct."

Vik's face managed a half smile. "You need to tell her the truth. She'll understand you had no choice."

"Will she?"

"From what I know of her, yes."

"I almost told her when we dropped her off just now at her apartment. She was so brave, so determined wanting to help."

The light on the main terrace illuminated. They detected movement on the first floor of the ivory residence as the BMW stood parked on an adjacent quiet street.

Leal shut off the engine and turned to Vik. "Just go in there and tell her like it is. Big words confuse Myranda, so make it as dramatic and believable as you can. You're wired for your own protection and can press the panic button any time." He grabbed his hand and located a thin undetectable patch, the latest technology in wiring. Thinner than a plaster and adjusted to skin color, the patch was wired with chips to transmit data to the DEI. "Courtesy of the NSA," Hudson had said.

"Hudson will alert me if anything goes wrong," Leal said.

"You going to stay?"

"Hudson and his men are a block away. They're here if anything."

"Where are you going?"

"To finish what started years ago."

Vik opened his door as drops of rain came down and darkness gained upon the sky. Leal leaned over to the passenger side. "I'll call you. It'll be over soon."

"You sure? People like Myranda never back down. How she got that information about me in the first place I'll never know, Leal. Not even my own family or places of employment have ever known that information."

"I have my suspicions. Myranda knows how to find anything. Nothing gets by her easily. She's kept this charade up for quite some time."

His cellphone rang.

Leal answered it and placed it on the in-car speaker. "Hudson here. Okay you can go in now. The wire is set up fine."

Vik jumped out of the car, grabbed his briefcase and walked up the windy hill to the estate. Leal watched as he advanced across the driveway toward the staircase. He watched for several minutes as Vik stepped up to the front door up, and was let in by a house attendant.

Had something stirred on the lawn? Maybe it was his heightened senses acting up again. Watanabe had once told Leal he had intense reflexes required of astronauts and pilots.

No. It was a figure moving across the lawn. Possibly a DEI agent getting in position. But that hadn't been the agreement. He hoped they wouldn't screw up. He squinted and hoped Vik wouldn't melt under pressure. Vik was no guiltier of the information in the file against him than he was.

He knew who'd set them up. If he hurried he'd make it to Connecticut in under two hours.

* * *

Jewel slid across the wet grass. The security cameras circumvented her wet frame. Flexibility was wired in her being and elasticity governed her bones. Years of gymnastics had continually made Jewel aware of her body. What it was capable and not capable of. She raised her head slightly looking for an open window as the rain slashed at her face obscuring the images in front of her. In the humid climate they'd been experiencing, she imagined someone would have left a window open. Vik had to succeed and if not, she would be right behind him. She wanted nothing left to chance. It was a long guess. Instinct told her Myranda had failed to give Devon the file on Leal.

It had taken all of three seconds when Cyrus dropped her at her apartment to make this move. Myranda wouldn't let anyone control her. Not even that Devon guy. That file was as precious to her as the gold on her deceiving neck.

The file was with her all the time.

It had to be.

Jewel had found the darkest items of clothing she owned, ebony cigarette pants and a long-sleeved rib top to match. She moved across the lawn, in a double effort to cower under the

321

security cameras and not trip on the sprinkler system. She hated to lie to Cyrus, but if she had mentioned her plan to him, he would have stopped her just as they had at the DEI. It had been a quick decision after Cyrus had dropped her off. Up the stairs, change, get the keys to the car and google Myranda's home address. A woman who dominated the society pages wouldn't be hard to find. The beaux arts building was one of few listed in and around New York. How many came with such lavish decor. Only Myranda would seek such attention.

Jewel reached the edge of the stone wall of the right spiral staircase. She glanced up at the dark clouds, staring into rain for all of five seconds and allowed the open skies to cool her cheeks with rain as she breathed in. She shut her eyes.

When she opened them, a sharp light pierced through them and blinded her for a few seconds. She cowered behind the stairs and heard light footed steps only inches from her. Heavy panting alerted her to the possibility of security dogs.

She waited.

The sounds stopped almost as soon as they had begun.

"What do you think you are doing?"

An adverse voice from a terrifying image of an unyielding man greeted her.

Jewel rose slowly, alarmed by his gruff tones and the steel length of his shotgun. A few feet below him, his companion's snarly eyes, and dripping gums told her the canine could snap her in two pieces should the man who held him release the lead.

* * *

Devon glanced over his shoulder certain he had locked the large doors that led out onto the lawn. He glared up the open stairway that mounted from the slate-paved entrance hall to the upper floors of the three-story house.

Cushioned within the forested landscape of New Canaan in Connecticut, Devon had just finished the refurbishing touches to the woodland weekend bungalow. Colonial in appearance, yet with contemporary flair, it stood on a private lane. That morning, he'd convinced Isabelle his wife to consider a getaway weekend and anticipated a long relaxed three days. The home had been in his family for several decades, which afforded them a secluded location on the edge of a picturesque hill overlooking the valley that led to the main town.

When he entered the kitchen, Isabelle stood by the sink, leaning against its clean edge as she glanced out the dark window.

"Looks like the rain's not letting up. Shame, I had hoped we could go pheasant hunting with the Ramseys tomorrow," he said.

Isabelle swung to face him. "Highly unlikely, my love."

She was unlike any other woman Devon had met. Having been raised by self-made millionaires, her parents were founders of Etolies Groupe, a Publishing conglomerate, affording them status on the Forbes list. She had her own money, and desired none of his. That's how he liked it. He worshiped her idealist and analytical mind. A woman who lusted after nothing was stimulating, unconventional at times, but fascinating. An heiress who could spend her own money. And not his.

Yet she lacked Myranda's ferocity. They'd met in a psychiatry lecture at Harvard, where he had first toyed with entering the field. Feminine to the core, Isabelle was congenial, conciliatory and very stimulating. Low maintenance was her charm and their weekends in their country escape were bliss. Here he could turn off his cellphone with no intrusions from work demands or Myranda, a topic he knew Isabelle was aware off, yet she never raised.

It had been their one agreement. Love was not a factor in the marriage. Intellect was.

"Have you finished your new drug project," asked Isabelle.

"You know me. I set myself efficient and unrealistic goals, so I can relax on weekends with you."

"That's how you always liked it. But, if the drug is not produced on time won't that ruin Trelles and your business reputation?"

He turned his back on her. "I don't care if people like me. Being respected for my work is more important than being liked."

Devon took the New York Scientific Journal he was reading and set it down on the frosted-glass cabinets in the galley kitchen and glanced outside the bay windows. "I'm going down to the back house to fetch some wood for a fire."

"Don't be long. Last time you disappeared before dinner you got stuck behind a medical journal. We came here to relax. Dinner is almost ready."

Devon shrugged and picked up the shaggy newspaper

looking forward to Isabelle's *Matelote*, his favorite French dish of fish stewed in cider.

"There's no wood for a fire. We've not been here since January," Devon said.

He glanced back at the living room from the kitchen, whose living area focused on a freestanding fireplace, and at the far end was his small study. A few logs stood in the basket, clearly not enough for his purposes. "I'll go check in the garage." He paced to the wooded door and placed a dark coat on his shoulders. "Be right back."

Devon opened a door by the front entrance, fished for a flashlight in the cloak closet. He left by the front entrance and trudged down the wooden stairs and took the back door out of the house that set him on a little paved path to the outhouse and the garage in the pelting rain. It stood a little distance from the main residence.

Devon nearly slipped on the steps leading to the courtyard entrance of the three-car garage which led to an outdoor swimming pool that was beside a detached, glazed summer house, overlooking landscaped gardens. He increased his speed as the showers assailed in streams. By the time Devon found the door handle, the back of his designer jeans were soaked through. He fumbled with his set of keys until he found the right one to unlock the metal lock, finally shattering it open, his fingers getting jarred in the process.

He cursed under his breath. The forced jolt had broken the lock in his haste to shelter from the rain. Ignoring the mishap, he barged inside and dusted the precipitation off his windproof garment. He turned on the light, a lone bulb suspended from the drab ceiling of the otherwise impressive garage. The barn-style room with carriage doors, white-pine walls, chestnut stairs and railings to one side was made of New Orleans brick.

Heavy rain pounding on the roof made Devon content he had opted for new tightly sealed and insulated additions to the garage. The concrete floors, stained to look like stone had cost a pretty penny.

Devon ran his hand along the charging stations for the electric cars and tablet-controlled lighting. He'd had the place renovated over the cold winter and insisted on hot and cold running water with a state-of-the-art central heating system. A lofted living section, complete with a kitchen and new bathroom, overlooked the space where his blue Bugatti and burgundy Porshe were parked.

He shook his body as a chill broke down his spine and advanced toward the wood-shelf in the far corner of the garage, a meter away from the Bugatti. He found a wood basket beneath the work table and began filling logs in the basket.

"Is this what my money bought you? The Bugatti?" a voice behind him said.

Devon zipped his head round to face Leal standing by the door. The basket he had picked up, crashed to the tiles, the firewood splattering over his feet.

He roared in pain clutching his foot. "What, what how, who the...?"

"After six years, Devon, I would expect a better welcome from a business partner- turned-coward-turned conspirator." Leal advanced toward him. "Don't pretend you don't know who I am."

"How did you get in here?"

"It was easy. There's only one property on this lot with the scent of Trelles money."

"What are you doing here? For a moment I thought it was someone else. Cyrus isn't it? How many brother's are there?"

"You know of all people, you were the one I feared to fool the most. Nothing tends to get past you, Devon."

Devon squinted. "I know that voice. You sound like... like Leal."

"Get ready to start where we left off, Devon. The part where you went squealing with your tail between your legs from a Montpellier hospital."

* * *

The Doberman Pinscher eyed Jewel with an imminent death wish.

Her voice stammered. "Hi—"

"Who are you?" asked the armed man.

Jewel searched her brain for a shrewd answer as she studied the man whose brown eyes and elaborately styled light blond hair suggested he took himself seriously.

Nothing came to mind.

The canine snarled, its loud bark piercing her eardrums.

"Who are you?" the man insisted.

With no crafty answer coming to mind, the truth was all she could think of. "Myranda Vaux's sister."

The man's eyebrows squished together. "I didn't know Mrs. Vaux-Trelles had a sister."

He backed off. "I'm sorry. I've not met any of Mrs. Vaux-Trelles' relatives."

"I'm here to surprise her with a short visit."

He pulled away his gun and held the growling Doberman back. "Let me take you in then."

"No, let me surprise her. We've not seen each other in a long time."

The man gazed at her with intent focus.

"Listen, once I see her. I'll put in a good word on how you cooperated."

Somehow that seemed to agree with him. "Okay then, the best way in is through the den. She has company, but after that she should be ready to have dinner in the dining room. I'll go and set a plate," he said.

She smiled. Her visit wouldn't last that long. She followed him through the house into the den, which seemed to be the nucleus of the home with its varieties of seating, a domed skylight and inviting fireplaces at each end.

The man disappeared through to the kitchen. "Make yourself at home," he said as she shut the door behind her.

She waited until all was quiet, before finding her way to the main area of the house. A grand staircase showcased contemporary Chinese art and the paintings of Salvador Dali along its wall. Her ears caught the clamor of voices on the ground floor, just beyond the staircase, possibly stemming from the adjacent living room.

She pressed her back against the stair wall. Two voices she knew well.

The conversation was anything but pleasant.

She strained her ears.

"Dr. Patil. You leave me no choice but to present that file to the authorities. How can you say you gave me the wrong file? I could've been infected like that woman in India."

"It was not intentional. The drug requires countless things to work well."

"Such as?"

"It blocks the effect of the hormone estrogen in your body. This blocking effect tricks the body into raising the levels of two other hormones needed for ovulation. These hormones are one, follicle-stimulating hormone, FSH and, luteinizing hormone, or better known as LH."

"You are buying time, doctor."

"No, even to the trained eye, mistakes can happen. You placed me under tremendous pressure and that's not how researchers work," Vik said.

Myranda could be heard pacing the floors. "Don't condescend me, Dr. Patil."

"Ms. Vaux, you came to me yesterday saying I needed to create a drug sample and all I had were a series of untested notes from your late husband. Not to mention that a drug is not created in an instant."

"What of it?"

"Let me say that twenty-four hours is not exactly how quickly medicine turns around. You came with threats. I went back, did my best and all I could think of was did I do it like Leal would have? Did I screw up? Your insistence clouded my concentration."

"You wouldn't dare test me, you low life—"

Jewel heard more pacing and the slamming of a drawer.

"Here! Where's the right drug now?"

Vik smirked. "I'm not giving it to you."

Jewel curled her fingers as she listened to the determination in Vik's voice. His life depended on his reputation, so did his medical career. *Give it to her, Vik!*

Myranda would expose and ruin him.

Jewel fought the urge to interfere. She shook it off and had to get to another file first. What was it Kaya had said? The maid Husdon had interviewed mentioned a jewelry safe that kept nothing but files and flash disks. If the maid had been correct, that file, possibly on a disk with hard copies had never left Myranda's bedroom safe. It was connected to the high-tech wireless home security system. A state-of-the-art safe that required communication of radio signals from triggered sensors to the control panel. A cellphone to be exact. If Jewel could find Myranda's cellphone, she could unlock the safe using it as the control.

Jewel edged into the hallway cabinet and stole up the oak

stairs. Her feet advanced up the high steps and she was thankful the stairs were carpeted.

Myranda's voice rose. "How dare you start this nonsense now?"

"I want my files before I give you anything," Vik said.

Jewel heard footsteps on the floors beneath her and hurried up the stairs concealing herself in the shadows. Peering over the rail, she watched as Myranda crossed the landing below and came storming back a few moments later with something in her hands.

Jewel waited until Myranda re-entered the living room. "Here, Dr. Vik, I'll have you know that on the fifteenth of May, seven years ago, you carelessly poisoned a woman, a study patient of yours in the Himachal Pradesh village of Manali."

"Let me see that," Vik said.

Jewel heard the conversation struggle back and forth. She crept toward the doors of exorbitant bedroom suites until she found what she believed was the master suite. She eased the door open. Once inside, her eyes scanned. No sign of a jewelry safe.

She moved to the bed and examined it. Her eyes fell on a cellphone by the bed. Jewel moved closer for a good look. She scanned the smartphone and swiped her hand over its smooth surface. The cellphone came to life, a dark blue screen, whose center blinked for a code.

Jewel had just enough light that came in from the hallway. She hadn't thought this through.

Chapter 25

"You're experiencing increased heart rate and lightheartedness. Surprised? I remember you didn't like surprises even when in the research lab. Surprise outcomes frustrated you. Perhaps that's where most of your failures hailed from," Leal said.

Devon took a step back, his back grazing the work bench. "It can't be! Why now? What do you want? How could—"

"So many questions. That's why you are a scientist, an inquisitor. I'm here to settle my conscience."

"What conscience? What sick moron would contrive games and cheat death?"

"Perhaps, you should try it. I doubt your talents would be missed." Leal advanced toward him. "No one had the first attempt we tried of Tharnex, but you. You know the one with the deadly side effects. You knew that a patient could get blood clots that could lead to a heart attack. I know you administered that attempt of Tharnex to that patient, and that's exactly what happened. It wasn't Vik. Once and for all I need to know... what drove you insane?"

Devon dropped his foot as the pain subsided. "You're supposed to be dead."

"So they keep telling me."

"I read the report myself. There's no way you could have survived that avalanche."

"Which report are we talking about? The one you stole from the Indian police? Or the one you and Myranda fabricated for the rest of the world? How much of my money did you use to pay off the authorities?"

Devon's face blanched and he swallowed hard. "Where have you been hiding?"

"In front of you."

Devon moved back as Leal advanced slowly.

Leal stopped by the table a meter away from him. "Give me the first sample of that vile, you know the fake one that you planted in Vik's drawer. It's causing all sorts of problems and it is time they were attributed to you."

"I've no idea what you are talking about."

Leal took a step forward. "I think you do, Devon."

"It was you in India, wasn't it? You tampered with my car. You couldn't live with the fact that I wouldn't use Jewel as guinea pig for what the DEI required. I insisted I would find a vaccine without using her. We didn't have her consent."

"Who cares? We had her mother's."

"Not good enough, Devon."

A good inch shorter than Leal, Devon squirmed closer, examining Leal's face. "The voice I know, but your face—"

"Does it haunt you?"

Devon grimaced and slid past him avoiding his intense scrutiny. "You should learn to keep your property safe. We could've been famous and had the medical world beckoning to us."

"Fame was never on my wish list."

Devon scowled. "That became pretty obvious. When I found out you weren't going to share your research with me, I had to resort to other measures. Vik was just a little persuasion. It wasn't meant for him, but for you to poison that girl."

"So you could hold my medical profession in a bind like you've done his."

Leal's eyes narrowed his voice lowering. "Why Jewel?"

"Huh?"

"Why incriminate her for something that was between you and me."

Devon threw his hands in the air and sniggered. "Every project needs a scapegoat. She happened to be mine. When I figured out her relationship to you after you left me battered in a Montpellier hospital, I knew I had my victim."

"You brought her into this—"

"No Leal, you did. You fell for her while still married to Myranda."

"Ethical all of a sudden? Let me remind you, you had an affair with Myranda the entire time I was married to her and you to Isabelle. I couldn't share a bed with two people in it. Tell me, does Isabelle know?"

Devon scoured. "Keep her out of this."

"How much of her inheritance fund have you swindled without her knowing?"

Devon shrugged. "I do what I need to do in the name of science."

"I see."

"Jewel was young and so foolish to fall for a two-timing bastard like you."

"Is that your best shot?"

Devon slung a fist at his face, propelling himself forward.

Devon's knuckles rocketed past Leal's face, and he dodged the missile as the miscalculated movement sent Devon rampaging to the floor. Devon's head collided with the side of the work bench and he gripped the side of his head, wringing on the floor.

"I've come here for one thing only. After seven years, I want the truth and a confession out of you. The truth about my grandfather's company that you slipped Myranda. How else would Myranda have known the true potential and value of Trelles Industries and my research?"

Devon's eyes shone with rage. He rose supporting his wounded jaw. "You're never getting that back. How could you resurface now as Leal the long-lost billionaire?"

"Is that what I'm worth now?"

"No one would believe you. I promised myself that with or without your precious formula and the missing code, I would finish the drug myself. Even if it meant playing your wife or the little ballerina."

Leal swung a roundhouse clout that crushed Devon in the stomach and sent him colliding with the work bench a second time. Work tools hurtled over Devon's head, making him loose stability as he fell back.

Leal shook his hand. "You and Myranda are the same. You deserve one other. It feels good to give my fist the satisfaction of six years of waiting."

"Myranda will sue you for everything you're worth."

"Hasn't she already?" He shook his head smiling. "Myranda will get what is coming to her."

Devon glided upward hobbling on one foot. His hands fumbled behind him tugging at a jammed drawer.

Leal took a step forward. "Now, hand it all over. Knowing their worth to you, the evidence can't be far."

Devon reached further in the drawer, his hand finding a M11

331

pistol. He swung the weapon in front of Leal's face. The steel gun brushed Leal's jaw.

Leal halted all movement, his eyes unflinching as they gazed into Devon's terrified face. "I've cheated death once. I'm sure I can do it again."

Devon slanted the gun. "How sure are you?"

* * *

"No, you don't," Jewel heard Myranda cry.

Her temples drummed with heat. What now? How was she going to unlock this and find the safe? She tapped in a series of codes.

Nothing worked. A new message flashed across the screen.

Security Breach
Phone Locked

Her face tightened and she tossed the phone onto the duvet. Her muscles tensed. The phone suddenly illuminated with a flashing message in red.

DNA scan required to activate

A round circle appeared in the center of the screen and then a second message.

Place your index finger on the round spot

Was this a fingerprint scan? She'd never pass. But then again it said DNA. *Wait a minute?* Being around Leal, she'd picked up a few things. She grabbed the phone and placed her index finger on the screen and felt a sharp scratch as the circle took a sample from her finger tip.

The phone illuminated. It incorporated a highly advanced DNA recognition scan system then flipped through a series of cyber gibberish before shooting out a message.

You are now ready to use your phone

So it was true? She shared DNA markers with Myranda. It had been a long shot. Jewel couldn't decide what was worse, being caught by Myranda a second time in less than seventy-two hours or the confirmation that they were sisters. She quickly scanned through the menu and found a security app. She tried it and a light turned on behind the mirror on the dresser in the far corner.

Jewel followed the light and hunched over the mirror. She scanned the app and soon located an unlock feature. The tall mirror set in a chrome rectangular frame slid to one side revealing a series of compartments.

She filed through more contents, a draft copy of Myranda's will, rare jewelry, written appraisals for her properties, stock and bond certificates, IVF treatment documents, until she found certified papers in a red plastic sleeve and three flash disks, encrusted in a burgundy see-through foil. Even without verification, she recognized the same letterhead she had signed six years ago in India.

The official seal of the Indian police services with its triple lions on the crest threatened to come alive as Jewel stared at it for several seconds. She filed through the attached papers, discovering not only a copy of her own signature but a set of related papers she'd never laid eyes on. Gathering her loot, she zipped the file, locked the safe, returned the phone and headed back toward the door. Her ear remained attentive to any movement within the grand house.

She placed the file against her breast and zipped up her thin leather jacket almost clipping her chin. The wait was over. She stole down the stairs, grazing her feet ever so lightly on the soft carpet. Her foot missed a step.

Jewel reached for the railing. Her hands missed the oak surface and she lost her footing plunging to the bottom of the stairs head first. Her face grazed the carpeting, causing a small burn on her temple.

The fall knocked wind out of her lungs and when her eyes focused she ran a hand along her jaw. Crimson stained her finger and sharp pain shot through her right leg. Movement drew her eye and she glared upwards.

A fast breath left her lips.

* * *

Isabelle peered through the high kitchen windows, her gaze in the direction of the garage. The gun shot had come from the outhouse. She turned off the faucet, shook her hands and dried them with a kitchen towel. Her eyebrows furrowed as she hurried to the door and grabbed her rain coat and a large umbrella.

Fighting the showers, she tripped over a step on the dark path and looked down at the house slippers still on her feet. She jetted up and forged ahead toward the garage doors. She shook the umbrella and her wet eyes focused into the light. Ignoring the drips of water in her hair, she barged into the room. Oozes of water spilled from her raincoat and mixed with a pool of what could only have been blood.

The glassy liquid, thick and tar-like had begun to darken on the tiles as it spilled outward along the floor. Her eyes broadened as she heard groans and movement under the table.

"Isabelle?"

She retreated. "Who's that?"

"Isabelle, it's Leal. Leal Trelles."

Leal moved under the overhead light and Isabelle took a trembling step back nearly tripping over some of the wood logs.

Her head shook in frantic jerks.

"You're dead." Her eyes fell on a groaning figure under the table. "What happened?" She caught a glimpse of a loose hand smeared with blood. "Devon?"

Leal followed her gaze.

Her eyes amplified at the sight of her husband's blood.

She gasped and fell over his unresponsive body. "You shot him!"

"Calm down, Isabelle. I would never do a thing like that. He came after me with a gun. He pulled it out of that drawer and I grabbed this pole here then flung it out of his hand. He was going to shoot me. The gun went off."

Even as Leal spoke, he knew that his few hours of ancient *Kali* training with Watanabe had saved his life. Fast reflexes and quick thinking were skills the art had taught him. The intrinsic need for self-preservation was the origin of the martial art. Watanabe had continuously reminded him that the warrior reaches his apex when he needs to, not when he wants to.

Isabelle threw herself by Devon's body, his blood soiling her white slacks.

Leal moved forward. "He's okay. He shot at me and I blocked him. It's just a flesh wound to his arm. Call an ambulance. I've held off the bleeding as long as I can."

Isabelle glanced up at Leal. Her eyes tearful, but with anything but worry.

He set a hand over hers. "You're in shock and feeling weak and nauseous. Where's the phone?"

She pointed to the back of the work bench.

Leal found the phone and dialed 911. Minutes later he returned to her side. "They'll be here in a few minutes. He fell by Devon's side and pressed the towel he'd found in the bathroom against the bleeding.

"I can't believe it's you."

Devon moaned on the floor. He rolled his eyes and looked up. "Leal, I'm sorry."

"Try not to talk, Devon. There's nothing to be sorry about. Perhaps if I'd been an attentive friend, we would never have fallen out."

Devon's eyes smiled despite the lack of emotion in his face.

Leal caught his eye. "You're a smart researcher and bio-chemist. Just a conceited moron. Why did you doubt yourself?"

"Yes, but you beat me to the formula."

Leal cradled Devon's head in his lap, lifting him off the cold floor. "It was never a competition, Devon. Why did you try to kill me in India by tampering with my car?"

Isabelle's face was sweating profusely. "You always inspired Devon. You two were inseparable our first semester at Harvard, now look at you." Her French accent was pronounced.

Devon's head careened as he reached Leal's elbow. "Leal, when Myranda got a prick of Jewel's blood, I thought I had you and I wanted no more competition. But the blood sample was no good. Myranda couldn't take a sample to save her life," he sighed deeply. "I couldn't break your girl, Leal."

"Who?"

"Jewel, she held on in India even to the point where it could have cost her much."

Leal squirmed almost dropping Devon's head. "It's time to correct that."

"I'm afraid you may be too late. Myranda had a man run into her mother a day ago. She knew it would weaken Jewel at the knees and break her."

"Why would Myranda do that Devon? She'd won?"

"Yes, Leal, but not you." Devon spoke slowly. "She never had you. Jewel had all of you. That was Myranda's last struggle with Jewel. She wanted a crushed spirit poisoning all that mattered to Jewel."

Devon cocked his chin up, the strains of discomfort visible in his face. "Myranda found out that it was Jewel's mother who'd conquered the infertility bug. She's gone mental. Obsessive and lost all sense of reality. Call it jealousy or not, but defeating the woman who overcame the disease seemed like victory to her."

"Try not to speak," Leal said.

Sirens blared outside. Several minutes later the emergency crew barged in and attended to Devon before placing him on a stretcher. Leal spoke to the cops who'd accompanied the ambulance at his request, filling out a police statement of no charges. Leal set a hand on Isabelle's shoulder pulling her into a comforting hug. "Go with him, he'll be okay."

"Leal," she grabbed his hand. "Thank you."

"I have to go."

Leal spoke with the ambulance attendants and gave the police the injury weapon before blundering into the rain. The sky broke, gushing drizzle streams over his head. They couldn't quench the anguish within. The torment in his mind continued. He needed to break free.

His phone buzzed alerting him that Vik had set off the panic button. He needed to hurry. He called his assistant at Mancini headquarters. "Do we still have the company helicopter in New Haven?"

"Yes, sir," a tired voice replied in Italian.

"Send her to this address I'm messaging you. I need the chopper fast. Now!"

* * *

"Get up!" Myranda said, her shrill voice echoing through Jewel's ears. The steel barrel of the shot gun stared Jewel in the face for the second time in less than two days. Jewel rose, rubbing her sore head.

Myranda put the gun to her temple, grazing the exact spot of the carpet burn. It stung Jewel like salt in a severely raw wound. Jewel's eyes moved to see Vik approach them in the hallway.

"Is that necessary?" he said.

"I could shoot her here. Nobody will even pick up the pieces."

Her voice fumed with every syllable she uttered. Jewel refused to move a muscle.

"What are you doing here anyway?" Myranda said. She grabbed Jewel's arm and yanked her toward the living room.

Vik followed the women in a state of numbness at the weapon, his eyes revealing an irritation she'd only seen in tigers. Myranda shoved her into an upholstered arm chair.

Jewel sank into its deep cushions. Myranda's eyes moved to her jacket studying the tip of the file that had surfaced from the fall.

Myranda's voice pierced the room. "What do you have there?"

Jewel put her hand to her chest shielding the file. "My life back."

Myranda reached for the file.

Jewel hauled it from her grip sending the plastic folder to the floor. The contents dropped to the carpet, ripping open a tear in the plastic.

"What the...?" Myranda began. "What're you after this time?"

"The truth."

Without taking the gun from Jewel's direction, Myranda sank to reach for the contents, her eyes fixed on Jewel. She retrieved the document. "I should set your mind to rest with all this nonsense. This business in India is over. Leal is gone. You can't bring him back and if you could, he's not your business. Can't you get that in your head?"

Myranda balanced the file with one hand and in one abrupt

337

movement, marched to the far end of the room and thrust it into the roaring fireplace.

"No!" The screech left Jewel's lips with amounted vehemence. She turned her eyes to Myranda.

Jewel begun to rise, but Myranda's weapon was quicker than her efforts. The barrel returned its aim in the direction of her head. Myranda's eyes narrowed. "Don't you dare."

Chapter 26

Was Myranda a good shot? Jewel held her breath. Myranda wouldn't hesitate to use the weapon. Soon her dark eyes found Vik's face. "Now who do I shoot first, the trespasser or the one who has breached contract? Either way, there's legal justification. Now hand over the vile, Dr. Patil." She neared Jewel's chair. "Or my gun goes off accidentally in her head." Her lips stretched into a criminal smile. "I could always say she broke in. It's the truth after all."

Vik gulped, rubbing a small medical bottle in his hand.

"Randi!"

Myranda zipped her head round. A dark figure stood in her entryway, hidden by the shadows cast by the overhead lights. Shock swept over her face as she kept the gun aimed at Jewel.

"No one called me Randi, but—"

"Leal?" the voice said.

Myranda's steady body loosened, her breathing intensifying. The figure stepped into the room.

"Looks like I'm having a night of intruders. Cyrus, what're you doing here? I don't care which one of you three does this, but one of you has to produce that drug."

Her fingers trembled on the gun making it shake. It could hit any of them. Jewel observed Cyrus's intrusion with interest. He was putting himself in danger. Myranda wasn't level-headed. Not anymore. Vicious, yes, but to add murder to her list of criminal activity was not something she would do consciously.

"Put the gun down," he said, his voice calm.

"Should I put you out of your financial woes as we did Leal?"

"So you admit it. You needed him dead."

"Leal was a fool. Uncommitted to Trelles. He didn't deserve that company and was only good for giving us the research solutions that kept it ahead of its competitors." She paced the carpet in her kitten heels. "I may have even loved your brother if he had let me. But, he was stupid, so stupid to go after a thing like this." Her gun returned its direction to Jewel. Myranda waved the gun in her face. "Vik, where is it?"

Jewel's eyes begged Cyrus to do something. He moved with caution. Something about his walk had altered. His eyes were no longer the shade of brown she knew, but blue, the exact shade of Leal's. His eyes rested on Jewel as he removed a small object from his pocket. "Vik never had it. I have the drug that can help you. Open your eyes, Randi, your husband has returned from the dead."

She shook her head, her eyes rapidly blinking. "No. It can't be. You are dead—"

Jewel sensed a lump sink into the well of her stomach. Was he playing Myranda? Using some hypnotic gimmick she was not aware of?

He coasted toward where Myranda stood. "Give me the gun."

Her head shook. "Not until I get that vile."

He eyed the bottle.

"Myranda, it's over," he said. "There's other ways to cure you."

Jewel's heart raced, pounding in her ears. Those words could only be from the doctor she'd loved six years ago.

"How can you be here?" Myranda demanded. She aimed the gun at Vik. Without warning the bullet zipped out of the barrel, sending a blast throughout the room. It missed Vik and sliced a crystal showpiece into two on the far shelf.

Vik tore the flask from Leal's hand.

"Last chance," Myranda said. "God help me, I won't miss."

"Here," Vik said. He threw her the bottle.

She caught it in one quick hand and moved toward the window.

Leal advanced toward her, his voice ringing with warning. "Don't do it, Myranda. It could kill you."

"You lie!"

"I'm not lying. That thing is like poison. But I can help you."

"How can I know you are Leal? You lie! We killed you six years ago!"

Leal's feet moved at even short paces toward her. "Seven years ago, I was approached by the DEI to find a vaccine to a problem that started in Benton. That disease broke out because of

340

your father Adan."

She lunged at him. "You lie! Papa did no such thing. How dare you?"

Her nails tore at Leal, slicing a cut above his chin.

Leal's determined stance remained. "Your father was fired from Solomon Bees, a sub-company of Ovatti Foods. He got angry, Myranda. He contaminated the waters at Ovatti headquarters where your mother worked."

"How could he do that? My father was a pathetic sales man."

"He's probably never told you, but he was a smart environmental scientist and knew what he was doing. The FBI have been after him all these years but failed to convict him. They needed proof. They have just arrested him as your medical condition and that of thousands of women speaks against him. Myranda you don't have to fight anymore."

"I won't believe you damn it! Stop it."

"The FBI has him in custody."

Myranda's voice raised several decibels and turned into a shrill. "Papa has done nothing."

Jewel witnessed the first set of tears she'd ever seen on Myranda, her eyes still spying on the unsteady gun in her shaky hand.

"Listen, Randi. The disease contaminated your mother too. That's how you got it. It was never Adan's intention, but he screwed up and by the time you were born it was in your blood stream."

Myranda flopped to the floor heaving as tears streamed down her face. "Your sister was born after she was cured. You can be cured too."

Jewel leered in anguish as Vik stood up holding the vile. "I'm calling for help."

Myranda raised the gun at him, her eyes bloodshot. "No!"

"Randi," said Leal. "Why do you think I allowed you to let me die and wipe myself from all things Trelles? That vaccine would have created confusion. The DEI knew Adan wouldn't be far, after he learned the true worth of a potential drug. Your father used you. He wanted that vile so he could control the disease and the solution. But it was always a prototype. It has a million side effects, some of which we've not tested."

"Whatever sick joke you think you are running, leave my father out of this."

341

Leal pulled out a second bottle. "I have the only drug that works. It can be taken orally and begins the path to fertility. I can treat you."

"Open it!" Myranda said.

Leal hesitated.

"I will shoot one person here, if you don't."

Leal unscrewed the cap.

"Give it to me."

Leal stepped back.

Myranda moved forward and grabbed the vile with one hand before swallowing the entire contents. With a pained stare, she lunged for Leal, the loaded gun still in her hand.

He shoved out of her way.

"Why her? Was it because she can have children and I can't?" Myranda's voice pierced Jewel like poison.

Leal stirred closer to Myranda. "Give me the gun?"

"The only way she leaves this room is in a bag."

Jewel gaped at Myranda as she released the trigger. The bullet sizzled toward her.

Leal threw himself forward.

Heat swept over Jewel as she watched Leal's falling frame thud to the floor. Her knees buckled and Vik glanced at each person before diving for Myranda's hand and snatching the gun.

Jewel threw herself down to Leal. His body rolled to one side, his hand on his chest and soon became still.

"Leal! No!"

Her mouth turned dry, her heartbeat racing as she shook his body for a response. Jewel laced her fingers in his until her knuckles turned white. Several moments passed before she turned her head toward Vik and seized his arm. "He saved my life. Again. I've lost him. Again."

Vik sank and gaped at Leal and then Myranda. His face turned ashen. "Jewel. Myranda's also not moving."

Jewel rose and walked slowly to where the gun had dropped. She stared at it for several moments.

* * *

Sirens could be heard on the grounds of the expansive estate. Hudson burst in the room with several DEI agents. "I think we'll take it from here."

Jewel stared at him, her eyes bloodshot.

Thirty minutes later, an ambulance arrived in the rain as two FBI agents, Hudson and another DEI agent spoke with Vik. Myranda's shivering body was placed inside the ambulance. The medics secured her belt and covered her with a blanket. Leal covered his eyes with a hand and rubbed the pain in his chest. The time he'd spent debriefing the authorities had weakened his muscles as well as the blast to his chest.

It was over. But not just yet.

"She needs to be kept sedated for a while," Leal instructed.

"Thanks, Doctor Trelles, we'll keep you informed of her progress."

Tightness formed in his gut as he saw Jewel descending the stairs of the front entrance. Her shoulders were wrapped in a heat-retaining foil. He headed toward her. Her face remained expressionless when she spoke to him. "I'm off," she said and turned her head. She suddenly stopped and faced him. "Do you always wear a bulletproof vest, Leal?"

She'd used his name. He took a few seconds so the emotion of the moment could sink into him.

"How many enemies do you have? How many lives do you have? How did you find us here?" she said.

Leal could feel Jewel's words tightening around his heart like an iron fist. Was he going to tell her more lies? "Vik raised the alarm button about forty minutes ago. We heard the struggle and it meant one thing, Myranda was armed. I wasn't gonna lose you."

She took a few steps down the wet stairs and passed him as he reached for her arm.

"Wait. Jewel, don't you want to hear the truth?"

"About what, Cyrus? Or is it really Leal?"

He took her hand and his skin grazed hers.

She pulled it away. "Who are you?"

"Please, let's just talk." Leal led her toward shelter in a lawn gazebo. She wrapped the blanket tighter round her shoulders as they sat down on the stone bench. The moment in the gazebo was familiar. A *maharaja* with his *maharani* sipping jasmine tea in the Himalayas.

* * *

Leal moved closer to Jewel. Her body shivered, but it wasn't the cold. When she opened her mouth and nothing came out Leal knew she was still in shock. He'd been a mystery to her since he'd first met her.

The rain continued a sizzling downpour. He wiped his sweaty palms on his denims, not used to being out of control. He needed to let down his guard. The shield that had kept out his emotions and personality, locked in a double-edged façade for years, had cost him her trust.

"I'll make it easier for you by asking the question," Jewel said. "Who are you? What was your name at birth?"

Leal's face strained into a difficult smile. "Leal Alexander Trelles."

"Who's Cyrus?"

A tingling scratched his throat as he spoke. "Cyrus was my identical twin brother. He died before I went into the First Grade."

Her gaze pierced him, searching. "I'm sorry."

He reached for her hand again, but she pulled it away. "Why didn't you tell me you were alive? For six years, I mourned you." A choke arrested her voice. "And you were alive... the whole time."

The pain in her eyes tore at his concentration as she braved her words, verbalizing every strained syllable. "And when you chose to come back into my life, you came in as a stranger."

Jewel shot up and moved to the edge of the gazebo. Leal followed, gripping her hand and trapping her between him and the gazebo's edge. He swallowed, his face tightening. "I couldn't tell you the truth?"

"Why?"

"I wanted to protect you and then I wanted you—"

"You were married, Leal. You let me love you. Why didn't tell me?"

"Because I'm an idiot living a double life. One here and one in Venice."

Her eyebrows drew together. "Yeah, I'll bet."

"I've lived a double life a long time and there was a reason."

"I can't hear anymore lies, Leal."

344

"It's the truth." His heart prayed she'd hear him out. "When my mother died at our birth, Nonna raised us. She longed to return to Venice and couldn't cope with the failing Trelles business here."

"Failing business? I don't believe your family has ever known what financial failure is. In the real sense."

"My father left us when my mother passed away. He had started a small clinic company that we later developed into Trelles Pharmaceuticals. That left my frail Nonna to raise us alone."

"Where did your father go?"

"We don't know. One day he set sail on the family yacht bound for France. His yacht was never found or retrieved. The police later confirmed he'd ran away with his mistress." Leal's face tightened. "It pained Nonna to see him waste so much of his life and they never ever saw eye to eye for years. Anyway, shortly before I came to Montpellier, the police started digging and believed Nonna had something to do with his death and disappearance. They would reopen the investigation. I was furious. Days later the DEI showed up at my office and offered an out if I gave them a nephthysis drug funded entirely by me. They would drop the whole thing. In exchange they'd give me access to as much as they knew about the disease and governmental credentials, field equipment and training just short of a CIA agent. This way I could also act as a medical spy for them on our enemies if they found a drug first."

Jewel digested the words. "So what really happened to your father?"

"I don't know. Whatever he did, I hated him for it and what he did to my grandma leaving a trail of his debts, bad company management, and a line of women wanting money. It was a mess. Even at age ten, I swore that I wouldn't let her suffer. That I would help her with her family business in Venice if I had to. Anyway, we stayed there until I was eleven. At that time, things got rough for us. I saw my Nonna come home one day. They were going to close the Venice business down. She mentioned that if only she was a man, she could claim the inheritance her family had left in Venice. Her father's will stated she needed to have a son or grandson take it over, or it would be split among her male cousins. She needed an heir to claim it. In my playful childhood way, I suggested why doesn't she create a male relative and pass

345

him off as the heir. It was meant as a childish joke. I will never forget Nonna's expression. She's the smartest woman among an army of generals."

"What did she do?"

"She suggested we use Cyrus's birth certificate to claim him as an heir and run the Italian business in his name. She wanted me to be free to pursue a medical career and she could run the business. Anyway. It caught on. Initially Nonna only wanted to keep her house. The villa in Venice. However, before you knew it, she kept Trelles and the Venice business afloat. I went to school, and by the time, I was eighteen, we had perfected Cyrus's identity to the tee. So I stepped in to keep business for Nonna and the front we had created to protect the family."

"No one found out all those years? The family?"

"Nonna's cousins had never met Cyrus and wanted to. We thought we could perfect our act until I turned eighteen, so I could take it over officially. But then, my inquisitive uncle Paolo came to New York just before I turned eighteen and started asking to see Cyrus as Cyrus had to be in active ownership of the business. That's when Cyrus became a physical being, in the form of my double."

"You went to Italy and pretended to be Cyrus? What logic did you use?"

"Twin psyche. I became the face of Cyrus there and Leal here in New York. Cyrus was a ghost who never made public appearances ever. We claimed he had an illness that kept him indoors, agoraphobia. At least not until Leal's supposed death."

"How did you—"

"By the time I was twenty, it got easier to be both brothers. Funny, I actually enjoyed it for a while. Until I started having real nightmares."

"You mean trouble from Nonna's family?"

"No. Cyrus. Angry with me for stealing his life. In my dreams, he would tell me he wasn't the person I was mimicking. It really messed with my mind that I had to eventually seek professional help."

Jewel's eyebrows knit. "Is that why you went to see that doctor at the villa in Venice the day we were there?"

Leal took a seat next to her. "Yes."

"But that still doesn't explain why you let me believe you were dead, Leal." Her eyes glistened. "I fell in love with you. I thought we had something. You let me spend a night with you thinking you were someone else, twice. That's hardly fair. I earned my right to your love, but you stole the feelings I gave you." Jewel's face softened. "You should've told me? Why didn't you stop being Cyrus if it was messing with your mind? Didn't your analyst help?"

"I kept the façade of Leal and Cyrus very well. It was flawless for a while. Until—"

"Until?"

"Until Med School, Devon Chesser and I started working on vaccines that the government got interested in. They started doing detailed background checks on us."

"Did the DEI know about Cyrus?"

He nodded.

"You and Devon were friends?"

"Once. I stopped working with Devon and built my own research. Meanwhile my work was recognized, donors poured in and I re-established Trelles Industries constantly producing drugs at low cost. The company grew into a multi-billion dollar privately owned business. I became hard to ignore and when we made thirty percent public, I was watched all the time. They could get me anytime. They could connect my family here with my family in Italy."

"What did you do?"

"Money buys many things but happiness. Anybody could be silenced or made to talk as I learned at great cost. The day the van went down in India, I decided we would kill Cyrus off and give him his peace. But Jeff gave me another option." Leal searched her eyes for forgiveness. "Why not kill Leal off instead."

"Why?"

"I would be dead to the world, and research in secret and most importantly test Tharnex. Yes we had initial success, but I wasn't convinced it was safe. I had to be sure. It was as simple as that."

"Leal, did you love Myranda?"

He shook his head slowly. "No. It was a business transaction. I had a prenuptial made knowing she couldn't conceive. I knew she could not have a child and made sure by not touching her."

"Leal—"

"Myranda and Adan were on the DEI's watch list. Marrying Myranda allowed me to spy on them and feed any information to the DEI concerning the Benton disease. They suspected Adan, but had little to prosecute him."

Jewel was silent for several seconds. She bit her lip and lifted her chin. "How did you get off that mountain, Leal?"

She'd asked the only question he'd ever dreaded answering, because... he'd left her there.

Chapter 27

Anguish ran through Leal's veins and his eyes dimmed as he shied from her intense stare. "Unlike you, Jewel, I never had the guts to compete in the Olympics, but I had all the training one needed to participate." He took a deep breath. "On a snowboard."

"What snowboard? I was with you. You didn't have a snowboard when the helicopter came for us."

"Actually, I did."

She hesitated and understood. "You mean the box you put in your backpack when we left Manali. I thought it was medical supplies. Wait a minute? You also had that in Salzburg. You were there to test your snowboard as well."

He nodded slowly. "The plan was for me to get mugged and beaten at Rotang Pass on the mountain, with you as a witness and others and get beaten badly by fake thugs Jeff's contacts hired."

"Are you serious?"

"Jeff arranged it all. They'd use local authorities to declare me dead. And you know the rest."

"A day before we went to Rotang, I couldn't do it. After we spent that night together, I couldn't leave you. The avalanche made the decision for us."

"You played with destiny and fate found you. I still don't know how you managed it."

Leal moved close to her. "For years I'd commissioned a sports company to produce a foldaway snowboard that was easier to carry and mount while on a mountain, yet have the sturdiness of any commercial snowboard. I almost always have a compass and satellite phone with me. Habits from years of snowboarding. I'd intended to try the board in the Himalayas."

"How did you get through the avalanche?"

"When it hit and once it rolled to a stop, I shot off three flames from a flare gun that exploded the side of the tent and blew the snow open. I then assembled the snowboard. The compass was okay, and the phone was dead. Then it hit me I had to leave the phone. The DEI had been bugging me for months on that phone. I'll forever be grateful to snowboarding for saving my life."

"Leal, we came to the site. All we found was a tent. No phone."

"The DEI were there, Jeff told me later. They wanted to remove any connection I had to them when they couldn't find my body. They removed as much evidence as they could and made sure I was dead. The mangled tent convinced them the mountain had gotten me. Those bastards. They never cared what happened to anybody, just their plans."

Jewel took a deep breath. "You could've saved me years of counseling."

"In all of this, I never counted on meeting you or falling in love with you. As much as I tried to keep you away from all of this, I couldn't. You were more real to me than anything I'd ever known. The only part that makes sense."

"Lying comes with a price and a relationship is based on trust. You told me that."

"I know, Jewel. Can you forgive me?"

She rose to leave. "I don't know who you are. I can't be—"

"Please, Jewel. I want you to know it all. Meeting you in Montpellier wasn't an accident."

"How far back does this lie stretch?"

"From the day you were born without nephthysis, the DEI has had your whole life and medical history on file. They've been prepared for years to do anything to stop economic espionage."

* * *

Jewel dropped her hand from Leal's sturdy grip. "What're you saying? You mean the government spies on us?"

Leal couldn't contain his seething emotions. "I plan to sue them on your behalf and for the years they stole from us. Jewel, I love you. From the moment, we were on that hill in Salzburg, I knew I was in serious trouble. I didn't tell you because you and Myranda were the two study patients with genes that could give answers. Two sisters from one of the first women with the disease. One sister developed nephthysis and you Jewel didn't.

The DEI gave me Myranda's blood work, but yours we had to steal. I wouldn't do it. I had to find an answer without touching you. I could only do that if Leal was dead and his research with him. I had to prove that the answer could come without anyone harming you or robbing you as they had Myranda. It was the only reason I married her to protect you both. And if I had met you first, I wouldn't have. That's all it was."

"Why didn't they ask if I could donate my blood for research?"

Leal rubbed his jaw. "They wanted no loose ends they couldn't contain. You were an Olympian, on an international stage and in the media. They gave me your data as a starting point. You were the only child born to any woman who'd had nephthysis. They believed your DNA had answers."

"Did you believe them? Is that why I was attacked in Montpellier?"

"Yes. Devon was employed by them. They wanted a solution. Fast."

"Tharnex."

"Believe me, baby, when I say I refused to use your data. I believed there had to be another way. They didn't seek your consent. The government wanted to keep the disease contained and away from public knowledge until we had a solution."

"What did you do?"

"In Montpellier, Devon insisted on getting a sample from you and develop something that could revolutionize fertility science. When I refused, the DEI gave me an ultimatum."

"That phone call in India."

"Yes. If Myranda and Adan knew what I was up to, they'd also try to market the vaccine under Trelles."

"And you didn't want to do that because you didn't want another commercial drug. You want to help people not run a commercial business. Such as those people at the clinic in India."

His eyes met hers. "It's the truth. You understand more than anyone."

"Enough, Leal. I've heard enough. I'm not sure I believe it."

"You and Myranda are sisters. Your mother was Adan's wife?"

Jewel contemplated for several seconds. She'd suspected that the minute she had left the hospital. "Mama had every right to leave Adan."

"Your mother couldn't live with the fact that she couldn't have any more children after the disease broke out at the factory."

"She had me."

"Exactly. Twelve women were initially affected, but she was the only one able to conceive. You, Jewel. You were the marvel baby. When Mahina's DNA failed all the researcher's tests, they turned to you. The phenomenon child."

Jewel wrung her cold fingers as the rain carved into the gazebo, wetting her feet. Leal had changed. He wore a sense of maturity and honesty. His strong jaw was tight with emotion and regret. If she only knew what to do. Should she believe him? Her eyes narrowed. "Did you test my blood? Sample my immunity? You're unbelievable—"

"No."

Jewel reached in her bag, drew Myranda's hand-gun and aimed it at him.

Leal's eyes widened. "Jewel?"

Her eyes narrowed. "You must've. How else did you get the answers? Did you use me as a research rat for Tharnex? Was that all I was to you?" The gun aimed straight at his crown.

"Jewel, I never touched you." His eyes moistened, his voice straining with every word, stalling back pained sentiment. "Where did you get that?"

"At eighteen I was tied to a hospital bed and nearly killed. Four years later a message appeared at my doorstep in India warning me of more danger the day before you left me. Then when you were gone. I did the only thing I could do. I got a gun license."

"I know I deserve it, Jewel, but—"

She took a deep breath. "You've lied to me from the moment I met you. How do I know you are telling me the truth? I can't afford to trust you, Cyrus, Leal. Whoever you are? What truth could you tell me now?"

"Jewel, please believe me. Devon and I were supposed to get a copy of your files and a blood sample then. The DEI requested it. I did everything to stop them. To protect you from them. That's why I came to Montpellier. I wanted to keep your records from Devon and the government. I switched your medical files in the hospital."

"How do I know you really wanted to protect me? Damn it, Leal! You left me. I don't believe you."

352

"You livened every passion in me. Every reason for a life worth living. Please believe me. You did something to me when you performed in the arena, as you do every moment I am with you." He choked on his words. "As you're doing now. I can't be alive without you, Jewel. You define me."

Jewel's eyes fell to the wet floor. Her mind heaving with unfathomable emotions.

Leal seized her cold hands into his warm palms, the gun still aimed at him. It moved to his heart in her trembling hand.

"There are so many things that aren't right." His lips brushed her wet cheek. "Jewel, let's start again, as if we've only just met. Please, forgive me. I had no right to deceive you. Let me correct the mess between us. Let me love you."

Leal pulled her frail shoulders to him. For a moment, she loosened her upper body. Wasn't this what she'd longed for? To find closure with Leal. To be loved by him. To hide in his sheltered hold for ever? She closed her eyes and let his soft kisses spellbind her. His misty tears stung her raw face. Leal was a sanctuary for her nomadic heart. One that had wandered for years yet never found home. He held the key to the shackles engulfed round her protected soul. Would she release it once and for all?

She opened her eyes. "No, Leal. No. This is wrong. You're married."

Leal didn't let go until she tore herself completely from his embrace. "I served Myranda divorce papers six years ago."

"I can't Leal. It's still not right."

His pained eyes pored into hers. "I filed for divorce in India, the night we went out."

"Still. There never was *us*."

"You don't mean that."

"I mourned you for six years. My family thought I was a lost psychiatric case, my friends too. And worse, Leal, I don't believe you."

"You can't say that."

"First I fell in love with Leal, then with Cyrus. Both times you earned your right to my heart, but mine was stolen. Both times I fell in love with a fantasy."

"It was always me."

"Was it?" She held a hand in front of his face. "You don't love me. If you did, you would have come for me. You would have trusted me with the truth." She grabbed the foil blanket and pulled it above her head. "Trust, after all, baby, was your idea."

She took several steps backward. Though his eyes petitioned for forgiveness, she gave in to reason and dropped the gun at his feet. She turned toward the main house.

The door closed behind her. Everything in him wanted to follow but he couldn't. The double edge sword he'd sharpened had pierced his own heart.

Chapter 28

The ambulance pulled up across from Jewel's apartment building.

"I'll get off here," she said. "Thank you."

"Are you all right ma'am? We can take you to see a doctor."

"I'm fine. I've had my share of doctor care to last me a lifetime."

She traversed the street under a pelt of thunderous rain. At the top of the stairs that led into the block of flats, she lost the will to move her limbs. Her legs trembled and as she took a step forward she missed her footing and collapsed to the steps. Heaven's watercourses mirrored her anguish, yet she failed to drop a tear. She'd cried enough? Six years to be exact.

She fumbled for her cellphone in the side pocket of her slacks. "Kaya?"

"Jewel? Where are you? I just tried your home."

Her lips trembled with trepidation. "I'm... I..."

"Where are you?"

"Ho... home."

"Stay there. I'm coming."

* * *

Twenty minutes later, Kaya's Mercedes nosed into a space across the street. She got out of the car, fought the minimal traffic, aiming to get across swiftly on the slippery surface. Jewel hadn't moved. She'd sat on the steps, her body drenched, her clothes tight, and her head swooning. Jewel trembled as heavy droplets streamed through her chocolate locks, and slashed her cheeks.

Kaya's easy steps ambled up to where she sat. "Jewel, sweetheart. What're you doing out here?" She wrapped her arms around Jewel's wet frame and helped her to her feet.

"Huh? I... Must've..."

"What are you doing out here in the rain?"

"I don't know. I told the ambulance to leave and then, I couldn't move."

"Are you hurt?"

"I don't know."

"Come." Kaya led her to the oak wood entrance. "Where're your keys?"

"I don't..."

"Never mind I have a set here." She set the key in the lock and pushed it open for them."

When they moved inside the drafty apartment, Kaya helped her friend out of her wet things and found a bathrobe for her. Draped in warmth, Jewel reclined on the couch, her face a mirror of agony.

Kaya busied herself with preparing a hot drink, willing every muscle in her to relax. "What happened? Was it...?"

Jewel's eyes spoke volumes revealing a picture of hurt and doubt. Jewel leaned into the sofa. "I should've listened to my instincts. I knew something was wrong in Salzburg, and then in India... I told you..."

Should she let Jewel speak or interject with some elevated logic or comfort? "What did you tell me?" Kaya said.

"It doesn't happen?"

"What?"

"The intimacy no one understands and the commitment we all desire to have."

"You have a connection with him."

Jewel's eyes turned to Kaya. "Do I?"

"You know you do." Kaya took a seat across from her. "Now, start at the beginning." She handed the mug over. "What did he say?"

"Leal is..."

Kaya bit her lip. Better now than never. Jewel had to know. "Leal is alive," Kaya blurted.

Jewel's jaw dropped. "You know?"

"I found out today?"

"How?"

"Hudson. They, the DEI, have known for a while. In fact, part of it was their idea."

"That's what *he* said."

"So he told you himself."

"He lied to me, Kaya. He was alive all these years and couldn't even tell me in Saint Louis."

Kaya's hand gripped her friend's cold ones rubbing them. "I'm sorry. Even I didn't see that coming. I don't know what to say."

"This proves everything that I said from the beginning. The Carlone curse."

Kaya searched her own heart. Was she right? Could she blame her?

Jewel pulled her hair into a tight bun on top of her head.

"Do you love him, Jewel? That's the only question you ever need to answer. Do you love him?" Kaya said.

"I can't believe him ever again."

"What're you going to do?"

"The only thing that you do with liars."

Kaya's eyes fell to the floor. Jewel had undergone her biggest setback yet. This time, Kaya knew there was no turning back to the healing place that Leal had cured in her heart. How does one recover from an injury caused by the healer?

FIVE MONTHS LATER

MANALI, NORTHERN INDIA

Jewel sauntered past the clinic. She strolled near the
building, and stopped by a rock overlooking the Manali heights.
Curiosity had grown in her and she knew she had to see it for
herself. A Manali clinic, giving medical care for free and restoring
a community. Vik had been let off from any charges without any
harm to his reputation. He'd emailed her a week ago and told her
about this place. Despite all the mistakes, he hadn't deserved any
the anguish he'd put himself through. Did he still live here from
time to time?

She took in the smell of the hills, fresh, crisp, and the
melange of cloves and coriander tingling her nose as she advanced
on the footpath leading to the clinic. Her flat Himalayan *juti*
sandals cradled her feet, as the morning sun seeped through the
rhododendron trees.

Jewel halted at the clinic's wide entrance and glanced
forward. She peered at a man's face and his presence set her pulses
pounding. He'd not changed one bit. His hair still full, his
scrutinizing eyes still so blue. His doctor-sense engaged and
responding to patients as they lined up outside. Leal knelt down
speaking to a young girl, one of his charges. He had a natural way
with children and the months had softened his mannerisms. He
seemed reserved and more empathetic, if that was ever possible of
Leal.

Something about him reminded her of how she'd warmed to
the cocky mountaineer who had raced her in Salzburg.
Everything came flooding back. The day she'd first fallen in love
with him. The first awkward kiss. The inexplicable way they
connected. Yet there was no doubt the chemistry between them
had been hypnotic.

Jewel purposed to turn around. Maybe coming here was not

such a good idea. He probably wouldn't notice her. Her sandals appeared heavy as she turned her back to him.

A hand landed on her left shoulder and she drew in a stream of fresh air.

"Jewel?"

She whizzed round. "Sofia, what are you doing here?"

"Helping at the clinic."

"Here?"

"Uh Huh. I've always wanted to be close to what Leal was doing. I'm helping for a few weeks."

"That's great, Sofia."

"And you. What have you been up to? Why didn't you tell us you were coming?"

Jewel opened her lips to speak but nothing came out.

Sofia's concern and interest was evident. She drew Jewel into a hug. "Leal developed a great vaccine. We've used it here with great results and the best part is he can control it completely."

"What does that mean?"

"You know, Leal never lost Trelles Industries. Myranda and Devon only thought they had gained it. Nonna first bought back the thirty percent shares, almost as soon as they went public and never told anyone. Each time a part of Trelles went public, Nonna used off-shore accounts under a pseudonym to buy them back until she'd acquired more than fifty-one percent. Devon and Myranda were so focused on new drugs they let business slip to the board. She was an anonymous silent investor. It never left the family. Leal never knew, but he also just needed to be away from Trelles to find himself. He's now doing the work he loves and the way he wants it done. He moved back to New York you know. He had to be near you."

"I didn't know that. I kind of knew about the house—"

"The Tharnex drug is his debt to society. He uses all profits to go to helping and developing new safe drugs for places like this. He's worked so hard and has more money to do so than when he started. Ah... and speaking of the man."

Leal advanced to where the women stood and their eyes met as Leal moved into frame several of feet away.

Sofia's lips curved into a proud smile. "Look who's here. I think I'll let you two catch up." She stepped into the clinic, with a contented expression on her face.

"You came?" Leal said.

Jewel nodded slowly finding extreme difficulty with her words. Leal pointed to where a young Indian woman sat on a bench outside the clinic with a tiny baby bundled in her arms. "That's Talil, Maya's son. She's got two more children."

"Is Tharnex what you used when we went to see her that day?"

He scratched the side of his face. "Yes."

She could feel the longing that stretched like a rubber band between them. Leal stepped toward her and sighed his eyes begging for forgiveness. "Did I lose you, Jewel?" He slowly engulfed her in his sturdy arms. "Please say I haven't."

Heat traveled to her cheeks and she glanced upward up at his face. "I've heard about what you've done here. I also read how Myranda was put in a hospital." She pored into his eyes. "How even though your divorce went through, you still went to check on her. Last week, they discharged her from hospital. I went to see her with my mother. She's okay. What you did for her is honorable."

Jewel took in a deep sigh conscious of his purposeful stare. "Kaya and Vik told me of this project here. How you are investing your personal wealth into this dream for humanity. I had to come and see it for myself. You've done so much for those that are not fortunate. I'm humbled by it, Leal. And I'm sorry for—"

Before she could finish her words, he set fervent lips over hers. The sweet throbbing of his lips made her shift closer to him. And after a prolonged time of drifting, her decisive heart made it home, to Leal.

He pulled back, just enough to contemplate the sentiment in her eyes. "Jewel. Can I hang onto you? I'm willing to do what it takes to have you in my life."

"Anything?"

"I should've told you about my marriage, but I'm free now. I never once loved Myranda, ever. I married her so I could study her medical files with no questions asked. The government were on my case and... Jewel, please. I never—"

"Touched her."

"You paid attention at the mediation." He suddenly went quiet. "How can I make you Mrs. Trelles? Would you ever marry a screwed up guy like me?"

Jewel's pulse raced. She held a finger to his lips and hesitated for several seconds before responding. "No, but I'd marry a genius

360

like you. You stole something from me years ago on this hillside, my heart; and I've never gotten it back. It's always been with you."

Leal was still and let her words sink into him as she tilted her head. "Leal, never change who you are, ever again."

He shook his head and ran his fingers through her loose hair before settling his warm palm on her cheek. "I won't, Jewel, I can't lose you ever again."

"And just in case you did, I'd still know where to find your adventurous heart."

"Where?"

"Here," She set his hand on her chest. "With me. You see, I may have been immune to a disease, but I wasn't immune to something more contagious... you."

His broad shoulders were heaving as he breathed. He kissed her again and brushed a lock from her eyes. "Will I get to see you perform again? How many times have I told you you'll perform again?"

Her lips curled. "Maybe."

"I heard about the competition you've entered in Moscow, as the choreographer for the US rhythmic gymnastics team, can I persuade you to be in the final?" he said.

Her eyes shied from his. "You've spied on me?"

"Oh and by the way, where's your Nikon. We could use a good photographer around here."

She pulled a camera from her bag and glanced up at him. "One more question."

His eyebrows drew together. "Yeah?"

"What was in your research? You said you didn't use my DNA to develop Tharnex. How did you do it?"

Leal's lips curled at the corners as he smirked. "I didn't."

"But how?"

"Tharnex was submitted to the DEI on the grounds that they would never keep my research to themselves as they treat the affected women."

"How did you develop it?"

"When the DEI thought your blood could help us in our research, I so wanted to disprove their theories. There had to be another willing volunteer to study besides you."

"Did you get a volunteer?"

"At age six, Cyrus died of a severe form of fatal disease that caused his liver and kidneys to fail by the time he was five called methylmalonic academia. It took me ages to figure out why though we had the same DNA and blood, he got sick and I didn't."

"I'm sorry, Leal."

"Mother kept a lock of hair of his, so I studied his DNA and compared it to mine. That's how the answer hit me. My body was building antibodies against the disease in a way his wasn't. The more I researched the more I saw the differences in our makeup. Eventually, I imitated the way my body fought the disease in a way his couldn't. I had to look closely at how my body's natural defenses against the disease kept me immune.

"This helped me develop immunity options for a vaccine. As identical twins we shared the same genes. I studied how gene expression could differ in identical twins. Diseases can be caused by a combination of environmental and genetic factors. Identical twins provide a perfect setting to examine complex interaction. While I shared the same genes with Cyrus, somehow I differed in how these genes were expressed. In a nutshell, I had to find a way for the body to increase production of follicle-stimulating hormones, some of it was not even physical but mental. The result was a series of studies that contributed to the safe development of Tharnex. The truth is, Cyrus helped me find the answer."

"You amaze me, Leal. You are helping a global fertility problem."

He winced and held her tight brushing her face with affectionate kisses before staring into space. "We are a step closer to eliminating fibroid tumors, the real fertility problem hasn't been addressed by anybody."

"What do you mean?"

"Infertility is on the rise, but not in women."

"What?"

"In men."

"Serious?"

"There's an infertility epidemic brewing as the government suspected ten years ago, but they started looking in the wrong place. If you ask the wrong questions, you get the wrong answers."

"So your work is only beginning."

"The truth is, an epidemic is upon us and unless we wake up and address the right patients, the rising levels of male infertility have become so perilous. It's now a real public health issue."

THANK YOU

For joining Jewel and Leal... and Cyrus on this journey.

If you enjoyed **THE CODE BENEATH** and have a moment to
spare, please consider leaving a review where you bought the
book, even if it's just a short line or two.

The reason I'm asking for reviews: reader reviews are the
lifeblood of any author's career. For a humble typewriter-
mademoiselle like myself, getting reviews means I can submit my
books for advertising. Which means I can actually sell a few
copies from time to time - which is always a nice bonus :) So
every review means a lot to me - and I'd like to take the
opportunity to give something back.

If you would like to know when my next book is released, you can
sign up here to be notified and to get news on specials and release
giveaways. And also know when my next book is released.

Thank you!
Rose
Crafting Suspense & Intelligence Thrillers.
<u>www.rosesandy.com</u>

ABOUT THE AUTHOR

ROSE SANDY
AUTHOR OF INTERNATIONAL THRILLERS AND SUSPENSE.

Rose never set out to be a writer. She set out to be a communicator with whatever landed in her hands. But soon the keyboard became her best friend. Rose writes suspense and intelligence thrillers where technology and espionage meet history in pulse-racing action-adventure. She dips into the mysteries of our world, the fascination of technological breakthroughs, the secrets of history and global intelligence to deliver thrillers that weave suspense, conspiracy and a dash of romantic thrill.

A globe trotter, her thrillers span cities and continents. Rose's writing approach is to hit hard with a good dose of tension and humor. Her characters zip in and out of intelligence and government agencies, dodge enemies in world heritage sites, navigate technology markets and always land in deep trouble.

When not tapping away on a smartphone writing app, Rose is usually found in the British Library scrutinizing the Magna Carta, trolling Churchill's War Rooms or sampling a new gadget. Most times she's in deep conversations with ex-military and secret service intelligence officers, Foreign Service staff or engrossed in a TED talk with a box of popcorn. Hm... she might just learn something that'll be useful.

To get an e-mail whenever the author releases a new title or just to simply have a chat, sign up for the VIP newsletter at www.rosesandy.com. Rose looks forward to welcoming you there.

ROSE SANDY ONLINE:

http://www.rosesandy.com/
rose@rosesandy.com

MY SPECIAL THANKS ON THIS BOOK GOES TO:

BEHIND THE SCENES
You are superstars!

Jason for being my everything and a super cover designer!
Andy L. for being such a great friend, editor and grammar
detective. We are such em-dash, comma, semi colon, double
negatives and dangling participle geeks!
Marilyn M. for the laughs and emotions we went through as you
read the manuscript. Ah yes… Leal was my problem child..Boy
did we root for him.
Lou and Julie for reading the first paper napkin ideas :)

THE FANTASTIC & BEST STREET LAUNCH TEAM ON EARTH
I couldn't have done it without you!
Thank you for everything, especially your feedback, laser sharp eyes and incredible support.

Cherry A, Ray, Dave, Lisa, Roz, Mark, Michelle, Roger, Kathy,
Lee, Richard, Brock, Brenda, Victoria, Nigel, William, Lucie,
Seamus, Kevin, Paul, Heather, Cherry, Andrea, Clive, Lyn, Donna,
Garry, Irene, Lorraine, Craig, Don, Jezza, Liz, Dave, Martyn,
Laura and Lester.

OTHER BOOKS BY THE AUTHOR

THE CALLA CRESS TECHNO THRILLER SERIES

BOOK 1—THE DECRYPTER: SECRET OF THE LOST
MANUSCRIPT
BOOK 2—THE DECRYPTER AND THE MIND HACKER

THE DECRYPTER: SECRET OF THE LOST MANUSCRIPT

"The detail is astounding!"
Amazon Customer

(Previously published as The Deveron Manuscript)
A Calla Cress Techno Thriller

**The secret of the manuscript is only the beginning... The
truth could cost her life.**
The first book in the explosive bestselling thriller series

Though her specialty is Roman collections at the British Museum
in London, history expert turned government agent Calla Cress
finds herself thrown into a bizarre international case. A code is
written in an unbreakable script on an ancient manuscript whose
origin is as debatable as the origin of life. Could its decryption
lead to a global cyber war?

When the highly guarded document goes missing from a Berlin
museum and ends up in her personal belongings with a long-
hidden secret concerning her parents, Calla is backed into a
corner. Forced on a run halfway across the world, Calla is pursued
from the underground scene of espionage intelligence into a
desperate hunt for truth and survival. Soon she discovers that
she's made of tougher stuff than she ever imagined. Her only
allies are few but resourceful.
There's: Nash Shields, a handsome yet mysterious National
Security Agency (NSA) intelligence analyst. Jack Kleve, a witty

technology entrepreneur.

The trio is thrown into a sophisticated conspiracy spanning continents and dating back several centuries. The secret of the manuscript is only the beginning... The truth could cost them their lives.

ABOUT THE DECRYPTER: SECRET OF THE LOST MANUSCRIPT

THE DECRYPTER: SECRET OF THE LOST MANUSCRIPT is a fast-paced, provocative, action-adventure techno thriller seeped in history that poses a question—what if the future of cyber technology had more to do with the past?

THE DECRYPTER AND THE MIND HACKER
(Previously published as Covert Interference)

*"I found myself intrigued about what could be the next step in
the evolution of cyber systems"*
UK Amazon Reader

**A CYBER CRIME WILL REWRITE
HISTORY...ONLY SHE CAN STOP IT.**
**The second book in the explosive bestselling techno
thriller series**

*Calla Cress took down the world's most dangerous man.
She made one mistake. She let him live.*

A billionaire behind bars, once the secret service's most brilliant
code breaker, is luring the world's smartest minds into his prison
cell. They leave in a coma and seconds later a lethal hack snakes
through one government system after another.
Meanwhile, Calla Cress, museum curator turned undercover
cyber-security agent, faces the biggest dilemma of her life. She's
harboring a dangerous secret buried in the deepest vaults of
technology history.
In a few hours, she'll have to make a decision that will change her
life forever. After an explosion rocks her hideout in Colorado,
Calla wakes up halfway across the world at the whim of a
powerful, unidentified organization demanding she produce the
whereabouts of a missing MI6 agent who can disarm the
billionaire's hacks. Powerful people are prepared to kill to obtain
the cryptic secret the agent kept.

There're a few obstacles: Calla has never met the agent who has
been missing for 30 years. Can Calla find the only person who
ever challenged the enigmatic billionaire?
With only a handful of clues left in a mysterious sixteenth-
century anagram encrypted with a sequence of codes, Calla, NSA
security adviser, Nash Shields and tech entrepreneur Jack Kleve
are thrust in a dangerous race across the globe. With each
haunting revelation, they soon realize the key to disarming the
hacks comes at an astonishing price.

ABOUT THE *DECRYPTER AND THE MIND HACKER*

THE DECRYPTER AND THE MIND HACKER is a fast-paced, suspense thriller, charging through government secrets, world history and computer fraud that will have you wondering whether technology has progressed beyond human intelligence, changing civilization, and perhaps human nature.

>>> Reader Acclaim for 'THE DECRYPTER AND THE MIND HACKER

"I found myself intrigued about what could be the next step in the evolution of cyber systems I look forward to more stories from the author especially involving Calla Cress."

"Calla Cress, still reeling from her recent discoveries, is thrown right back into danger. This is an exhilarating read that will have you begging for more."

"Hard to put down once you start reading it."

"Great story line with twists and turns and a good alternation of action and scene setting which will keep you on the edge of your seat."

"I can see how this would look on screen but it may be my wild imagination! The end will shock you!"

17208686R00223

Printed in Great Britain
by Amazon